By Elizabeth Boyle

IT TAKES A HERO
STEALING THE BRIDE
ONE NIGHT OF PASSION
ONCE TEMPTED
NO MARRIAGE OF CONVENIENCE

If You've Enjoyed This Book,
Be Sure to Read These Other
AVON ROMANTIC TREASURES

ENGLAND'S PERFECT HERO *by Suzanne Enoch*
GUILTY PLEASURES *by Laura Lee Guhrke*
HOW TO TREAT A LADY *by Karen Hawkins*
MARRIED TO THE VISCOUNT *by Sabrina Jeffries*
THE PLEASURE OF HER KISS *by Linda Needham*

Coming Soon

A DARK CHAMPION *by Kinley MacGregor*

ELIZABETH BOYLE

It TAKES A HERO

AVON BOOKS

An Imprint of HarperCollins*Publishers*

This is a work of fiction. Names, characters, places, and incidents are products of the author's imagination or are used fictitiously and are not to be construed as real. Any resemblance to actual events, locales, organizations, or persons, living or dead, is entirely coincidental.

AVON BOOKS
An Imprint of HarperCollins*Publishers*
10 East 53rd Street
New York, New York 10022-5299

Copyright © 2004 by Elizabeth Boyle
ISBN: 0-7394-4134-5

Printed in the U.S.A.

To Matthew.
Thank you for the much-needed lessons
in patience and for teaching me the joy
that comes in the smallest of hugs.

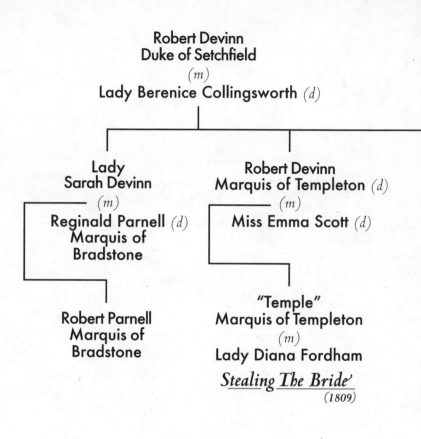

Robert Devinn
Duke of Setchfield
(m)
Lady Berenice Collingsworth *(d)*

Lady
Sarah Devinn
(m)
Reginald Parnell *(d)*
Marquis of
Bradstone

Robert Devinn
Marquis of Templeton *(d)*
(m)
Miss Emma Scott *(d)*

Robert Parnell
Marquis of
Bradstone

"Temple"
Marquis of Templeton
(m)
Lady Diana Fordham

Stealing The Bride
(1809)

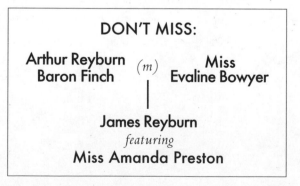

DON'T MISS:

Arthur Reyburn
Baron Finch
(m)
Miss
Evaline Bowyer

James Reyburn
featuring
Miss Amanda Preston

SEE THE EXPANDED FAMILY TREE AT ELIZABETHBOYLE.COM

Elizabeth Boyle's
Danvers
Family Tree

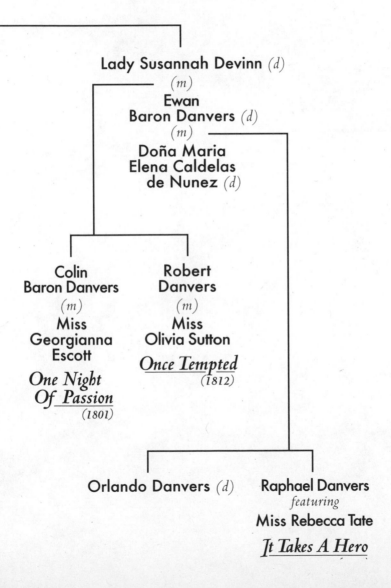

Lady Susannah Devinn *(d)*

(m)

Ewan
Baron Danvers *(d)*

(m)

Doña Maria
Elena Caldelas
de Nunez *(d)*

Colin
Baron Danvers

(m)

Miss
Georgianna
Escott

*One Night
Of Passion*
(1801)

Robert
Danvers

(m)

Miss
Olivia Sutton

Once Tempted
(1812)

Orlando Danvers *(d)*

Raphael Danvers
featuring
Miss Rebecca Tate

It Takes A Hero

It Takes A Hero

Prologue

Miss Emery's School for Genteel Young Ladies
Bath, England
December 1816

> *The hillside blared with the trumpet's strident cry.*
> *"Ahead! Charge ahead!" cried Colonel Darby.*
> *And his troops did so, with Lieutenant Throck-morten leading the brigade against the ruthless and barbaric Mughal hordes.*
> *Miss Darby, seated astride Champion, watched the battle from the safety of the hillside, a spyglass to her eye. At her side, her ever faithful wolfhound, Ajax, stood at guard. Her breath caught in her throat as she watched her beloved Lt. Throckmorten rush into the thick of battle, the dust and smoke swallowing him immediately from her sight.*

Lady Lucinda Witherspoon paused in her reading and glanced up at her rapt audience. While the lights in their dormitory should have been out hours ago, the young ladies under Miss Emery's charge braved both the chill that seemed never to leave their school, as well as Miss Emery's ire, to huddle around Lady Lucinda's bed to hear this final chapter of *Miss Darby's Darkest Hour.*

Over the last two years they'd read all four volumes of Miss Darby's adventures just like this, hidden in

Lady Lucinda's room beside a stub of candle one of them had pilfered from the music room or the parlor when none of their teachers was looking.

Miss Emery prided herself on economy, so the candles were hard to come by. And if frugality was a virtue in Miss Emery's world, then fiction, in the esteemed lady's estimation, was as close to the torments of hell as any young lady dare tread. The school's mistress had banned the *Miss Darby* tales from the first moment they started to appear, saying: "Miss Darby and her radical notions of independence and outlandish manners are unforgivable."

The girls at Miss Emery's disagreed.

"Botheration, Lucinda! Read on," complained Miss Geneva Thayer. While Lady Lucinda outranked Miss Thayer socially, Miss Thayer was an heiress and that counted for much in the pecking order of Miss Emery's establishment.

Besides, it had been Geneva's abundant pocket money that had ensured the illegal book could be smuggled into the dormitory.

"Oh, please go on, Lady Lucinda," one of the younger girls urged. Several heads nodded in agreement.

For in truth, no one could equal Lady Lucinda's dramatic flare for reading. Besides, it was essential she finish *Miss Darby's Darkest Hour* this very night. In the morning, school would be dismissed for the Christmas holidays, and most of the older girls, Miss Thayer and Lady Lucinda included, were to make their bows come spring and would not be returning.

Lady Lucinda drew the flickering candle closer.

"Find him, Ajax," Miss Darby shouted. The brave wolfhound forged into the fray, blazing a safe path for Miss Darby and Champion to follow. Despite the

smoke and fighting on either side of her, Miss Darby
continued her dangerous sally.

"Lieutenant Throckmorten!" she cried out. "Lieu-
tenant Throckmorten, can you hear me?"

To her dismay, the lieutenant was nowhere to be seen.

Lady Lucinda paused again, this time to turn the page.

"Oh, dear," Lady Penelope Bittleman whispered. "I fear something dreadful has happened. I'm never wrong about these things. Mother says I have the sight."

"Pish!" Miss Mary Mavery said. "Lieutenant Throckmorten is a brave man. He'll be fine." She was the most practical of her classmates, but her admonition didn't stop a spate of tears from falling down Penelope's cheeks.

Lady Lucinda, at the renewed urging of the others, read on, this time with a bit of haste to her tenor.

Suddenly she saw him, her beloved Lieutenant
Throckmorten.

"See, I told you," Miss Mavery said. Several heads nodded.

Then to their horror, Lady Lucinda, who had been scanning the lines ahead, gasped, "Oh dear. Oh, no!"

Not a girl moved, every pair of eyes riveted on the slim volume Lady Lucinda held. Nary a breath was drawn as she continued to read.

To her horror, she spied a tattered piece of blue silk.

"The scarf Miss Darby gave Lieutenant Throckmorten in *Miss Darby's Perilous Journey*, as a symbol of their undying respect for each other," one of the younger girls whispered.

*Her beloved, her dearest betrothed lay on the ground,
his scarlet coat tattered and bloodstained.*

"Blood?" Lady Penelope repeated, then wobbled slightly before giving over to faint, toppling onto the girl next to her.

Lady Lucinda spared a glance at her friend then continued.

*Miss Darby leapt from the back of her horse and knelt
beside him, but even as she went to touch his cheek, she
knew the Fates had dealt her a most heinous blow.*

"No!" gasped Miss Thayer.

Lady Lucinda nodded. "I can't go on," she said, her voice quivering, tears welling up in her eyes.

"Oh, but you must!" one of the girls begged. "For us, for Miss Darby."

A handkerchief was produced and passed forward. Lady Lucinda accepted it gratefully. After regaining her composure, she read the fateful line:

Her beloved Lieutenant Throckmorten was dead.

Handsome, dashing Lieutenant Throckmorten dead? Could the world be so cruel?

*"Lieutenant Throckmorten, my dearest Geoffrey," Miss
Darby sobbed, holding the lifeless body of her beloved to
her heaving breast. "I shall bear my grief to the world in
memory of you. I shall never marry. Never."*

For a time, none of them spoke, though heartbreaking sobs echoed through the dark chamber as they grieved with their favorite heroine for the heartwrenching loss of her betrothed.

Lady Lucinda glanced around at her schoolmates. "I shall never marry."

Most thought she was just repeating the line from the book, but as they saw a dangerous light glow to life in her eyes, they saw something else burning there.

A revolution of sorts.

If their dearest Miss Darby, the young woman whose adventures filled their dreary lives with romance and excitement, was determined never to marry, then neither would they.

Lucinda held out her hand, and one by one, every girl in the room placed hers atop the other.

"Never marry," they repeated like a sacred oath.

Chapter 1

She held me spellbound from the first moment I spied her. For it was like a spark fell from heaven and lit my heart afire. I fear I will never be whole again without her in my life.

Lieutenant Throckmorten to
his batman, Thomas Rivers
in *Miss Darby's Daring Dilemma*

London

The Season of 1817 should have begun like any other, in fact it should have been the most engaging Season in ages. Napoleon was no longer a threat. English officers and gentlemen alike were ready to celebrate, and more importantly, many were of a mind to marry.

The mothers of unwed daughters throughout the land should have been in alt.

Instead they were in a panic.

Their daughters were refusing to cooperate. Refusing to be wed!

Who had ever heard of such a notion? Not marry? Why not just declare oneself a savage and be done with the matter.

Well, such foolishness wasn't to be borne. Especially

not by Malvina Witherspoon, Countess of Tottley, the mother of Lady Lucinda. She hadn't spent a fortune sending her darling daughter to Miss Emery's exclusive school only to have her arrive home and announce that she would never take a husband.

Never. Ever.

"It is all this wretched Darby creature's doing," Malvina declared one morning to a circle of equally desperate mothers. "And it is time we put a stop to this nonsense once and for all."

Heads nodded enthusiastically, since they knew the countess had good reason to want to see this state of anarchy put to an end.

If the rumors were true, and most likely they were given the ungodly hour Lady Tottley's summons had arrived, Lady Lucinda had refused, *yes, refused*, the young and handsome Lord Barwick, heir to the Hemswell dukedom.

There wasn't a moment to lose. It could very well be one of their daughters refusing such an eligible *parti*. And so it was that the good mothers of London had gathered together to formulate a plan of attack. The author of the *Miss Darby* chronicles, known only as M. Briggs, was probably hated with more ferocity and incurred more wrath by the occupants of Lady Tottley's morning salon than Boney at the height of his despotic reign.

The murmurs of complaint and gossip were interrupted by a discreet knock at the door. Crumpton, Lady Tottley's infamously stodgy butler, poked his long nose through the crack in the door. "Ma'am, there is a *gentleman* here who claims to have been invited."

His tone spoke volumes. That he no more believed the man in question was a gentleman, nor that this interloper had been invited.

So it was a rare treat for all those in the room to see

Crumpton's mouth fall open in dismay when her lady-ship responded with an enthusiastic wave of her hand.

"Send him in at once, Crumpton."

"But, my lady," the butler protested, "this . . . this . . . person isn't accepted. I have it on good authority that he's considered—"

"Don't be such a ninnyhammer, Crumpton," the countess said. "These are desperate times and we can no longer cling to social boundaries if we are to see the world righted."

Fans fluttered and more than one slanted glance asked the same question.

Who had Lady Tottley invited that had Crumpton in such a state?

They didn't wait long to find out, for a few moments later the door opened a second time, swinging inward in defiance to the soft, hallowed confines of this oh, so very feminine sanctuary.

As their savior entered, filling first the doorway, and then, in many ways, the room with his long-legged stride and wide shoulders, there was a soft echo of gasps and even a few sighs at the sight of this all-too-infamous man.

His dark gaze sped around the room, examining and discarding a hasty inventory of property and persons as if he suspected that danger lurked close at hand.

Not that the man wasn't receiving the same detailed inspection from every woman in the room. It wasn't his fashionable dress that caught their attention, for he wasn't wearing anything of note other than plain buff breeches, scuffed and stained boots, and a black worsted jacket.

No, it was the man beneath the plain and unnotice-able wrappings that couldn't be so easily hidden.

And what a man he was.

A hairsbreadth past thirty, Raphael Danvers stood well over six feet tall and his presence left no one in doubt that he was a man in his prime. Oh, he may have gained his proper English name and citizenship from his illustrious father, Baron Danvers, but his dark mien and rakishly foreign good looks spoke of thousands of years of Spanish nobility—hawkish, penetrating eyes, a jaw line hammered and tempered from a Castilian forge, and a masculine fire that emanated from him like the unforgiving Iberian sun.

Since his return from the Peninsular wars, there hadn't been a happily married, matronly, or thankfully widowed woman in London who hadn't wondered what it would be like to bask beneath his raw, untamed heat, strip the unfashionable clothes from his muscled body and see just how unacceptable Rafe Danvers could be.

And to Mr. Danvers' credit, he was inclined to indulge them.

"My lady," he said, nodding his head slightly to the countess.

She should have been miffed that he hadn't managed a decent bow, but she knew, like most everyone else, that Rafe's long years at war and unconventional upbringing had not garnered a healthy respect for his betters. Besides, at present, she was doing her best to set aside her own decadent notions of a deserted hunting lodge, ten foot snow drifts, and Rafe wearing only a . . .

"Ma'am?" he asked, an impatient edge to his query.

Malvina took a deep breath and cleared away her wayward thoughts. "Yes, Mr. Danvers, quite on time," she managed, waving her hand at the only available chair. "Please, sit. I have need of your assistance with a most distressing matter."

"Malvina, you don't mean to . . ." This outburst came from her old friend, Harriet Bittleman, the Marchioness of Funtley. From the look of shock and dismay on Harriet's face, it was obvious she'd deduced the countess's plans. Furthermore, she'd also gauged the scandal that would embroil them all if anyone, especially their husbands, discovered what they were about to do. "Do you realize what will become of us, of our daughters, if anyone learns that we've . . . we've . . ."

"Yes, I do," Malvina said, snapping her fan shut and tossing it down on the elegant side table at her elbow. "But I will not stand idly by while our long years of toil are ruined. I will see my Lucinda married, and I care not by what means." She shot a meaningful glance at the others, one that cowed them all into considering a far more shameful future—one that had them being trailed for the remainder of their years by a bevy of spinster daughters.

"Uh-hum," Mr. Danvers said, venturing a polite cough into the tense room, before he rose to his feet. "Did you say 'marriage'? Now look here, I'm not going to be bartered away like some—"

"Sit down, sir," Malvina told him.

It was rumored that Rafe Danvers had fought side by side with the Spanish guerillas during the war, that he'd partaken in skirmishes so dangerous, so gruesome, that nothing could frighten the man.

Obviously he'd never entered into an altercation against Lady Tottley.

"I'm not in the business of—" he began to argue.

"I said *sit*, sir!" Malvina ordered.

Not even a unit of French sharpshooters could match the countess's ruthless intent when she'd set her mind to something. So when she issued her sharp retort, Rafe dropped to his seat as if ducking enemy fire.

"Now," the lady said, "I would ask you to hear what

I have to say before you dismiss our proposal."

Mr. Danvers crossed his arms over his chest and heaved a sigh, one that suggested his patience was barely contained and that not even the countess's legendary ire was going to hold him for long.

"Have you heard of the troubles?" she asked.

He shook his head.

She took a deep breath and added, "With this season's debutantes?"

He shrugged off this bit of information. "As you may be aware, my lady, I don't spend much time in society."

"Oh, sir," Lady Funtley enthused. "You haven't heard what happened last week at Almack's?"

Again his dark head gave a slight, insolent toss.

"No?" she asked. "I don't know how you couldn't have heard about it."

The other women joined in, offering their own *on dits*.

"The ballroom was empty, mind you, empty . . ."

"Refuses to wear anything but mourning . . ."

"And then there was the duel—" one of them offered.

Mr. Danvers latched onto that piece of gossip as if it were a lifeline out of the cacophony. "Oh, yes. The duel between those two foolish chits. I did hear something about that nonsense."

"Nonsense?" Malvina said. "Hardly nonsense. They could have been killed. All over whether or not this wretched Miss Darby will be wearing full mourning or half mourning by next Season."

"Why didn't they just ask Miss Darby?" he ventured, shifting in his seat, one scuffed and stained boot after the other stuck out in front of him.

"Ask Miss Darby?" Lady Funtley repeated as if she hadn't heard him correctly. "Ask her, you say? Why that is droll, sir!"

His dark brows drew together. "No, I'm serious. Why didn't they just ask this Darby gel and be done with it?"

This left Lady Funtley so flustered, she fell into an unprecedented silence.

"They didn't ask the lady in question," Malvina explained, "because she doesn't exist. She is a mere fiction, a character in a spate of heinous novels. And it's because she does not exist that she must be stopped. Don't you see, sir, you must see her influence put to an end. Immediately."

This explanation only left his brows furrowed deeper, as he tried to fathom how some fictional character could be behind the ruin of everything these ladies held dear. Or that he had a hope in hell there was a shred of sanity between the entire lot of them.

He rose again. "My lady, I can see that this situation weighs heavily on you and your friends, but I have far more important obligations to attend to than chasing after figments and fancies."

Malvina rose as well. "This figment, as you so blithely put it, is bent on ruining the very fiber of English society."

"Lady Tottley," he said, slowly and calmly, "I don't see that society is in any danger. Least of all here in Mayfair. Besides, I can't take on any more cases right now. My current obligations are far too pressing."

"Yes, yes. Codlin's misfortunate accident," she said, waving her hand dismissively as if they were discussing what color gloves to wear, not the most grisly murder London had seen in fifty years.

The other ladies, at the mention of the incident, weren't so unmoved. Most looked away and several drew delicate lace handkerchiefs to their now pale lips.

"I don't consider a man being gutted like a mackerel as *accidental*." He paused for a moment, ignoring the gasps around the room, his eyes narrowing to two dark slits. "The investigation into Sir Rodney's *murder* is far too important for me to be wasting my time here." He went to excuse himself, but Malvina blocked his path.

"I don't see how some nabob's indecent passing matters all that much," Malvina told him. "*Sir* Rodney, indeed! Codlin's elevation last year was an abhorrence. Really, Mr. Danvers, the man is dead. There isn't much you can do for him now."

"I doubt he would share your opinion, my lady." A wry smile twisted at his lips. "My talents lie in solving problems, my lady. Real problems. Living, breathing ones. Or at least ones that drew a breath at some time. Now if you don't mind, I bid you good day."

He started for the door, weaving through the crowded room like a man dodging out of the way of a wayward mail coach.

Malvina nodded at Lady Funtley, who immediately rose and stepped into Mr. Danvers' oncoming path.

He skidded to a stop but not before he nearly toppled into the brave marchioness.

Lady Funtley reached for his arm to steady herself, and when her fingers wound around his sleeve, her eyes widened at what must have been the heat and strength to be discovered beneath. "Oh, my," she managed to say.

Every lady in the room knew what she meant. And every woman envied her the experience.

"You will be compensated, Mr. Danvers," Malvina told him as he attempted to shake a determined Lady Funtley from his arm. "*Well* compensated."

"I doubt even *your* pin money, my lady," he said, "could begin to cover my fees. The East India Company is offering a thousand pounds for the discovery of Sir

Rodney's murderer and I intend to collect that reward."

"I wasn't talking about money, sir," she said. "I was speaking of something more valuable."

At this intriguing bit, Mr. Danvers found the wherewithal to extract himself from Lady Funtley.

Malvina stared directly into his dark gaze and was pleased to spy a flicker of interest in the man's eyes. In the past fortnight, she'd gleaned every bit of information she could about Raphael Danvers and she suspected she possessed the one thing that could induce him to help her, help all of them.

"A house," she said simply. "With land and income. The deed is yours if you uncover the author of this havoc. And more importantly, see that this M. Briggs never puts pen to paper again."

Bramley Hollow, Kent
A fortnight later

"I won't do it," Cochrane said. "No, sir, I won't do it."

Raphael Danvers glanced over at his assistant, then nodded his head in the direction of the quaint little village in the valley beyond. "Come now, Cochrane, I thought you were braver than that. It's just a village. Hardly even that. You've gone into the worst rat infested corners of Seven Dials for Pymm but this—" Rafe waved his hand at the view. "This frightens you?"

The young man nodded vehemently.

Rafe took another tack. "I hear tell the inn serves the finest beef pie in all of Kent." Honestly, he had no idea if Bramley Hollow even had an inn, but if there was one thing his newly inherited assistant didn't fear it was his next meal.

Cochrane bit his lip and eyed the village anew. Yet,

after a few moments he shook his head. Apparently, not even his unrelenting appetite was enough to prod him into entering the infamous matchmaking village of Bramley Hollow.

"I promise I won't let you be wed against your will," Rafe told him.

The lad didn't look the least bit convinced. "I hear tell it happens afore you know it. One minute you are asleep in your bed and the next—you wake up married with a houseful of mouths to feed."

"As long as they haven't your stomach to fill, you should be fine." Rafe nudged his horse forward and a few moments later smiled to himself when he heard the young man let out a long sigh and follow.

Cochrane had previously been employed by Mr. Pymm, the Foreign Office's legendary spymaster. But with peace now at hand and Napoleon securely locked away on St. Helena, Pymm had finally gained his ever-sought-after retirement. With nary a glance back at Whitehall, Pymm had packed his bags and left London, though not before he'd sent Cochrane over to Rafe's lodgings—instructing Danvers to take the sixteen-year-old lad under his wing and see that the boy gained some gentlemanly manners.

Not that Rafe knew much about being a gentleman, or how he was going to keep the still-growing adolescent in potpies and shoes.

He suspected the infamously parsimonious Pymm had sent Cochrane into his care so as not to be beggared by the boy's rapacious appetite.

"We could be in London," Cochrane grumbled. "Finding Codlin's killer and eatin' a decent meal."

Rafe had to agree with Cochrane, he'd rather be back in town. He'd been dead set against Lady Tottley's offer. The house was probably a tumble down wreck and what did he care if the Marriage Mart had been declared officially closed for the Season?

Say he did find this *Darby* author and put everything to rights? He'd be run out of town by every unmarried man in London for ruining what was turning out to be the Season of the century.

Yet here he was, traipsing down this nearly forgotten country road in search of Lady Tottley's villainous author.

In his defense, he would have stuck to his first reply to her offer, an unhesitant "No!" if Lady Tottley hadn't then gone to Georgiana, Lady Danvers, his illustrious sister-in-law, and complained vehemently about his refusal to help.

Now Rafe loved Colin's wife, Georgie, but damnation she had a way about her that was more interfering than an excise man. As it turned out, Georgie was in a fine state over the entire problem for it seemed their daughter Chloe was being just as stubborn about this *Darby* mess as Lady Lucinda Witherspoon.

To Rafe's credit, he'd held strong against Georgie's pleas and admonitions, until she'd demanded a family convocation.

Rafe hated family convocations. They usually involved a long table with his brothers and their wives at one end, him at the other and a lot of arguing.

Hardly his idea of an evening well-spent.

He much preferred the lively pursuit of an eventually willing lady, a hackney waiting to take him home before she got any further ideas about him staying the night, and once home, a good bottle of port ready for his indulgent hand to pull the cork and measure out a healthy dose.

No, instead, he'd squandered a perfectly good

Thursday night listening to the Danvers' wives threatening him with all sorts of invitations, escorting Chloe all around town, not only at night, but during the day when he was more inclined to be sleeping.

At this rate he'd never get any work done—pleasurable or rent paying.

So in a moment of utter desperation, he'd agreed to solve Lady Tottley's case, if only to regain his blessed independence from female interference.

If there was a blessing to this case, Rafe decided, he'd gotten a good day's ride out of the bargain. In Spain, he'd spent weeks at a time in the saddle, scouting and hunting French troops. He missed the freedom of the open country, something London and his work afforded him little time to enjoy.

"I've no mind to find myself married," Cochrane was repeating.

"Then I promise I'll keep you well out of the matchmaker's way." As Rafe intended to do for himself as well. "But into Bramley Hollow we must go, and Bramley Hollow we shall brave."

To locate the elusive author, Rafe had gone to the publisher, Ahey and Sons, to ask for directions to M. Briggs, but the esteemed Mr. Ahey had laughed outright at such a request. Undeterred, Rafe and Cochrane spent the next week frequenting the inn favored by the man's overworked and underpaid apprentices, and one night had treated the lot of them to a feast of beef steaks and bottomless tankards of ale. Before midnight, they'd had the directions that Mr. Ahey had declared "absolutely unavailable."

And as luck would have it, the property that Lady Tottley had offered him wasn't that far afield from the little village of Bramley Hollow, so Rafe would be able to assess his payment and make good his promise to Lady Tottley to see the author properly persuaded to give up his profession.

"I heard tell last night," Cochrane said, "that the East India Company upped their reward for finding Codlin's killer to two thousand pounds." The boy whistled. "You could pay the rent with that kind of blunt. You know, so we wouldn't have to duck out the back all the time."

Rafe ignored the jab about his less than reliable finances and got to the point. "Where did you hear about the East India offer?"

"I just 'eard it," the boy said, shrugging his shoulders and suddenly gaining a new appreciation for the scenery as if he'd never seen a tree in his life.

Rafe made a note to keep better track of the boy's whereabouts. He could get into trouble wandering about London alone at night. Not that that had probably ever given Pymm a moment's pause.

"Is this house you get worth more than two thousand pounds?"

"Most likely."

This seemed to cheer up Cochrane, though not enough to dampen his suspicious nature. "Don't you think it's rather a generous offer, giving you a house and all, when all we've got to do is to find some bloke and break his arms so he can't write?"

"Cochrane!" Rafe sputtered. "We aren't in the business of breaking people's arms. We solve problems. Discreetly, professionally."

"Like you did that Lord Harold last month?"

Rafe sighed. He would have to bring up that case.

Lord Harold, a worthless sot if ever there was one, had been attending house parties and using his hosts' homes as a playground for pilfering—stealing silver and other small items of value to pay off his gambling debts. His family, notably his brother, the Marquess of Carston, had wanted to avoid scandal at any cost, as had Lord Harold's equally well-heeled victims.

Rafe and Cochrane had caught up with the unrepentant thief in Surrey about to leave a party with his pockets and trunks stuffed with his latest plunder. Instead, they'd seen the goods returned and "escorted" the young wastrel to the coast where passage had been booked by his brother for a one-way trip to the lonely reaches of Halifax.

Needless to say, Lord Harold hadn't taken to this turn of events all that willingly, and Rafe had finally planted a facer to end the young man's caterwauling and whining.

"Lord Harold was the exception," Rafe said.

"What about that fellow who was beating up the girls at Madame Rochelle's? Or that bloke who thought he could run away with the viscount's daughter? You gave them a bit of the business, didn't you?"

"They both needed a little more attention, that's all," Rafe admitted, wondering if these were the sort of moral lessons that Pymm had intended Cochrane to gain under his tutelage.

Then he shot a second, more narrowed glance over at his assistant. "What do you know about Madame Rochelle's?"

The boy shrugged. "You sent me there last week." Again his interest in English flora rose to new heights as he intently studied the passing hedge.

Wait just a damn moment, Rafe thought. Sent his assistant to Madame Rochelle's? "I did no such thing," he countered.

"Yes, you did. You said quite specifically to go around and collect our late accounts and so I did."

"Madame Rochelle's account wasn't late," Rafe pointed out as they rounded a corner and came within sight of the village.

"It's paid in full now." Cochrane grinned, then he nudged his horse and raced the last length into town leaving a groaning Rafe behind.

While he was less than bemused with the idea of Cochrane at Madame Rochelle's, at least he wouldn't have to give the lad the talk he'd been meaning to. One Pymm had alluded to in his instructions as "explain to the boy the necessary evils of women and keep him free of pox."

Rafe made a note to himself that from now on he'd take care of unpaid accounts and leave Cochrane behind to do the paperwork.

Beneath him, his horse pranced and sidestepped, as if it too were reluctant to enter the notorious little hamlet. Reaching down, he patted the high-strung animal and spoke softly in Spanish to it as his grandfather had taught him, then nudged the soothed beast forward.

Bramley Hollow seemed at first glance like any other English village—well tended, if not sleepy by London standards, but Rafe, like Cochrane, knew this village was unique in that it boasted a matchmaker, and had kept one at the ready for hopeless spinsters and wayward and unwitting men for over a thousand years. It was enough of a reputation that most avowed bachelors gave Bramley Hollow a wide berth.

Cochrane looked around the respectable little cottages and shops as if he'd just been dropped in the middle of a savage village and was ready to take flight at the least provocation from the matrimonial minded natives.

"How are we going to find this Briggs fellow?" he asked. Cochrane shared Lady Tottley's opinion that the *Darby* author was a man.

Rafe wasn't so convinced. After the family convocation, Georgie had pressed the four volumes of *Miss Darby's* novels into his hands and told him to read them. He'd scoffed at the idea, but out of curiosity, and because he was currently between mistresses, he had picked up the first book and begun reading.

There on the pages of a book, Rafe discovered something, someone who left him intrigued.

Miss Darby.

From her headstrong ways to her fearless devotion, Rafe was captivated by this figment of a fervent imagination. Not that such a woman could ever exist in real life, but time and time again, he found himself wondering what it would be like to encounter such a lady.

And there were also clues to be found within the binding of the slim volume. The independent and outspoken heroine might have been created by a man, but Rafe knew women. He'd loved enough of them to have an inkling of their unspoken desires and this Miss Darby clamored of long-held hopes and undeclared dreams.

No, in his estimation the author was most likely some bluestocking with stars in her eyes, living out her dreary life through Miss Darby's adventures. The type of chaste lady who'd never caught a man's eyes, let alone a stolen kiss, and would consider that insufferable bore, Lt. Throckmorten, a fine catch. Oh, yes, they'd find the lady with her twelve cats at hand, dreaming of a life that had passed her by.

And with a bit of his notorious charm and a warning hint as to how ruinous the lofty Lady Tottley's ire could be, the spinster's pen would be tucked away for years to come.

"This fellow isn't going to want to be found," Cochrane said. "We could be stuck here for days." That prospect had him looking longingly over his shoulder toward London.

"We'll ask at the inn to start."

This caught Cochrane's attention. "The one with the pies?"

Rafe laughed. "Business first, pies later."

"Don't see how we are supposed to break arms on an empty stomach," he grumbled.

"We aren't going to break any limbs."

They continued riding into town when a sign caught Rafe's eye.

ROYAL POST OFFICE

THADDEUS STONE, POSTAL MASTER

Rafe grinned. Now here was a bit of luck. This Mr. Stone would be just the person to help them, without having to bribe an innkeeper for directions. This would save what few coins he did have, especially now that Cochrane had apparently used the Rochelle payment for purposes other than rent.

He reined to a stop and told the lad to wait for him as he entered the post office.

To his chagrin there was a customer inside, a woman chatting to the young lady behind the counter. He looked around for the postmaster, but saw no one other than the pair of females before him.

This could either work to his advantage or . . .

"Oh, Miss Tate, you must do something about the colonel. You simply must," the postmistress was saying. "Everyone is talking about the other night."

Miss Tate's bonnet shook furiously. "What do you want me to do, send him—"

The female chatter ended abruptly as the postmistress looked up from her gossip, her mouth falling open. Then she gave her friend a warning shake of her head.

Rafe shifted from one foot to the other, then doffed his hat. "Good day," he offered, adding a smile meant to leave both of them weak in the knees.

The woman behind the counter shot him a quick narrowed glance and then moved closer to her friend.

Then Miss Tate turned around.

From behind, she had looked like the typical country mouse, in her plain brown bonnet and nondescript gown, market basket in hand. But as she first shot a glance over her shoulder and then slowly spun on one heel, he found himself wondering, but for a second, if he'd just discovered his very own Miss Darby.

Chapter 2

Remember me when I am gone with a nosegay of forget-me-nots and fond regrets. . . . Oh, and, father, don't let that odious Cecilia Overton talk you into giving her my best blue bonnet.

Her chin is far too pointed to wear it to advantage.

Miss Darby (while in the throes of fever)
to her father, Colonel Darby
in *Miss Darby's Darkest Hour*

As quickly as Rafe found himself transfixed by the lady before him, he realized how wrong he'd been. For up close, Miss Tate did not possess the qualities of the imaginary Miss Darby, but she did exhibit nearly every trait on his list of potential suspects:

1. The lady was obviously a spinster. There was no first blush on her cheek, no dewy light to her eyes like some Bath miss fresh from school.
2. In her market basket was a book, which a quick glance revealed as Sir John Sutton's *Translations of Early Latin*. The lady was a bluestocking of the first order. Early Latin? What lady read such stuff?
3. Her pinched lips and the set of her jaw was enough to scare off any man who might con-

sider the temptation of stealing a kiss—even
that insipid Throckmorten.

The only thing missing was the horde of cats at her
skirts, mewing for the cream and bits of chicken she in-
dulged them with on a daily basis.

She made a polite cough, and it was then that Rafe
realized he'd been caught staring at her, gawking if he
was honest about it.

And he would have stopped if he hadn't looked into
her eyes and found himself captured anew. They were
so very blue, a color that reminded him of the warm
and sultry Mediterranean. And even more, they
sparkled with mischief and intelligence, a dangerous
combination in any woman.

Her brows rose slightly as he looked at her, as if to
say she was compiling his attributes as well. But what
her estimation of him was, he couldn't tell, for not a
hint of interest filled her blue eyes.

No interest? Rafe felt his rakish reputation tarnish
ever so slightly, and he didn't like it in the least.

In fact, it was as if she'd dismissed him without a
second thought. The last time he'd been so summarily
dismissed by a woman he'd been twelve.

"May I help you?" the postmistress asked.

"I'm looking for someone," he said, moving forward,
slanting another glance at this imperious Miss Tate to
see if perhaps his eyes were playing tricks on him.

If she had been disinterested in him before, her attention was now focused on her fingernails and she'd
completely missed his attempt to undermine her indifference.

"Oh," the postmistress said, sounding relieved. She
shared a bemused glance with her friend. "Yes, I should
have known." She pointed down the street. "First lane

after the pair of dovecots. Esme's cottage isn't hard to miss. Her door is painted bright blue."

"Esme Briggs?" he asked, wondering how the lady knew who he was looking for without even asking.

She shook her head. "No, sir. Esme Maguire. The matchmaker."

The matchmaker?

Cochrane's worst fears were about to be realized.

Rafe shook his head. Probably a little too adamantly. "No! No! I'm not looking for the matchmaker," he told her, his hands waving in front of him.

"You aren't?" she asked, a little surprised.

"No!" he said. "Certainly not."

"Then whom, sir, are you looking for?" This question came from Miss Tate. Her query startled him out of his reverie, and then he realized something else about her. Her words weren't formed with the strict tones of an English lady, but held a lilt to them that whispered with an odd note like exotic spices on the nose.

They teased at his ears like the sultry tones of a well-experienced lady, one who knew how to tell a man exactly what she liked. And once again, he found himself taking another gander at this enigmatic spinster before him.

"I'm sorry, you are?" Rafe asked.

"Miss Tate," she said. "Miss Rebecca Tate." She inclined her head ever so slightly, yet her sharp gaze never left his.

So she wasn't the elusive M. Briggs. He didn't know if he was disappointed or relieved that he wouldn't have to tangle with her.

"And this is Miss Sarah Stone," she added, "the postmistress of Bramley Hollow. And you would be?"

"Danvers," he offered. "Raphael Danvers, at your service." Remembering some hint of manners, he added an elegant bow. "I'm looking for an M. Briggs," he said, reaching into his jacket and pulling out a packet of papers, as if he were merely trying to complete an errand. It was a ploy that had worked well in the past. These ladies didn't need to know the packet was the eviction papers his landlady had served him with this morning.

The postmistress shared another glance with Rebecca, only this time there was no humor in their silent communiqué.

The postmistress cocked her head. "Did you say *Miss Briggs*?"

Now I am getting somewhere. He'd have his directions and be gone from Bramley Hollow before Cochrane's dire predictions of an unplanned wedding came true. "Aye. I'm looking for Miss Briggs."

The postmistress's brow furrowed. "And what business do you have with the lady, sir?"

He wanted to tell her that his business was none of hers, and in London that would have been well and good, but he reminded himself that this was the country and a modest, more mild approach would serve him to better advantage.

"These papers are from a solicitor in London. A very confidential matter, or so I am told," he lied. Manners were one thing when they were a means to an end, but honesty had little place in his line of work.

Especially when there was so much at stake.

Miss Tate smiled at him. "How kind of you, sir, to bring something so important all the way from London to Bramley Hollow."

It was then he noticed a few tendrils of red hair peeking out from beneath her bonnet. The rebellious color seemed at odds with the prim spinster before him. Rather such silky, enticing tresses were far better suited for spilling over the tangled sheets of a moonlit boudoir, and in an instant he imagined the lady herself naked in his bed. But then he glanced at Miss Tate again, seeing only the plain lady in the hideous bonnet and wondering what had happened to the momentary temptress of his imagination.

"I said how kind it was of you to come all this way," she repeated, her brows arched in annoyance. "Very generous, indeed."

Of course she was annoyed. He was staring again.

Rafe shook his head, not so much at her question, but at his own odd thoughts. Naked spinsters? What was he thinking?

Perhaps there was something to Cochrane's fears about this village and its matchmaking reputation. He hadn't been here more than five minutes and already he was seeing a seductress in the guise of a spinster.

Cochrane would probably say that was how it always started . . .

"Nothing so generous," he told her. "Actually this charming village was hardly out of my way and I make it a habit to lend a helping hand when I can. Besides, when my friend spoke so highly of Miss Briggs, I knew I'd be only too delighted to make her acquaintance." He supposed he was laying on the charm a bit thick, but perhaps this as yet unsusceptible miss wasn't going to be such a challenge to charm after all.

He couldn't have been more wrong.

"Indeed," she mused, crossing her arms over her chest. "Now was that Miss Mary Briggs or Miss Millicent Briggs?"

Rafe coughed. "Two of them?" Just his bloody luck.

"Perhaps it says inside the packet," she said, holding out her hand. "You can trust that we are both the epitome of discretion."

The postmistress nodded enthusiastically.

Yes, and he was about to be named a Knight of the Garter.

"Mary Briggs," he said, offering up one of the names. Besides, if he was wrong, there was always his next course of action—bribing the innkeeper and explaining to Cochrane that his next meal would not be forthcoming.

Miss Tate nodded. "Of course! Miss Mary Briggs would make more sense. If you would like, I am sure Miss Stone would see your packet delivered promptly and you could be on your way."

While her lips curved sweetly, her eyes held all the predatory wiles of a cat stalking its prey.

"No, it really isn't any trouble," he said, tucking the papers back into his jacket for safekeeping.

"And it would be no trouble for Miss Stone, for in truth, it is her job," the insistent miss said, folding her arms across her chest. "Especially since, I assume, you have no real business here."

Little minx, Rafe thought. With little or no effort she'd boxed him into a corner—challenging his story and essentially calling him a liar—all the while with a pleasant, deceptive smile on her face.

Mierda, he cursed silently, reverting to his mother's native language. *She was more wily than Napoleon.*

Rafe almost felt sorry for the man who woke up and found himself matched to this termagant.

Then again, it was no wonder she was still *Miss* Tate. For what did it say about a lady when she couldn't even find a husband in Bramley Hollow?

The postmistress picked up her friend's cue. "You must be in a hurry, sir. Please feel free to leave Miss Briggs' packet with me and I will see it delivered to her forthwith."

The pair of cats smiled at him, looking as innocent as two young country misses could. Why he could almost smell the sweet roses and fresh manure behind their offer to help him.

"I thank you, ladies," he said. "But I fear I am under strict instructions to deliver the packet to Miss Briggs personally."

"Yes, I suppose you would want to do that," Miss Tate said, her eyes sparkling with new mischief as she slanted yet another glance at her friend behind the counter. And not to be diverted from her self-appointed mission to aid him, she then turned and said, "Mr. Danvers, if you are under such strict directions, then please allow me to take you to Miss Briggs."

"Rebecca!" Miss Stone whispered. "What are you doing?"

"Offering to help this man," she said to her friend while smiling at Rafe.

"Oh, you needn't go to any bother," he insisted, having never meant something more in his life, though he suspected his protest wouldn't matter in the least to this Miss Tate. The pushy miss was determined to make his business her business. "Perhaps you could just give me the directions, then I can be gone and leave you ladies to your . . . uh, conversation."

Miss Tate crossed the room, her steps direct and full of purpose, so very unlike her sleek and smooth counterparts in London. As she passed him, her skirt brushed his leg, and if he'd been in town he would have been of half a mind to check his wallet and watch fob after coming so close to such a wily wench, but as he looked at her again, smiling up from beneath her simple straw bonnet, he wondered if he was just being foolish.

Miss Rebecca Tate and her charming and unsullied

village of Bramley Hollow were about as far from
Seven Dials or the Rookeries as one could get in England. Obviously he was becoming as jaded as his
brothers claimed, especially when he viewed a country
spinster to be as disingenuous as a London abbess.
Miss Tate was most likely just being as congenial as
most people from the country tended to be.

That's it, she was just being generous and kind.

He shot one more glance at her blue eyes and went
with his original instincts about the lady.

She was trouble.

"There is no problem, sir," she was saying. "I am
more than happy to assist someone who is so generous
with his time." And he would have believed her innocent then if not for the bemused mockery in her eyes
that said only too clearly that she knew as well as he
that he was lying about his connection to Miss Briggs.
"Are you coming along? Or do you have other packets
you need directions for?"

Rafe cringed, but decided he'd trust her for now to
take him to Miss Briggs. Once they got there, he'd
leave her on the lady's doorstep to go seek her gossip
elsewhere.

She made her way out the door but stopped on the
steps, her gaze fixed on Cochrane. "Quite a procession just to deliver a packet." She looked from him
to Cochrane then back to him, as if she expected an
introduction.

She wasn't getting one.

Rafe shot his assistant a black look, a warning as it
were, before he asked Miss Tate, "Is Miss Briggs far?
For I see you don't have a ready mount." He was hoping she'd take the hint and just give him the directions.

"And why would I need one?" she asked. "Bramley Hollow isn't that grand, sir. Everything I could

possibly need is merely a stone's throw." She shied another glance at Cochrane, who'd now doffed his cap and was smoothing down his hair. "Unless you need your friend, why don't you just follow me? Miss Briggs isn't far." With that, she turned and strolled down a narrow path, market basket swinging in her hand.

"Wait here," he told a disappointed Cochrane, before striding after his newfound and unwanted helpmate.

When he caught up with Miss Tate, she was stopped before the gate to the churchyard.

"You seem rather an odd sort to be looking for the author of the *Miss Darby* novels."

This stopped him. Did everyone in Bramley Hollow know that Miss Briggs spent her time penning these scandalous tales?

She must have noted his surprise. She leaned forward, cupping her hand to her mouth. "You aren't the first to come here seeking her out," she whispered.

There was a wicked light in her blue gaze that teased him and once again he found himself staring at her, unsure whether or not to trust his own eyes.

"I'm not?" he managed to ask, still trying to reconcile the spinster before him with the siren who seemed to lurk beneath the lady's plain exterior.

"Oh, no," Miss Tate said, leaning back against the gate, her market basket plopped by her feet. "I think she had three visitors just last week."

So much for the bundle of coins he'd wasted on those worthless clerks. Obviously Mr. Ahey's apprentices were making a small fortune selling the directions to the popular author.

"I actually do have business with her," he said, finding some gratification in the truth.

Those damn, infuriating eyes of hers held a bemused air, but she hardly appeared impressed—with him or his assertion.

"Ah, yes. The packet to be delivered."

"You don't believe me?" Rafe wasn't used to people not heeding what he said. In his line of work, people either feared him or just wanted to avoid him.

But they didn't mock him. And even if it took a few coins to get the truth out of them, they always told him what he wanted.

Her slipper nudged at a bunch of blue flowers blooming at the foot of the gatepost. "It's just that none of the others went to the trouble to bring a packet, though one professed to have an offer of marriage, while the last one claimed she was a long lost relation. Poor Miss Briggs. Besieged by all sorts of knaves and imposters."

She reached down and plucked a few of the wayward blossoms.

"So which are you, Mr. Danvers?" she asked, straightening up and arranging the purloined stems into an orderly little nosegay. "For truly you don't look like one of her acolytes, those foolish young girls who forget the *Darby* tales are just fiction—" She paused and that assessing gaze ran from the toes of his less than polished boots to the top of his hat. "Then again you hardly appear the type to come ringing a righteous peel over her head either, like the vicar who arrived last month."

"I have a business proposition for her," Rafe said, holding firm to the truth. It was a business proposition of sorts. *Stop writing or else.* "And if you don't mind, if you could finish escorting me to her, then I can be done with my business and return to London."

Her glance seemed to say, *Where you belong*, though her good manners held sway. "Why we are already there."

He glanced up at the yard, and then at the cozy vicarage sitting like a tidy mushroom beside the ancient stone church.

The vicar's residence? Oh, Lord. This wasn't his day.

He'd bet even money he'd been sent to break the arms of the vicar's spinster sister.

If Spain hadn't been enough hell for one existence, then this day was proving itself a close second.

"Here?" he managed to ask, trying to determine how far into Dante's rings of hell he was going to have to wade through after he'd "persuaded" some kindhearted old lady to quit writing.

She'd probably offer Cochrane a plate of sugared biscuits right before they got down to the business of wrenching a promise out of her never to write again.

"Yes, right over there to the left," she said, pointing across the yard to the far corner.

And in the opposite direction of the house. He nearly sighed with relief until he saw where she was going.

Having opened the gate, Rebecca was picking her way through the yard, her skirt swinging this way and that as she wove past the headstones and lichen covered stone monuments raised for Bramley Hollow's more illustrious former residents. She paused and glanced over her shoulder. "Come on. This is what you came all the way from London to discover."

He followed, now convinced he was part of some great jest the postmistress and her friend liked to play on unsuspecting visitors.

"Here she is," she said, pointing at a simple headstone.

Rafe strode across the graveyard, ready to end this charade.

"Careful as you go," Miss Tate said, pointing at his boot which hung in mid-stride. "You are about to step on Abigail Roundsfield, and she would be quite put out by the insult."

Rafe moved his foot over, just avoiding trespassing on Mrs. Roundsfield's slumber.

"If this is some kind of prank, Miss Tate," he said, "let me assure you I am not the kind to find such diversions amusing."

She glanced him over again. "No, I suppose you aren't."

Rafe bristled. Well, she needn't say it like he was some aged high-stickler. Why he'd have her know . . .

"Here we are," she was saying, interrupting his silent outrage at being so summarily dismissed. "Though, I think you will agree, 'tis hardly a laughing matter."

And when he glanced down, he realized that she hadn't been joking with him—just leading him to a dead end, quite literally. For at his feet was the very lady he sought.

Mary Briggs, Spinster
1732–1784
Forgotten in life
Forgotten no more

And by the time he'd regained his composure, he discovered his escort was already out the gate and walking back into town, whistling a most unbecoming tune, and swinging her basket as if she hadn't a care in the world.

"Now wait just a damn minute," he said, crossing the yard and not caring two farthings if he disturbed Mrs. Roundsfield's sacred dreams.

It didn't take him long to catch up with Miss Tate. "That wasn't funny," he said, pointing back at the graveyard.

She paused and glanced over her shoulder at him. "No, I suppose not," she said, before continuing down the road.

"Miss Tate," he ground out. "You offered to help me."

"Yes, I suppose I did. But did it ever occur to you that Miss Briggs doesn't want to be found?" She folded her arms over her chest again. "And if you are truly doing a favor for her solicitor then I think you would have her *complete* directions instead of having to ask around like some cheaply had Bow Street runner."

Bow Street? This is what she thought of him? Obviously his town charm didn't translate very well to the countryside.

Then to his further chagrin, Miss Tate didn't wait breathlessly for his reply, instead she left him standing in the road, like one might say . . . a cheaply had runner.

At this point, Cochrane came walking up to the churchyard, leading their horses. He glanced at the departing Miss Tate and then at Rafe.

"No luck, sir?"

"In a manner of speaking," Rafe told him, as he pointed at the lonely plot in the corner. One that was now decorated with a small bouquet of blue flowers.

Cochrane tied up the horses and crossed the graveyard, tiptoeing through the grass as if he feared someone was going to reach up and grab his offending toes. When he reached Miss Briggs' headstone, he pulled off his cap and bowed his head in respectful observation.

But Cochrane's good graces for the pegged out spinster ended quickly. He heaved a sigh and then settled his cap back on. "So are we bound for London?" Hope filled his question.

"Not yet," Rafe said, grabbing up his horse's reins. The road where Miss Tate had been ambling along moments earlier was now empty. He couldn't very well go about town banging on doors to find the infuriating little minx or to find the elusive *Miss Darby* author either.

Oh, she was nearby, there was no doubt in his mind and Miss Tate knew exactly who she was.

If it wasn't the lady herself.

He hadn't survived all those years behind enemy lines, dodging French piquets by not listening to his instincts, and right now they were clamoring that this seemingly innocent spinster needed closer inspection.

He let out a low growl and swung up into his saddle in one effortless movement.

"The way I see it," Cochrane began, having scrambled out of the graveyard, then up onto his horse. "If this gel is dead, then we can tell Lady Tottley that we've done our work and collect your house. Just because the reaper beat us to the business doesn't mean we shouldn't get something for coming all the way out here. Especially since there doesn't appear to be any pies about."

It wasn't a bad plan, but Rafe preferred to earn his money by doing what he'd been hired to do.

And that was stopping the publication of any more *Miss Darby* novels. Suddenly his earlier promise to Cochrane that they weren't here to break any limbs seemed rather empty.

Especially after meeting Miss Tate.

"Seems our work is done," Cochrane said, turning his horse toward the road north.

"No," Rafe told him. "We aren't finished yet." Not by a long shot.

Bribing clerks with drinks was one way to find someone. The other was to use one's connections.

Connections . . .

Demmit, why hadn't he thought of that earlier?

While Bramley Hollow may boast one of England's most infamous matchmakers, it also could claim one of England's greatest busybodies.

"Time we pay a social call," Rafe said.

"Will there be food?" Cochrane asked.

"Most likely," he told his relieved assistant. And hopefully a serving of Miss Briggs' address.

Miss Rebecca Tate returned home whistling a ditty she probably shouldn't know, and not caring if anyone heard her. She glanced back over her shoulder and smiled at the glowering figure of Mr. Danvers standing beside the graveyard.

Pompous fellow. But weren't they all? These London dandies and scatterbrained misses, making the trip to Bramley Hollow like it was some great pilgrimage and seeking out their own bit of fame by trying to find the mysterious author of the *Miss Darby* novels.

Why, if the stories continued to grow in popularity, Bramley Hollow would be overrun with these nitwits.

She had to give Mr. Danvers credit. He was quite the most inventive of the lot. All dark and dangerous like some infamous Bow Street Runner, carrying on as if he held the very fate of the world and Miss Briggs was the key.

"Bah!" she muttered under her breath. His packet of papers was probably nothing more than his tailor's bill.

No, she thought, changing her mind. He didn't look the sort who spent a great deal of time fussing about his looks. His coat and neckerchief, tied in a very hasty knot, spoke of a man who didn't like to be held to fashion's fastidious rules.

In truth, he most likely didn't need a commanding suit of clothes to get his way—his charm and disarming smile probably had the female population of London falling at his feet offering their aid in whatever he sought.

She could see why. It would be easy to believe the lies that tumbled from his lips like honey, trust that the unfathomable depths of his dark eyes could be navigated without peril to one's heart.

Poor Mr. Danvers, she thought remembering the shock on his face as he stared down at Miss Briggs' grave and realized he hadn't gotten his way.

Most likely it was the first time he'd ever had a woman deny him. Served him right. Really, it wasn't as if she were the type of lady worth all his flattery and gawking. Yet in the glow of his charm and smile, he'd made her feel like one of those Originals in town who kept all the men at sixes and sevens. He'd gazed at her like she was some daring Incognita, a wicked lady in heart and deed.

Perhaps, Rebecca mused, she was as wicked as Mrs. Wortling, their housekeeper, liked to tell her uncle. And while she considered herself a practical lady, since most poor ones were by necessity, she had no delusions about who or what she was. A plain, country spinster.

As Rebecca drew up to her gate, the shrill voice of their resident harridan rang out with a discordant trill.

"Colonel, sir, come down off the roof. I have it on good authority your watch is over and there ain't a bit of them Benjali blokes lurking about."

Rebecca cringed. Her uncle was on the roof again.

She glanced around to see if the neighbors had noticed. If they had, they would be giving the cottage a wide berth. Especially after the colonel had shot at John Benton a few months back, mistaking him for a Punjab scout.

"Who goes there?" the colonel bellowed from behind the chimney.

Rebecca stopped at the gate and glanced up at the roof. Lord, there he was again, Brown Bess in hand. She swore she'd locked it and the powder up after the last incident.

" 'Tis me, Colonel. Rebecca," she called to him. "I've been to town." She held up her basket for him to see.

"Lieutenant Bex. Good man," he said, cautiously poking his nose around the brick and mortar. "Thinking of provisions when we are all but surrounded."

"Only by Englishmen, sir. Now come down and I'll see if I can get Mrs. Wortling to serve us an early tea."

"Tea? At a time like this? Never, my good man. Besides, we seem to be out of shot and powder."

Good, she thought. He hadn't managed to find where she'd hidden it. She'd told him time and time again not to shoot at the neighbors. Even if it was only to keep up appearances.

Around her feet a large mangy ginger colored cat wove and purred. Rebecca set her basket down and snatched up the animal. "What if I were to send up Ajax?" she offered.

"Corporal Ajax, you say? He's on report. Should be in stocks. If it weren't for his connections, I'd have seen him drummed out months ago."

"Been in the cream again, eh, fellow?" Rebecca whispered to the ill-mannered cat. She'd found Ajax aboard the ship that had brought them home from India.

While Rebecca made it a rule to avoid stray, handsome men, she hadn't been able to resist the ragged tomcat—though in hindsight, perhaps she should have tried a little harder.

Ajax was a beast of a feline—always breaking into the larder and spilling the cream, scratching up the furniture or any human leg or limb that happened to be nearby. And while she might outwardly agree with Mrs. Wortling and the colonel that the cat was a menace, secretly Rebecca rather admired her fiendish and independent companion.

As she continued to scratch behind his ragged ears, Ajax purred in contentment, looking deceptively amiable though most likely plotting his next raid on the pantry.

Rebecca glanced up at the roof once more. "Come down, Colonel. The baker had those raisin buns you like and I was able to commandeer a nice tin of pekoe that Mr. McGraw assures me is very fresh."

"Harrumph," he snorted. "Sounds like bribery."

"Can't keep a sharp mind when your stomach isn't full," she said, quoting one of his favorite bits of advice.

"Right you are, Bex," he said. Taking one last look through his spyglass, he surveyed the empty road and the surrounding countryside. "Seems clear for now," he muttered. He pushed it closed and stuffed it into his belt. "Suppose a spot of tea and a bit of food wouldn't be out of the question. Tell Ensign Trotter I'll expect his report on the perimeter lines before tea."

Mrs. Wortling huffed. "Miss Tate, that man should be in Bedlam. Ensign Trotter, indeed!" She stomped off toward the house.

Her uncle's imaginary aide-de-camp, Ensign Trotter, kept Mrs. Wortling in a fine state. She didn't like the idea that she was supposed to care for someone she couldn't see, let alone provide the extra service that wasn't included in her wages.

Rebecca held her breath as her uncle ambled across the stone roof. One day these lofty rambles were going to leave him with a broken neck. She rushed over to the ladder that he'd leaned against the house—most likely after she'd left to do her shopping—and held it steady as he climbed down.

Now she had to add the garden shed to her list of places to keep locked. Right along with the shot and powder.

When he got to the bottom, he looked into her eyes and smiled. "Ah, Bex, my girl," he said, reaching out to touch her cheek. "You take good care of me. What would I do without you?"

"What would Richard and I have done if you and Aunt Dorie hadn't taken us in all those years ago?" She wove her arm into the crook of his, guiding him toward the cottage door. As they passed her market basket, she swooped down and picked it up.

"You two scamps gave Dorothea someone other than me to worry about," he told her. "But what would she say if she could see you now? Five and twenty and still not married, stuck here taking care of me in my dotage." He let out a long sigh, as if her lack of matrimonial state was all his fault. "She always wanted you to marry that Lieutenant . . . Lieutenant . . . oh the devil take him, what was his name?"

"Habersham," Rebecca supplied, having heard this lecture a thousand times before. "Lieutenant Habersham."

"Ah, yes. Habersham. Good man, that Habersham. Danced with you enough. Brought you loads of posies.

Should have married him before he shipped home, Bex. Would have seen you properly settled."

She smiled at her dear protector. "There is one simple reason why I didn't marry Lieutenant Habersham. He didn't ask me."

Colonel Posthill snorted. "Then I take back what I said. He's a demmed fool, I tell you. A fool."

That and other things, she thought as she caught up the latch and opened the front door.

Immediately there was an onslaught from Mrs. Wortling.

"I'm glad to see you've got him off the roof, Miss Rebecca. Gone mad as a hatter this time. Called me an ugly old toss-pot when I wouldn't give him the shot." She pulled a large grayed square of linen from her apron pocket and sniffed loudly into it.

Rebecca would bet that Mrs. Wortling had been called a lot worse than a drunkard in her spotty career as a housekeeper. Still, at the very least she needed to keep the peace and tried to smile sympathetically at the woman.

She was, after all, their fifth housekeeper in as many years, and had lasted twice as long as any of the others.

"A woman has her character, her reputation to maintain," Mrs. Wortling was wailing. "It wouldn't do my name any good for the neighbors to be hearing me called a 'toss-pot.'" She blew another loud, wet snort into her handkerchief.

"I am sure no one heard him, Mrs. Wortling." And if they had, they would probably have agreed. Rebecca doubted there was anyone in the village who didn't know their housekeeper was prone to tip the bottle.

"I should hope not," the housekeeper said, reaching for the shopping basket and then taking a peek under the cloth. "Tsk, tsk, tsk. You forgot to get the colonel's Madeira. He's almost out," she chastened.

Almost out because you've gone and drunk it, Rebecca wanted to counter. They'd taken to locking up the liquor cabinet, but that hadn't deterred the illustrious Mrs. Wortling. Rebecca suspected the woman picked the lock.

Still, confronting their only servant or complaining to the woman wouldn't do. Mrs. Wortling had the same look about her that the last housekeeper had held moments before she'd thrown up her hands in despair and quit.

It had taken them nearly two months to find Mrs. Wortling, and Rebecca had been nearly at her wits end between trying to maintain the house, carry on the colonel's correspondence, and keep them financially afloat.

"Tea, Mrs. Wortling, if you please," the colonel said, sweeping into the room and settling into his chair, looking and sounding like the regular country gentleman that he was supposed to be.

"Harrumph," Mrs. Wortling snorted before stomping off to the kitchen.

"Bex," the colonel said, looking up from his paper. "Did you write to Mr. Billingsworth about that tract on the Roman ruins nearby?"

"Yes, sir."

"Hmm," he murmured. "Wonder why he hasn't seen fit to respond. We'll give him until the end of the month. Then be a dear and write him another reminder." He sighed. "If my translations are correct the lost wages of Hadrian are buried not far from there. Such a treasure will make us rich, not to mention famous."

Treasure! Rebecca held back a loud groan. How she wished she'd never heard the word. It held nothing but empty promises and unending disappointments.

She glanced over at her desk, with its mountain of papers and letters and bills. Not for the first time, Rebecca wondered what it would have been like to marry Lt. Habersham, now Viscount Pease, and live a life of luxury, instead of the poverty in which they struggled.

Not that she knew any other way to live.

Oh, there was the colonel's retirement pay, but he had never held a regiment, never made a very good showing in the army, so the half pay he received was not nearly enough for them to live on.

Luckily, his cousin, a local baron, had offered them this cottage in which to live.

But what would she do if something happened to the colonel? Then where would she be? Continue living on Lord and Lady Finch's good graces? Not if she had her way.

Pulling a small ledger from her writing desk, Rebecca looked over her contingency plan. All she needed was a little more money, then she'd find the security and stability that had alluded her all her life. It was all she'd ever wanted and she wasn't going to let anyone stop her.

Glancing up, she saw two figures ride by, Mr. Danvers and his young companion. To her relief, they didn't stop, but continued riding. Hopefully, he'd given up and was leaving Bramley Hollow for good.

And good riddance to him, she thought, trying to dismiss him from her thoughts, but it wasn't that easy. His dark good looks and charm had left her ruffled and disquieted. So much for her practical resolve to avoid such men. They only reminded her of all she had lost so many years ago, and of all she still desired.

Well, if there was one good point to consider, it was that if the arrogant lout came looking for her, his reception would be the colonel and his trusty Brown Bess. That ought to send him running back to London.

Looking over her list of things to do she added one more item.

Leave the powder unlocked.

Chapter 3

Though I am never one to carry tales out of turn, I do believe Miss Darby carries a terrible secret in her heart. What vexes me something terrible is, I can't for the life of me determine how we can get her to divulge it. Discreetly, of course.

Lady Lowthorpe to Miss Cecilia Overton
in *Miss Darby's Daring Dilemma*

Rafe Danvers had never actually met the infamous Lady Finch, but his brothers, Colin and Robert, and their cousin, the Duke of Setchfield, all swore that if one ever got in a bind, the baroness was perhaps the only person in England (besides the now missing Mr. Pymm) who would know the answer to any puzzle.

Though the baroness stayed for the most part at her husband's Kent estate, that didn't stop her from keeping her nose firmly stuck in the *ton* and all its gossip. She employed no less than three couriers whose sole positions were to ride back and forth to London with her legendary correspondence, in addition to her full-time (and much beleaguered) secretary who copied out her advice sheets and kept her vast records of marriages and children and events and sins. Her letters were considered either a welcome boon of good information or a blistering barrage of advice that would leave the recipient's ears burning for weeks to follow.

No one dared slight the lady or countermand her advice, for one day they might need Lady Finch's good graces to save them from a peccadillo, or worse yet a scandal, that with only a few of her well-placed endorsements could wipe the path of disgrace free and clear.

"I don't think this is a good idea," Cochrane said as they rode closer to the gates. "Mr. Pymm always said Lady Finch was in with the devil himself. A good example of what happens when you let women read and write."

"Pymm said that?" Rafe asked.

Cochrane nodded. "That and more. She sent him a letter once. I don't know what it said, 'cause he burned it, but I dare say whatever she told him singed his pride more than that match did the parchment. Had him muttering her name like a curse for a good seven months."

Rafe laughed. Must have been some letter. He'd never gained such a favor from her—either in admonishment or in advice.

He supposed she left those particular privileges to his sisters-in-law. After all, Olivia, Robert's wife, had been Lady Finch's secretary for seven years.

As they passed through the gates of Finch Manor, Cochrane gaped at the massive pair of stone lions guarding either side of the entrance.

A timbered manse, an old gatehouse Rafe reasoned, sat just inside the walls, while a long drive stretched past it and up toward the main house.

Situated on a small knoll, Finch Manor was an elegant collection of stone and marble, grand evidence of the passion for building that had struck several generations of Finch lords. Rafe knew the current baron loved botany and had added a great glassed orangery to the south wing, along with classical gardens all around the house.

"Gads," Cochrane muttered, taking a glance up at

the three-storied house that spread out before them. " 'Iffin that Bettlesfield Park that Lady Tottley is offering you is even half the size of this one, they'll have to make you one of those lords."

"I doubt that is going to happen," Rafe said. Given his less than sterling service in the army and his tarnished reputation around town, he'd have to save the entire royal family from a mob of anarchists before he'd have a hope in hell of ever seeing even a meager "Sir" before his name.

But as he gazed at the manicured lawns and the smooth yellow stone building, he felt an odd ache tug at his chest.

This was a home. A place one settled and stayed. The kind of place where one actually unpacked one's trunk.

He didn't hold out any hope that the property Lady Tottley had dangled before him could be as well-kept as the meticulous lawns and blooming gardens of Finch Manor, but the green hills and trimmed hedges of Kent spoke of an ordered life that so far in his thirty some years had eluded him.

And until the countess had offered it, he'd never held any interest in gaining property, for to be rooted in a house, one had to belong to a place.

And Rafe Danvers had never fit in. In Spain, his English blood had kept him at arm's length from his aristocratic relations. In England, his Iberian heritage was just as frowned upon. The army had been too full of rules and regulations and ridiculous notions that a man could lead troops into battle just because his father had the price of a commission.

His return to London hadn't been much more welcoming, especially once he'd decided to do the unthinkable—offer his services for hire. But then again, he really didn't care what society thought.

At the door, Rafe produced his card to the butler and explained his connection to the family, especially his sister-in-law, the Marchioness of Bradstone.

The man grinned at the mention of "Mrs. Keates," and welcomed Rafe and Cochrane into the foyer before setting off to tell her ladyship of her visitors.

Cochrane stood in the middle of the round marble entryway and gaped up at the columns and paintings and lush blue drapes.

"A far cry from Seven Dials, eh, Cochrane?" Rafe asked.

"I never," he muttered back.

The butler returned and led them through the house to the dining room. It had wide windows that let in the late afternoon light and beyond was a garden and gazebo awash in spring flowers.

The table was elegantly set for dinner. A young lady in widow's weeds faced them, while a gentleman of some years sat at the far end of the table, his nose buried in a journal.

"So I finally meet the infamous Raphael Danvers," a voice booming with enthusiasm called out.

Rafe turned and fixed his gaze on a regal figure in a mauve gown and purple turban. Lady Finch.

Cochrane looked ready to bolt.

"Lady Finch, I presume," Rafe said bowing low. "It is an honor to meet you."

"People always say that to me, but few mean it," she laughed.

"My family owes you a great debt, and therefore I do consider it an honor. You've helped my brothers and now here I am also seeking your counsel."

At this, her eyes lit with interest.

Rafe had never doubted for a moment that Lady Finch wouldn't rise to the occasion, especially when the opportunity to meddle came begging at her doorstep.

She drew closer to him, studying him with a scrutiny that would have been considered rude by most. Rafe, having grown up with a twin brother, was used to the minute examination.

"You have your brother Robert's fierce mien, but from what I hear, you also possess Colin's sharp mind."

"Thank you, ma'am, though I doubt either of them would appreciate your assessment."

She laughed. "I suppose not. Not given what else I've heard about your more interesting exploits," she said, whacking his arm with her fan and then glancing over his shoulder. "And who do we have here?"

"Beg your pardon," he said. "May I present my assistant, Cochrane."

Cochrane managed a halfway decent bow, though he kept a wary eye on the baroness. Apparently Pymm had used stories of Lady Finch on the lad like parents used the boogeyman to frighten children into proper behavior.

"Cochrane what?" the lady asked, coming around Rafe to get a good look.

"Just Cochrane, ma'am," he managed to stutter.

She drew closer, her sharp gaze fixed on him. "You have a familiar look to you. Who was your father?"

"I don't rightly know, ma'am. Mr. Pymm took me in when I was just a wee lad."

"Pymm, you say?" she managed, glancing over at Rafe.

He nodded to her.

"Harrumph! That old weasel took you in of his own free will?"

"Aye," Cochrane said. "Raised me like his own son."

Rafe watched as the lady took one last searching gaze of Cochrane's features. From the arch of her brow, he suspected she doubted the boy's assertion of Pymm's paternal charity.

"Cochrane, would I be correct in assuming that Mr. Danvers hasn't fed you yet today?" Lady Finch asked.

He shook his head. "Not since breakfast, ma'am."

"A crime," she said, good-heartedly. "Please, you both must join us for dinner."

Rafe shook his head. "We didn't mean to intrude on your meal and would be just as happy to wait until you are finished."

He ignored the indignant and painful nudge into his back. Turning down a free meal was sacrilege to Cochrane.

"I insist," Lady Finch said. "It is only my secretary, Mrs. Radleigh, and Lord Finch and he is no company whatsoever when his Orchid Society journal arrives."

Lord Finch glanced up and managed a nod to his guests, then went back to his reading.

The lady of the house let out an indulgent sigh. "As you can see, we keep country hours here and do not stand on ceremony." She nodded to the butler. "Addison, could you please set places for Mr. Danvers and our famished new friend, Cochrane."

"You may find your larders emptied," Rafe warned her.

"It will give the kitchen staff something to do," she said, as a grinning Cochrane happily took the chair Lady Finch waved her hand toward.

She smiled after him, and then took her place at the head of the table. She motioned Rafe to take the one beside her. "What brings you here to Finch Manor, Mr. Danvers? Don't tell me it is true that Lady Tottley has hired you to end these *Darby* troubles I've been deluged with."

This took him aback. Lady Tottley had sworn her co-conspirators to secrecy.

"Never mind," Lady Finch said. "I can see from your face you've taken a vow of silence on the matter. So tell me everything. Especially since it was my suggestion."

"Yours?" he asked.

"Oh, yes. I've been inundated with letters from every mother with a marriageable daughter pleading with me to help them. I may have hinted to Malvina she hire you to help her find this author and gently suggested that you might be able to persuade them to stop writing."

"Now I know whom to blame," Rafe said.

"You may thank me in the end," she said. "That is if Lady Tottley rewards you as generously as I advised her. She had better have dangled something pretty substantial before you to entice you to take time away from your work on the Codlin case." She patted her lips with her napkin. "Now, humor an old lady, and tell me what she offered and I'll help you in any way I can, for I can't imagine someone as purse tight as Malvina Witherspoon offering anything that would make it worth your time, not with the East India Company having raised their reward to two thousand pounds."

Cochrane waggled his brows at Rafe, an *I-told-you-so* sort of gesture.

Rafe set aside his wonder at Lady Finch's sources and smiled at her. Actually her offer was better than he'd hoped for. He'd thought he'd have to divulge a lot more than just his payment to gain her aid.

"Bettlesfield Park," he told her.

The lady's eyes narrowed. "Did you say *Bettlesfield Park*?"

"Yes. The house and property if I stop the *Darby* author from publishing any more tracts."

Lady Finch's reaction didn't do much to instill confidence. She burst out laughing, and continued so, until tears ran down her wrinkled cheeks. "Oh, my dear boy, tell me this isn't true?"

He shifted in his seat. "Yes. It is." Rafe dug into his jacket and produced a miniature of the house. "She showed me this and said it was a fine estate."

Taking his offering, Lady Finch peered down at the delightful country vista and well-situated manse and began laughing anew. "A fine estate—of all the nerve. I hope you weren't planning on moving in any time soon."

So his suspicions had been right. Still, the property had to be worth something—for he was only interested in the cash it would gain him. "No, I was going to sell it. What do I need a house for?"

"I suppose you don't," she said, though she didn't sound convinced. She handed him back the deceptive portrait. "Malvina won the property in a game of whist about four years ago and it's been a noose around her neck ever since."

"Is it worthless?" he asked, more than willing to return to London and wish Lady Tottley many happy years with her unwed daughter at her side.

"No, just in need of repair."

Lord Finch, seemingly still captivated by his orchid journal, made an ignoble snort.

Lady Finch shrugged. "The baron is probably right. A lot of repairs. But the land is good and you should have no problems finding someone to buy it."

"So why hasn't Lady Tottley been able to sell it?" he asked, still suspicious that his possible fortune was now dwindling to a meager purse.

"She's had offers, but mostly from mushrooms and other cits who want to set themselves up with a country address. She's rather high in the instep and has refused them all so far, much to my relief." Lady Finch sighed. "I suppose you won't be so particular though and I'll end up with another one of these ridiculous and pretentious nabobs for a neighbor."

Rafe smiled at this. "I haven't the means to be choosey, so it will be the first fool I can find."

"You shouldn't have any trouble there, for London is full of them," Lady Finch remarked before returning to her meal. "And though I see now that you are going to be the ruination of Bramley Hollow, I'll still help you. But I'll ask a boon in return."

Rafe felt an uncharacteristic twinge of guilt, and in a weak moment said, "My lady, if there is anything I can do to repay your favor, you have but to ask."

She glanced up from her plate and studied him. "Since you've offered, there is a matter of some importance that I would like your assistance with."

"Anything."

"Not for me, but for someone else."

Something about the way she said it sent a warning clamor down his spine. Yet before he could inquire further, a young man entered the dining room.

"Rafe? Rafe Danvers? Is that you? Demmit, I thought I'd gone round the bend when I saw you ride past the gatehouse," he said, hobbling into the room, leaning heavily on a silver tipped cane.

"Jemmy," Rafe said, more in shock than in delight at seeing James Reyburn, the Finch heir and only child. Like his mother, Jemmy was a recluse, though for different reasons.

Years earlier the young man had impetuously stowed away on Colin's ship and ended up in Rafe's guerilla band searching the Iberian Peninsula for an ancient treasure.

But the fresh-faced, idealistic young man he remembered held little resemblance to this pale, haggard man before him. Rafe saw only too clearly the terrible price Jemmy had paid for his noble dreams of war.

One hand clung to a cane, which he obviously needed to walk, his once shattered leg dragging along, sad evidence of the nearly fatal injuries he'd suffered at the Siege of Badajoz. There was also a long scar on one side of his face and he looked pale and thin. Hardly the rakish and robust daredevil Rafe remembered who'd come to Spain determined to make his place in history.

And when Rafe glanced over at Lady Finch, he knew without a doubt what she wanted.

She wanted him to help her save Jemmy.

Dios, what had he gotten himself into?

"What are you doing here?" Jemmy asked, as Addison set a place and filled a plate for him.

"I've come to ask your mother's aid in finding someone."

"Yes, and he was nearly to telling me whom, when you arrived," Lady Finch said. "I thought you weren't hungry and deemed us too boring to eat with?"

"I didn't know you were having company," Jemmy told her, winking at Rafe. "So who are you looking for? A murderer? A thief? Some foreign spy? Bramley Hollow is hardly a hotbed for insurrection and unrest."

"No one of that nature. I'm looking for the author of the *Miss Darby* novels."

Jemmy put down his knife and fork. "What? You're looking for some spinster scribbler?" The young man broke into wails of laughter. "Oh, you must be up the

River Tick if you're chasing after harmless blue-stockings."

"Scarcely harmless," Lady Finch said. "Those novels have caused a revolution amongst the *ton*. Daughters refusing to marry, can you imagine such a thing? Almost as bad as heirs who refuse to take their obligations seriously."

Jemmy ignored his mother's jab at his own unmarried state and turned to Rafe. "So you think this chit is here?"

"Yes. My information says that the M. Briggs who is writing the books lives here in Bramley Hollow."

"Here? Imagine that," Jemmy said. "If you ask me, those *Darby* books are a shocking waste of time. Utter nonsense. I wonder that anyone gives them a bit of regard."

"I wouldn't be so quick to judge," Lady Finch told her son.

Rafe couldn't resist asking, for there was something a little too defensive in the lady's words, "Have you read the *Darby* books, my lady?"

At first she started to shake her head, then stopped. "Oh, I must confess I've read every single one. I couldn't put them down." She sighed. "Would be a shame to see the stories end, but I can see Malvina's point. Can't have all these girls running about decrying marriage. Now that's utter nonsense." She shook her head. "And you? Have you read them?"

Rafe shifted in his seat. 'Twas embarrassing to admit the truth. "I've only just started the first one, *Miss Darby's Daring Dilemna.* Though purely as part of my case." He wasn't about to admit, especially not in front of Jemmy Reyburn, that he'd been up till the wee hours reading the demmed thing.

"And what do you think of them?" she asked.

He ignored the smirk on Jemmy's face. "They aren't quite what I expected," he confessed. "This Miss Briggs does know how to spin a story. But that Lieutenant Throckmorten is an insufferable boor."

"Agreed. I was glad to see him die at the end of *Miss Darby's Darkest Hour*."

Rafe's gaze shot up. "He dies?" Not that he cared, for Throckmorten was only a figment of Miss Brigg's fertile imagination, but it was a shame to think of Miss Darby as brokenhearted.

"Ha!" she said, pointing a finger at him. "You are as besotted as the rest of the *ton*."

"I suppose," he admitted, not willing to tell the lady that now he would have to burn an extra candle tonight to see how exactly Throckmorten's utterly dull life ended.

"Are you so sure the author is here in Bramley Hollow?" Mrs. Radleigh asked. It was the first time she'd entered the conversation, but her question was well put.

"I have it from the clerks in her publishing house that the manuscripts come from Bramley Hollow and the payments are sent here as well."

"But who could it be?" Lady Finch mused aloud, more to herself.

"Perhaps it is one of those nabobs you love so much," Jemmy teased. "Especially since all the *Miss Darby* books take place in India."

Rafe shot him a sidelong glance. "I thought you said you hadn't read the books." He grinned down the table at Lady Finch. "Utter nonsense, wasn't that what he called them?"

She smiled. "I believe his exact words were 'a shocking waste of time.'"

"Well it was a waste of time to read them." Jemmy

conceded, then grinned. Then he leaned forward, his elbows resting on the table, a mischievous light in his eyes. "But at least I know how Throckmorten died."

"Has everyone read these books but me?" Rafe asked.

The entire party nodded, including Lord Finch and Cochrane.

"*Et tu?*" Rafe asked his assistant.

"Pymm said it would show me the evils of what happens when a gel gets too headstrong," Cochrane said between bites, ignoring the snort of dismay from Lady Finch's end of the table. "But I thought that Miss Darby is probably a real swell sort of lady. Wouldn't fuss if a fellow didn't have the best of manners and all." He swiped at his chin with his sleeve and went back to his dinner, as if suddenly embarrassed to have all eyes upon him.

Rafe glanced at Lady Finch and found her studying Cochrane once again, her expression maternal and something else, as if she were making notes to herself.

Poor lad, he thought. *That woman is going to take you under her wing.* Cochrane may have learned his trade from the spymaster, but he was about to meet the master meddler. He didn't stand a chance.

Better him than me, Rafe thought, before returning to the subject at hand. "I think you might be on to something, Jemmy. The author would have to be someone who knows India, or is well enough read to have a good command of the locale and customs. A nabob's daughter, perhaps."

"Cits and mushrooms," Lady Finch said. "Nuisances, one and all. Buying up every sort of manor and acting like kings. No manners, no breeding, just an obscene amount of money that allows them to think they should be included with the gentry."

Jemmy shot Rafe an arched glance. *Now, you've done it.*

"Are there many of them about?" Rafe asked, realizing this was as good a place as any to start. Maybe he'd find that infuriating Miss Tate once again. He'd like to see if her blue eyes still held that mocking skepticism once he'd unmasked his quarry. Without her witty aid.

"How many? Too many, according to mother," Jemmy told him. "Take you at least a week, most likely two just to call on all of them. But I doubt just making a social call will work, for whoever it is must be very good at keeping their scribbling a secret if mother hasn't discovered them before now. Besides, to get into their houses, you'd have to take mother along with you."

Lady Finch groaned, looking as if she were about to be ill at such a prospect. But she was saved from that horrendous fate by her husband.

Lord Finch glanced up from his end of the table. "Why not just invite them all here? All the likely suspects and that sort of rot. Have one of those supper parties you're always pestering me about. Ought to be able to winnow your likely author from the field."

Rafe and Jemmy glanced down at Lady Finch. She looked about to choke on a forkful of cheese tart.

"Here? To Finch Manor?" she managed to sputter. "You want me to invite those . . . cits into my home? Preposterous!" She shuddered. "Why, if word got out that I had lowered myself to entertaining nabobs and mushrooms, my good opinion would hold no continence with anyone of any social standing."

"All anyone will remember, my lady," Rafe told her, warming to the idea since it would expedite his time in Bramley Hollow, "is that you assisted in unmasking the author of the *Darby* tales. In that light, your heroic sacrifice will be regarded as merely another indication of the great lengths you will go to aid your peers." He added a charming smile and a wink to his plea.

The lady picked up her fan and fluttered it at him. "Go on with you, Raphael Danvers. You are as silver-tongued as your father once was. And I'll have you know he was quite a favorite of mine when I was out."

There was another snort from the baron's end of the table.

Lady Finch ignored him.

"The idea of a supper party does have merit," Rafe said. "For I couldn't call on these people without you accompanying me and you did say you would help me." He glanced over at Jemmy. "How many visits would it entail?"

"Weeks worth," he said, clearly enjoying the idea of his mother being sidetracked for a good fortnight or so.

Glancing over at Mrs. Radleigh, Lady Finch asked, "How many likely families are there?"

"Fifteen at least," the young woman replied. "And I imagine they would all come if you invited them to dinner."

"Fifteen?" Now it was Jemmy's turn to express disapproval. "Why not just invite the entire Indian subcontinent and be done with it? No, I think you two should go out and visit each one. Uncover them in their own lair, so to say."

Jemmy wasn't getting rid of his mother that easily.

"It won't be necessary to invite them all," Lady Finch said. "We can eliminate a good many of them for any number of reasons. I have no more desire to see this house overrun than you do, Jemmy."

"Thank heavens," Rafe heard him mutter under his breath.

"Who do you think would be our most likely suspects, Mrs. Radleigh?" Lady Finch asked.

Her secretary paused, her brow furrowed. "Major Harrington and Mrs. Harrington, most decidedly," she said. "And Charlotte, of course."

"Their daughter," Lady Finch said, nodding. "She seems an intelligent enough sort, possibly capable of writing two lines of sense."

Mrs. Radleigh nodded in agreement. "I'd say she's your most obvious choice. But there are also the Gadbury sisters."

"Yes, good suggestion," Lady Finch said, tapping her fan against her chin. She glanced over at Rafe and said in explanation, "They were raised in India and certainly know the country and habits. And both have a fondness for literature. Yes, either of them could be your author."

"Miss Alminta or Miss Honora?" Jemmy sputtered. He set down his wineglass and motioned for Addison to refill it. "You can't think that one of those ape leaders is Miss Briggs? Why the very idea of them being *Miss Darby's* creator is preposterous. Why Miss Darby is elegant and sophisticated, which neither of those two ladies, kind though they are, could ever imagine." His brows furrowed together and he sat back in his seat.

"I think I'll have to consult you as my resident *Darby* expert, Jemmy," Rafe teased. "You sound quite enamored."

"I'll loan you *Miss Darby's Perilous Journey*. Read how she escapes a pack of Barbary pirates and you'll see what I mean." Jemmy sighed. "She's one dashing chit."

Lady Finch cleared her throat. "So we have the Harringtons, the Gadburys, and who else?" she asked, bringing the conversation back to a more respectable subject.

"The Swantons," Mrs. Radleigh offered. "Mrs. Swanton is educated and she certainly isn't afraid to voice her opinion."

Lady Finch groaned. "That bothersome woman? Why she's the most grating, meddlesome, interfering—"

A polite fit of coughing broke out at the other end of the table. Jemmy looked about to fall out of his seat, while Mrs. Radleigh held her napkin to her twitching lips.

Lady Finch's iron brows arched. "Strike Mrs. Swanton. She couldn't possibly be who we are looking for. Anyone else?"

Jemmy cleared his throat and then said, "What about Kitling's second son?" The sly, innocuously innocent tone of his voice hinted at something else in his choice.

"Sydney?" Lady Finch said. "That idiot? You can't be serious."

"I was at Oxford with him and he was considered quite talented. They gave him the poetry prize his first year."

"Only in hopes that he wouldn't enter again," Lady Finch said. "We'll spend the evening listening to the woes and agonies he's suffered composing his latest canto."

"Yes, but I saw him riding past the gates the other day on a new mount and a well polished pair of Hessians. His father certainly didn't open his purse strings for those extravagances—we all know how tightfisted Sir David is."

"So he's come into some money?" Lady Finch asked, nodding to Mrs. Radleigh to make a notation in the book her secretary had beside her.

Jemmy shrugged. "He's managed to gain some blunt somehow. Who's to say it isn't from writing? He even bought rounds the other night at the inn."

Lady Finch's iron brows rose at this bit of news, but she didn't ask how Jemmy had come by it. Instead she turned to Rafe. "What I am willing to sacrifice to assist you, sir, you will never know, but the price is rising with every moment." She sighed and turned to Mrs. Radleigh. "If we invite the Harringtons we will have to invite Lord and Lady Kirkwood." She shot a glance at Jemmy as she added, "And do make sure to include Lady Victoria on the invitation."

"Mother!" Jemmy protested. "You'll not turn this night into one of your misguided attempts at matchmaking."

"Misguided?" She fluffed her napkin and settled it back down on her lap. "I'll have you know that there is an immeasurable number of couples in England who count their happiness as a direct result of my 'misguided matchmaking.' "

"And how many more that wished your unsolicited advice had gone astray?" he countered.

Mrs. Radleigh's napkin was back up at her lips.

"Bah!" Lady Finch told him. "Lady Victoria may likely be our author."

"Victoria? I think not," Jemmy said. "I would be more inclined to think it is Mrs. Radleigh than Kirkwood's daughter."

All eyes turned to Lady Finch's secretary.

"Me?" she said. "I hardly think so."

"You lived in India," Jemmy said. "And your husband was in the military. And you are always writing."

"Letters for your mother," she countered. "When would I have the time to compose novels?"

"True enough," Jemmy conceded, then winked broadly at the rest of the diners.

Lord Finch nodded to Addison. The butler filled the baron's wineglass. "If you are going to include all the likely suspects, you'd best invite Colonel Posthill and Miss Tate."

"Miss Tate?" Rafe asked, his ears perking up at the familiar name. "Miss Rebecca Tate?"

Jemmy's eyes narrowed. "You know Bex?"

"Bex?" he asked.

"Miss Tate. Bex is what the colonel calls her."

"Is she an infuriating minx with red hair?"

Jemmy laughed. "You've met our Bex," he said, before his gaze narrowed. "You've wasted little time if you've already made the lady's acquaintance."

"She was at the Post Office this afternoon when I made inquiries there."

"Isn't she the one who led you on that merry chase through the graveyard?" Cochrane interjected.

Curious looks broke out around the table.

Rafe shot Cochrane a dire look meant to tell the young man this might be his last meal.

"Never mind," Cochrane said, happily digging into the plate of beef Addison was offering.

"Fetching, isn't she?" Jemmy was saying. "But be warned, better to invite her up here than to try calling on her. The Colonel is apt to send you to an early grave if you arrive unannounced on one of his off days."

"Off?" Rafe asked.

"He's a bit daft," Jemmy said. "Likes to keep a Brown Bess at the ready, in case of invasion and all. Even bought a cannon and had it fixed in his garden pointed toward France. Fires it off periodically just to keep the enemy in check, or so he likes to say. The fellow refuses to believe that Bramley Hollow isn't on the verge of being overrun."

Lady Finch motioned for one of the footmen to remove her plate. "The poor colonel took a fever a few years ago and hasn't been the same since," She folded her napkin and placed it on the table. "He is a distant cousin of Lord Finch and when the poor man returned to England, and under rather difficult circumstances, we offered him the use of the Bramley cottage."

"And Miss Tate?" Rafe asked purely out of professional curiosity. Fetching though she might be, she'd led him on a merry chase and that he didn't appreciate. Besides, he still hadn't shaken his suspicions about her—or that first heart-stopping glance she'd shot at him over her shoulder, with the same deadly accuracy as a French sniper. Oh, there was more to the lady than just a spinster with a wry sense of humor. "Who is she?"

"His niece," Lady Finch said. "On his late wife's side. Miss Tate and her brother Richard used to live here in Bramley Hollow when they were children. Her father fancied himself something of a treasure hunter, but he never found a blessed thing. Rather, he ran through nearly every penny they had chasing myths, until he beggared them completely trying to get the entire family to India after some nonsense or another. As luck would have it, both he and Mrs. Tate died on the passage. Fortunately, the colonel and his wife took the children in when they arrived in Calcutta."

Jemmy leaned forward. "I doubt Bex is your author, what with the colonel's illness and all. He's mad as a lark most of the time. He's run them through a passel of housekeepers, while Rebecca spends a good deal of time appeasing the neighbors because the colonel's spent the afternoon shooting at their chickens. The gel hasn't got two seconds to spare most of the time."

"The colonel is, however, a rare fellow when he's lucid," Lord Finch added. "Unbeatable in chess. And devoted to Bex. And when he is in his right mind, an admirable scholar. Why, he's always asking for one of

Evaline's couriers to fetch him some Persian tract or odd translation."

That explained the Sutton volume in her market basket, Rafe reasoned, though it didn't shake his suspicions.

"And the brother? Richard?" Rafe asked. "Where is he?"

There were downcast glances all around.

"Dead. Died fighting on the Peninsula," Lady Finch finally said. "Broke the colonel's heart, for he thought of Richard like a son." She sighed. "Richard was a dear boy. He came to see us just after Jemmy left for Spain and stayed with us until he could arrange for his own commission."

"Still, if anyone deserves a bit of your meddling, mother," Jemmy said, "it would be Rebecca." He turned to Rafe. "A bit old for the Marriage Mart, still she's the type of girl who could sneak up on a fellow, and before he knew it, find he's fallen for her."

Only if he'd been struck on the head, Rafe thought, thinking the man who found himself in love with that vexing bit of muslin ought to reserve a seat at Bedlam right next to her uncle's.

But still the image of her sparkling eyes and pert lips left him oddly unbalanced. He tried to tell himself it was just because she'd gotten the better of him—at least this time.

This time? Gads, he needed to get out of Bramley Hollow post haste when some spinster got him feeling all cork-brained.

"How soon could you manage to put together this dinner?" Rafe asked.

Lady Finch smiled. "Would tomorrow suit you? If I must have these people in my house, let's get it over with quickly before we all come to our senses."

Jemmy groaned. "Say you do find this author, what then?"

"I've got to convince them to stop writing," Rafe told him.

"Seems a shame," Jemmy said. "I'll miss those books."

After dinner, Lady Finch insisted Rafe and Cochrane stay with them. Before he could refuse, she ordered rooms prepared and Cochrane's preferences for breakfast passed on to the cook. Rafe witnessed firsthand the indomitable Lady Finch in action.

So when it came time for Jemmy to leave for the gatehouse, Rafe offered to walk down with him. The idea of being cooped up in the same house with a woman known for her matchmaking schemes and penchant for gossip was enough to send him hightailing outside with the feeble excuse that he wanted to catch up on old war stories.

The war, Rafe suspected, was the last thing James Reyburn would want to discuss. And he was right.

"You've unleashed the dragon, I hope you know," Jemmy told him, his cane crunching into the gravel of the drive. "She'll not rest until she helps you discover this poor author. Badger you and nag you until . . . well, until . . ."

"Until you move into the gatehouse?" Rafe suggested.

Jemmy nodded. "Yes. I suppose so." He grinned and continued his slow, beleaguered pace toward his solitary residence.

"She's worried about you," Rafe said, after a few moments of silence.

"I know."

Demmit, so was he. He'd never realized how badly Jemmy's injuries had crippled him, or that he avoided society because of them. And a large part of Rafe felt

o

the sting of guilt that he had never bothered to discover the truth about Jemmy for himself, so caught up was he in his own life.

"Now that I've seen you, so am I," Rafe admitted.

"Thank you, but I don't need—"

Rafe stopped in his tracks. "Yes, you do. Jemmy, you can't hide from what happened to you. You're alive, for Christ's sake. You saw how many people didn't come home. You've got to live, if not for yourself, then for the poor bastards buried back there. Gads, it's not like there is anything to stop you."

And all of sudden, Rafe realized how much he envied Jemmy. Probably always had. An heir to a respected barony, wealthy, respected by society. Here was a young man who had a firm place in the *ton* and instead he hid away from it.

"Come to London," he said, trying a lighter tone. "We'll go out and do the town right. You can buy," he offered. "Besides, you can't hide forever."

But his words had no effect. Jemmy's jaw set in a determined line that was most likely inherited from his mother. Pride and fear burned in his gaze. "I damn well can," he said. "And I damn well will."

He hobbled off, up the steps of the gatehouse and closed the door. Moments later, a single candle moved through the house, then was snuffed and the place was cast into darkness.

Not unlike the occupant.

And Rafe realized that the small favor that Lady Finch had asked of him, to help her son, was going to be far more difficult to fulfill than he'd imagined.

Chapter 4

There is a vast difference between a rapscallion and a gentleman. A discerning lady knows which to kiss and which to marry.

Lady Lowthorpe to Miss Darby
in *Miss Darby's Reckless Bargain*

Rafe stood at the gates of Finch Manor long after Jemmy had gone inside and cursed the past fortnight.

Why had he ever answered Lady Tottley's summons? This simple assignment was turning into far more work than he wanted to invest.

First of all, how the devil was he going to help Jemmy Reyburn? The very idea curled in his gut like sour milk. For he suspected that if he were to nudge Jemmy back into society, he may well find himself on that same reluctant road.

"And it wouldn't hurt you none either," a voice said.

Rafe looked up to find an old woman standing in the middle of the road. With a knit shawl tossed over her shoulders and a plain little bonnet on her head, she might have been just another wrinkled village crone, but the lady shot him a saucy wink and swung her flower filled basket like a flirtatious milkmaid.

He glanced down the road in either direction and swore she hadn't been there a few moments before.

When he looked at her again, she was grinning.

"Never you mind where I came from. What matters is where I am going. Home it is, and you are going to walk me there. I'm not as spry as I used to be and you look capable enough." She shot him another wink and slid her hand into the crook of his arm and started down the road, towing him along until he fell into step beside her.

For a wee bit of a thing she had a grip like a dockhand.

"I wasn't planning on—" he said, glancing over his shoulder at the gates.

"Never you mind about Lady Finch. You just tell her Esme borrowed you for a bit." Her fingers gave his arm a squeeze. "Now why don't you tell me what you are looking for?"

"Looking for?" Rafe looked down at his newfound companion and wondered if everyone in Bramley Hollow knew of his quest. "I'm not—"

"Nonsense! Of course you are looking for someone. No one comes to Bramley Hollow unless they are looking for someone."

Esme. That name now rang a bell. What was it the postmistress had said earlier?

Esme Maguire. The matchmaker.

Rafe came to an abrupt halt. "Now listen here, I'm not here to . . . to . . ."

"Get matched?"

"Exactly."

"Of course you aren't," she said, tugging on his arm anew and setting them back on their amble down the road. "No one is. Or at least not that they'd confess."

"I can assure you, madame, I am not the marrying type."

She tipped her bonnet back and studied him. "You just haven't found the right lady yet."

"I suppose you could remedy that?"

She tugged her shawl closer. "You have only to ask."

Rafe decided the better part of valor was to say nothing.

The matchmaker laughed. "Silence won't save you, Mr. Danvers."

A shiver ran down his spine. "You know who I am?"

"Everyone in Bramley Hollow knows who you are. You couldn't have done yourself a worse disservice by introducing yourself to a certain young lady."

"Miss Tate," he said, under his breath.

"Not Rebecca, you dolt," Esme said. "The postmistress, Miss Stone."

"Oh, it's just that I thought—" He stopped when out of the corner of his eye he saw her smiling. "I didn't mean—"

"Of course you didn't, Mr. Danvers. Of course you didn't."

Rafe didn't like the way she chuckled as she finished her assurances, but he said nothing further and walked in companionable silence.

The spring evening couldn't have been more perfect as the days started to stretch longer, leaving the night to steal what time it could.

He'd always marveled at the serenity of the English countryside. After years on the war torn plains of Spain and the parched fields of Portugal, the green, fresh grass and the spicy scent of wild roses tangled in the hedges lulled him into Esme's confidence.

"I didn't mean to imply that I thought Miss Tate was a prattle-box."

Esme smiled.

"It's just that she's—"

"Yes?"

"Nothing." He was most definitely better off not saying anything. Yet in the silence he found himself thinking of that annoying minx. How she'd teased him with impunity. The chestnut fire of her hair. He'd never been one for redheads, but perhaps he'd just never seen a shade he liked . . .

Liked? He shook his head. The day he found himself using "liked" and "Miss Tate" in the same sentence was the day he needed to hightail it back to London as fast as he could.

"So how does one become a matchmaker?" Rafe asked, his silent reverie becoming more unnerving than the notion that he could accidentally fall into one of Esme's marital traps.

"By chance," Esme said, as if that was explanation enough. "Now you tell me, have you found who you are looking for?"

Obviously Miss Stone had done her job well. Not only did everyone know who he was, they knew why he was here.

So much for the element of surprise.

"No," he said.

"You will," she assured him.

"Then you're here to help me?" he asked, putting on his most charming smile.

The lady laughed and ignored his question. "That's the best you can offer? I was led to believe you were a charming devil." She shook her head. "You do need my assistance."

"I do well enough," he said, feeling a bit affronted. He was starting to think that the English countryside was a foreign country when his London manners held no sway.

"I suppose you might," Esme said after taking another assessing gander at him. "But not for what you were intended to do."

"And what is that?" he asked without thinking.

"Love someone."

He flinched. What was it about this village that had him asking questions to which he didn't really want to hear the answers?

"I don't think that's possible," he told her, meaning every word of it.

"It isn't for you to decide."

Rafe definitely needed to take control of this conversation before he indeed found himself matched and married. The direct approach seemed the best. "Do you know who the author of the *Miss Darby* novels might be?"

Esme laughed. "No. And even if I did, I wouldn't tell you. I rather like those books." She came to a stop before an arched gate. "Here you are."

"Is this your home?" he said, glancing up the lane at the cozy looking cottage.

"No," she said, pulling her hand free from his arm and straightening her shawl. "But it is where I leave you." Then she reached into her basket and pressed a bounty of long stemmed flowers into his arms. Before he could protest that the thorns were going to bleed him dry, she scurried up the road, whistling a tune not unlike the one Miss Tate had left ringing in his ears earlier.

Rafe grit his teeth. There she was again, that vexing little minx invading his thoughts.

Then she invaded more than that.

"What are *you* doing here?"

He turned around and discovered that perhaps he hadn't quite escaped Esme's intrigues.

For the matchmaker had left him at the doorstep of Miss Tate.

Rebecca stood on the path and stared at the man at her gate.

His dark hair was brushed back, giving way to his sculpted features: the deep cleft in his chin, the hard line of his jaw, the perfect turn of his lips. In his dark jacket and breeches, Raphael Danvers looked more like a barely civilized pirate than a gentleman.

The kind of man who smoldered with an untamed fire, barely contained by a thin veneer of manners.

She told herself he didn't affect her in the least. Not a whit. As long as he didn't smile, glance at her or stand in her general vicinity, she would remain immune.

Oh, why couldn't this Mr. Danvers just give up and go home? And, more importantly, leave her in peace.

Rebecca glanced back at the cottage. Through the window she could see the colonel bent over another of his translations, so absorbed he wouldn't miss her for the time being.

She hurried down the path with every intention of sending her unwanted guest packing back to London with a peel ringing in his ears that would take a good month for him to shake loose, but she stopped just shy of the gate.

What the blazes did he have in his hand?

Flowers? For her?

Off all the underhanded, sneaky, predictable . . . her indignation started to fade when she realized the blossoms were roses. Pink roses. Her very favorites.

And from the looks of them purloined from Lord Finch's hothouse. Now she could add theft to his list of sins.

The first and foremost of those being his utter audacity.

He glanced down and spied the errant blooms and tried to put them behind his back, as if to hide his offering. "I hadn't planned on . . . I mean . . . I never intended . . ."

Rebecca considered all the sharp-witted ways she could skewer him, but she couldn't. Something stopped her, leaving her just as tongue-tied.

What was it about this man that made her forget every vow she ever made to find a nice, sensible, practical vicar?

Yes, a vicar was just the man she wanted.

Because right now, Mr. Danvers had her praying for things that had nothing to do with proper sensibilities.

"I thought you said you weren't here to be matched?" she said, crossing her arms over her chest.

"I'm not."

He needn't say it so emphatically; it wasn't as if she were demanding he come up to scratch.

"Then who are the flowers for?" She couldn't resist persisting, if only to see him shift uncomfortably from one foot to another.

"No one. They were given to me by"—he glanced up the empty road— "a friend." He looked down at the blossoms in his hand as if he weren't too sure what to do with them. "Would you like them?" He shoved them toward her in a motion that was both awkward and reluctant, as if he'd never given a woman a bouquet before.

She found that hard to believe, but then again men like him probably didn't need the aid of flowers and gifts to gain a woman's attention.

Rebecca was ready to say no, but they were her favorite, after all. And they would look so nice in her mother's vase on the mantelshelf.

"Thank you," she said, taking them hastily, trying to avoid any contact with him. Too hastily, it turned out, for she caught hold of a large thorn which stuck in her finger.

"Ouch!" she yelped, shaking her hand and dropping

the roses in a shower of blossoms to her feet. "Oh, bother," she cursed, as she tried gingerly to pull the thorn free.

Before she realized what was happening, he caught hold of her hand and plucked the thorn out with a quick tug. Then he reached inside his jacket and pulled out a square of linen and wound it tightly around her injury.

Rebecca's breath caught as he held her hand, tended her, and when his fingers cradled her hand one last time to examine his handiwork, she wondered that the flowers hadn't been singed by his touch . . .

A spark of something whispered up her arms and down her spine—a thread of desire, like a long forgotten memory tugging to be freed. A dangerous memory of passion and what it was like to be touched by a man.

And when she glanced up and into his eyes they held a spark of surprise that must have mirrored her own.

She pulled her hand back. "Uh, thank you," she muttered, as she reached down and picked up the dropped stems, taking care this time not to get stuck by the thorns hidden in the lush and verdant greenery . . . or the charming smile and handsome face of the man who'd offered them.

Such wounds, she knew only too well, didn't heal readily. If ever.

"What are you doing here?" she asked, suddenly wary, both of his masculine power and the temptation still teasing her senses. "I would have thought you'd be back in London by now."

"I haven't finished my business yet."

"Ah, yes, your delivery."

"I do have business here," he insisted.

"Of course. With Miss Briggs," she said, fixing a serious countenance on her face, while trying not to smile at the memory of him gaping down at the lady's grave. "I'm sure she was delighted today with the pleasure of your company."

His brows furrowed, and his jaw set. She could imagine he wanted to deliver a well deserved set down, but he couldn't, not when he needed her help. That gave her the upper hand, or so she liked to believe until she found herself pinned by his dark gaze.

Gads, she didn't know what was worse, his disarming smile or his tempestuous frustration.

"You needn't sound so satisfied," he was saying. "You are the most incorrigible miss I've ever met."

Rebecca tried hard not to preen under such high praise. "You asked for directions to Miss Briggs and I gave them, I don't see that I did anything that deserves your censure."

He made a low noise in the back of his throat that sounded like Ajax when he spied another cat in his territory.

The oh-so-masculine sound sent a shiver of warning down her spine. What was it about this man that made her think of her overbearing, ill-mannered tom?

Might it be that he was just as rakish and inclined to get his own way? She would do well to remember that half the kittens in Bramley Hollow sported Ajax's ginger coloring.

"Actually, I've enlisted Lady Finch's aid to help me."

"Lady Finch?" she managed to stammer. Oh, this was a disaster. Rebecca's heart fluttered and she fixed her attention on the pale pink blossoms in her hands. "How do you know Lady Finch?"

It was a foolish question. Everyone knew Lady Finch.

"She's a close family friend. In fact, I'm staying at Finch Manor for the time being."

So close? It was obviously time to start packing. Rebecca wondered where it was that she'd put her valise. Instead she took a sniff of flowers and feigned indifference. "You have? I would think that if you knew who you were looking for, you'd make your delivery and be gone."

"I would like nothing more."

"So what are you waiting for?" she asked, waving to the empty road.

"For you to confess the truth that you are the author of the *Miss Darby* chronicles."

Rebecca's mouth fell open. No one had ever suspected her, not once, and this man just waltzed into Bramley Hollow and lay such a claim at her feet. It was too much to believe. So she laughed. Laughed in his face, laughed at his audacity.

Laughed to hide the fact he knew the truth.

"And if I were this author, Mr. Danvers," she offered, "why don't you tell me why you are really here? And not this fiction about a solicitor and papers."

He heaved a deep breath and looked at her.

"The truth, sir," she told him.

"I was hired to find the author by a lady of some means in London."

"So you are a runner."

He shook his head. "Not exactly."

"Then what are you if you aren't a thief taker?"

"I prefer to think of myself as a gentleman who assists my peers with problems they find difficult or disagreeable."

A gentleman? She nearly scoffed aloud. There was nothing gentle about this Raphael Danvers.

Oh, he might possess the markings of a nobleman, from the hawkish line of his nose and strong jaw, to the commanding presence he made when he walked into a room. But everything else about him spoke of a dangerous man, rakish and devilish, and most decidedly not a gentleman.

"I help people when they have no one else to trust," he said, as if trying to nudge her out of her disbelief.

"What does this lady in London want with the *Miss Darby* author?"

His jaw worked back and forth as if trying to come up with an answer that would aid his cause. Heaving another sigh, he said, "She wants the lady to stop writing."

"Stop writing?" Rebecca sputtered. "Well, it certainly doesn't sound to me like you are here to help this author."

He flinched, as well he should. Arrogant man to come here and think he could just dictate someone's livelihood.

"And what are you going to do if she refuses?" Rebecca said. "Make some dastardly threat? Break her arm?"

He flinched again, and Rebecca considered it a warning. That was most likely what he'd been sent to do.

"And you think I'm the author of these *Miss Darby* stories?" She brazened out the truth by laughing again.

"Yes." He said it with a dangerous certainty that shook her down to her sensible shoes. "And I have every intention of proving it before I leave this village."

"Proof?" She snorted. "You'll find no proof, sir, for you have the wrong woman. You are wasting your time chasing after me."

In more ways than one.

"I may not have my proof yet, Miss Tate. But mark my words, I will. *I will.*" The challenge in his eyes sent a warning tremor down her spine.

"Who have we here?" came a voice from the doorstep, like the saving grace of a dinner bell.

Uncle. His timing was impeccable, but that didn't mean he was here to help her. Knowing her uncle and his disposition, he'd probably ignite the situation like throwing hot grease on a kitchen fire.

Rebecca held her breath as Colonel Posthill continued to say, "Mrs. Wortling said you were out here courting with some stranger and I told her it was nonsense. Called her an old rum-pot for making up such ridiculous stories and now she's in a fine kettle. Our Bex never has swains, I told her, and now look at this, you've gone and made a liar out of me, sir."

Rebecca forced a smile onto her lips and tried to make the best and shortest work of her uncle's arrival. So she told him, "The gentleman was just leaving."

"Nonsense!" her uncle declared, coming down the steps and marching smartly up the walk. "I won't have men calling on my niece without . . ." he paused for a moment and stared at the flowers in her arms. "What have we here?"

"Just some flowers," Rebecca said, wondering if this could get any worse.

Her uncle made sure it did. He eyed Mr. Danvers from head to toe. "Now who are you, that you think you have leave to bring my niece flowers without first seeking my permission to pay your addresses?"

Rebecca swallowed. Oh, yes, worse was decidedly possible. "Uncle, this is Mr. Raphael Danvers. Mr. Danvers, my uncle Colonel Posthill."

"Good to meet you, Mr. Danvers. You aren't from around here, are you? Then I must ask what you are doing bringing flowers to my niece?"

"I wasn't really here to see your niece. I was out walking with Mrs. Maguire, and the lady—"

Rebecca looked up at the heavens and prayed for a sudden bolt of lightning to strike her dead.

Better yet, may it hit Mr. Danvers.

"The matchmaker brought you here?" The colonel said loud enough for Mrs. Benton across the garden wall to hear him.

Delightful! By morning, the entire village would know that Esme had brought her a suitor.

"Now Mr. Danvers," her uncle continued, "if you are here to court my niece, I must know a few things about you."

Rebecca held her breath.

"First of all, how are you," her uncle asked, his head tipped slightly as if to better gauge his response, "with a cannon?"

She turned a fast glance at him. A cannon? Why it was brilliant! Nothing like a freshly fired cannon ball to send one's enemies scampering for higher ground. Her uncle would have Mr. Danvers running back to London before midnight, if he didn't accidentally shoot the rogue first.

But her happiness was short-lived when Mr. Danvers said, "A cannon? Why I have a great fondness for them. Is it a three pounder or six?"

Rebecca's mouth fell open. Even the colonel looked taken aback, but he recovered much more quickly than she did.

"A nine pounder. And a fine one, I might add. Come along, come along. We'll fire off a few rounds and I'll see if your boast is worth any merit."

"Delighted, sir," Mr. Danvers said, following behind the colonel. "I haven't fired a nine pounder in years. Not since I was experimenting with powder loads at school and accidentally destroyed the statue of Cromwell in the middle of the commons."

"You don't say?" the colonel said, a light of appreciation glowing in his eyes.

"Mr. Danvers, uncle, you cannot fire off the cannon."

They turned and looked at her with the same question in their eyes. *Why ever not?*

Then they grinned like a pair of errant schoolboys and headed for the rear garden, discussing weights and range as if they were about to defend the village from the entire Continental army.

"Oh—" Rebecca stammered as she tried to come up with the most unladylike curse she could think of. But a small breeze stirred and brought with it a gentle hint of roses.

She inhaled deeply, and suddenly her ire faded. The demmed rogue had brought her flowers.

It wouldn't hurt, she decided, to put them in water—before she sent him packing.

Remember you are in Bramley Hollow, Rafe told himself. For the sake of his carefully guarded bachelorhood, it probably wouldn't do to spend the evening staring at a woman, especially not when that lady was Rebecca Tate.

But demmit it was hard not to look at the chit.

She glowered at him like she'd like nothing more than to consign him to the darkest reaches of hell. But what she didn't realize (or maybe she did) was that in her passionate fury, her prim spinsterly demeanor fell away.

There was something altogether disconcerting about a lady who refused to be charmed. Something altogether appealing.

The colonel was in the process of loading the charge for his next shot. They had fired eight rounds already and the man was determined to hit the target they'd set up in the field behind the house.

Rafe had already hit it three times in a row.

"I think I'll match your skill with this one," the colonel was saying.

"I think you have too much powder," Rafe advised, taking a few steps back.

"No such thing," the colonel said enthusiastically.

A derisive snort rose from Miss Tate's position.

The chit certainly had a way with words, he thought. Perhaps, she wasn't the author of the *Darby* novels. It was hard to believe that such lyrical prose came from a lady whose favorite phrase sounded like a cat with a hairball.

As the colonel tamped down the load, Rafe wandered over to Rebecca's side. "Care for a turn?" he said, casting her a wayward grin.

Charm, that was what he needed to do, charm the lady into giving away her identity. And if her uncle had been telling the truth, and Rafe saw no reason to doubt it, considering her less than welcoming stance, Miss Tate wasn't exactly the belle of Bramley Hollow.

If there was something Rafe knew a little about it was gaining a lady's confidence. How hard could it be to charm one spinster?

But her tight smile did little to instill confidence in his efforts. "Would you trust me with a cannon?" she asked. "I fear my aim isn't as precise as yours."

He could well imagine what she'd aim at. Still he wasn't about to let her sink his efforts just yet. He leaned forward and whispered in her ear, "Perhaps you just haven't had enough practice."

Her eyes widened at the implication of his words and from the outraged moue that formed on her lips, he had no doubt she knew exactly what he meant.

So Miss Tate wasn't quite as inexperienced as she appeared.

And that in itself took him aback. What did she know of men? The mysterious lady caught and held his attention once again.

And if he'd meant to tease her with his double enten-
dre, he should have at the same time kept his distance
from her, for he had gotten close enough to smell the
lingering hint of roses about her, and spy the pale hint
of freckles on her rose-tinted cheeks, enticing stars that
provoked him to consider tracing their haphazard path
across her face with his fingers, with a lingering kiss.

Her arms once again crossed over her chest. "I assure
you, sir, I am able and ready to defend myself."

Rafe backed up, his boot bumping into something.

An indignant yowl set up at his feet and he looked
down to find an enormous cat eyeing him with a mixture of indignation and distrust.

Not unlike its mistress.

Well, if he couldn't charm the lady, perhaps his en-
trée was this ugly beastie. He reached down to give the
old fellow a scratch on the ears, even as Miss Tate cried
out, "Don't touch him!"

At first he thought she feared for her cat's welfare,
but only too late discovered the warning had been for
his benefit.

In a flash, the cat turned from ragged beast to a raging fury. It jumped up on his sleeve and dug in with all
four paws. It ripped and shredded at his jacket and the
more he tried to shake it off, the more determined the
wretched feline became, clinging to him, spitting and
hissing, its fur out at all points.

"Oh, Ajax," she cried. "Get off of him. Get off of Mr.
Danvers."

Rafe heard her cries but was too busy trying to save
his arm to let her words register.

"Get off of me," he barked at the beast, and for a moment it paused, hanging from his sleeve, glaring up at
him as if gauging how serious he was. "*Stand down*," he
ordered, glaring back at the animal.

It made one more swipe at his tattered coat and then leapt off his arm. It shook itself, as if trying to remove any traces of evidence, then sauntered off, tail high and waving with all the pride and markings of a victor.

Looking down at his coat, he knew the demmed thing had every right to be cocky.

"Oh, dear, oh my," Miss Tate said, her hand covering a smile. "Your coat, I fear it is ruined."

He glanced down. His coat *and* his shirt. Not to mention the stinging scratches in his flesh. He held it out for her to see and her eyes widened as she surveyed the damage and her glee turned to something else.

Concern.

Rafe held back a grin. Concern wasn't a bad place to start.

He flinched as she reached out to touch his arm, as if it pained him greatly. It stung a little, but nowhere near the pain he feigned as she looked up at him.

"You shouldn't have tried to pet him," she said, taking him by his uninjured arm and leading him to a nearby bench.

"I thought it was merely a cat."

"He's not very friendly," she advised.

That was an understatement.

Now that he was settled on the bench, she sat beside him and tenderly took his sleeve in her hands. Ever so gently she pulled back his torn sleeve.

"Ooooh," he groaned, trying to retrieve his arm out of her grasp.

"Does it hurt?" she asked.

"Terribly so," he told her, hoping his pained expression and strained words would be enough to get her to let go. "I think I might be bleeding."

"Oh, no," she said, hanging on tighter, and pursuing her ministrations with even more due diligence.

Just his luck, he got the only lady in England not squeamish about the possible sight of blood.

Jemmy Finch had been right when he'd said that Miss Tate was anything but typical.

"What were you thinking?" she was saying. "Petting a cat."

"I usually have a way with animals," he said. *And ladies*, he thought vexed at her continued indifference.

"Ajax is not your typical feline."

"Neither is his mistress," he said, glancing into her eyes.

Her pale cheeks blushed to a rosy hue and even the wary light in her eyes started to soften. Rafe took that as a good sign, leaning forward, gazing down at her lips and wondering what it would be like to steal a kiss from her usually tart mouth. To see if beneath her bluster and prickles was a fire to match the one now smoldering in her eyes.

Once again, he'd miscalculated his own allure.

"Try to kiss me, sir," she said, dropping his arm as if it had suddenly grown white hot. "And you'll leave here with Ajax attached to your breeches."

A little flesh off his arm was one thing—his lower regions were another.

"Kiss you? Why I wouldn't—" Rafe started to protest.

"Oh, please, do us both a favor and save your charm for a lady foolish enough to be dazzled by your errant smile. You intended to kiss me in hopes that I would melt under your skillful attentions and then be so dazzled I would reveal all my secrets to you."

"Miss Tate, I'm a gentleman," he told her. "I would never—"

To which she snorted rather inelegantly, rose from the bench and stalked toward the cottage.

He couldn't help noticing that the defiant swing in her hips wasn't so unlike Ajax's victory wave.

Chapter 5

In the military there are two methods of waging a campaign: a direct assault or subterfuge. Both work well on the battlefield of love.

Miss Darby to her dearest friend,
Miss Cecilia Overton
in *Miss Darby's Daring Dilemma*

Rafe was still clinging to his denials the next morning as he rode over to inspect Bettlesfield Park.

Miss Tate had so thoroughly and decidedly set him on his ear before she'd retreated to the safety of her cottage, he'd been unable to utter another word . . .

But there was little defense when she'd stated the truth. He'd been about to kiss her.

Still, the lady didn't realize she'd only thrown down the gauntlet before him. And now he was more determined than ever to prove his case.

He was going to enjoy seeing how she fared tonight over dinner at Lady Finch's—without her wretched tomcat to protect her.

Oh, he'd break down Miss Tate's defenses, it was just going to take some careful planning. And perhaps a kiss or two . . .

In the meantime, he'd inspect his payment, if only to determine if the prize was worth the trouble. Not that he didn't suspect that a kiss from Rebecca Tate's lips would result in all kinds of mayhem.

The troublesome ones, he mused, were always worth the bother.

His horse whinnied and he reached down to pat its neck. "Not that much further, my friend," he told it in Spanish.

The small estate of Bettlesfield Park bordered the Finch lands, and so he rode cross-country, following the landmarks Jemmy had detailed for him with military precision.

After years in Spain riding with his guerilla troop, he'd never been one for taking the open road when he didn't need to. He'd crisscrossed Spain's lonely expanses without the aid of roads, so the English countryside was a wealth of bounty in comparison.

Around him flowers bloomed, peeking out from around fence posts, giving the thorny hedges a deceptively inviting blush, while the grass glowed with a vibrant shade of green.

A low stone wall marked the end of the Finch holdings and the beginning of Bettlesfield Park.

He kicked his horse and it sprang forward, clearing the wall with little effort, dancing in protest as Rafe slowed its pace once they'd gained the other side, for there in the distance was his first glance of the house Lady Tottley was offering.

For a moment Rafe thought that perhaps Lady Finch's dire warnings had been overstated, for the house and gardens appeared quite fine to his untrained eye. But as he drew closer, he could see the lady hadn't been mincing her words.

A tumbledown wreck, she'd called it. Her description had a bit of kindness to it. Bettlesfield Park would be better off being pulled down for the stone.

The clatter of his horse's hooves echoed through the desolation that surrounded them and he shifted in his saddle, craning his neck this way and that to take it all in.

There were few windows still left whole or just merely cracked, but the rest of the panes gaped like open ugly wounds.

That is, what he could see of the windows. Ivy, left to its own wild and insatiable nature, covered most of the walls. The steps to the front entry were cluttered with leaves and debris, while the door stood open, hanging lopsidedly on one creaking hinge.

Lady Finch had been right when she'd said it would take a fortune and a fool to bring the place to rights.

As he jumped down from his horse, a host of birds rose from the bushes and sought safety inside the upper floors.

His house was a demmed rookery. He had birds in his attics. Oh, Colin and Robert would find all kinds of irony in that notion.

As he was about to push the door open the rest of the way and venture inside, he heard something odd—a whistled tune coming from around the side of the house. The melody caught his ear and lured him from the steps. Before he knew it, he was picking his way through the waist high lawn and tumble of weeds, and seeking the source of the enticing strains.

Just as he hopped over a low stone wall a gasp rose from the garden beyond.

"You!"

He looked up to find the object of his vexation seated cross-legged atop a large stump, a pen in hand, and a small, traveling desk spread open on her lap.

Miss Tate no longer, Rebecca's prim demeanor had

been replaced with a loose braid that fell nearly to her waist. She wore a simple green gown, but around her shoulders lay a fanciful shawl. Her feet were bare, a sight that enticed him. He didn't know if he'd ever seen an English lady with bare feet, outside his bed that was. Her toes wiggled in the sunshine, leading up to delicate ankles and an inviting pair of shapely calves.

She looked . . . well, she looked . . .

Fey.

The word came unbidden to mind. Hadn't his Irish nanny filled his head with stories of the fey—troublesome, tempting folk—but he'd never believed in them until now.

She hastily capped a small bottle of ink, and then stowed her pen. "So now you've taken to following me to prove your ridiculous theory?"

"No," he said, still taken aback by the sight before him. She captivated him as she had last night in the garden when he'd been about to kiss her. Now, more than ever, he was flooded with regrets for not having succeeded.

"So then what are you doing here?" she sputtered as she tried to gather up the pages stacked around her. Just then a gentle breeze caught the leaves and sent them fluttering over the ill-kempt lawn like autumn refuse.

"Bother!" she exclaimed before clamoring off the stump and chasing after her lost possessions.

As she dashed about trying to catch them up, he started to doubt the certainty of his convictions.

This was the creator of Miss Darby? The Miss Darby in her fine helmet and boots, who rode a charger effortlessly into battle or snagged a python from beneath the Raj's dining table with her father's best fishing rod with the same finesse with which she poured tea?

An *Incomparable*, ever at the ready, and never floundering about like a freshly caught trout.

Though, he had to admit, Miss Tate had several incomparable assets, for her all-too-tempting shape was in fine view as she leaned this way and that trying to retrieve her wayward papers.

Then in a very astute display of the differences between the elegant lady of fiction and this real life spinster, Miss Tate toppled into a hedge in an unsightly tangle.

"Oooh," she wailed as she tried to right herself but only got caught deeper in the shrubbery.

What was it about this woman and her affinity for thorns?

Rafe rushed to her side. "Careful," he advised as he started to pick her up out of the briars. "You are well caught," he added in jest.

"So you would like to think," she said, shaking off his help and righting herself with all the dignity of her accursed cat.

What the devil had she called that beast?

Ajax. Now why did that name sound so familiar? Then it struck him. Ajax wasn't just the name of Miss Tate's hellbent tom, but also of Miss Darby's beloved wolfhound.

"Aha!" he said, pointing at her.

"Aha, what?" she asked, shaking out her skirt, then tossing her thick red braid back over her shoulder. Unruly strands curled about her face.

"Ajax!" he said. "The name of your cat and Miss Darby's dog are one and the same. I think that is hardly a coincidence."

She shook her head, and skirted past him like one might a tattered beggar on the street. "You truly do this for a living?" she shot over her shoulder.

"Well, yes."

"Then it is no wonder your cuffs are so thread-bare." She sighed. "I named my cat after Miss Darby's dog because I thought they shared the same fierce determination."

Damn her. It was a reasonable explanation. There were probably hundreds of Ajaxes scampering about England now given the novels' popularity. And even a few Darbys for that matter.

She caught up with another of her pages and scooped down to retrieve it. Tucking it in with the rest of the collection, she hugged them to her chest and stomped back to her desk. "What are you doing here?"

"I would ask the same of you," he replied. "Writing novels, I presume?" He nodded at a page she'd missed that was fluttering into what might have been a knot garden at one time.

"Harrumph." Her brow furrowed as she followed it. "None of your business," she told him as she stuffed a jumble of pages into her traveling desk, snapping the latch shut and turning to face him, her hands on her hips. "If you aren't following me, then what are you doing here?"

"Inspecting the property."

"Shouldn't take you very long," she remarked.

He laughed despite himself. "I suppose not."

"Is this another of your *gentleman's* services?"

"In a manner of speaking. When I prove you are the author of the *Miss Darby* novels"—he paused as she punctuated his sentence with another indignant, and very unladylike snort—"I will be paid with the deed to this house."

Her response was much the same as Lady Finch's. She broke out laughing. "I was right. You can't be very good at what you do if you're willing to take this ruin in payment."

"I don't intend to live here," he told her.

"Not unless you like living in a . . . a . . ." Just then a bevy of birds flew out the open attic windows far above them.

"A rookery?" he asked.

This time, they both laughed, and the sudden camaraderie, even if it was only for a few moments left Rafe unsettled. This was a potential suspect. The first rule of investigation was never to get overly chummy with one's quarry. Which definitely included kissing them . . .

"So you noticed the squatters," she was saying. Her teeth captured her lower lip and she glanced shyly away from him.

Oh, he'd noticed. More than he wanted to.

"Now that I've revealed my purpose for being here," he said, "why don't you tell me what brings you to Bettlesfield Park?" He nodded toward her traveling desk. "Writing love notes or misleading guidebooks to Bramley Hollow's lost attractions?"

She laughed again, and when she smiled her entire face lit up. Perhaps it was the tumbled surroundings or the afternoon light, but the lady had left her spinster armor behind and before him stood an intriguing miss.

Really, what harm was there in one kiss? Perhaps in this case the rules required a little bending, he told himself. All in the line of duty, of course.

He went to step around a tumbled statue blocking his path, to pick up the piece of paper she'd missed, when she called out, "Stop!"

Rafe paused and looked up at her. Her eyes were

wide and her mouth open in a wide "O". "I was right,"
he said. "Must be missives of love or the proof I need to
discover your secret identity, Miss Tate." His boot rose
to step over the obstacle.

"No!" she warned him. " 'Tis dangerous."

"Dangerous?" he scoffed, ignoring her advice and
taking just that step. His boot crunched atop something
that creaked, then gave way. Before he could catch himself, he toppled downward.

He bounced once or twice then landed in a heap at
the bottom of what must have once been the garden
well.

Dirt and debris showered down upon him, and
when the dust finally settled he managed to sputter a
loud curse. Struggling to his feet, he looked up.

There, high above his head was the concerned visage
of Miss Tate.

"Are you *well*?" she called down, her brows arched
in jest.

Well? Was that her idea of a joke? So much for any
hope of maidenly concerns for his welfare. In truth, he
should have known better. This was Miss Tate, after all.
He bit back the first reply that came to mind and
ground out an, "Aye."

"I don't suppose you can climb up?" She leaned over
the edge and held out her hand.

The well wasn't that deep, only about twelve feet but
too high for him to reach her outstretched hand. He felt
around the walls, but the thin roots that poked through
and the few remaining boards offered no help. "No,
I'm stuck." All his years in Spain, all his daring raids
and sorties into enemy territory, and he manages to
nearly break his neck in a forgotten Kent well.

"It seems you are once again at my mercy, Mr. Danvers." If her words didn't sting, the fact that all he could see was her grinning visage was salt enough for his wounded pride.

"Would you mind going for help?" he asked.

"That depends," she called down.

Rafe held back yet another retort. He was painfully aware that he was at her tender mercies. And tender and mercy were hardly words that seemed to fit into Miss Tate's vocabulary.

"And on what would that be?" he asked as kindly as he could manage.

"That you return to London and leave this *Darby* business alone." An edge of desperation tinged her words.

Rafe could barely restrain himself from rubbing his hands together in glee. Either Miss Tate was the lady he sought or she knew who was. "I would love to leave this place, but I have a reputation to maintain, Miss Tate. I can't give up now. Not with such a fine house as Bettlesfield Park in my sights. Think of it, I'd be living here in Bramley Hollow. You wouldn't deny a new neighbor in need?"

"Harrumph. I might remind you, you'll have to find your author first before you gain your prize."

He was beginning to dislike her rampant skepticism as to his abilities.

But then again, she wasn't the one at the bottom of a well.

"Are you going to stop hunting for this author?" she repeated.

"No!" he barked. He was losing patience with her, even if she was the only hope he had of ever gaining his freedom.

"I think it is patently unfair that you think you can march into a village and demand someone stop their profession, their very livelihood, all under the guise of a gentleman. A gentleman, indeed! And what do you get for this atrocity? A broken down estate. You should be ashamed," she scolded. "If you had one ounce of nobility in your heart you would leave Bramley Hollow this instant."

But he hadn't any nobility, he wanted to tell her. His very lack of nobility had gotten him tossed out of nearly every school in England, out of the army, and on several occasions nearly out of his family.

If she wanted honor and dignity and moral integrity— the elusive virtues that supposedly came with those blessed with aristocratic bloodlines—she should go seek out his brothers, Colin and Robert. They wore theirs like a silver mantle, though even with their lofty ideals they had let theirs tarnish a bit from time to time.

No, if any of the Danvers brothers could lay claim to unarguable nobility it would have been his twin brother, Orlando.

Lando, as he'd been known, had always displayed the highest degree of courage and nobility that any single man could possess. And there wasn't a day that went by that Rafe didn't think of his lost brother. The half of his soul that would have known exactly what Miss Tate was talking about.

And agreed wholeheartedly with her.

"Well, are you or aren't you going to leave?" she was saying.

"Miss Tate, I would be more than happy to leave," he said, "if I weren't at the moment trapped at the bottom of this well." He had not agreed, he noted to himself, to give up finding his prey. "Would you please just go for help?" He decided to count on the fact that at heart,

Miss Tate was a decent sort, hardly the type to leave one down a well to meet their fate.

He was wrong.

"No," came the adamant reply.

"No? You mean to say you'd leave me down here?" he asked.

"Of course not," she told him. "It's just that there is no need to go for help. I believe there is some rope in the shed." She disappeared from sight for a few moments, then popped her head back over the edge. "Don't go anywhere," she called down merrily.

Delightful minx, he thought, planning all the ways he would throttle her when he got to the top.

Rebecca didn't go to fetch the rope—at least not immediately. First of all she carefully picked up the last piece of paper, the one Mr. Danvers had been reaching for when he'd fallen down the well.

"Damn his pestering hide," she cursed under her breath. What the devil was he doing following her to Bettlesfield Park, of all places? He hadn't been satisfied with flowers and his attempted kisses; he had to follow her about like an annoying stray.

And boasting that he was about to become the owner of this place. What utter nonsense! Then again, she could just imagine what he would do with it—probably turn it into his own personal country boudoir, like the last resident had done—filling the rooms with cheap red velvet, copied Turkish hangings, and throwing a series of notorious house parties, his nights spent tempting and ensnaring one lady after another.

The idea of him seducing a cadre of ladies brought on a new storm of ire, and she didn't want to consider why that was. She didn't care in the least whom he seduced.

But one thing was for certain, he wasn't going to be doing it at Bettlesfield Park. Not as long as there was a breath left in her body.

She opened up her desk, and was about to stuff the remaining page inside when her gaze fell to the lines thereon.

> *Miss Darby's heart wrenched as she read the news. It couldn't be true. She didn't believe it. How could he have lied to her? Deceived her so utterly, so terribly, so . . .*

"So overwrought," she muttered, making a note to correct the paragraph later.

Looking around and over her shoulder, she reached inside her desk and poked her finger into the empty inkwell. Only it wasn't an ordinary inkwell, for it had no bottom, only a button which she pushed and out sprang a hidden compartment in the bottom of the desk.

She grinned at the ingenious French dispatch box her father had acquired to hide his more important research—notes and descriptions of lost treasures he'd never found.

But her father's failures aside, the box also did well to keep the pages of her next book, *Miss Darby's Terrible Temptation* away from prying eyes.

After tucking the loose pages into the drawer, she closed it and it clicked shut, leaving only some innocuous correspondence visible in the top section for the curious.

Such as Raphael Danvers.

Then a wicked thought occurred to her. Oh, it was a terrible temptation, she thought as she glanced over at the barely discernable well.

Perhaps she should let him stay down there. At least

overnight. Maybe that would make him more inclined to return to London where he belonged.

After a moment or two of considering that rather pleasant fantasy, Rebecca heaved a sigh. Oh, bother, if she had to get him out, she might as well be done with the task and away from the rogue before someone discovered them out here alone and came to some scandalous and entirely untrue conclusions.

She started down the haphazard path toward the little stone house that had once been the gardener's domain, so lost in her own thoughts of Rafe pleading and promising anything if she were just to release him, her boot caught on a tree root and she went topsy-turvy into what had once been an ornate maze.

Now it was just a thorny hedge.

"Eee-ow!" she cried out.

"Miss Tate? Is that you? What happened?" came an anxious cry from the well.

Oh, yes, now he was troubled about her welfare. She imagined he was only worried because she was his sole remaining hope for getting him out of his latest predicament. That in itself probably had his blood running cold. She grinned at that comforting thought, and then called out, "I'm fine, Mr. Danvers," as she regained her footing. This time she made her way a little more attentively.

The garden shed was probably one of the few places at Bettlesfield Park that hadn't been looted and pockmarked by the locals and passing tramps. Hidden in a grove of rhododendrons, the shed had long been forgotten.

Even Rebecca hadn't remembered it until she'd spied the edge of the roof poking out from between a couple of branches the previous fall. It had taken some work to find the door, but inside she'd discovered all the gardener's tools still safely tucked away, including a coil of rope. The shed had come in handy from time to time, when she'd found herself caught out here in a sudden downpour, or just to escape Mrs. Wortling's complaints on a rainy day. The old potting table made an admirable desk in a pinch.

She caught up the rope and made her way back to the edge of the well.

"I think this will reach you," she called down.

"Tie it onto something sturdy before you throw it down," he yelled up at her.

Did her think her so daft? Perhaps two nights down the well would be more appropriate.

"Do you know how to tie a knot?" he called up. "A good one?"

"Yes." Then she couldn't resisted adding, "I read how in one of my uncle's books."

An agonized groan rose from the depths. "Miss Tate, if you don't know how to tie a knot, then you'd best go fetch someone who does."

"No need. I am quite an astute student. Really, Mr. Danvers, if you would slowly and diligently study the facts instead of jumping to conclusions, you might learn a thing or two. You might even make a living from this profession of yours." She grinned at the muttered curses echoing up. Having secured the rope to a toppled statue of some long forgotten saint, she gave the line a good tug. Satisfied that it would hold, she picked up the rest of the line and was about to toss it in, when she stopped and eyed the frayed end.

Smiling to herself, she tied one more knot before calling out to Mr. Danvers, "This ought to be just what you need."

The rope came flying down and stopped right in front of Rafe. He started to catch hold of it, but came to an abrupt halt, staring at the dangling mischief before him. Even he had to laugh at her latest attempt to put him in his place.

There before his face hung a noose.

A very well tied one, he noted.

The woman certainly knew how to add insult to injury. And in that wry moment, he recalled Jemmy's words yet again.

She's the type of girl who could sneak up on a fellow, and before he knew it, find he's fallen for her.

He wondered if Jemmy had meant that literally.

Not far from Bramley Hollow, the esteemed Major Harrington's game warden had arrived at his office a half an hour earlier, babbling mindlessly and sounding half mad. It had taken two good belts from a bottle of whisky to get the man to put two coherent words together.

Lacking in much patience as it was, the major had finally bellowed out, "Show me!" to which the poor frightened warden had tossed up his breakfast at the very notion of returning to the grisly scene that had sent him riding for the main house as if the countryside were on fire.

"Demmit, then. Where is it?" Harrington had demanded next.

"The hillside," the fellow managed. "Above the meadow. Along the path. The big oak before the fork."

The major ordered his horse saddled, then retrieved the pistols he kept in the case on the mantel. They'd saved his life more than once, and it never hurt to err on the side of caution.

"Father?" his daughter Charlotte called out as he strode toward the front door. "Father, are you going riding?"

He bustled past her. "Yes. Be back before tea."

"Well, if you can spare a moment, I'll have John bring my mare around as well. We can ride together."

The major stopped in his tracks, spinning around almost immediately. "You'll do no such thing."

"But Papa—" she started to protest.

"None of that," he said, taking some of the tension from his voice. It wouldn't do to frighten her needlessly. "Go see to your mother. Spend some time with her today and I promise we will ride first thing tomorrow."

Charlotte shot him an odd glance, and then spied the pistols stuck in his belt. "Is there trouble?"

"Nothing but some rabbits in the meadows. Pesky devils are wreaking havoc on the field I want to use for training the new horses." He smiled at her. "Go on now. See to your mother. She was complaining just the other day that you weren't keeping up your studies of *Debrett's*."

Charlotte shot another speculative glance at the pistols, then retreated upstairs.

The major waited in the foyer until she was gone and then called for their Indian servant. "Mahesh!"

The English servants were fine enough. But for this—if it was what he suspected—he wanted someone with the same devilish breeding to be on guard.

Mahesh arrived silently and bowed.

"See to the ladies," the major ordered. "Don't let them out of the house and don't let anyone in."

Mahesh inclined his head. "Is there anything else, sahib?"

Major Harrington tugged at his moustache as he considered his next words. Then he leaned forward and whispered, "I fear the Kailash has returned. Be on guard."

Mahesh had served the major for nearly twenty years, and in that time, Harrington had never seen the man show a single emotion, but the fear that ran through Mahesh's eyes made the major's gut clench.

"Are you sure, sahib?"

"I don't know. Not yet. Not until I see what it is that fool warden is babbling about." He shoved the pistols into his belt. "Stay sharp, man. I won't have anything happen to Charlotte or Mrs. Harrington."

Mahesh nodded.

The major strode down the steps and leapt up on his horse. He might be approaching his sixtieth year, but he hadn't led some of the best cavalry units under Cornwallis and Wellesley for nothing.

Two grooms were already mounted and waiting for him, both of them armed. Obviously, the warden hadn't been all that discreet when he'd come blundering into the stable yard.

He looked them over. One looked no more than thirteen, evidenced by the lack of beard.

"You there," the major said.

"Yes, sir?" the youth asked, doffing his cap.

"Go back to the stables. I don't need both of you."

The boy looked sorely disappointed but did as he was told. If it was as the major suspected, the boy didn't need to see it.

Nodding to the older man, they rode off, and it wasn't long before they were climbing the hill alongside the meadow and approaching the tall, ancient oak that stood like a lone sentinel above his estate.

"Stay here," he ordered the remaining groom.

The major rode around the massive trunk, at first unable to see what the game warden had been babbling about like a wild man.

"Demmed fool," the major muttered. "Don't see what he was talking about. Probably been drinking again." As he had just about come to the decision that he would fire the man without paying his back wages, something caught his eye.

His horse shifted and pawed nervously about, dancing sideways from the tree.

Pulling at the reins, Harrington said, "Steady there, steady there, old girl."

He rode closer, then started around the tree, only to be greeted by the display that had put his game warden into such a fever.

At first, he felt only anger and disgust at the sight.

Demmit. That was one his daughter's best gowns nailed to the tree and sliced to ribbons as if having been used for saber practice.

Worse yet, the once pristine white muslin was decorated with fresh blood, and the sickly sweet scent of it sent his horse dancing despite his sure grip on the reins.

Harrington's gut filled with sick dread.

The bastard had gotten into the house, or at least the laundry. He'd gotten close enough to . . . The major didn't even want to consider what this fiend could have managed. Could still . . .

He glanced yet again at the grisly sight before him. He couldn't help thinking that this was how Codlin must have looked when his poor housekeeper had stumbled upon his mutilated body. He shuddered, and nudged his horse closer, intent on ripping the gown down before anyone else saw it and burning every last shred, when a bit of wind stirred around him and sent a piece of paper fluttering on the nail that held it.

A note. A warning. And what it said, sent the major reeling back, then fumbling out of his saddle and retching into the bushes like a green recruit.

His eyes, wide with terror, read the words again. Though written in Bengali, he'd learned enough of the language to know what it meant. To know he hadn't much time.

You're next.

Chapter 6

Of all the things I regret now that I have lost my beloved Lieutenant Throckmorten, the worst is that I never bestowed upon him a single kiss.

Miss Darby (in the strictest confidence)
to Miss Cecilia Overton
in *Miss Darby's Darkest Hour*

"**R**eady for your trip back to London, Mr. Danvers?" Miss Tate asked when he finally managed to climb out.

"Not quite yet," Rafe told her, ignoring her lightsome tone, one that suggested he'd just taken a misstep at a country dance rather than an impromptu tumble down a dry country well.

It certainly didn't appear he was going to get any anxious feminine displays from Miss Tate.

Oh, Mr. Danvers, how brave you were and how strong you must be to have survived unscathed.

Or . . . *Are you sure you don't need a surgeon, Mr. Danvers?*

Oh, no, not from Miss Tate. She appeared more bemused by her own wit, barely paying him a bit of heed as she poked odd stones and bits of rubble back into the well with the toe of her boot. After peering over the edge for a few more seconds, she slanted a glance in his direction. "Not exactly someplace you want to spend too much time hanging around," she teased.

That she made him smile, despite his bruised pride, was to her credit. "Your rescue was quite innovative."

"I did try to warn you."

"So you did," he said, brushing off the dirt and twigs clinging to his jacket. The only recompense of being too poor to hire the services of a valet, he decided, was that when he arrived home in utter disarray and ruin, he didn't have to endure the requisite dismay and scolding from some fustian fellow. Though if he stayed much longer in Bramley Hollow, he wouldn't have much of a wardrobe to speak of, let alone tend.

"If you would just heed my advice—" she was saying.

"Such as?"

"Go back to London."

Rafe took a step closer to her. "Not until you admit you are the woman I want."

Now he had to confess, that statement could have come out better, but once he made his demand, he wondered just exactly *how* he had meant it.

For as the words fell from his lips, she glanced up at him, like a startled doe, shooting him one of those glances, the fey sort that caught him unaware—her lips parting slightly as if she wanted both to deny his request and respond most willingly. Suddenly he saw her, her red hair unbound and her lips offering another answer.

You know who I am, Rafe. And I want you as well . . .

Dios, he cursed. What the hell was he thinking?

Meanwhile, the spinster's armor came back on as she sputtered and spit like Ajax. "Well, I . . . I . . . I never—"

Rafe held up his hand to stave off her indignant litany, regretting his words already. This harmless flirtation was becoming dangerous with each passing moment, just as this assignment was turning into a series of pitfalls. Quite literally.

"I would suggest, sir," she was saying, having regained some of her composure, "now that you've finished inspecting the underside of the Park, you finish your tour and begone before you find yourself in need of further assistance."

"Yes, quite funny," he told her. "How lucky for me that you are so adept in tying knots. Tell me, besides aiding and abetting the postmistress, misdirecting visitors about Bramley Hollow, and completing an apprenticeship with the local hangman, what brings *you* out here? I don't see that you've got the time to spare."

She tossed her head, and turned on one heel. "You're right. I don't. So if you will excuse me, I'll take my leave." She went back to her belongings, gathering up her traveling desk and a bag that she slung over her shoulder.

Now he'd done it. He'd forced her into full retreat. And the last thing he wanted was for her to leave. At least not until he'd gotten a chance to . . .

"Listen, I didn't mean to disturb you," he said quickly. "Please continue finishing your novel—"

She smirked for his benefit.

"Really, make no note of me. I truly just came to see the property. I'm sorry to have bothered you."

She shook her head. "No, I was done with my *correspondence and household accounts* and should go home. My uncle will likely be into more mischief if I am away too long. I heard enough lectures this morning from the neighbors about last night's antics to last me quite a while."

At this he grinned. "Your uncle does love a good cannon shot."

"As do you, sir."

Besides the obvious accusation in her voice, he thought he detected a hint of admiration.

From Miss Tate? Maybe he'd hit his head on the way down the well for now he was hearing the impossible.

She picked up her bonnet and toyed with the strings. "I never did have a chance to thank you for the flowers." Glancing up at him, she offered a small smile. The concession was hard won, but well worth the effort. "I thank you, and bid you good day." She started for the path as if she couldn't be gone from him fast enough.

Rafe scrambled for some reason to entice her to stay. Then she unwittingly gave it to him as she stopped by the gate and turned to him.

"If you go into the house," she warned, "do be careful as some of the floorboards are loose."

That's it, he realized. The inspection. The now horribly-dangerous-without-her-aid inspection. He rushed to press his case. "Miss Tate, may I ask one more favor?"

"Yes?" That impatient tone had returned to her voice.

"Perhaps you could lead me on a tour of Bettlesfield Park so I don't find myself trapped again? It would be a shame if I were to meet my fate here while you were home having tea."

"I don't think I'd call that a shame."

Of course the little minx wouldn't. This was the same woman who'd tied a noose for his benefit. He'd fall to his death in this wreck and she'd probably go to his funeral just to grin at the cortege.

She wasn't fooled by his request either. "Let me understand this, you trust *me* to see you safely through this ruin?"

Rafe eyed her. "I have to believe that eventually you'll lead me to where I want to go."

Even as he had said the words, he'd envisioned her wearing only a chemise and leading him into an elegant boudoir, her hand tugging at his, pulling him toward a massive bed.

Rafe, I want you so . . . Come with me, Rafe.

He coughed again, and this time he gave the side of his head a good tap. He'd have to ask Lady Finch if the village boasted a surgeon and go visit the fellow, for obviously he'd injured something in his fall.

"I suppose I could spare a few minutes," she was saying, her hands on her hips, while glancing up at the third story, a wry smile turning her lips.

Probably gauging whether a tumble from that height would be enough to remove him from her life, since the well had failed in that regard.

"I assume it won't take long to see," he said. "I only want to be able to give whomever I sell it to a fair description."

"Hmm. I suppose that would be important," she said, her fingers toying with the fringe on her shawl. "If you actually gain Bettlesfield Park, which you won't."

"That remains to be seen," he said, "not that I'll possess it long enough to worry about whether or not the roof leaks."

She set down her desk. "It isn't such a terrible ruin, I'll have you know." The passion in her voice came as a surprise. Practical Miss Tate defending Bettlesfield Park?

"It isn't?" he couldn't help asking.

"No, actually it has many redeeming qualities. If only—" She stopped and looked at him and then shook her head. "Never mind. It matters not."

"If only what?"

"It doesn't matter," she said. She set her bag atop her writing desk and looked back at the house with a new light in her eyes. "Oh bother, since you asked, I think it's a terrible crime to let such a wonderful house just tumble down. And if you did, by happenstance, come into it, which I am not saying you will, but if you did, promise me you won't sell it to one of those pompous nabobs or cits who'll tear it down and build some gilded monstrosity and ruin not only the vista but the neighborhood?"

Her eyes took on a fiery passion, one that sent a thread of guilt through Rafe. He didn't understand why everyone cared so passionately about what became of this place.

Lord, it was barely upright. What on earth did she think could be done with it? It wasn't like it could be a home.

A home . . .

Could it be? That in the very practical eyes of Miss Tate, Bettlesfield Park wasn't just a pile of stones, but the image of a home.

And in that realization, Rafe found himself wondering that if Miss Tate could believe a home might exist in such a ruin, then mayhap there was one out there for him.

A home for him?

Now he was convinced he'd hit his head.

Still, he could see that the house meant much more to Miss Tate than just a leaky roof and a place where birds found refuge. It was the dream of what could be had— not the charitable offerings of a distant relation, but a home where she was the mistress and would remain so until the end of her days.

A place he would sell without a second thought, she dreamt about. Yearned for with a passion that captivated a secret longing in his own heart that he'd never known he'd possessed.

A home . . .

Suddenly, he found himself asking, "What would you do to this place?"

"Me? You want to know what I would do with it?" Besides the usual skepticism in her voice, there was also a hint of hope—her tightly held dreams breaking free from the chains that held them fast.

Mierda! When was he going to learn to keep his mouth shut? He could feel her enthusiasm creeping into his own heart like a battlefield fever. Well, there was nothing he could do now short of throwing himself back in the well.

"Yes, you," he said. "What would you do to Bettlesfield Park if you were the mistress of this house?"

She cocked her head and stared at him, as if weighing the intent behind his question. "Do you really want to know? Even after yesterday and the bit with the rope just now?"

"Yes," he said. "You seem to have a fondness for this place, if not a familiarity, and I would be interested in hearing your opinions. And I promise I will even pass your suggestions on to the new owners."

"No need to take notes, for this house will never be yours," she said, nodding her head toward the hint of a path in the garden. "This way."

"If you are convinced this house will never be mine, then why give me a tour?" he asked following her.

Miss Tate paused. "Perhaps if you see what happens when others interfere where they have no business, you will come to realize the error of your ways."

It was Rafe's turn to cock a brow at her. "I doubt that will happen. I rather like 'interfering' as you put it. I got to meet you, after all." He couldn't help adding one more attempt at flirtation, but all it was met with was a hearty "harrumph" and a view of her back as she marched up the path.

"Where do you want to start—with the gardens or the interior?" she asked.

"I've seen enough of the gardens," he laughed. "Let's see inside this palace of yours."

She nodded and started around the house.

"Isn't the front door that way?" he asked, jerking his thumb in the other direction.

She shot him a wry glance.

"Yes, right," he muttered. "I suppose you have your own private entrance."

"Actually, I have several."

Why didn't that surprise him? But if he thought Miss Tate was done surprising him, he had another thing coming.

"You've spent a great deal of time here," he commented, following her carefully as she picked her way through the shrubberies and came to a hidden entrance.

"Of course I have," she replied, stepping gingerly into the house. "I grew up here."

"You lived here?" he was stammering.

Rebecca didn't look back to see the shock on his face. Since he was staying with Lady Finch, she assumed he already knew about her family's ignoble fall from grace. But his question indicated that the gossipy baroness was being uncharacteristically circumspect.

An odd notion, but knowing Lady Finch she had her reasons.

They'd arrived at the door near the kitchens, and Rebecca pushed aside the hedge that obscured it and entered the house. "Watch your step," she warned him. "The floorboards are loose."

Rafe followed her gingerly.

"My father was a fortune hunter," she said, leading him past what had been her mother's morning room to the back stairway. As she reached the first flight, she spotted the quizzical look on his face. "What I mean to say is that my father had a great desire to discover lost treasure."

"I thought he was a scholar."

So Lady Finch had been talking.

"He was," she replied. "When it suited him."

"We could start from the top and make our way down," she offered, nodding at the stairs.

"Is that necessary?" he asked, looking this way and that at the gloomy interior.

"Yes," she told him, catching him by the arm and dragging him up into the abandoned mansion. "You can't give an honest and detailed assessment of a place unless you've seen *all* of it."

"Practical advice, Miss Tate," he muttered. "Though I think you mean only to see me into an early grave."

"There is more to the place than meets the eye, sir."

"Yes, if one lives through the tour."

She knew, without a doubt, that if he'd gone through the house on his own, as had been his original intent, he would have gotten no further than the main foyer, with its roost of pigeons and dirty floor and returned to London with the intent of unloading the house on the first unwitting buyer he could find.

Yet Bettlesfield Park deserved so much more, she thought as she led him through the main bedrooms and the upstairs parlor, pointing out the marble on the mantle in the second guest room and the stain in the floor that her brother had left with one of his science experiments.

She hoped that mayhap he would see that the house deserved to be filled with laughter and joy once again.

"Hard to believe a house could become so ruined in what," he asked, "fifteen years?"

"It wasn't the finest estate when my parents owned it," she admitted. Bettlesfield Park had been an aging relic, but that hadn't stopped the Tates from struggling to make it a home.

That is, until her father had been lured to Calcutta with the promise of finding untold riches.

The kind of treasure that will make this place splendid, he was wont to say. But his great gamble had cost so very much.

Rebecca could feel Mr. Danvers' gaze upon her, but she didn't dare hazard a glance in his direction. She wanted neither his pity nor his opinion. But why she felt compelled to tell him her story, she wasn't sure either, but she plunged forward anyway.

"A man who'd been with the East India Company approached my father with an ancient tract that he'd picked up in Calcutta detailing a huge treasure trove that was kept in a sanctuary in the northern reaches. He offered to fund our trip to India for a share of the profits. A lion's share, but that mattered not to my father when there was a treasure to be found." Wandering down the main staircase, they paused on the second landing. "When my parents died, the man took Bettlesfield Park as a repayment for his lost investment."

"And turned it into a bordello?" Rafe asked, looking up at the tattered red silk hangings and ill-rendered mural on the ceiling of Zeus seducing Danaë.

"I fear so," she said, shaking her head at the wretched painting. "Don't get Lady Finch started on the subject, for she considers those the dark years for Bramley Hollow. Luckily for the neighborhood, though not so happily for the house, he ran into a spate of ill-luck and gambled it all away." Rebecca sighed and continued down the steps, sidestepping the loose ones until she reached the marble in the entryway, and then continued toward her father's beloved library.

Rafe walked around the room, stopping from time to time to poke at yet another hole in the wall. "I would like to know why this house is so pockmarked. From the looks of it, you'd think that it had withstood a French siege. That or your uncle has been using it for target practice."

"Pests," she replied, hoping he knew little of home ownership.

"I hardly think all this damage is the result of pests," he muttered, nudging his boot at a loose floorboard.

Rebecca said nothing to enlighten his skepticism. "The only thing left is the ballroom," she said, drawing him from the library and any further speculations. Much to her chagrin he changed the subject in an even more uncomfortable direction.

"So how is it, Miss Tate, that living in Bramley Hollow as you do, you stay unwed?" he asked as he followed after her.

Rebecca tried not to flinch. She knew it was a question asked often behind the closed doors of local society. "By avoiding the matchmaker," she told him as lightly as she could. "Besides, it isn't like I'd be deluged with suitors otherwise."

"I don't see why not," he said. "You're a—" he stopped himself and then eventually said, "A practical lady," using her own words.

"You don't need to be kind," she told him. "I know what I am. A lady past her marriageable years, with a half-mad relative and no dowry. There aren't too many men who want to burden themselves with a wife with so many encumbrances and deficits."

"I don't think your uncle is a deficit. You never know

when you'll need a dab hand with a cannon."

Rebecca nudged him with her elbow. "You should be ashamed of yourself for encouraging him as you did last night."

The rake grinned. "I have a fondness for cannons."

"So the entire village now knows."

He laughed. "Yes, Lady Finch rang a peel over my head this morning. Said she was going to write my brother immediately and chide him for my upbringing."

"Someone ought to," Rebecca replied. "But why your brother and not your mother?" If he could ask personal questions, she decided she might as well satisfy her curiosity about this enigmatic scoundrel.

"My brother raised me and Lady Finch holds him responsible for all my sins," he said, hardly sounding a bit repentant. "My parents died in a carriage accident when I was but a child."

"I'm sorry."

"No, it was a long time ago. Besides, my brother did an admirable job with me, all things considered. You might not believe this, but I was a bit of a hellion."

"You?" She feigned innocence, but she could well imagine that he'd been a devilish rogue even at a young age. "I don't think much has changed in the ensuing years. I agree with Lady Finch, a letter to your brother is most definitely in order."

He groaned. "You'll have me hauled before my siblings and lectured fiercely."

"Does it help?"

"Never."

"Do you have many brothers and sisters?" she asked, suddenly curious.

"Just two older brothers," he said. "Well, actually they are my half brothers. My mother was my father's second wife."

There was something about the way he answered her, that left her feeling that he wasn't quite telling the truth. Like he was leaving something out, but she didn't feel comfortable pressing a man she hardly knew for intimate details of his life.

But she was curious, too much so, she thought as she asked, "Where was your home?"

He laughed and shook his head. "I've never had one." Her face must have displayed her disbelief, because he continued by explaining. "My father was a diplomat and we moved quite often. When my parents died, I went to boarding school, but given my spotty scholastic career, I went to several establishments before my brother Colin gave up in exasperation and brought me aboard his ship."

"You went to sea?" She couldn't help but hide her admiration.

"I think he thought that there would be little room for me to find trouble onboard a warship—"

A warship? That didn't bode well.

"Oh, dear, the cannons!" she said.

He nodded. "That and other things. When he was about to toss me overboard, my other brother, Robert, stepped in and took me with him into the Army. I did better there. Plenty of cannons and such, but the regulations—" He shuddered. "I wasn't exactly a model officer."

"I imagine not," she said. As she glanced at him, a notion most unnerving uncoiled within her. There was something disarming and appealing about his unrepentant ways. And before she even weighed her words, she said, "I envy you your independence, Mr. Danvers."

"Don't, Miss Tate. My independence has gotten me

into all kinds of scrapes." He stepped closer to her, catching her arm and steering her around a hole in the floor. "Besides, you are the most independent lady I've ever met."

Rebecca stilled, for his hand was cradling her elbow, holding her close. She dared a glance up into his eyes and the dark appreciation she saw there sent a warm tremor down her spine. Like he had last night, his gaze dipped and lingered over her lips and she felt them open slightly, as if of their own volition. Oh, the temptation he presented bedeviled her senses. So when he stepped closer to her . . . she panicked and shook him free and picked up her skirts and fled briskly down the hall.

"This way," she told him, not daring to look back in her startled wake. "The ballroom is quite exquisite."

Independent, indeed! She was a scared little goose. If she were so independent, she would be testing her theory about the temptation of his kiss right this very second.

"How is it you are unwed, Mr. Danvers?" She saw no reason not to let him dangle a bit.

"Not you as well," he said, feigning agony, his hand over his heart. "I fear I am a contented bachelor and see no reason to change that."

"Well, you are in Bramley Hollow. 'Tis a dangerous place for a 'contented bachelor.' "

"I plan on taking a page from your example and keep my distance from that wily matchmaker."

"You'd be better to worry about my uncle," she told him. "I think he was quite taken with the idea of you bringing me flowers. He declared you a devil of a shot and a fine gentleman this morning. Come around the cottage again and he'll have you before the parson and me at your side."

"And you'd let him?"

"Not likely," she declared a little more adamantly than she should have.

He crossed his arms and leaned against the wall. "And why do you think you can outwit your uncle?"

"Because I'm a better shot than either of you."

He laughed and shook his head.

She came to the double doors that led to ballroom, and paused, staring at them. "That's odd. I don't recall them being shut." She tried the latch, but the door wouldn't budge. "Or ever being locked for that matter." Without asking for his help, she put her shoulder to the panel and gave it a shove.

The door held fast.

"I suppose we'll have to forgo this room," she conceded, biting her lip. " 'Tis a shame, because it is my favorite room in the house."

"Is there another way in?"

"We could try the garden doors, but we'd have to break the glass to get them open." She put her hands on her hips. "I don't understand how this door came to be locked." Looking over her shoulder at Rafe, she added, "It isn't like there is much around here that does work, let alone locks. We'll just have to get a pry bar from the shed."

"Let me try," he offered, stepping around her and twisting the latch for himself.

When it didn't budge, she shook her head. What, did he think she didn't know how to open a door?

He winked at her before throwing his shoulder into the locked panels. They rattled on their hinges, sending a cloud of dust showering down on them. And still they held fast.

"I don't think the new owner will appreciate a broken door," she told him.

"Miss Tate," he said, rubbing his aching shoulder. "I doubt that adding one broken door to the list of repairs in this house is really going to make a noticeable difference in the price."

"I suppose not," she said. "If you'll just wait, I can—"

He took her by the arm, guiding her away from the locked entry. Once she was well out of harm's way, he glanced over at her and winked again.

Rebecca's mouth gaped as she watched the unlikely gentleman before her transform into a whirl of power and strength. He took two long strides back, then came at the double doors like a fury.

His foot hit just beside the latch and the door burst open in an explosion of wood splinters and dust.

She'd never seen a man move so fast or with such deadly intent. "No, I don't suppose the pry bar is necessary," she managed to utter.

Mr. Danvers grinned as he stalked into the ballroom, like Ajax after defeating yet another interloper in his territory.

What had she been thinking? She'd been telling herself that this man wasn't anyone she should worry about. But now she saw how she'd been lying to herself in the worst sort of way.

His mercantile jacket and scuffed boots spoke of a thin purse and careless manners. Yet when he'd unleashed his so-very-masculine power at the locked door, her entire body had trembled. Watching him left her with only one breathless thought: *What it would be like to have a man possess her with that same undeniable passion?*

There was no doubt that this was a man most decidedly capable of untangling all of a woman's desires. And all of her secrets. Oh, she needed to tread very carefully.

"What the devil—" she heard him mutter from inside.

While she'd remained in the hallway gawking at the open door, he'd long since gone inside the ballroom.

As she walked through the ruined portal, her body thrummed with awareness at the destruction he'd left in his wake. It would be wise to remember the wreckage, she told herself.

She found him kneeling before the fireplace, his fingers poking at the ashes in the grate. Then he rose and looked around. "Someone has been living here."

"Tramps, perhaps," she offered. "But they are usually here in the winter, not this time of year."

"No, someone has been living here. Recently."

"How do you know?" she asked, looking at the dirty grate and the dust shrouded room.

"I know," he said. His confidence spoke volumes. "You see these footprints, here and here," he said, pointing at them. "The rest of the room is full of dust, except for those places. And here, beside the fireplace, look at this." He waved his hand at the floor as if she should be able to see the evidence inscribed in the wood.

When she shook her head, he explained further. "This entire spot is clean. It's the size of a man. He was sleeping here, but he's done a remarkable job of cleaning up—as if he didn't want to be found. But it is always impossible to fix the dust."

Rebecca didn't want to know how he knew of such things. Of hiding oneself, of tracking another human being, of dust and the clues to be found in a seemingly innocent, albeit filthy, grate.

Her secrets didn't stand a chance against this man and suddenly she realized just how far over her head she was.

She might as well be the one at the bottom of the garden well.

"I'll have to tell Lord Finch," she said. Then she explained further. "The baron is the local magistrate. He'll send the constable out to investigate, though I doubt Mr. Holmes will be all that impressed with your findings."

He shook his head. "There is something odd about all this. Why would someone want to hide out here?"

Rebecca shrugged as if the answer was far out of her ken. But his question sent a barrage of fear through her gut. Someone had been hiding themselves at Bettlesfield Park? Lurking about the neighborhood like a thief? And a sophisticated one, at that.

Suddenly she needed to be home. Home to the colonel and away from her suspicions, away from Raphael Danvers.

She spun around and started to flee, heedless of how it looked, of where she was going.

"Careful," he called out as she nearly stepped into a hole in the floor.

Suddenly she found herself captured in his arms. His far-too-capable embrace.

Rebecca had never been held by a man, at least not like this, commandeered by his strength, hauled up against his chest, into a wall that promised sanctuary.

"I just remembered, I promised my uncle . . . I said I'd be home . . ." she stammered.

His eyes narrowed. He didn't believe her. Not in the least.

"Your heart is pounding, Miss Tate," he said, not letting her go. "What has you so frightened?"

"Nothing," she told him trying to shrug off his grasp. "Now please unhand me."

"No," he said. "Not 'til you tell me what has you so pale? So terrified. And don't try to tell me some Banbury tale about almost falling."

She should have known that like the ashes in the grate and the dust on the floor, Mr. Danvers would have no trouble seeing right through the lies that fell so clumsily from her lips.

"Rebecca," he whispered, using her given name like a caress, like he had the right to such a familiarity. "Tell me. I can help you." His hands reached up to cradle her face, to turn it toward him so her gaze met his. He searched her face as if he could find the meaning behind her fears.

And where she had felt panicked and terrified but a few moments ago, in his arms she felt shielded from the worst the world had to offer.

Something she knew a little about.

His touch smoothed away her distress, like the fading ripples of water on a pond. "Tell me, what is wrong? What sent you racing out of here?" His fingers caught a loose strand of her hair and brushed it back into place. The tenderness in his touch sent tremors down her spine. So gentle, so very precarious.

"I realized . . . I need to . . ."

"You need to tell me the truth. I can help you."

No, he couldn't. No one could.

His gaze fixed first on her lips and then on her eyes. There was a look there so dark and unfathomable in the jet of his eyes. So very dark and dangerous. As if he desired her.

Why ever for, she couldn't imagine, but denying him was impossible.

And she was lost, awaiting him to find her like a hero from one of her novels. But Raphael Danvers was no hero—a rake and a scoundrel, most certainly, but no hero. He'd done things in life that no gentleman should claim—and as she found herself gazing once again at the firm set of his mouth, she had to imagine that he wouldn't kiss like a gentleman either.

"Tell me, Rebecca," he whispered. "What has you so frightened."

"You," she whispered.

"You're not scared," he said. And to prove his point, he dipped his head down and captured her lips with his.

Her eyes fluttered shut as his tongue eased her trembling lips open. Oh, she should protest this intimate invasion, issue a set down that would leave him sufficiently put in his place.

Instead she quaked beneath him. His tongue teased hers, daring her to sally forth, unleashing a cannonade of desire within her. Her arms wound around his neck, pulling him closer. His lips were not enough, she wanted him to unleash the maddening passion that had been tormenting her since she'd first spied him.

His kiss deepened and he groaned, the untamed hunger of the sound calling to her own unanswered desires.

Her shawl fell away, her hair became unbound, his fingers gently combing through the tangled strands.

She was falling, falling so dangerously. And this man was the type who wouldn't save her when he caught her . . .

Even now, he was stroking her back, his hands running reverently over her hips, up her sides until he cradled her breasts.

She moaned, the sensation of his thumb easing over her nipple sending her knees crumpling beneath her.

Oh, he caught her, and kept kissing her, teasing her with his touch, leaving her willing to let him do oh-so-much more.

He gathered her closer, and as he did, he stepped back, obviously having forgotten how he had originally gotten her into his arms—by keeping her from falling into a hole in the floor.

His boot crashed through and as he fell, she found herself sprawling into a heap. Rafe didn't land too far from her and chuckling at his misfortune, he heaved himself back up and then extended a hand to her.

"Miss Tate," he said, "I swear you will be my undoing." He laughed again.

Her hand went not to his, but to her lips, where the cold air was a stunning contrast to his heated kiss.

"Oh, my," she managed to gasp. She'd been about to . . .

This time, her practical nature had a chance to be heard and it clamored a warning that couldn't go unheeded.

Rebecca scrambled to her feet, snatched up her shawl and fled from the room.

Fled the untamed man who had nearly been her undoing.

Rafe tried to follow her, but she slipped out of the house through an opening in the wall that had been poorly mended with a few boards nailed over it. The space was just too small for him to get through.

By the time he'd gotten out the front door and back around to the garden, she was nowhere to be seen.

"Demmit," he cursed. What had he done?

He'd kissed her without thinking. Oh, he'd been thinking but not with anything resembling good sense.

And what about the practical, sensible Miss Tate? She'd been like wildfire in his arms, igniting his passion with her response. The kind of response that would take a lifetime to explore.

A lifetime? He raked his fingers through his hair and cursed. He needed to get the hell out of Bramley Hollow.

He was about to turn around and go collect his horse, but he spied something sitting atop her former perch.

In her haste, Miss Tate had forgotten her traveling desk.

On any other case, her negligence would be considered a boon in his favor. Cochrane would have had the demmed thing open by now, without even a moment's hesitation.

He looked around the empty landscape. There was no one about, except for a few birds trilling in the hedges. Just him and most likely the evidence he needed.

So what was he waiting for?

Perhaps if you see what happens when others interfere where they have no business, you will come to realize the error of your ways.

Her words chided him. If he did reveal who she was, what would that mean to her ordered existence? She might have her legions of fans, but her enemies, the mothers of those rebellious daughters, were the ones who held sway in society. They would see her ruined and ostracized without a second thought.

Not even Lady Finch would be able to save her reputation once those tabbies in London got done with her. They'd discredit her to her publisher and any society that she tried to find a home within.

He couldn't let that happen to her, to them.

To them?

Rafe gulped for air. How had this chit gone from an annoying minx to "them?"

Marching over to the desk, he knelt beside it and studied the unusual design. It looked almost like a military dispatch box than a lady's traveling desk, but leave it to Rebecca to have something unexpected.

He took a deep breath and flipped the lid open. Inside, he found her hastily stowed pages, along with two capped inkwells—one full and one empty—and at the bottom, several quills in various states of sharpness. Ignoring the nubs and penknife, he went straight for what interested him: the pages. Sifting through them, he searched for telltale prose.

Instead, he found,

Dearest Mary,

I know this letter is long overdue . . .

Dear Sirs,

I am writing on behalf of my uncle to request that he be allowed to borrow a volume from your library . . .

Household Expenses for May 1817 . . .

Rafe kept reading one after another, turning the pages over and scanning every paragraph to find the evidence he needed.

But it was nothing more than what she had said—household accounts and correspondence. Not even the household accounts gave any indication that Miss Tate had spent an exorbitant amount on a writer's necessities: paper, ink and quills.

No, her monthly inventory looked just as it should, the accounts of a practical woman trying to hold together a household on a meager income and the charity of her uncle's relations.

The pages fell from his fingers as the truth hit him.

She wasn't the woman he sought.

He should be elated that he wouldn't have to destroy her to get his prize, yet why did he feel so disappointed?

Maybe it was because for a time this afternoon, Miss

Rebecca Tate had become his own personal Miss Darby: resourceful, brave, adventurous, and so entirely enticing. And now . . .

He stuffed the pages back in the case and shut the lid, closing his heart as well to such foolish notions. To spinsters who could capture his imagination with their capricious ways and passionate kisses.

Picking up her belongings, he decided to take them with him to Finch Manor. He'd ask Jemmy to return them to her this evening, discreetly of course.

Yet as he carried the case back to his horse, one nagging question burrowed up out of his disappointment.

If Rebecca wasn't the *Miss Darby* author, then what had frightened her so?

He hadn't even kissed her at that point. And when she finally had fled, could it have been their kiss that sent her racing from his arms?

For if he was completely honest, her kiss had terrified him right down to his boots.

Chapter 7

While you think that by accepting my proposal, my fair Miss Darby, you would be merely my second wife, believe me that you would be first in my heart.

Prince Sanjit to Miss Darby
in *Miss Darby's Reckless Bargain*

Rebecca rushed home, her feet flying over the path, mindless of the flowers and sunshine brightening the spring day. Normally such sights would have left her filled with joy, but today she saw none of it.

Who could have thought that when the sun had dawned this morn, that her life would be so turned upside down before tea time?

Someone was lurking about Bettlesfield Park? The thought chilled her for it could only mean one thing. And why had this trouble chosen now to return to her life?

She started up over the stile at the boundary fence and paused at the top. Oh, if only that was all there was to her distress.

Rafe had kissed her. Kissed her without any thought of decency.

Oh, he was certainly no gentleman. He'd kissed her until her knees had gone weak and she'd been about to toss aside every bit of propriety she possessed.

She fumbled down the steps and jerked to a blundering halt at the muddy bottom as one final condemning thought occurred to her. If she could so easily dispatch Mr. Danvers as no gentleman, what did that make her? For she would have continued the kiss, continued to allow him liberties, if it hadn't been for that wayward hole in the floor.

Perhaps there was some reason to be glad that Bettlesfield Park was in such disastrous condition.

She glanced back over her shoulder at the house and hugged her shawl tighter. Until she was assured that Mr. Danvers was gone from Bramley Hollow, she was going to have to find another place to seek solace. Even still, how would she ever find peace there again when her childhood home was now riddled with new memories—unsettling, undeniable memories of kissing a stranger.

"Oh, what have I done?" she whispered into the soft breeze winding through the meadow. "What is to become of me?"

Hopping down from the wall, she continued home resolving to forget everything about this afternoon. The heat of his body pressed to hers. The dark smoldering blaze in his gaze that had set her knees quaking. Or the moment when he'd pressed his lips to hers, his tongue teasing her to open up to him, demanding and unrelenting, as if it were his due.

The devil take him, she thought. How would she ever forget?

Forget . . . Botheration! She'd forgotten her desk. Oh, drat the man. He'd left her so befuddled she'd gone and left her belongings in the garden.

She stood her ground for a time, considering whether or not she should go back and risk facing him, but she decided it was the better part of valor to flee while she could.

Her desk would still be there tomorrow, while hopefully, he wouldn't.

As she came to the edge of the village, past Esme's cottage, Rebecca picked up the pace, suspecting that the matchmaker, with her uncanny sense of the secrets of the heart, would come racing out of her cottage declaring Rebecca "matched."

Matched to Mr. Danvers? She shuddered. Not to that charming rogue. She'd disavowed that sort years ago when Lt. Habersham had left Calcutta without a single word to her.

Yet a little voice danced inside her head.

Imagine spending the rest of your life in his arms . . . being plied with his kisses . . .

How could any woman forswear such a passionate gamble?

Rebecca blew out a loud sigh. She was growing as addled as Miss Honora, the spinster up the road.

No, she was too practical to believe such nonsense. Mr. Danvers had kissed her hoping to discover what she knew about the *Darby* novels. And like some dizzy Bath school miss, she'd almost fallen for his wiles. Rebecca marched up the road with a new determination to her steps.

It wasn't long before she found herself at the rose covered trellis that marked the entrance to their cottage. Maybe she could hope that Mr. Danvers' fall into the hole had knocked some sense into him. And that perhaps she would never see him again, which would be a blessing in and of itself. Never be kissed like that again, not by a rake, and certainly not by her future vicar. She should be thrilled to be done with him, but suddenly all she wanted to do was give herself over to a very impractical spate of tears.

As she entered the cottage, Mrs. Wortling was hustling about—a rarity to be sure—with the iron in one hand and the Colonel's dress jacket in the other.

"Rest assured, Colonel Posthill, I'll have your uniform shipshape. I'm a dab hand with an iron."

"I was in the army, madam, not one of those brine soaked fools England seems to regard as so essential."

"Army, navy, I see no difference. A man in a uniform is a sight to behold."

She turned and spotted Rebecca standing open-mouthed in the doorway. "Wouldn't you agree, Miss Tate?"

"What is going on?" she managed to ask.

"You had best get along with you. You've an invitation to dine tonight." Mrs. Wortling returned the iron to the kitchen and came out with Rebecca's best sprigged muslin. "I took the liberty of putting a few touches on this one." Cocking her head, the housekeeper gave her an assessing glance. "What is different about you?" She sighed and thrust the gown into Rebecca's arms. "Upstairs with you and get ready. Wouldn't do to be late."

"Late to what?" she asked, directing her question to the colonel, who stood before the mirror in the hall tying his cravat.

Rebecca laid the muslin over the back of a chair, and made her way to his side. After watching her uncle attempt to tie his neck cloth, she reached over and finished the simple knot for him.

Glancing up at the mirror, she found him smiling at her.

"What is this about a dinner invitation?" she asked.

"Lady Finch sent a command down this afternoon. Going to have a party to introduce your Mr. Danvers to the neighborhood."

"*My* Mr. Danvers?" She didn't even realize she'd said the name aloud until Mrs. Wortling laughed.

Well, more like cackled like an old crow.

"Oh, that caught your attention," she said, poking her head out from the kitchen. "He must be rich, because I hear tell he's inherited Bettlesfield Park. Or he's buying it. Most likely he won it dicing, for I thought last night he had the look of one of those London sharpsters." She looked back at Rebecca. "Maybe your best muslin isn't a good idea. I'd hate to see you lose your heart to a gamester. My sister did that and look at her now. Seven babes and nary a sign of the worthless sot. Not that my sister cares, for she swears that devil's kisses were well worth the price she's paying now." Mrs. Wortling shook her head and let out a skeptical "harrumph" that offered her opinion on the subject— no man's kiss could be worth a life of poverty.

But Rebecca knew exactly what kept Mrs. Wortling's sister enthralled—the memory of kisses capable of tempting a woman beyond her good sense, beyond reason.

"Yes, I think your dark dress would be better," the housekeeper was saying. "Mourning has a way of putting most men off. Most, I tell you." She made another heavy sigh. "I hope this Mr. Danvers isn't one of those that likes—"

"Mrs. Wortling, don't you have some more pressing to attend to?" the colonel asked.

The woman's brow furrowed at being interrupted, but when the colonel was in his right mind, the housekeeper knew to keep her place.

She hustled back into the kitchen, but that didn't stop her from muttering, "Don't be blaming me if this gentleman turns out to be some plaguesome cad."

Too late, Rebecca wanted to tell her. Instead, she caught her uncle by the elbow and steered him into the library, closing the door behind them and checking it once again to make sure it was shut tight. "What do you mean that we are dining at Finch Manor? It isn't Sunday."

They always dined at Finch Manor on Sundays.

"I told you. Lady Finch sent an invitation around just after you left and asked us to dine with her and your Mr. Danvers."

"He is not *my* Mr. Danvers," she told him through clenched teeth. Why couldn't the colonel have sent the Finch footman scurrying for safety, offering their regrets with a hail of shot blasted from his ever-faithful Brown Bess. "And I'm not going."

"Balderdash!" the colonel said, as Mrs. Wortling came in with his coat. He held it up to inspect her handiwork and then nodded in approval. The housekeeper sniffed and returned to the kitchen, though Rebecca knew the lady probably hadn't gotten any further than the hallway so she wouldn't miss a word of the brewing dispute.

Mrs. Wortling loved dissention in the ranks almost as much as she loved Madeira.

"Uncle, we can't accept," Rebecca said, this time a little less urgently. No need to put him on alert, let alone give Mrs. Wortling something to gossip about with the butcher's wife.

"I see no reason why not," he said, shrugging on his jacket.

" 'Tis a long walk and will tire you out," Rebecca told him, smoothing the wool over his back, and tugging the hem down so his uniform looked crisp and stately.

"Lady Finch is sending her carriage," he said. "She is ever the thoughtful woman."

Lady Finch thoughtful? Only when it suited her purposes. But what reason did the lady have for trotting out her husband's poor relations? Rebecca's suspicions grew. "Who else is going to be there?"

Mrs. Wortling answered this, calling from the hall-way, "According to Mrs. Benton, Lord and Lady Kirk-wood, Major Harrington and his wife, the Gadbury sisters and since they are going to be there, that hand-some Mr. Kitling."

Rebecca groaned. It wasn't some welcome to the neighborhood party as her uncle seemed to believe. Lady Finch had deliberately invited everyone who had any connection to India. Anyone capable of writing the *Miss Darby* novels. It wasn't a social event, but a witch hunt.

"I haven't anything to wear," Rebecca said, panic ris-ing in her chest.

The colonel pointed at the muslin. "Looks fine to me. You'll be the prettiest gel there." He picked up the gown and pressed it into her hands. "Now do your primping or whatever it is you ladies must do before one of these affairs."

"I'm not going," Rebecca told him. Spend an evening with Mr. Danvers? She'd rather face a firing squad.

And drat the man! He'd known all about the dinner as she'd fled the Park like a frightened rabbit. No won-der he hadn't pursued her. He already had his second trap baited and set.

The devious wretch!

"Bex, did you hear me? You have a half an hour until the carriage arrives. Go on upstairs and get yourself buttoned up."

She shook her head.

"None of this," the colonel said, striking a com-manding stance. "You are coming along and I'll hear no more of this mutinous babble. About time you had a suitor and this Danvers fellow strikes me as just the man. Dab hand with a cannon, besides."

Rebecca did her best to ignore the "amen" coming

from the kitchen. She was surrounded by traitors about to cast her before a tiger. A tiger with jet black eyes and a ravenous appetite for unwitting spinsters.

Meanwhile, the colonel was warming to his subject as if he were once again in command. "Perhaps it is time to consider seeing about that Season in town you've always wanted. I suspect Lady Finch would know how that is all done."

"A Season? In town?" Rebecca's throat went dry. "We haven't the funds. Besides, I can't leave you. I won't leave you." She couldn't leave him—not if there was someone lurking about the fringes of Bramley Hollow.

"You're a loyal gel, Bex, but you have to consider your future. I won't be around forever. Probably past time that I saw to yours." He folded his hands behind his back and rocked on his heels. "Now go on with you. And no more long faces. Perhaps this Danvers fellow will take a fancy to you and you won't have to go to town and do the pretty."

Right now facing the perils and pitfalls of Almack's sounded preferable to another encounter with Mr. Danvers. For she had her own secrets to keep and she knew without a doubt he was the one man capable of uncovering them.

One dangerous kiss at a time . . .

"My dear friends," Lady Finch said, entering the room with Rafe on her arm. "Here is my good friend, Mr. Raphael Danvers, and his associate, Mr. Cochrane."

Rafe knew in an instant, he'd prefer an evening spent at the Rose and Lion, Pymm's old Seven Dials haunt, guarding his purse and hoping his throat didn't get slit than spend tonight in the company of Bramley Hollow's good society.

The faces turned toward him held an air of skepticism that was nearly palatable. As Lady Finch feared, her guests were suspicious at this hasty and unprecedented dinner invitation.

Cochrane bowed curtly, then headed for a far corner. Lady Finch had spent the day hammering manners into the uncivilized young man, and from the looks of it, her lessons were working.

The rest of the company wasn't quite so concerned about civility—Miss Tate in particular, for she barely afforded him the courtesy of a glance.

She stood beside her uncle, a fierce and determined set to her lips and a taut trim to her shoulders, and nary a hint of the woman who'd melded into his arms, wild and passionate in her ardor.

Rafe shifted from one foot to another. Had his kiss been that bad? He'd never had any complaints before. Certainly he should apologize for pursuing her over the *Darby* nonsense, but now he probably needed to add his regrets over their interlude at Bettlesfield Park.

Only he didn't feel like apologizing.

He'd rather spend the night trying to tempt another such kiss from her. But before he could do that, he had to determine which of Lady Finch's guests had a secret passion for writing.

"Lord and Lady Kirkwood, may I present Mr. Danvers," Lady Finch began, wrenching him from his reverie and towing him through the room to begin the introductions.

The best chair in the room, Lady Finch's chair to be exact, had been commandeered by Lady Kirkwood. As a countess, she outranked Lady Finch, despite the fact that Lady Kirkwood had been born plain old Sally

Smythe-Bimpton, the fourth daughter of a poor country curate. Luckily for Sally, being the prettiest of the sisters and the smartest, she'd been sent to London to be a companion to a distant and elderly relation, and managed in a few short months to gain herself a marriage to the second son of Earl Kirkwood. After ten lucrative years in India, they'd been summoned home upon the death of his older brother, and a year later assumed the Kirkwood title when the old earl passed away.

All of this Rafe knew, because Lady Finch and Mrs. Radleigh had supplied a complete history of their guests and the elements of their past that made them a likely candidate. Lady Finch and Mrs. Radleigh both counted Lady Kirkwood and her daughter, Victoria, as the most likely suspects.

The countess inclined her head slightly at the introduction. "That Lady Finch has shown us the hospitality of her home speaks most auspiciously of you, sir."

Lord Kirkwood stood behind his wife, mumbled his greetings and turned his attention back to the drink in his hand.

So summarily dismissed, Lady Finch steered him toward the next couple. "And here we have Mrs. Harrington, and over there by the window, is her husband, Major Harrington."

"Charmed," Rafe said, putting on his best town polish.

The lady smiled, and her husband paused long enough in his pacing about the room to nod in greeting. The man tugged on his watch chain and pulled it out from the pocket of his waistcoat. He glanced at the time and then out the window.

"I do say, I was quite surprised when we got your invitation this morning, Lady Finch," Mrs. Harrington was saying. "The major was inclined to send our regrets, but an invitation from you, why how could it be denied? Don't you agree, Lady Kirkwood?"

"Yes, quite," the countess said in bored tones that belied her sharp, curious gaze.

He thought it was telling that Mrs. Harrington sat as close as she could manage to Lady Kirkwood. A military wife on campaign. This time for the social advancement of her family.

"Mr. Danvers, you say?" she asked. "Are you related to Baron Danvers?" Clearly she'd been reading her *Debrett's*, just as Mrs. Radleigh had predicted.

"He is my brother."

"Hmmm," she murmured, smoothing out her handkerchief with her fingers. "Raphael Danvers, you say? Are you sure you are related to the baron? Why just this morning I was glancing through my new *Debrett's* and saw only a brother Robert listed." She glanced at Lady Kirkwood and then Lady Finch and smiled. "I find it indispensable to ensure that no ineligible *parti* arrive on our doorstep."

"You won't find me in *Debrett's*," Rafe told her. "I'm not listed."

"Lucky devil," Jemmy said, toasting such good fortune from his spot near the sideboard. He was in the process of filling a glass of Madeira for the major.

"Not listed?" Mrs. Harrington blinked several times as if she were trying to ascertain why Lady Finch would invite them to dinner with a man not listed in *Debrett's*. "Not listed? I do say, how odd!" A few seconds later she sniffed in dismay, then promptly returned to her fawning over Lady Kirkwood's new shawl.

After the Harringtons came the less notable members of their limited society, the Misses Gadbury. Since little was known about the sisters, they were regulated to the sofa opposite the countess, with the safety of a long, low table between the social gulf. Lady Finch barely had her introductions out, when one of the sisters spoke up, extending her hand in greeting and smiling at Rafe like a practiced coquette.

"I am the eldest," Honora informed Rafe, after she first dumped a tiny dog out of her lap, then extended her hand for him, "by all of eight minutes. Though most say I look several minutes younger."

"Honora, we are identical," Alminta said, holding an exact match of her sister's miniature dog. "There isn't a bit of difference between us."

"Ah, but there is," Rafe said. "Miss Honora has a tiny scar over her eyebrow."

Miss Honora preened. "Sir, you are very observant." She touched her brow with her fingers. "I fell from a stool as a child, trying to reach a jar of honey on the top shelf. Our *aya* scolded me something fearful, while mother was bereft that I might have ruined my face."

"I see nothing ruinous about it," Rafe told her. "But even without the scar, I would have been able to tell you apart. For I was a twin as well."

Out of the corner of his eye, he saw Rebecca's head turn quickly at this news, her brow raised like a question mark.

He hadn't mentioned Orlando earlier because he hadn't wanted to . . . well, he hadn't wanted to draw on her sympathies by using his brother's memory.

"You *had* a twin?" Miss Alminta asked, before her sister had a chance to comment.

"Yes, Miss Alminta," he said. "He died a few years ago."

"Murdered, wasn't he?" Sydney Kitling asked from where he stood near the fireplace. At least, Rafe assumed the man was Kitling.

"Murdered?" gasped Mrs. Harrington, while Lady Kirkwood's fan fluttered.

With this revelation out in the open, he didn't glance at Rebecca. He didn't like discussing Orlando's death—it was, and he suspected would always be, like an open wound in his soul. No, her sharp gaze and keen mind would see right through his façade of barely restrained indifference on the subject. See the guilt and blame that hung around his neck like a noose.

He should have been there for Orlando. Should have never let his scholarly and forthright twin enter into the family profession of espionage. For Orlando had trusted where he shouldn't have, a lesson Rafe held close to his own closely guarded heart.

Meanwhile, Kitling seemed well pleased with the stir he'd created. With one hand resting on the mantel, he leaned against the heavy oak lintel like some character from a tragic novel. His choice of evening dress evoked his time in the East and his self-proclaimed position as the local poet—he wore a turban and a paisley sash wound across his chest instead of a waistcoat. "I seem to remember reading about it in the papers while I was in Calcutta. Murdered at Lord Chambley's. During a ball, wasn't it?"

Rafe grit his teeth and nodded. Kitling was every bit the smug bastard that Lady Finch had intimated. If Kitling turned out to be the author, Rafe knew his vow to Cochrane, that they weren't in Bramley Hollow to break any limbs, was going to be quickly forgotten.

Lady Finch rushed in. "Yes, dear brave Orlando Danvers. Working for the Foreign Office at the time. Gave his life protecting our King and beloved country."

Mrs. Harrington seemed anything but impressed at this addition to the story. *Murdered*, she mouthed at Lady Kirkwood and shuddered for good measure.

The Gadbury sisters clucked and fussed over this news.

"I would be bereft without my dear sister," Miss Honora said.

"As I would be without you," Alminta replied, reaching over to pat her sister's knee.

"And I would be lost without either of you, my fairest ladies," Kitling said, sauntering across the room and then seating himself between the sisters. He glanced up at Rafe. "Good to have someone new in the neighborhood. I fear everyone here is already bored to death with my harrowing accounts of India."

"I'm fond of stories of the sub-continent," Rafe told the man, hoping he was handing the fellow enough rope with which to hang himself.

"Now you've done it," Major Harrington muttered as he paused in his pacing about the room. "Hogwash for the rest of the night, mark my words."

Kitling ignored the major, as did everyone else.

Lady Finch pasted a smile on her face and led Rafe to the pair of ladies seated in the corner. "Mr. Danvers, this is Miss Charlotte Harrington and Lady Victoria Manvell."

"Charmed," Rafe said, bowing to the ladies.

Charlotte's gaze shot to her mother's, obviously to gain approval for this introduction, while Lady Victoria shot Rafe an assessing glance that went from the top of his head down to his boots, calculating the exact worth of his costume and therein, his possible income.

As if satisfied with her total, she shot him a dazzling smile. A sort of "oh, you'll do" look that made the hairs on the back of his neck stand up higher than they had the time he'd accidentally ridden into a French cavalry unit camped near the Portuguese border.

He could see now why Jemmy avoided the lady. She

held a spark of trouble about her worse than a match near a powder keg.

Yet if there was anyone who seemed to be the living embodiment of Miss Darby, it was Lady Victoria. She carried herself with immeasurable confidence and had an air of feminine mystique about her that would draw the men of London to her like moths to a flame.

But Rafe had crossed her off his list of suspects almost immediately. The girl was missing one thing that Miss Darby, and he suspected her creator both possessed—a certain spark of unrelenting passion and intelligence that would make the lady standout even in a room filled with Originals.

And those characteristics Lady Victoria did not possess. Rather, she wore her allure out like an array of colorful ribbons for all to see.

So why did his gaze keep straying in the direction of a nearly forgettable spinster in a shapeless muslin gown?

"How very nice to meet you, Mr. Danvers," Lady Victoria was purring as she eyed him once again. "But you must tell us why you've come to the quiet world of Bramley Hollow. You look like a man who would find country life rather, shall we say, *restraining*."

A coughing fit rose from Miss Tate's corner, interrupting Lady Victoria's flirtation.

"Dear me, Bex," the colonel was saying, "what the devil is caught in your craw?" He gave his niece a good pat on the back that sent her sputtering forward.

It didn't escape Rafe's notice that Miss Tate wasn't included in the chummy company of Charlotte Harrington and Lady Victoria. It was obvious she wasn't comfortable with them, nor they with her.

He knew exactly how she felt. Listed or not listed—

English society was as particular as a Bath school-mistress.

Lady Finch waved at Addison to bring Rebecca a drink, then she continued her introductions. "And you've already met Colonel Posthill, Lord Finch's cousin, as well as his dear niece, Miss Rebecca Tate." For the benefit of the others in the room, she added, "Yesterday in the village. Miss Tate was so kind as to give Mr. Danvers the directions he was seeking."

"It is a pleasure to make your acquaintance again, Miss Tate," he said, bowing over her gloved fingers. He lingered a little too long there, for all too soon she was wrenching them out of his grasp.

"Yes, I suppose it is," she said. "I'm surprised to see you, sir, for I thought you were going back to London." Her eyes held the rest of her statement. *And please do so in all good haste.*

"Miss Tate!" Lady Victoria exclaimed, rising from her spot and coming to Rafe's defense. "Why would you want Mr. Danvers to leave when he's only just arrived?"

Rafe now found himself trapped between the two ladies. Help, female help that is, always came at a price. One he wasn't willing to discover. Besides, Lord Kirkwood looked capable of still firing a straight shot and the last thing he wanted to do was be called out by an irate father.

And besides the earl, there was also Colonel Posthill to consider. Rafe had to imagine that if the addlepated officer ever discovered what had happened at Bettlesfield Park, Rafe would find himself the victim of random cannon fire.

"I can't imagine why Miss Tate would want you to leave, do you, sir?" Lady Victoria asked, her hand wrapping into the crook of Rafe's elbow.

He tried to shake her off, but found himself anchored by the ingenious flirt.

Miss Tate glanced down at the other girl's possessive stance and smiled, though in Rafe's estimation it looked more like she was baring her teeth.

"I just find it unusual that he was bound for London yesterday, and here he is settled in for a cozy visit at Finch Manor," she said. "Nothing more than curiosity. Just as you were inquiring as to his reasons for being here." She turned to Rafe. "I don't believe you ever did answer Victoria's—"

"Lady Victoria, if you don't mind," the young woman said in frosty tones that echoed her mother's.

Rebecca nodded. "How forgetful of me, *Lady Victoria*. I fear you will always be just plain Victoria Manvell to me."

The room fell silent, as if a gauntlet had been thrown down.

"That's right," Kitling was saying. "You two came out together in Calcutta. I remember. Wasn't there some dust up over a lieutenant or some such scandal?"

Rebecca's cheeks pinked with embarrassment, while Lady Victoria's flamed with anger.

Lady Kirkwood stepped in immediately. "Scandal? I hardly think my daughter was ever—"

"Mother!" Lady Victoria hissed. "Please!"

Her mother glanced around, recognizing her daughter's unspoken reminder as to the extent of the company they were keeping, and she instantly recomposed herself with the cool disdain of one to the manner born. Then she steered the conversation back to where it had gotten off track. "Really, I don't see why Mr. Danvers is here is all that important. Suffice it to say that he is here and a guest of Lady Finch's." On that note she retook her seat, while her daughter returned to her place beside Charlotte.

Mrs. Harrington moved into the void, perhaps trying to cement her position with Lady Kirkwood, by saying, "I must say the girls look splendid together. What perfectly lovely additions you'll both make to this Season," she said to Charlotte and Lady Victoria.

"Oh, yes, our Season," Lady Victoria said, warming to the subject now that it revolved around her. "How delightful it will be to have my beloved Charlotte there. I had been so bereft at the notion of going to London without my dearest friend beside me." She smiled for the benefit of all. "I mean to see Miss Harrington well matched. After all, I do come from Bramley Hollow and we have a certain reputation to uphold."

"To town just like that? This is a surprise, Mrs. Harrington," Lady Finch said, settling down on a nearby chair. "I had thought you and Major Harrington had decided against going this year."

Mrs. Harrington smiled profusely. "I had thought so as well, but then the major came home this afternoon and declared we were off for London without any delay."

"How abrupt!" Lady Kirkwood fussed, sending a scandalized glance at the major, who paid her no heed because he was too busy glancing out the window.

"Oh, I'm quite used to it," Mrs. Harrington was saying. "Why I remember once in the West Indies we had less than an hour to leave our house. After a lifetime of following the drum, I've become quite adept at packing in haste."

Lady Kirkwood still looked doubtful at the entire proposition. "But where will you stay? Of course, we keep a house in town, but leases are quite hard to come by so late in the Season, especially in the *fashionable* neighborhoods."

"Actually we do have a house in town," Mrs. Harrington said. She made a ruffled little flip of her handkerchief. "In Mayfair."

"You don't say?" Lady Kirkwood said, as if she didn't believe a word of it. "How convenient."

"Yes. I inherited it from a distant cousin last year and as luck would have it, the tenants recently departed for Italy. The house is ours for the Season." She leaned forward and said softly, "We intend to give it to Charlotte when she weds."

Lady Kirkwood nodded approvingly.

"Season, you say? Time of year for that?" Colonel Posthill asked, wading into the female conversation with both feet. "Been thinking of sending Bex up to town to see how she'd fare. I know she's always wanted a Season."

Rafe shot a glance at Rebecca to find her flinching with embarrassment, her eyes shut and her hands balled at her sides. Unwittingly, her uncle had just shot her into enemy territory.

"A Season? For Miss Tate?" Charlotte declared, barely stifling a giggle. "Why she's too old!"

Lady Finch clamped her mouth shut, while Lady Kirkwood and Lady Victoria both colored. Obviously Charlotte had missed the point that Rebecca and Lady Victoria had come out together years earlier in Calcutta.

"Don't think of Bex as old," the colonel said. "A bit stodgy at times, but I don't know about being too old. Especially when all she's after is some nice, respectable vicar. They have those in town don't they?"

Charlotte dissolved into giggles, while Lady Victoria's nose poked in the air at such meager matrimonial expectations.

But the worst of all was Rebecca. She'd blushed a deep shade of red, her mortification and humiliation running to the bone. Rafe couldn't stand to see her standing there, enduring Charlotte Harrington and Lady Victoria's taunts.

Wasn't anyone going to save her?

And before he realized what he was doing, he stepped to her defense.

"How can someone as fair as Miss Tate be too old?" Rafe asked. "Nonsense! Why I think Miss Tate will be declared an Original before her first ball. She has those rare qualities that will always hold her in good stead, while lesser women, younger women," he made these statements in the general direction of Victoria and Charlotte, "could only hope to have such a luminary quality. They will fade, while Miss Tate will continue to rise each night with the radiance of a full moon." His praise was met with stunned silence. "At least that was what I told Cochrane here after I met her yesterday."

"Oh, that he did," Cochrane chimed in. "Said she was a rare one." The boy grinned, leaving off the rest of what Rafe had called the gamine spinster.

The colonel grinned. "Aye, that's my Bex. A rare one indeed."

Rebecca stared at Rafe openmouthed, as did the rest of the ladies.

"Mr. Danvers, you are a rakish devil," claimed Miss Honora. "Teasing us all. Not that our Rebecca doesn't deserve such high esteem, but you are a charmer, that is certainly evident." Shooing Sydney up from his spot, she patted the sofa beside her. "Do come over and tell us the latest news from town. For I would wager that you know some deliciously naughty *on dits* that they never put in the gossip columns and Lady Finch is too much of a lady to reveal."

He crossed the room, willing himself not to look at Rebecca as he passed her. But look he did and their gazes met for a furious second.

One question blazed in her eyes. *Why did you come to my defense?*

And if they were alone, he would have confessed the truth. Because he couldn't forget her kiss—her lips pressed to his. The way her body molded against him as if seeking shelter from a tempest. And what a wild tempest it was, blowing aside reason, pulling from the depths of his heart a stormy conflict to which he'd thought himself immune.

And as he'd continued to kiss her, even against his better judgment, he'd found himself running his fingers through the stray tendrils of her silken hair, tracing a line down her jaw, along the trembling pulse of her neck, down to the rounded curves of her . . .

"Mr. Danvers?" Miss Honora asked politely, again patting the sofa.

"Oh, I'm sorry Miss Honora," he said, bowing slightly in apology. "I fear you caught me woolgathering."

"Men are apt to do that in my company," the coquettish lady mused.

Her sister made an inelegant snort. "More likely a touch of sun, for we saw you ride by earlier and thought you most daring to venture out without an appropriate *chapeau*."

"I thought you looked devilishly handsome," Miss Honora added. "Now do tell us about yourself. We have few stories to offer but I suspect you are a man of great deeds. You have the stance and seat of a military man. I said it the moment I saw you ride by, didn't I, Alminta?"

"Yes, but then you do have a passion for a red coat and a jaunty tricorn."

"That I do." Honora was anything if not persistent, for she went right back to her inquiries. "Were you in the war?"

Rafe shifted. His military service wasn't something he liked to call attention to, especially amongst society. At best they viewed him as a deserter, at worst a rank coward to be shunned.

"Danvers? Danvers?" Mrs. Harrington piped up. "I thought that name was familiar. William, wasn't there a Major Danvers in Spain?"

"Yes. One of Wellington's information officers." Major Harrington replied, returning to his nervous pacing about the room.

Rafe wondered if the man was always so agitated.

"My brother, madame," he demurred. "He is now the Marquis of Bradstone."

"And married to my dear Mrs. Keates," Lady Finch. "Three secretaries before Mrs. Radleigh."

Mrs. Radleigh held up four fingers.

"But there was another one," Mrs. Harrington persisted, her finger tapping her ample chin. "Another Danvers in the Peninsula."

He should have known that while the major didn't remember him, Mrs. Harrington would. Army wives possessed memories as long and as deadly as the Corunna retreat.

"Don't you remember, William?" Mrs. Harrington persisted. "He struck his commanding officer and then ran off with a band of those Spanish devils." The woman gave her audience a moment's pause. "Not that it wasn't to be expected, he was half—" she glanced up at Rafe, her gaze taking in his dark features and pitch black eyes and her lofty words fell to a dead stop.

"Spanish?" Rafe finished for her.

"Yes, I daresay," she managed, her handkerchief pressed to her lips.

"Oh, you're Spanish?" Miss Honora asked, sounding only too disappointed. "I had thought, well really hoped, you were a gypsy."

Lady Finch groaned at this notion. The poor lady could see the tabbies in London having a field day with such a report.

I hear tell poor Emmaline is entertaining Gypsies and nabobs. I fear she's gone around the bend.

Rafe explained his circumstances. "My mother was Spanish, my father was Lord Danvers."

"I don't recall *Debrett's* listing a Spanish wife," Mrs. Harrington said, as if she was beginning to doubt his entire legitimacy.

Lady Finch stepped in to fill the scandal ridden silence. "Lord Danvers was a very distinguished diplomat," she explained. "So I am sure the omission of his second wife was purely a mistake due to his long years out of the country, serving our dear King with such fortitude and dedication," she said, promoting her guest's connections with her whole heart.

That was pushing the truth, Rafe thought, for no one had ever called his father's career distinguished. He'd been a rapscallion at best, and a thorn in the side of the Foreign Office with his peccadilloes and scandals. Including his elopement with Rafe's mother, the daughter of a Spanish grandee. He'd nearly been tossed out of the diplomatic corps for that disastrous faux pas.

"Is the current Lord Danvers a diplomat as well?" Lady Victoria asked.

Rafe laughed. "Colin? No. He was in the navy."

"Until he was court-martialed," Jemmy added happily.

His mother and Rafe glared at him.

"Turned pirate, didn't he?" Sydney asked. "I remember reading a list of goods he'd seized. A rare privateer your brother."

A pirate? Lady Kirkwood mouthed to her husband, as if the word was too shameful to be repeated.

"Demmed traitor, more like it," Lord Kirkwood muttered.

An awkward silence fell about the room.

The older ladies shot worried glances at the young ladies, while Kitling let out a short guffaw.

Rafe was used to his family being the target for speculation and outright defamation, since it had only been recently that his brothers had chosen to make public their clandestine service for the King and England during the long years of war with France.

No, most of the *ton* thought the Danvers and their relations were the worst sort of crackpots and ne'er-do-wells.

And Rafe was the worst of all. He'd barely escaped court-martial and a hanging for giving his superior officer the beating the man had deserved after ignoring orders and nearly getting their entire company slaughtered.

Lord Kirkwood shot him an angry glance and then turned his back, muttering to his wife, "Some party, this!"

Before Lady Finch could turn the conversation, Jemmy jumped in. "Being tossed out of his unit didn't stop Rafe here from making his mark in the war. He carried ammunitions to our troops trapped behind enemy lines. Raided French strongholds. He even helped find the King's Ransom."

"The King's Ransom?" Miss Honora asked. "Oh that sounds terribly interesting! What was it? How did you find it?"

"I didn't actually," Rafe countered. "By the time it was found, I was long gone."

"Oh, give some credit where it is due," Jemmy said. "You and your compatriots led Major Danvers across Portugal, to the very foot of Badajoz. Without your assistance, the major may never have found the treasure."

"Treasure?" Kitling perked up from his slouched stance near the fireplace. "Did you say a treasure?"

Jemmy nodded and then enthusiastically told the tale, finishing his exaggerated, albeit enthusiastic rendition with, "I thought Rafe here was a goner when we arrived to find those wretched Frogs had captured everyone. They had him in a bad way, beat him nearly senseless but he wasn't about to betray his mission."

There was a snort of disbelief from Lord Kirkwood. But this time everyone ignored him.

"How did you escape?" Lady Victoria asked Rafe in a breathless voice.

"Jemmy and my brother, Robert, created a diversion that sent the French scrambling. Then we were able to overcome them."

"But the more important thing to consider," Mr. Kitling said, "is did you get your share of the treasure?"

Lady Victoria's gaze flicked from Kitling to Rafe. "Oh, did you?"

"No," Rafe said. "And I wouldn't have taken it. It belonged to the Spanish people."

This was followed by another "harrumph" from Kirkwood. "Rabble don't deserve such riches."

"Not even a single gemstone?" Kitling asked, with an air of incredulity that echoed Kirkwood's skepticism.

"Oh, I would adore finding a treasure," Miss Honora said.

"Treasure, indeed!" Lady Kirkwood declared. "Foolery. Look what chasing after treasure did to Miss Tate's father. Left him neck deep in debt and dead of fever. Absolute foolery."

Jemmy spoke up. "The King's Ransom allowed Wellington to offer hope to the Spanish people, especially after the tragedy at Badajoz. They rallied to the English cause, organized themselves and were able to help us drive Boney out of the Iberian Peninsula." He held his ground and stared directly at a disbelieving earl. "My lord, nearly everyone in this room lost someone or something on those dusty plains. Rafe's contributions may not be well known, but without him and men like him, England would have lost countless more fine young men before finally defeating our enemies."

Lady Kirkwood looked up from her fingernails. "Let me get this straight, Mr. Danvers. Your eldest brother was convicted of treason, your other brother gave away a fortune, and your twin brother was murdered."

Rafe squared his shoulders and smiled at her. "That about sums it up."

She glared at Lady Finch for including her in this travesty of a social gathering.

Much to everyone's relief, there was a discreet cough at the doorway. The Finch butler, Addison intoned, "My lady, dinner is ready at your convenience."

Rafe could have sworn he heard Lady Finch say, "Good heavens, about time."

"Shall we?" Lady Finch announced, offering her arm to Lord Kirkwood. Lord Finch stepped forward, after being prodded by Jemmy to take Lady Kirkwood's arm.

Kitling offered one arm to Miss Honora and the other to Miss Alminta and the threesome followed their hosts through the adjoining door to the resplendent dining room beyond.

Jemmy sidestepped Lady Victoria, and offered his arm to Charlotte. The unrepentant son of his hosts had the audacity to wink at Rafe over Lady Victoria's shoulder.

Satisfied their daughter was suitably matched, the Harringtons marched into the dining room with military precision.

That left Lady Victoria waiting, none-too-expectantly. The young woman smiled, an artful and calculated tip to her lips, as she sauntered in Rafe's direction. "Ah, Mr. Danvers, would you do me—"

"*Victoria*," her mother called out. "Do come immediately." Lord Kirkwood returned and took his daughter by the arm making sure there was no question who escorted her into dinner.

That didn't stop the unrepentant girl from tossing him a come-hither smile over her father's shoulder.

My parents may not approve, her gaze decried, *but I do.*

"Followed your conscience, I daresay," Colonel Posthill said, as he came up to Rafe's side.

"Pardon, sir?"

"Your conscience. You followed your gut and did what your honor told you needed to be done." The old man nodded. "Ignore Kirkwood. He's a fool, always has been." Then he patted Rafe on the back, and said, "I for one commend you. Took more courage, I'd guess, than your entire regiment possessed. Never let anyone tell you differently." The man straightened his coat, his posture military erect and his head held high, as if he were about to dine with Wellington himself.

Rebecca stepped past Rafe and took her uncle's arm. When she got to the door, she glanced over her shoulder, her eyes alight with the same pride that had filled the colonel's words.

For whatever reason, one Rafe didn't want to explore too deeply, he was glad that of all the people in the room, his disreputable past had gained her approval and understanding.

For the evidence was there for all to see in a single tear falling upon her cheek.

Chapter 8

The brave of heart always looks his enemy directly in the eye so the devil will see only a resolute desire to prevail.

Colonel Darby to his troops
in *Miss Darby's Darkest Hour*

O*h, drat the man*, Rebecca thought as she took her seat in the dining room. How dare he turn up honorable!

She had resolved herself that he was a despicable cad, only to discover that he'd fought for Spanish freedom at the risk of his own reputation, his very honor.

Why in that light, he was downright noble.

And why hadn't he said anything about his twin this afternoon when he'd been telling her about his family? Though the lack of disclosure explained much about this mysterious man—the loss obviously pained him still.

She knew how that felt, only too well.

Then if the evening wasn't full of enough surprises, he'd risen to her defense with all that nonsense about her being like the moon. Like the moon, indeed! More of his Spanish enchantment, she supposed. Yet when he had glanced over at her, he made her feel all those things, like she was some rare beautiful woman. Maybe it was just his usual charm, maybe he made every woman feel like that, but that didn't stop her heart from fluttering, from believing that such magic could be possible after such a short acquaintance.

Blast and curse the man, Rebecca thought as she stared down at her plate. She might have even admired him, if it weren't for the fact that he kissed like the very devil, left her all tangled up and believing in the most impractical notions.

Her future vicar would never leave her feeling so . . . so . . . delirious.

She stole a glance across the table at him. Though he'd dressed for the occasion, Mr. Danvers still had a disreputable air about him, which pleased her for reasons she couldn't fathom.

What was it Jemmy had called him? *Rafe.*

'Twas a name that fit him, she decided. The kind of name a woman whispered in the night.

Rafe, come to me. Love me, Rafe.

A plea she had no doubt he would answer most expertly.

The object of her momentary fantasy looked up and in her direction, as if he heard her silent plea, knew her scandalous thoughts—including the way his kiss had left her unsettled and longing for more.

Rebecca quickly fixed her gaze back on her plate and took a deep breath. Oh, she was loathe to admit it, but she was inclined to agree with Lady Kirkwood—Rafe Danvers was completely unacceptable.

The company at the table appeared strained, but Sydney Kitling, seated to her right, came to the rescue. "Mr. Danvers," he said, "it seems you and I are of the same ilk."

Rebecca nearly laughed aloud at the look of skepticism that clouded Rafe's eyes.

Sydney and Rafe similar? If day and night collided perhaps.

"How is that, sir?" Rafe managed to ask.

"Oh, yes, do tell," Lady Victoria said, clearly be-mused by the ridiculous notion.

Sydney sat back in his chair, only too happy to be the center of attention. "Because neither of us stands a chance in hell of inheriting. Born to a noble world, tossed out into the cold arms of another, wouldn't you say?"

"Hardly that dire," Rafe replied.

Sydney leaned forward. "I'm always interested in how a gentleman goes about making his way. You know, how one gets on without the comfort of knowing you'll stand to come into some pile of rocks and a regular income for French brandy and other necessities."

"Luckily for me, I've never developed a taste for such necessities, so those worries don't keep me awake at night," Rafe told him.

Rebecca had no doubts it wasn't a *what* that kept Rafe Danvers awake at night, rather a *whom*.

But Sydney wasn't satisfied with Rafe's dry response. Obviously he smelled the mystery surrounding Rafe like everyone else and was going to persist until he solved it. "So how is it that you manage to pay your rent?"

Rebecca gaped at the rude inquiry, but her shock was soon replaced by the revelation provided by Rafe's young assistant, Cochrane.

Seated at the far end of the table, the lad piped in, "Oh, he don't. Most months we have to use the back stairs to avoid the landlady. That is until we get paid."

Lady Finch groaned, while Mrs. Harrington imme-diately edged her chair away from Rafe as far as she could without landing in Colonel Posthill's lap.

Sydney laughed. "Been there myself a time or two, lad."

"Do you mean to say that you work, Mr. Danvers?"

Lady Victoria asked. "How interesting! What is it that you do?"

With every gaze fixed on him, Rebecca wondered how the rapscallion was going to escape now.

"He assists people," Lady Finch said hastily. "With their problems."

"What sort of problems?" Miss Honora asked.

"I think Mr. Danvers likes a level of discretion for his clients," Lady Finch replied, obviously trying to hide the fact that she'd invited a runner to dinner and that her guests had been set up to help him. She signaled for the next course.

Not even the soup could save Lady Finch.

"Oh, no," Miss Honora protested. "We haven't heard from Mr. Danvers."

"Perhaps it isn't any of our business," Miss Alminta pointed out. "It is impolite to pry, sister."

Unfortunately for Rafe, Honora was not plagued by the restraints of good manners. "Sister," she said, "what if we discover ourselves with a problem that cannot be solved? Wouldn't it be nice to know someone who takes care of such things?"

"Miss Honora," Kitling said, "you know I will always be there to aid you and Miss Alminta in any way possible."

"Yes, of course, Sydney," she said, dismissing his gallantry with a wave of her hand, her gaze fixed adoringly on Rafe. "But I suspect Mr. Danvers would be far more capable in such matters."

Rebecca bit her lips, while Kitling turned a mottled shade of red, and for once, said nothing.

"I hardly think you will come across the kind of problems I solve," Rafe assured the lady.

Miss Honora appeared unconvinced, and Rebecca

wouldn't put it past her romantically inclined neighbor to invent some dire dilemma just to see Mr. Danvers stay in Bramley Hollow.

Sydney, having recovered his composure, wasn't about to be left out of the conversation. "Any money in solving problems?"

"There can be," Rafe said. "As long as you collect the payment."

Cochrane coughed and sputtered.

Rebecca imagined there was a story behind the boy's discomfiture that Lady Finch certainly wouldn't want repeated at her dinner party.

"I hear tell there's a fortune being offered to find that Codlin fellow's killer," Kitling said as he held out his glass for a footman to refill. "Looking into that, are you?"

Rebecca didn't glance at Rafe, but at his assistant. The lad's nose dipped even lower toward his plate.

Well, that confirmed Kitling's question. They were investigating the murder. She didn't know whether that frightened her or brought her a measure of comfort.

"Are you truly investigating Sir Rodney's murder?" Miss Honora asked, the admiration in her voice notching up another level. "Sydney has been reading the accounts to us from the newspapers and I find it all terribly fascinating." She shivered. "Murdered in his own home."

"I daresay, some nights I can't sleep thinking about it," Alminta declared. "Terrible tragedy."

"Codlin?" Mrs. Harrington asked, glancing at her daughter then her husband. "I don't see that is a fit subject."

"No, no indeed," Lady Kirkwood declared.

Again, Miss Honora continued blithely on, unwilling to let go of her curiosity for the sake of pleasant conversation. "But are you?" she asked Rafe. "Looking into the Codlin murder?"

He wiped his lips with his napkin and settled it back on his plate. "Yes. I've been studying the matter."

"Oooh," Miss Honora said, her eyes alight. "Did you come here to find his killer? Among us?" She looked around the table, apparently ready to stand as Rafe's second if need be.

"Miss Honora!" Lady Kirkwood intoned, as if she had never been so insulted in her life.

"No," Rafe told the lady. "That isn't what brings me to Bramley Hollow."

"Still," Miss Honora said, "it would be quite a lark to discover who killed poor Sir Rodney."

"Poor Sir Rodney?" Mrs. Harrington huffed. "Odious man. I don't see what all the fuss is about. The world is better off without the likes of him."

"Muriel!" Major Harrington said. "That is enough." His words rang through the room like the retort of the colonel's cannon, startling nearly everyone.

Everyone but Rafe, Rebecca noticed. His gaze narrowed and fixed on the major.

"You knew Codlin?" he asked the man.

"Yes." Major Harrington drove his knife into the cut of beef before him, making it obvious that any further explanation was not forthcoming.

"Have any theories on why he was murdered?" Rafe asked, leaning back in his chair.

The major shifted in his seat for a moment, then regained his composure, taking the stance of a military man trapped on all sides. "Like my wife said, he was an odious human being. Not one to make friends readily, nor did he keep them. Just ask Posthill over there." He pointed at the colonel. "Posthill knew him, as did Miss Tate, when we were all in Calcutta."

The colonel looked up from his meal. "What's this? Who do I know?"

Rebecca took a deep breath. *Please, uncle, tread very carefully.*

"Codlin. You remember him, don't you?" Major Harrington said in a loud voice.

"My uncle is confused, not deaf," Rebecca said.

"Codlin, you say?" Colonel Posthill asked. He scratched his chin. "Hmm, I don't recall a Codlin about. You'll have to ask Ensign Trotter if he is on the company roster. Sorry I can't be of more help, but I can't keep track of every man, now can I?" Her uncle glanced at her. "Bex, where is Trotter? The lad isn't out drinking again, is he?"

"No, sir," she told him. "I believe Ensign Trotter is standing watch this evening."

He nodded. "Good man, Trotter. Always ready to keep a sharp eye on our perimeter lines. Feel better already. When he gets off duty send him over to Major Harrington to help find this Codlin fellow." He returned to his meal with gusto.

Rebecca smiled and shrugged at the rest of the table. "I fear that is the best he can offer. His memory is so unreliable."

"And you, Miss Tate?" Rafe asked. "Did you know Sir Rodney?"

She shook her head. "I know he visited my uncle once on Company business, but I was never introduced to the man."

Rafe looked from her to Colonel Posthill to Major Harrington. "And were you friends with him?" he asked the major.

"Certainly not!" Major Harrington declared. "And I will not be badgered so, not by the likes of you!"

His words were spat out with such vehemence, they made even Rebecca flinch. But Rafe appeared unscathed in the face of the major's ill-temper. There was something to admire about Mr. Danvers' fortitude and cool demeanor.

"My apologies, sir. I meant no offense." Rafe leaned forward and looked the major in the eye. "But I intend to see justice done. For when a man is murdered, no matter his character, it is still a crime."

"Harrumph!" muttered Mrs. Harrington as if she found such noble intentions ridiculous.

The table fell silent, and Lady Finch signaled for another course to be served. Any distraction to help save her sinking party.

"Will your business, whatever it may be, keep you here in Bramley Hollow long, Mr. Danvers?" Lady Victoria asked.

"No, I doubt it," he said. "I plan on returning to London very soon."

Not soon enough, Rebecca wanted to add.

"How delightful," the young lady said. "Then I can expect to see you again, sir, in London." Her mother shot her a scandalized glance. Lady Victoria ignored her.

"I don't mix often in society," Rafe told her.

"Good reason for that," Mrs. Harrington muttered under her breath.

"Then I must cling to the hope that I have the chance pleasure of your company yet again," Lady Victoria said, nearly purring.

"What do you hear from town? How is the Season progressing?" Lady Kirkwood asked her hostess, trying to direct her daughter's attention away from Lady Finch's questionable guest.

"Oh, yes," Charlotte Harrington enthused. "What is happening in town? I cannot believe I am truly going this year."

Lady Finch happily launched into a discussion

about the fashion mistakes of several well-known ladies and a few well placed bits of advice on which mantua makers to avoid.

Charlotte and Lady Victoria chattered on about their plans, ignoring Rebecca as they did on most occasions.

Rebecca smiled as best she could, nodding when appropriate, but she found the talk disenchanting. What did she care for prattle of new gowns, balls and musicales when her life was set in a path as insurmountable as the high mountains of Tibet?

"It seems an advantageous time to go to town in search of a husband," Kitling drawled, leaning back in his chair, with his arms folded over his chest. "You ladies will have the men all to yourselves. From what I hear, with all this *Darby* nonsense there is talk of turning Almack's into a poorhouse." He chuckled, but it was obvious Lady Kirkwood and Mrs. Harrington saw nothing funny in such a notion.

"Heresy," the countess sputtered. "Why the very notion of perfectly good vouchers going to waste while these foolish girls squander everything their mothers have worked so hard to see to fruition is an abomination."

Mrs. Harrington nodded. "Exactly my thoughts." She shot a slanted glance at her daughter.

It was as if she had literally prodded Charlotte with a hot poker. The girl forced a grim line to her mouth and said, "I've never read the *Miss Darby* novels. I find such fiction tedious and by no means improving."

Rebecca thought Charlotte was going to have to practice her lines a little better if she were going to use them on the patronesses of Almack's.

"The author should be tried for treason and given an appropriate punishment," Mrs. Harrington said.

"I would think a medal is in order," Jemmy remarked. "Sounds like town has finally become a safe haven for a gentleman."

Lady Kirkwood ignored him. "Why someone hasn't discovered that miscreant's identity and sent them packing, I don't know."

Rebecca took a hasty sip of her wine and did her pointed best not to look at Rafe. Better to remain a coward than confront the enemy, she decided, no matter what the intrepid Miss Darby might do in the same situation.

"Perhaps the beleaguered patronesses should hire you, Mr. Danvers, to find this purveyor of corruption," Kitling joked. "Break their arm, or some such rot, eh?"

"I don't break arms," Rafe said, despite the coughing from Cochrane's end of the table. The boy looked ready to interject another comment, but the dark glance from his employer silenced him immediately. "Though I hardly think writing novels warrants such drastic punishment."

Lady Kirkwood was not done with her diatribe. "But you do agree, sir, that this author is a criminal? A despicable creature?"

He took a deep breath and sat back in his chair. "I would venture that while current opinion tends toward that description of the person, the author could just as easily be someone at this table."

"Sir!" came the affronted gasp of Lady Kirkwood, while the rest of the table set to speculating who was the most likely suspect amongst them.

Rebecca raised her resolute gaze to meet Rafe's. What she saw there terrified her—his unyielding desire to unmask his prey.

You will not undo me, sir, she silently challenged.

His gaze mocked hers. *Perhaps I already have.*

"Mr. Danvers, you do tease," Lady Victoria said.

"And what is your opinion of the *Darby* books, Lady Victoria?" Rafe asked.

"You don't mean to imply my daughter is capable of—" Lady Kirkwood looked ready to have a fit of apoplexy.

"Oh, mother, Mr. Danvers is only doing his job," Lady Victoria said, smiling at the man as if she'd be willing to submit to a full interrogation. A very private one. "You really want to hear my opinions?"

Rebecca carved at the piece of meat in front of her, stabbing it with a little more vehemence than necessary. So now that he had finished "questioning" her at Bettlesfield Park, he thought Lady Victoria was the author of *Miss Darby*? That vapid, ridiculous, spoiled . . .

"I'd love to hear what you have to say," Rafe was saying.

I just bet you would, Rebecca thought.

"I simply adore the *Miss Darby* novels," Lady Victoria exclaimed. "I was a watering pot for a month after I read the last one. Poor, dear Lieutenant Throckmorten, how I grieved for his loss."

"Victoria," Lady Kirkwood said. "That is enough."

"Mother, you know as well as I that I am not the author of these books. And it isn't like you haven't read every single one of them. Twice."

Lady Kirkwood turned a bright shade of red at this disclosure.

"Well, I think Miss Darby is a splendid chit!" Jemmy said. "You could have used her a time or two in Spain, eh, Rafe? Like when you were tracking that French messenger along the Guadiana and he was so determined to foil you, he tossed his dispatch box in the river!" Jemmy started to laugh.

"Oh, my," Miss Honora said. "How ever did you get it back?"

Rafe grinned at her. "I tossed the Frog in after it."

There was a moment of silence, and then everyone at the table laughed as if they had never heard such a jest.

"But truthfully," Kitling said, "why go to the bother of dunking the poor fellow, when the contents inside were most likely ruined."

"Not like you would think," Jemmy said. "Most French dispatch boxes have a secret compartment in them. Sealed in tight to keep their missives safe from harm and prying eyes."

Rebecca's chest constricted and her gaze wrenched upward to meet Rafe's to see if Jemmy's fateful words had registered with him.

And to her horror she saw the light of discovery blaze to life in his dark, fathomless gaze.

Most French dispatch boxes have a secret compartment . . .

"Oh, dear," Rebecca cried out as she sent her wine-glass tumbling over, claret spilling over the table.

She rose from her seat, blotting at the stain with her napkin, apologizing profusely to Lady Finch. "I fear I've ruined your cloth, my lady. Please forgive me."

"Accidents do happen," Lady Finch said, waving for one of the footmen to clean up the rest of the mess.

Accidents, indeed, Rebecca thought. How ironic! It was as if the Fates were bound and determined to aid Rafe Danvers in his mission to uncover her.

And the light in his eyes, when she dared once again to look at him, revealed the truth—like her, he didn't believe in accidents or fate. But unfortunately, he was only too happy to pounce on those fortuitous gifts from above, especially when they showered down upon him with the naked truth as clear and evident as drops of claret on a white tablecloth.

*   *   *

Rebecca wandered through the neatly kept aisles of the enormous Finch orangery. While there were the requisite large pots of citrus trees, the baron's beloved orchids took up much of the space, tended like they were his children. And they showed it in their rare displays of delicate blossoms.

Around her the conversations rose and fell, like the varied winds of the seasons. Colonel Harrington's wintery bluster, Mr. Kitling's flowery discourse like the rich, warmly scented breezes of summer. And blithely moving about the room fell Lady Victoria's billowy, tinkling voice, like the music of spring, light and airy and welcomed by all.

And by the lady's side walked an attentive Rafe Danvers. He appeared to hold each of Lady Victoria's words with untold interest.

But the fragrant air and the calm beauty of the long gallery offered no solace to Rebecca's panic.

Rafe knew. Knew her innocent travel desk was a French dispatch box. Knew that inside it lay the keys to proving his case against her.

So what was he doing strolling along the aisles with Victoria Manvell? Some runner! Why, he was within a hairsbreadth of discovering the truth and what did he do? Invite Victoria to take a turn about the gallery with him. Of all the insulting . . .

Rebecca didn't particularly believe that the winsome blonde held his attention, not for a moment. It was part of his carefully wrought plan to uncover her identity, for what else could it be? As much as she didn't want Rafe Danvers paying *her* the least bit of heed, when the rakish devil and Lady Victoria paused in their stroll and the earl's daughter looked up at him with a flirtatious smile, her head tipped just so and her lips parting expectantly, Rebecca found herself ducking behind a particularly full orange tree, one that afforded her an excellent vantage point for . . .

Oh, dash it all, spying. She was spying like the worst sort of schoolgirl, but she didn't care. If anything, life with Mrs. Wortling had taught her there were worse transgressions than eavesdropping.

Besides, if Rafe Danvers was going to run around Bramley Hollow kissing every woman in sight, Rebecca knew it was her moral duty to make sure every likely suspect was warned that their heart was about to be used and toyed with most scandalously.

Not that she thought Lady Victoria cared a whit about those things, the deplorable flirt. She was probably only clinging to Rafe because he'd praised Rebecca earlier.

But whatever was Rafe doing with her? Could he really believe that Lady Victoria was capable of penning the *Miss Darby* novels?

Rebecca sniffed. She could hardly see what the earl's daughter had done during the evening that would lead him to such a conclusion.

Then another thought occurred to her. Perhaps he wasn't looking at Lady Victoria as his potential windfall, but as a financial savior in another realm.

As an heiress and bride.

What if she'd done too good of job showing him the house, and now he wanted to keep it? If Rafe decided not to sell Bettlesfield Park, he'd need a dowry the size of Lady Victoria's just to make it habitable.

Rebecca chewed her lip. Lady Victoria the mistress of Bettlesfield Park? She'd level it down to the last stone with the colonel's cannon before she'd let that happen.

She glanced out the tall arched window and past the far meadow, where she could spy the distant roof of Bettlesfield Park.

She always forgot how close Finch Manor was to her former home. Why she could skirt across the meadow and have her writing desk this very night, and Rafe would never have a chance to lay his hands on it.

When she glanced back over toward the palm, she couldn't see him or Victoria. *Good riddance*, she thought. Knowing Victoria and her lack of good judgment, she'd probably lured the man into a secluded corner. Like she'd done with Lieutenant Habersham all those years ago.

Rebecca glanced once more around the room to make sure no one was watching and then eased the garden door open, making her way into the garden. If she was quick, she would be back to Finch Manor before the tea cart arrived and anyone missed her.

In the meantime, Victoria could have Rafe Danvers and all his wiles to herself. Not that Rebecca cared.

Most decidedly not.

Not even if he . . .

Swept her into his arms and devoured her mouth with his sweeping kisses . . . Caressed her shamelessly with his skilled touch, made her . . .

"Woooof." She slammed into the solid wall of a man's chest, the air in her lungs swooshing out.

"Oh, I'm so sorry," she began, "I was in a hurry and thinking of . . . of—" she stammered until she glanced up and realized just who was blocking her way.

Rafe.

"Lost in thought or composing another one of your letters?"

"I hardly see that it concerns you," she replied, trying to dodge past him, but he moved effortlessly into her path again. "Besides, what are you doing out here? I thought you were occupied elsewhere."

"With Lady Victoria?" he asked. "Nice of you to send that pampered little chit into my arms just to distract me."

Victoria had been in his arms? Why that . . .

"I never—"

Rafe stopped her with a hearty laugh. "Unfortunately, I'm not all that fond of flirts." Leaning closer to her ear, he whispered, "I like a little bit of chase to my pursuits."

Rebecca couldn't help but wonder where that put her in his realm of preferences. Right now she'd be willing to risk a mad dash and a chance to prove him wrong.

"What has you in such a hurry, Miss Tate?" he asked, slanting a glance over his shoulder at the distant roof of Bettlesfield Park. "Did you lose something?"

Her gaze shot to his. She saw the truth there as if it were spelled out on parchment. Dear lord, he'd found her desk. He already had it. Now all he had to do was open it and he'd . . .

She spun around, heading back to the house.

Rafe caught her in two strides, and held her fast. "Like I said, I like a bit of a chase."

She shook at his unwanted grasp, but he had no intention of letting her go.

Not until he had some answers.

"Unhand me," she whispered. "Or I'll . . . I'll . . ."

He smiled, wolfish arrogance challenging her to do her worst. "Why don't you tell me what's inside your desk?"

She clamped her mouth shut.

He could hold her until the sun rose because she

wasn't going to tell him anything. He could berate her, he could threaten her, and she wouldn't tell him a thing.

But Rafe Danvers had more dangerous means of persuasion in his arsenal. His thumb stroked the inside of her wrist, sending traitorous, tempting tendrils of desire through her limbs.

She tugged her arm again, but he still held her, still teased her with his touch. She sent him a scathing glare, hoping he had no idea of the turmoil he was causing.

"A ha' penny for your thoughts," he whispered.

"They involve the investigation of your untimely demise."

"My demise?" he asked, faintly amused. "That doesn't sound very practical of you, Miss Tate."

"I think it would be very practical."

"Ah, but there would be consequences, repercussions when you were caught," he advised.

She already was. More than she cared to admit. "How about if we settle for your hasty return to London?"

"I could be gone tomorrow if you'd like—"

"Delighted in fact." She tugged again at his grasp, with no success. She couldn't struggle or call for help, for she'd cause a scene. And a scene right now was not what she needed. "So does that mean you're giving up?"

"I never give up."

He wouldn't, she thought grimly. Why couldn't he be like the rest of the inconstant, faithless men in the world?

"And right now I see no reason to," he was saying. "Especially when something seems to be keeping me here." His lips curled into a dangerous smile. "I imagine you could answer all my questions. Solve all my problems."

"No, I doubt it."

"I could be persuasive, *mi amor*," he said in that sultry, Spanish tinged lilt of his.

"Don't flatter yourself," she told him, lying through her teeth and hoping he couldn't tell. "Your charms are rather like your manners, lacking on all counts and easily forgotten."

"You seemed quite engaged this afternoon." He pulled her closer.

Rebecca's heart began to pound anew, her senses reminding her just how engaged she had been. How close she'd come to . . .

"There should be no secrets between us." His breath teased her ear, his arms winding around her waist, pulling her to him.

No secrets? Her entire life was an enormous tangle of them. And this was just the man to unwind them. Strip her bare. Literally if she let him pull her any nearer to him.

Out of the corner of her eye, she spied the handle of a small trowel left by a gardener on the fence post. She reached for it with her free hand and caught it up.

"Unhand me, sir, or I will be compelled to use this," she said, bringing around her newfound weapon.

He looked at it, one brow quirking upward. "What do you intend to do with that, Miss Tate? Dig me an early grave?"

She frowned down at the dull edge and realized it presented about as much danger to a man like Rafe Danvers as a newborn kitten.

Heavens, it wouldn't even frighten Miss Alminta.

"Please, let me go," she pleaded. "I can not help you. I will not help you. I—" Her words stopped short when inside the orangery there came a strident cry of outrage.

"Tell me where it is, Posthill, you doddering idiot," Major Harrington railed, "or you'll see us both consigned to hell!"

Rafe let her go as she straightened up, his body instantly tensed and poised, a warrior at the ready. He pulled her behind him and started down the path at a fast clip.

As he thundered toward the house, Rebecca wondered at him. Who was this man who'd invaded her life, her heart in such short order?

Friend or foe, right now she needed a hero. And it seemed he was the only one willing to help her save her uncle.

And perhaps, if she could find a way to trust him, to trust her heart, he might even save them all from the danger and folly that had followed her and her uncle for far too long.

Chapter 9

What else is there in life worth living for but secrets and those willing to reveal them to us?

Lady Lowthorpe to Miss Cecilia Overton
in *Miss Darby's Daring Dilemma*

"Tell me where it is," thundered Major Harrington. "Can you not see that our very lives are at stake?"

Rafe had gained the doorway to the orangery just ahead of Rebecca.

"Oh, dear," she gasped. "Oh, no, this cannot be."

What it was about, Rafe didn't know, but he'd seen enough desperate men in his life to know that Harrington was beyond angry, beyond agitated. It hadn't escaped his notice that the man had been nervous and cagey all night, and while he had at first thought it was just part of the major's character, now he could see that something was erupting inside the man, spilling forth at the poor witless colonel.

Rafe's simple trip to the seemingly innocent village of Bramley Hollow had cast him neck deep in trouble. Seven Dials was starting to look positively bucolic.

"Listen to me, Posthill, you've got to pull yourself together," Harrington was saying. He had the colonel by both shoulders and was shaking the older man like a terrier with a rat. "Tell me where it is. Think man, use your wits, whatever you have left, for our very lives depend upon it."

"Unhand me, you knave," Colonel Posthill said, jerking away from Harrington. For a man who was supposed to be fragile of mind, Posthill looked very capable—dangerously so. "This is all your fault," he shouted at the major, prodding him in the chest with a stubby finger. "None of us would be in this predicament if you and the others hadn't cheated Richard like a pack of thieves. You brought this on yourself, you arrogant, greedy—"

"Why you—" Harrington shot back, his temper rising to the forefront. "I'll not stand for being called such names, not from any man, and certainly not from some disgraced half-wit."

"Half-wit! How dare you!" The colonel caught up a rake and broke it over his knee. Tossing aside the tongs, he held the ragged handle like a sword, driving the edge up and under Harrington's wagging chin so he had the man propped up like a puppet. "You pompous windbag!" he seethed. "I should have seen you court-martialed when I had the chance. I should have told them the truth, told them that you and Codlin—"

But the colonel didn't have time to finish his damning statement. Harrington moved quickly and decisively, dodging the impromptu weapon, and throwing a facer that sent Posthill sprawling backward onto the paving stones.

"Uncle!" Rebecca cried out as she rushed to her guardian's side. "How dare you!" she raged at Major Harrington. "You know he isn't well, you know he wouldn't, couldn't have harmed you."

"He was about to kill me," Harrington said, wiping

the back of his hand across his mouth. "You all saw it—
he was trying to murder me."

"Bah!" Rebecca spat at him. "My uncle isn't capable
of such a thing. Murder, indeed!"

Rafe didn't think that was entirely the truth. The colonel had looked quite capable.

And what had Posthill said just before Harrington
stopped him? *I should have told them the truth, told them
that you and Codlin—*

The hairs on the back of Rafe's neck rose, while his
gaze pinned on Harrington. He hadn't believed the
man's denials before but now it would be impossible
for the major to dodge the connection.

And from all the signs of it, a most dangerous one.

He glanced down at Rebecca, crouched beside her
uncle's still form. A cold dread filled his gut as he realized the threat encompassed her as well.

Rafe had braved all sorts of peril that should have
left him dead and he'd never really been afraid. But
now as he gazed at Rebecca, he knew only too well the
icy stranglehold of fear. A cavalier attitude about one's
own life was one thing, but now his life included her.

He could try and deny it all he wanted, yet suddenly
Rebecca Tate's welfare rose above all his concerns.

Not now, he told himself. *Not her.* But like the tide of
trouble rushing through Bramley Hollow, Rafe suspected he could no more outrun the danger swirling
around her as he could ignore the way her kisses ig-
nited his untried heart.

Rebecca smoothed her uncle's wrinkled brow. Beneath her gentle ministrations, the colonel stirred and
moaned.

"He's cracked," Harrington said, pointing a finger at
his adversary.

Mrs. Harrington rushed to his side, to be joined seconds later by Charlotte. "Basil, you're injured," his wife said, plucking a handkerchief from her sleeve, dabbing it against his bloody knuckles.

He pushed aside her fussing, winding the cloth around his hand with military efficiency. "You saw what he did," he was saying. "The colonel went unhinged for no reason. He's a danger to the public and should be locked away. And if you don't see to it, Miss Tate, I will. Your uncle is a dangerous man."

"To whom, Major Harrington?" Rebecca asked, struggling to her feet. She faced the tall man, a David in muslin against a colossus in a scarlet coat. "He only fears his enemies. And those of England. Which are you?"

Rafe had to admire her mettle and nerve, but knew that while she might have the spirit to fight Harrington, she was in over her head.

"How dare you," the major sputtered. "Why you impertinent little bitch. And here I was risking my own neck and trying to warn your uncle and this is how the lot of you repay me? He tries to kill me and you dare insult me. Why I ought to—"

Rafe tugged her out of harm's way even as the major drew his arm back, then he stopped the man's hand in mid-swing.

A quick glance assured him that Rebecca, teetering on her heels, was in good hands. She'd been caught by a grinning Cochrane.

The lad had leapt into the clash with the reflexes of a pickpocket and was even now swiftly retrieving a narrow, wicked looking knife from his boot. The lad hadn't grown up in London's roughest neighborhood without his fair share of scrapes and fights, able to respond with the deadly assurance of a battle hardened veteran.

Perhaps Pymm had sent the boy to Rafe for reasons other than the cost of his upkeep. To see that there was always someone to watch his back. To keep this Danvers brother safe, as he had failed Orlando so many years ago.

"How dare you!" the major blustered. He twisted at Rafe's grasp, but was unable to break free. "This is none of your concern."

"When it comes to striking a lady, it becomes my concern," Rafe said, in a voice that brooked no resistance. "For like Colonel Posthill, I too have no use for cowards."

Harrington's eyes blazed wide, his brow a furrowed line across his forehead. But like most recreants, he knew when to cut his losses. So instead, he sent Rebecca a scathing glance and snorted. "Found another champion, have you? Wonder if he'll be as constant as the last one—your faithless Lieutenant Habersham."

The man's words caught Rafe unaware. *Another champion?*

Harrington used the moment to his advantage. His free hand dove into his jacket and produced a pistol. "Now I'll say it again, Mr. Danvers. Unhand me."

Like hell, Rafe wanted to tell him. For while he had a healthy respect for a loaded pistol, when Harrington had dared to raise his hand to Rebecca, something inside of Rafe had snapped.

Like a bolt of lightning, his anger had ripped from his heart and torn asunder his equilibrium. And now it had him willing to face fire to right her world. To protect her.

"Major Harrington!" Lady Finch cried out from the doorway where she stood with Lady Kirkwood.

The countess took one wide-eyed glance at the entire proceedings and started to waver in faint.

Made of sterner stuff, Lady Finch waded into the

fray looking quite capable of murder herself. "What is the meaning of this?"

"Oh, Basil!" Mrs. Harrington pleaded. "Please, what are you doing with a pistol? At a dinner party, of all places? Think of the scandal. Think of Charlotte's future, her reputation."

The man hazarded a glance at his daughter's shocked and tearstained face and growled. "Bah," he spat, yanking his hand free of Rafe. He glowered for a moment longer, then shoved the pistol back into his jacket much to the relief of everyone in the room.

After straightening his coat, he ran a hand over his brow, smoothing out his features before he faced their irate hostess. "My apologies, Lady Finch, for this unseemly display. But I find your choice of guests," he said, shooting another glance of loathing at the prone form of Colonel Posthill, as well as one last dismissive glance at Rafe, "to be lacking in manners." He spun on one heel and called to his wife, "Muriel, Charlotte, gather your things, we are leaving."

But Rafe wasn't done with him yet. He caught the major by the shoulder and stopped him. "Sir, what did the colonel mean about you and Codlin?"

Harrington shook himself free. "None of your business."

Mrs. Harrington was already in tears.

"Your temper has ruined us," she railed as the major stalked from the room, leaving Charlotte and her no choice but to follow along in his angry wake.

Lady Finch glanced over at the fallen form of Colonel Posthill. "Dear lord! Is he hurt?"

"I don't think so," Rebecca told her, her hand patting his.

Rafe dropped to his knees and examined the injured

man. The tiles on the floor were cold and not the best place for a man of his age to lay. "He should be taken upstairs where he can be tended to," he said. "Can you arrange that, Lady Finch?"

"Yes, of course. Immediately!"

"No!" Rebecca said so adamantly that he and Lady Finch turned and stared at her.

"I only mean that—" she began, biting her lip for a second. "I meant to say . . . I just think, well, that it would be better if he were taken home."

"Nonsense!" Lady Finch told her. "He can have the second best guest room upstairs." She waved at Addison to start making the arrangements.

Rebecca rose abruptly. "My lady, your offer is very generous, but I think in his state that if he awoke in unfamiliar surroundings it may agitate him further."

Lady Finch appeared about to argue when Colonel Posthill struggled up, catching hold of Rebecca's arm. "Trotter! Trotter, where are you? The devils have breached the walls and I've been hit, good lad!"

Rebecca winced and then knelt beside him again. "We are well and safe, uncle. You merely stumbled." Her glance to everyone else told them quite clearly not to contradict her. "Just try to relax."

"Must stop them before they reach the armory," he clamored as he struggled to gain his feet, only to waver and fall back. "I appear to have been more gravely wounded than I first suspected." He glanced over at Lady Kirkwood. "Brandy, Ensign Trotter. Fetch the bottle from my tent and be quick about it."

Lady Kirkwood's eyes grew round.

"Uncle," she whispered, "that is our good neighbor, Lady Kirkwood, not Ensign Trotter."

His eyes narrowed. "I say, what is she doing here? A

spy for the French?" This time Posthill managed to stagger to his feet and teeter over to the countess. "*Parlez-vous français?*"

"*Oui, monsieur*," Lady Kirkwood replied.

The colonel's gaze swung back to Rebecca. "Aha! French, just as I thought!" he declared. "Seize this fellow! We've been infiltrated!"

Lady Kirkwood's hand went to her throat as she gasped. Lord Kirkwood stepped in front of his wife glowering not just at the colonel, but also at Rebecca.

"Miss Tate," he said, "your uncle is in need of more than just a spare bedroom to see to his ills. The man is unsound."

Rebecca looked about to offer another set down and Rafe didn't think a second confrontation was necessary so he stepped forward. Again.

This was becoming a bad habit, he decided.

"Colonel Posthill," he said. "I think it is time we all retired for the night. May I escort you back to your tent? That is for your safety, sir."

"Harrumph," the colonel snorted. "I hardly think I need your advice. Why, I was picking off those rebellious colonials before you were sucking at your nursemaid's teat." He stepped back and swayed unsteadily. "Hmm. Seems I've had too much to drink. Perhaps I could use some assistance to find my bed. Won't be much help to the regiment in the morning if I'm face down in some ditch."

"Exactly, sir," Rafe told him. "I'd be more than happy to escort you *and* Miss Tate home."

He guided the old man out of the room past a glaring Rebecca.

If she was outraged now, he could assure her, her mood wasn't going to improve once they reached her cottage.

For Rafe wasn't going to leave until he had some answers.

Rebecca seethed the entire ride home. A half an hour to become increasingly indignant at the very presumption of Rafe Danvers.

And that didn't even include her outrage at her uncle. Blast his hide, he'd gone too far tonight.

Men! she wanted to sputter as she stared out the window and ignored the pair of them, though she was hard pressed to succeed in that endeavor. Rafe and her uncle were seated side by side singing a rousing Spanish song that she suspected the translation wasn't in the least bit proper.

She crossed her arms over her chest and sighed. Oh, she hadn't minded when Rafe had stepped between her and Major Harrington or how he'd come to her uncle's defense, but now she wanted him well and gone.

There was too much at risk and too much to be gained to allow him to delve into their secrets.

When they arrived at the cottage, Mrs. Wortling greeted them at the door wearing her wrapper, her hair sticking out from her nightcap, and a stubby candle in her hand. "Is 'e in his cups?" she asked, eyeing the colonel, then Rafe, with a skeptical eye.

Rebecca considered asking the woman the same question considering the copious cloud of liquor that came wafting at them as she spoke.

"He is not drunk, Mrs. Wortling," she replied, walking into the house.

The lady held the candle higher. "He looks it. And I'll tell you right now, I'm not cleaning it up 'iffin he starts casting up his accounts all over."

"The colonel was injured, madame," Rafe told her,

sweeping past the housekeeper and into the house, guiding the colonel with every step.

"Up the stairs, the last room on the left," Rebecca told him.

"Injured?" Mrs. Wortling asked. "Did he shoot at someone again?"

"No," Rebecca told her. "It was Major Harrington. He argued with the colonel and knocked him out."

Mrs. Wortling rolled an extravagant glance heavenward as if she bore the terrible burden of all of their problems. "Did you warn the major not to come within range of the cottage for a week or so? I'll not be blamed if yer uncle blasts him all the way to Sussex."

"Mrs. Wortling, is it?" Rafe asked from where he stood at the foot of the stairs. "Why don't you go seek your bed. There isn't anything more you can do tonight. And I'll see to the colonel's welfare."

"Harrumph," the woman snorted, as Rafe helped the colonel up to his room. "Oh, he's a high and mighty one. Ordering me about." She glanced up at his retreating figure on the stairs and sniffed. "Mark my words, Miss Tate, make sure the colonel is all that man sees to. He has the look of getting what he wants from a lady without so much as a 'by your leave.' I'd get the colonel's cannon ready, if I were you."

"I assure you, Mrs. Wortling," Rebecca told her, "I won't need the cannon to be rid of Mr. Danvers."

And as much as she wanted to believe her well meant words, when he came downstairs, his dark gaze melted her resolve.

No, Mrs. Wortling had been entirely wrong about Mr. Danvers.

She'd need an artillery unit to protect herself.

"Thank you for your help, Mr. Danvers," she said as primly and politely as she could. She held the door open, and let her gaze sweep outward, hoping he'd take the hint and move in that direction without asking her any of the questions burning in his eyes.

"If you think I'm leaving without some answers, you are more addled than your uncle."

Rebecca chewed on her lip. *Damn him.* Why did he have to meddle into business that wasn't his concern?

But it was. The moment Harrington had slipped about their connection to Sir Rodney, their secrets had fallen into Rafe's domain.

Especially with the money the Company was offering to have the embarrassing case solved.

"I don't know what you mean," she brazened. "Now, I bid you good night. I'd like to see that my uncle is resting comfortably," she said, stepping back into the house and starting to close the door in his face.

His hand shot out and he stepped forward faster than Ajax dashing in from a rainstorm.

"Not so hasty, Miss Tate," he said. "I'm not going to be dismissed so easily."

Her heart wanted to believe that it was more than just the reward that held his interest. Then again, perhaps spending the evening in Miss Honora's company had her seeing heroes where there was only a bounder.

"Major Harrington seems convinced you are all in danger. Why is that?" he asked.

"Perhaps that is a question better posed to the major," she told him, still pushing futilely against the door.

"I'll tend to him first thing in the morning," he said in that dogged tone of his that seemed to underline his tenacious resolve.

"Then I suggest you go seek your bed and get a good night's rest, for that interview will be sure to tax even your determination."

"It isn't Harrington that I'm worried about."

He was worried about her? Rebecca paused and met his gaze. Whatever was he doing looking at her like that? His strong jaw set in a steely purpose, his lips, both hard and forgiving, drawn together into a daunting line. He was mesmerizing in his masculine power. No man should be so tall, so handsome, so magnificent of form.

Not even Lt. Thockmorten was so perfect, and she'd drawn him from the deepest secrets of her heart.

And as he looked down at her, he sent a quiver down her spine that whispered of passionate resolve and she realized truly how little she knew of men. This one in particular put her insides into a tangle of hot and distressing longings.

"I don't see that . . . I mean to say, you needn't—"

But she wanted him to! Wanted him to catch her up and carry her off to some secluded bower and promise her that she would be safe forever more.

Then in gratitude she let him ravage her with his lascivious passions that would leave her delirious and eventually, sated.

Oh, botheration, she was starting to script her life like she was the heroine of her own novel.

"This isn't your concern," she told him. *I'm not your concern.*

"I beg to differ. Someone should be looking out for you. What were you thinking challenging the likes of Harrington? You could have been hurt." He heaved a sigh and then raked his fingers through his hair. "What if I hadn't been there to stop him?"

"But you were," she whispered, amazed by this show of emotion—all over her. Rebecca Tate, the spinster of Bramley Hollow.

There was a telltale rustle in the kitchen.

"Mrs. Wortling," she whispered as he stared over her shoulder. "She's most likely eavesdropping."

His eyes narrowed and then without a word, he drew her outside the cottage and into the garden, far from an ear pressed to the door and prying eyes.

She went with him, pulled along despite her resolve to resist his charms.

Avoid his kisses.

The moon had risen and shone its magical light down the path. He caught her in his arms and pulled her close.

"Demmit, what am I going to do with you?" he muttered. For a moment he stared down at her, and she felt both his hunger to taste her lips again and confusion over this uncommon passion that seemed to bind them together.

She could sympathize, she didn't understand it either.

Desire it, oh, yes, but understand this inexplicable thread between them? Hardly.

She closed her eyes and tipped her head back, awaiting the endearments that were sure to follow, the passionate devotions of how he feared for her very life, and then the heat of his lips as they met hers.

Her dreams were quickly shattered.

"How is your uncle connected to Codlin? What was Harrington talking about when he wanted to know 'where is it?' What was he looking for? Does your uncle know? How is all this connected to Sir Rodney?"

The questions peppered her like shot from her uncle's Brown Bess. Her eyes flew open, and she staggered back from the warmth of his arms, cut to the quick, as her dreamy visions of romance turned into the Spanish Inquisition.

He hadn't brought her out in the garden to seduce her, but to interrogate her. Bully her into helping him solve his case.

"Why you presumptuous—" she sputtered. "You drag me out here," she waved her arms at the setting, the ideal of every girl's romantic vision, "and claim to want to help me, when all you really want to do is find Sir Rodney's killer."

He threw his hands up. "Well, of course I want to find the man. He's a murderer."

Rebecca let out an exasperated sigh. "And the Company's reward has nothing to do with it?"

"Of course the money matters. It's how I make my living."

Yes, she saw that now. Seducing ladies to gain his ends. Oh, bah, she'd been a moonstruck fool to believe otherwise. Like the kiss earlier at Bettlesfield Park, he'd only meant to tease her into his charmed confidence and then he'd be gone, gone like . . .

Drat and bother men. All of them. She stomped toward the house.

"Rebecca," he said, striding after her. "Where are you going? I need to know the truth of all this if I am to keep you safe."

"I don't recall asking you to do so, nor can I afford the price."

It was his turn to flinch. "It's not like that."

"Then how is it? Pray tell me, sir, how is it?"

He stammered and shuffled his feet. "*Dios!* I'm just trying to be honest with you."

"Honest? You lure me into the garden and pretend like you . . . like you . . ."

His eyes narrowed. "Like I care?"

"Yes."

"I do."

His confession sent her reeling. He cared? It wasn't true.

But what if it was? a very impractical voice whispered from her heart.

"How can you?" she managed to whisper. "You don't even know me."

"I know this," he said. Before she could step out of his reach, his hand snaked out and caught her and tugged her into his chest.

She opened her mouth to protest only to find her lips covered with his.

He claimed a kiss as if it were his due, as if he were the only man destined for such a privilege. And kiss her he did, his tongue defiantly meeting hers, teasing her into a tangled, passionate dance.

One of his hands had wound itself into her hair, pulling and toying with loose strands, freeing others.

He deepened his kiss, while his breathing turned ragged with need. He pressed her closer, until she understood just how much he desired her—hard and demanding.

For a wild heartbeat, she believed, truly believed that he cared because she was his. Matched by the fates.

But Rebecca couldn't forget that at the heart of his desires, was a country house and two thousand pounds. And rich and beautiful women like Lady Victoria to tempt him.

For Rafe Danvers wasn't about to let anyone or anything stand in his way of laying claim to these. He'd said so, and she believed him, more than she could his enticing kisses. And as much as she needed his help, she couldn't risk the price.

Her heart.

Wrenching herself free, she put both hands on his chest and shoved him away. "Don't you ever kiss me again."

And with that said, she marched for the cottage.

"Rebecca, I'm not done with you."

"Oh, yes you are, you high-handed, arrogant lout," she told him before she slammed the door in his face, and slammed the bolt in place with a determined thud.

"Ah, there you are, Lieutenant Bex," the colonel called out from the stairwell. "Where is the shot? The powder? I fear the walls are in danger of being—"

"You needn't continue," Rebecca said, catching her uncle by the arm and towing him into the library. "We are alone and Mrs. Wortling is most likely sound asleep." Passed out, more likely. The only blessing to the woman's penchant for nipping in the liquor cabinet is that it kept her snoring for most of the night.

"Whew! That was close." The colonel wiped his brow and settled into his favorite chair. "You did splendidly, Bex. Followed my lead like the best little thespian."

Rebecca shook her head and dropped into the chair beside him. "You nearly gave us away tonight," she scolded.

"Bah!" he said, waving his hand at her concerns as if they were just a few lingering gnats. "But I must say, I just about dropped short when Mr. Danvers said he was investigating Codlin's murder. Fancy the coincidence of that."

It was the last thing she wanted to consider, but now there was no getting around their involvement. She knew only too well that Rafe Danvers wouldn't stop until he'd discovered the truth.

"You need to be more careful," she scolded again. "You can't let anyone suspect that you have the full use of your faculties."

The colonel nodded. "I thought I covered myself quite well with Lady Kirkwood. Did you see her face when I called her a French spy?" He laughed, as did Rebecca, forgetting for a second that she was angry with her uncle. Lady Kirkwood had turned the same shade of green as the perfectly situated plumes atop her head when he'd called for her arrest.

But the humor didn't last long, for they both knew only too well the evening had been like a bell tolling on their charade.

"We haven't long, have we, Bex?" he asked.

"No," she acknowledged. "But I am close to finding Mr. Purcell. I had a very encouraging letter from an acquaintance of his who thought he had taken a new address in Spitalfields. I'll write to him again tomorrow and implore him to return Richard's haversack to us."

If only she could get to London. Then tracking down her brother's friend would be so much easier. In person, the former Lt. Purcell wouldn't be able to ignore her as he had the countless letters she had written him over the years requesting he send her Richard's belongings. Other than his one short note after he'd returned to England promising to bring Richard's haversack to Bramley Hollow at his earliest convenience, there had been no other word from the man.

For without her brother's journals, they would remain unable to locate the very thing Codlin's killer was looking for.

The Kailash Ruby.

A legendary gem, it promised its bearer eternal life. But beyond that disputable claim, it was also the size of a hen's egg and worth a fortune.

And her father's only legacy. While the rest of his treasure hunting had been more myth than precious metal, the Kailash Ruby had turned out to be everything his notes had claimed.

Yet as quickly as it had been found, the elusive stone

had gone missing, and it had become the colonel and Rebecca's dream to regain it.

"We can't go seeking the ruby until I've learned how to undo the curse," her uncle told her. "I've still got some work to do on the translations to figure out how to keep it from driving us mad while we return it to the temple."

"Uncle, I don't want to have this argument with you. I am not going to return that ruby to India."

"But the curse, Bex. You can't dismiss all the terrible problems that have beset us since it was stolen. The texts are quite explicit—it is never to be handled directly or disturbed. Its corrupting forces cannot be so blithely dismissed."

She waved her hand at him. "I doubt all that money will make us anything but deliriously happy."

Her uncle got up and uncorked the bottle on the sideboard, then frowned when he found it empty.

"Consider this," she offered, "by selling the ruby, we will be able to keep even Mrs. Wortling satisfactorily supplied with Madeira."

The colonel's busy brows rose in a disgruntled line. "We are not going to keep it. It has done nothing but cause death and destruction. Look what it did to Codlin."

Codlin. Rebecca glanced up at her uncle, her mind awhirl on another possibility. Oh, why hadn't she thought of this before? "What if we were to find him first?"

"Find who?" her uncle asked, looking behind the books on the shelves in hopes the housekeeper hadn't found his private stash of whiskey. It wasn't like either of them worried that she might stumble upon them while cleaning—the thick dust on the shelves was evidence enough of her lack of devotion to her position in the household.

"Codlin's killer, of course," Rebecca was saying. "Think of what we could do with that reward the Company is offering."

"Ah, here it is," he said, pulling aside a thick tome and retrieving a half full bottle. "Leave that job to Mr. Danvers. We are in enough danger as it is," he advised. "Though the extra money would finance our trip to India and there would most likely be enough left over to go on an expedition across the Congo afterward. I have several myths and maps that suggest there is a city of gold there—and nary a curse to burden us when we bring it all home."

Home! He was a fine one to talk. They didn't even have a home. This cottage was their refuge only because of Lord Finch's benevolence.

"That two thousand would be better served toward buying us a house of our own and seeing us clear of debtor's prison," she shot back.

Her uncle sighed. "You are too practical by far, Bex."

"Someone has to be," she muttered.

"Sent you packing, did she?" Jemmy called out from the study as Rafe made his way into Finch Manor.

"In a manner of speaking," he said, willing to admit defeat to a friend. He strode into the room and threw himself down in a large chair before the fire. "That woman is enough to drive a man to madness."

"Rebecca is a smart gel. She's not going to be flummoxed and put in a dither by your rapscallion ways."

"Oh, she was in rare form when I left. Called me arrogant and high-handed." Rafe stared moodily at the fire. He left out the loutish part for good reason.

Not that he needed to tell Jemmy. He was already laughing. "Then I guess you tried your infamous charm on her?"

Stretching one foot out in front of the other, Rafe wasn't sure how to answer that. He didn't need to.

"And when that failed," Jemmy continued, "I suppose you demanded answers and told her she had to give them to you."

He folded his arms over his chest and nodded.

"And she probably told you to go soak yourself in the mill pond."

"In so many words, yes," Rafe admitted. "There has got to be some way to—" He shot up from his chair. "Demmit! How could I have forgotten?" Glancing over at Jemmy, he excused himself and went up to his room where he had stowed her writing desk. Gathering it up, he brought it downstairs.

"What's that for?" Jemmy asked. "You intend to write her an apology?"

"No, prove she's the *Darby* author."

At this, Jemmy sat up, his gaze locked on the box, then flying up at Rafe. "Really?"

Rafe nodded. Perhaps once he had the proof he needed to reveal her identity, he could use it as leverage to get her to let him help her. It wasn't the most honorable means, but he was running out of choices.

"Where did you get that?" Jemmy asked, getting up from his chair, cane in hand and hobbling over to the sideboard where Rafe had set Rebecca's dispatch box.

"Miss Tate left it at Bettlesfield Park this afternoon."

Jemmy glanced at him, his brows rising with questions. "She left her desk behind? I wonder what had her in such a hurry that made her forget something so important?"

Rafe ignored him. "I brought it here with the intention of returning it to her this evening. That is until you started telling that story about the French dispatch box."

Jemmy let out a low whistle. "And you think this is one."

"I'd bet my reputation on it."

"So how do we open it?"

"I used to smash them open with the butt of my rifle, but I doubt Miss Tate would appreciate receiving her desk back in pieces."

"Hardly sporting," Jemmy agreed.

Rafe flipped the lid open and took out the correspondence and accounts he'd found earlier in the top portion. "Now all we have to do is discover how to open the hidden compartment." Rafe tapped and pried and turned the box every which way, but couldn't for the life of him discern how to open it.

"Too bad," Jemmy said, having long since retreated back to his chair and a bottle of port. "Probably a mess of pages inside there, considering she's gone and emptied that one inkwell."

Rafe glanced at the box again. The inkwell! While the other one was stained and nicked, the second one appeared to have never been used. He poked a finger inside and discovered to his amazement a button, which he pressed.

The box swung open, revealing a drawer on the bottom half, and as Jemmy had predicted, stuffed with pages.

Rafe picked up the first one and began to read.

*"There is no shame in a broken heart, my dear girl,"
Lady Lowthorpe said. "Mourn the loss of your beloved
and then resolve to find someone else. Lieutenant
Throckmorten would never have wanted you to suffer
this terrible decline."*

*"I fear," Miss Darby said, in a voice weak and grief-
stricken, "My heart will never be whole again."*

"It's her," Rafe said, feeling none of the elation he should be. He'd found his mark, uncovered the author's identity. Now he had to do the impossible—convince her to stop. If only he didn't have her censorious words from the other night still ringing in his ears.

What right do you have to tell someone to stop writing?

What right indeed? None whatsoever. And yet here was the proof he needed, and just out of sight was the house and property that would be his.

Rafe groaned.

"Can I offer you a bit of advice?"

He glanced over at Jemmy and nodded.

"You can't push Rebecca. Doesn't like charity. Very self-reliant. Drives mother to distraction, because the more she tries to meddle in Rebecca's life, the less it works."

"And what would you suggest?"

"Time."

Time? How ironic his friend would offer that advice. It was like his own past haunting him. What had he told Olivia, his future sister-in-law when his brother Robert had been reluctant to declare his heart?

Give him time—he'll come around.

"I don't have time," Rafe said.

"Of course you don't. But swaggering about and making demands obviously isn't going to work."

"You seem to know her quite well," Rafe said, casting a sideways glance at his friend. "Have you, well, considered—"

"Rebecca?" Jemmy shook his head. "Oh, mother would be delighted. Christ, she'd be happy if I married the drover's daughter at this point, but I couldn't do that to Rebecca."

"Do what?"

"Marry her. I couldn't give her what she wants, what she needs."

"Why not?"

He nodded at his ever present cane, at his useless leg. "Rebecca deserves a man who can prod her to live her dreams. To push her out of her careful existence and lead her on a merry chase." He laughed. "I don't even think I could give the drover's daughter a good go of it." He glanced over at the low flames in the fireplace and shook his head.

Rafe could see what had Lady Finch so flummoxed, so frightened for her only child.

"Rafe," Jemmy said. "Whatever you decide to do about Rebecca, hear me well. If you hurt her, if you harm her in any way, I'll kill you."

"I'm not about to—"

Jemmy shook his head. "I saw the way you looked at her. No man looks at a woman that way unless he's . . . well, you know what I mean. And I'm not saying you have, but she's a decent chit, not one of your London lightskirts. And from that scene tonight and what you've told me, it sounds like she's caught up in some terrible trouble. Sounds to me like she needs a hero, not a bounder in her life. Tread carefully, my friend."

Jemmy rose, cane in one hand and the bottle in the other and made his slow and beleaguered way to his solitary gatehouse.

Rafe watched the astute young man leave and thought it a profound loss that Jemmy had closed his heart to love. The man had much to offer if only he would let go of the past.

And apparently Jemmy wasn't the only one in Bramley Hollow whose past followed them about like leg irons. What had Harrington said, when he'd taunted Rebecca?

Found another champion, have you? Wonder if he'll be as constant as the last one.

Rafe shook his head. Lt. Habersham. And it seemed that the faithless bastard had broken her heart.

He tried to tell himself it would never come to that if he were to help her.

But most of all, he wanted to know if his fears weren't so unlike Jemmy's.

Chapter 10

Your Highness, a decent and respectable English-woman never comes second in a man's household nor his affections.

Miss Darby to Prince Ranjit in
Miss Darby's Reckless Bargain

Rafe wished he could feel quite pleased for having discovered the proof that Miss Rebecca Tate was the author of the *Miss Darby* novels. Instead, he found himself filled with an uncharacteristic dread as he stood at the gate of her cottage and looked up at its bright green door.

It didn't help that his earlier interview with Major Harrington had been nothing but an exercise in futility. The man's stalwart Indian servant, Mahesh, had all but slammed the door in his face, after stating that the master of the house did not receive uninvited callers.

Hopefully, he would have a better reception here. Staring down at the package in his hand, he realized it was a poor offering in the form of an apology and offer to help.

Miss Tate, here is the proof you are the woman I am looking for.

Rafe grimaced and shook his head. No. No. No. That wouldn't do, it sounded like the preamble to something altogether different.

Miss Tate, I discovered your dispatch box at Bettlesfield

Park yesterday, and after I broke into it, low and behold, there was the proof I needed to destroy your life.

Yes, that ought to put him in her good graces. Rafe heaved a sigh. Why was it he could charm the petticoats off of just about any woman, but the mere fact of facing Rebecca Tate—not to mention having to apologize to the chit—put him into knots that he doubted the saltiest of sailors could unravel?

He banged his head against the archway, pledging never again to take any case that involved a woman.

The spicy scent of roses assailed him and he opened his eyes and looked around him. Flowers! That might do the trick. They'd helped his cause before.

After gathering up a handful of blossoms and getting thoroughly pricked and stabbed in the process, Rafe took a deep breath and marched up the walkway, ignoring his smarting fingers . . . and pride.

Think of the money you'll get from the sale of Bettlesfield Park, he told himself as he rapped on the door. *Consider the information you may gain regarding the Codlin murder.*

He was shown into Colonel Posthill's library by Mrs. Wortling, who surveyed him from head to toe with a suspicious glare that said she'd be searching him for household items later.

Rebecca knelt before the fireplace, her back to him, barely acknowledging Mrs. Wortling's gruff, "That gypsy fellow's back. Come to see you, miss, or so he claims."

Heart pounding with inexplicable nerves, he tried to tell himself this is what he'd agreed to do—albeit reluctantly—but now he had to see it to the bitter end.

He never quit. Ever. Wasn't that what he'd told her yesterday with a measure of arrogant assurance?

You haven't succeeded yet, a small voice not so unlike Rebecca's lilting tones taunted him.

But he would, he reassured himself. He would stop her. And then . . . well, he didn't want to consider what next. He still had to find Codlin's killer, and then there would be another dangerous case . . . and another. Far away from Bramley Hollow and the tempting little spinster who resided here. She'd be safe and he'd be . . . adrift once again.

If only he could find a way to convince her that not writing was the best thing for her. For both of them.

Just how to do that, he wasn't so sure.

"Uh, hum," he said, wondering if she was going to even greet him.

Crumpling the paper in her hand, she tossed it into the flames, then rose and smoothed out her skirt before she turned to him. Her features, already fair by nature, held an uneasy pallor, and her mouth strained to rise into even the barest of smiles.

Immediately, Rafe was struck by one terrifying thought. Something was wrong. Terribly wrong, and it wrenched at his heart in the same way it had when he'd thought Harrington was going to strike her.

"Mr. Danvers, how nice of you to call." She barely glanced at the package he held or the flowers.

"I brought you something," he said. "I thought you might be missing this." He held out the package, flowers atop it, and waited for some display of gratitude or even, given that this was Rebecca, some admonition about him "interfering."

"Thank you," was all she said, before she turned and poked at the fire.

After standing there aimlessly for a few moments, he settled the dispatch box atop the piles of maps and began unwrapping it for her to see.

What the devil was wrong with her?

He peered around her skirt and noticed that the

piece of paper she'd been reading had fallen out of the fire into the ashes at the grate. It was barely charred. And apparently she didn't realize that whatever she'd taken such care to consign to the flames, had escaped its fate.

Resisting the urge to march across the room and snatch it up and demand an explanation, Rafe instead asked her, "You know why I've come, don't you?"

"To return my desk, I suppose."

"Yes, that," he said, coming closer to her, hoping to turn her attention away from the fire. "And to apologize."

She stared at him, one delicate brow arched in skepticism. "There is no need to apologize for doing your job."

"No, I'm not apologizing for that. For last night. For being so . . . so . . ."

"Overbearing?"

Rafe held his impatience in check. "Yes, that."

"And presumptuous?"

He took a deep breath. This was harder than he supposed. Apologizing for missing a promised dance or an afternoon rendezvous was one thing. But for offering his protection, well that just seemed ridiculous. Didn't she see that she needed him? For whatever it was that had her at odds last night, now had her looking ready to bolt and run this morning.

"Yes, presumptuous," he admitted.

"And maybe even—" she began.

"Fine, enough," he sputtered, having no need to listen to a litany of his faults. He had his family for that task. "I just wanted to offer my sincere regrets for my behavior last night."

To his chagrin, she brushed off his offering as she had the dispatch box. "Really, there is no need to apologize. I thank you, sir, for returning my desk," she said.

"But as you can see, I am busy with some work for the colonel, and I would like to finish it." She tried to brush past him, to make her way to the map table, but he stopped her, using every bit of restraint to take her lightly by the forearms. He wanted to tug her to his chest, to shield her from harm, but he knew that would only drive her further from him.

And closer to danger.

"Rebecca, what is it?" He thought he saw her flinch, as if she feared the intimacy that seemed to spring to life so readily between them.

Instead of falling into his arms and pleading for his able assistance, Rebecca shook him loose. "Nothing. Thank you for my desk and good day."

She moved toward the door, and while her back was turned to him, he swooped down and retrieved the note, shoving it into his pocket before she noticed.

With it secure, he discarded all of Jemmy's sound advice. "You can't just ask me to leave. If you think we're finished just because you say—"

"I beg your pardon?" Her arms folded over her chest, her eyes blazing with fiery indignation.

He clamped his mouth shut and then raked his fingers through his hair. "What I mean to say is that I know about your desk."

"That it's a French dispatch box?"

"Yes, exactly," he said, latching onto her offering. "And once I opened it, I discovered—"

"Your proof that I am the author of the *Miss Darby* novels?"

"Exactly." This wasn't going so badly, he told himself.

"Did you pry my desk open or were you able to discover the locking mechanism without breaking it? I only assume it was one or the other since you didn't have to smash it entirely to gain your boon."

Rafe shifted from one foot to another. Well, she needn't put it like that. Like he was some shady housebreaker.

She glanced up at him and shook her head. "Can you get to the point? Obviously, you discovered the hidden compartment and the pages for my next book."

His moment of triumph hardly managed even a weak "huzzah."

Especially when she heaved a sigh and continued by saying, "Really, Mr. Danvers, you aren't very good at this. I can see why your rent goes unpaid."

"I do well enough," he said, bristling at her doubt. Why was it that no one in Bramley Hollow seemed to believe him capable of the simplest of tasks? Maybe it was because he had been competent at his profession before he'd set foot in this topsy-turvy village. "I assure you, Miss Tate, I am quite capable of the task at hand."

"Harrumph. If it hadn't been for Jemmy's fortuitous story last night, you would never have discovered the truth about my traveling desk."

Rafe bristled. "Granted his revelation helped, but I assure you, Miss Tate, I would have uncovered your identity nevertheless."

She stared heavenward. "When you got done blustering and demanding and stomping about like a—"

"I do not stomp."

"Of course not," she conceded with the assurance one might give an errant toddler. "I would assume you've now come to make your demands." She stared at him until he nodded. "What will you do, Mr. Danvers? Tell me I have wreaked terrible havoc upon society and attempt to shame me into quitting? Since you know me better than that, we'll both save you the lecture and agree that I don't succumb to shame."

Kisses, he thought. *She'd succumb to his kiss.*

But the problem with that method of persuasion was what it did to him. Left him all tangled up and thinking about renovating tumbledown country houses.

Rebecca, on the other hand, was just getting started. "Has your employer authorized you to use whatever force is necessary to complete your work?" She held out her right arm. "I write with this hand, so if you would like to render it useless, do so and be done so I can get on with my life and find some other source of income to keep the colonel from being sent to Bedlam, while maintaining a roof over my head."

And she needn't be so practical about it. He didn't break people's limbs for a living.

Not as a rule. Not unless absolutely necessary.

He stared down at her outstretched arm and cursed.

Dios! She was going to be the end of his career. The end of his reputation. He was a scoundrel. People hired him because he was ruthless. Unmoved by plights of pity or pleas for leniency.

Now he'd be the one looking for employment, not her. As it was, she still had a roof over her head, while his penurious landlady had most likely already sold what few worldly goods he did possess to pay what he owed her.

"Put your arm down," he said. When she still held it out with stubborn resolve, he took hold of it and towed her over to a chair where he gently pressed her down into it. "I'm not here to cause you bodily harm."

She glanced up at him, and all he wanted to do was bodily. Tug her into his arms and stoke his fingers through her tempestuous red hair, soothe her taut lips with kisses, pull her so close her breasts pressed to his chest, her hips against his.

Don't think about her that way, he told himself. *Don't think about the soft curves that begged for a man's touch. The way her smile makes you believe that the stars can sing the very secrets of love.*

No, he had to find a way to make her decision to quit writing seem like her own idea. Make it enticing enough that she would snap it up without a moment's hesitation.

Then he remembered something else he'd learned about her last night. What was it the colonel had declared before everyone?

I know she's always wanted a Season.

That was it! The solution to all his problems.

"This doesn't have to be the end of your ability to care for your uncle," Rafe told her. "You could make a deal with Lady Tottley. You could have a Season in London. Have her sponsor you in exchange for quitting writing. Maybe you could even find your vicar and get married."

And even as he said those words, he knew he'd just made the biggest mistake of his life.

Get married? Rebecca didn't know what to say. He thought the solution to all her problems was just to prance off to London for the Season and find some unwitting fool to marry her?

Rafe Danvers was lucky the fire iron was safely across the room and not within arm's reach, for he'd have found it imbedded in his thick skull.

"Just go to London?" she repeated. "For the Season?"

He nodded slowly. "Uh, yes. Your uncle said last night that you'd always wanted to have one."

Her uncle had also accused Lady Kirkwood of being a French spy, but she didn't feel the need to point that out to him, for as her indignation started to wear off, she realized the full implication of what he was saying.

Go to London? Why that was perfect!

"And this is what Lady Tottley is offering?" she asked cautiously, trying to hide the hope in her voice, the only bit she'd felt since she'd found the note left on the hallway table this morning.

He hemmed and hawed a bit. "Well, she hasn't said as much—"

"So she didn't actually offer a Season in town?" Rebecca prodded.

"No," Rafe conceded. "But she would."

"Harrumph," Rebecca snorted knowing she sounded just like Mrs. Wortling when she couldn't find the brandy.

"I could write her and tell her of your demands. Say that you would be willing to quit writing if she were to bring you to London and—"

"I'll go," she declared, stopping him cold. "I'll do it."

Rafe stepped back from her and stared. "Just like that? You'll give up writing and go to town?"

She nodded. "But I have a few demands."

"Of course," he said. "I wouldn't expect otherwise."

She got up and cleared a spot on the map table, setting aside a pile of correspondence and two large volumes. Opening up her desk, she retrieved a quill, the small bottle of ink and several pieces of paper.

He eyed the stack of parchment. "You think we'll need that many pages?"

"I've never had a Season in London," Rebecca told him. "And if I am to give up my livelihood, then I intend to have the best one possible."

He sighed and sat down at the table, picking up the pen and scratching out the first part of the letter, outlining the offer. When he got done with the basic premise, he said, "And your demands, Miss Tate?"

"I'll need a wardrobe. Gowns, gloves, hats, shoes, and . . . and . . ."

"Other unseen items?" he suggested, a wicked smile pulling at his lips.

"Yes, whatever it takes to make a lady decent. But I suspect you know more about what goes beneath a proper lady's gown than I do."

"I am far too much of a gentleman to admit to such knowledge."

Rebecca snorted, borrowing once again from Mrs. Wortling's limited vocabulary.

"Yes, well, let me list those as 'unmentionable necessities.'"

Incorrigible fellow! Let him smirk all he wanted, but what he didn't realize is that a new wardrobe would require numerous trips around town giving her ample excuses to be away from Lady Tottley's and out searching for Lt. Purcell.

And Codlin's killer.

"I'll need dancing lessons," she said over his shoulder.

"One dancing master," he wrote. "French and *very* patient."

She ignored him. "I also want to see the Elgin Marbles."

"Modest young ladies do not view the Elgin Marbles."

"Bah!" Rebecca said. "Have you seen them?"

"Yes."

"Did they corrupt your morals?"

"Hardly." Rafe dipped the quill in the inkwell. "Though in truth, my morals were already far from perfect before I ventured to the museum."

Rebecca saw no reason to argue with that. "I suspect my character will survive the experience, sir, so if you would be so kind." She tapped the page where he'd left off.

Adding the request, he glanced back at her, expectantly.

She didn't keep him waiting long. "A membership at a local lending library and an account at Hatchards."

"This list has all the earmarks of designating you as an incurable bluestocking."

She tipped her nose in the air. "Just write down my requirements, if you please, and keep your comments to yourself. This is *my* Season."

"Indeed it is," he muttered.

"Please add that I want to attend the opera, the ballet and the theater."

"Those should all be easily secured," he said, "since they are proper entertainments for a young lady."

She ignored the barb. "I also want the colonel to come with me. I will not leave him here in Bramley Hollow with only Mrs. Wortling to see to his care."

Rafe glanced up at her. "Are you sure that is wise? I doubt Lady Tottley is going to want her house turned into an Indian garrison."

"The colonel comes with me."

He mumbled something about endangering the citizenry of London, but he wrote it down. "Anything else?"

"Yes," she said. "Vouchers to Almack's."

"Almack's?" He groaned. "Why would you want to go there?"

" 'Tis every girl's dream." And she'd recently read that Mr. Purcell had been part of a party of young gentlemen there.

"You aren't every girl," he told her. This should have pleased her, until he muttered under his breath, "Thought you had more sense than that."

"Almack's, sir, or I finish *Miss Darby's Terrible Temptation* this very week."

Rafe wrote it down. "That everything?" he asked wearily.

She glanced over the letter and nodded. "How long do you think it will take to hear back?"

"I'll send Cochrane along with Lady Finch's courier when he leaves with this afternoon's packet of her correspondence. They'll return tomorrow night."

She nodded. "Very well."

"No more writing?" he asked.

She nodded in agreement. "Why don't you see it off yourself?"

"Ready for me to be gone so soon?"

It was on the tip of her tongue to say "yes," but her manners won out. "Not at all."

"You are a poor liar, Miss Tate."

"And you are a troublesome man."

He looked up at her, a sparkle of mischief in his eyes. "Then we are well matched."

His words took her aback, unused as she was to men flirting with her. It was flirting, she assumed, for he'd had the same devilish look about him before he'd kissed her yesterday.

Both times.

And for one impetuous moment, she wished she'd demanded that he escort her around town. Dance with her at Almack's. Tease her with his smiles, and when no one was looking, steal a kiss from her only-too-willing lips.

Hardly proper or practical considering what she needed to get done in London had nothing to do with balls or routs or musicales, but when Rafe Danvers was in the room, Rebecca felt so dangerously alive. And when he looked at her with those penetrating dark eyes of his, she felt herself drowning in his passionate nature.

But the moment was broken by a screech in the kitchen and a loud yowl.

Ajax! she cursed silently.

There was a clatter of a heavy pan and another screech, then a streak of yellow fur into the library. The wretched tom dove under the map table, taking advantage of the long cloth that covered it.

"This time I'm going to stew that beast," Mrs. Wortling said as she came barreling into the room, cleaver in hand.

"Is there a problem, Mrs. Wortling?" Rebecca asked in an innocent voice.

"That beast has dumped the cream and gotten into the mutton."

Rafe glanced away, and she would bet it was to hide a smile.

"I don't know where he's gone. You've most likely frightened him away for good," she told the housekeeper.

"Doubt that," Mrs. Wortling said. "Cats and men have a way of staying put when they know there's a free meal to be had." She glanced over at Rafe. "Is he staying for tea? Because I have too much to do to make another plate."

"No, ma'am," Rafe offered. "I was just taking my leave of Miss Tate."

The housekeeper's relieved look said "good riddance."

"I will see to our agreement, Miss Tate, with all alacrity."

"Thank you, Mr. Danvers," Rebecca said, wishing Mrs. Wortling would leave, but she was too busy hunting around the room for sign of Ajax.

"Would you mind seeing me to the door?" he asked her.

"Not at all."

Away from Mrs. Wortling and her cleaver, Rafe looked down at her. "Are you sure there isn't anything else I can do for you? Help you with?"

She knew what he was asking, and as much as she wanted to unburden her heart on someone, she couldn't risk it with him—a man she barely knew and found so desirable. He muddled her senses and practical nature to the point where she wondered if she could trust her own judgment.

"No," she told him. "You've done more than enough, I assure you."

"If you are—"

"No, I'm not," she told him hastily before she lost her resolve.

"Then until tomorrow," he said and, to her chagrin, went out the door and down the cottage path with nary an attempt at anything resembling the previous night's impetuous kiss.

She ignored the gnawing disappointment that crept down her spine. For once she wished he'd been her overbearing knight—or at the very least a charming rogue out to steal a kiss.

Kisses, indeed! she admonished herself. They only led to trouble and if there was anyone who didn't need help causing a lady havoc, it was Rafe Danvers.

Rebecca turned from the door and found the colonel standing on the stairs. His left eye was swollen shut and ringed by a growing bruise, foul evidence of his confrontation with Harrington.

"You should have told him the truth, Bex. He could have helped us."

"No, I think not. Besides, we can't afford his fees."

"I don't think the fees would be an issue." The colonel took a step down. "He cares for you, and he'll be hell and fire when he discovers that you and I are right in the middle of this Codlin muddle."

"He's only interested in the two thousand pounds that the Company is offering for finding Codlin's murderer."

"Then why did he bring you a handful of flowers if he didn't care."

She glanced at the hastily plucked roses atop the table and wondered how many thorns he'd endured to gather them. But that was beside the point. "I've received flowers from a man before and it turned out to be nothing more than my own imagination."

"Habersham? Are you comparing this Danvers fellow to him?"

Rebecca didn't want to tell her uncle there was no comparison. Oh, she'd once thought Lt. Habersham's gentle kiss was the end of the world and beyond. But one moment in Rafe's arms had ruined her for any other man.

Compare the two? Ridiculous.

"Tell him the truth, Bex. He'll help us find what we need. Moreover, he'll keep you safe. Do a fine better job than I can."

"What? And let him walk away with the Company's reward?" It was bad enough she'd just handed him Bettlesfield Park. "Actually Mr. Danvers is going to help us without his even realizing it or it costing us a farthing," she told her uncle. "He is leaving to arrange a trip to London for us with lodgings in the heart of Mayfair."

Instead of being delighted at this turn of luck, the colonel's face darkened. "I won't have you . . . I won't allow you to . . ." He coughed and sputtered. "Now,

Bex, protecting you is one thing, but offering his *carte blanche*—"

Rebecca realized what her uncle was saying.

"No! No! It isn't that way," she told him, rushing to the foot of the stairs. "It's Lady Tottley. She's going to pay for all of this. We'll be staying with her."

"What?!" he sputtered. "This Lady Tottley wants to give you her *carte blanche*?"

Rebecca laughed. "No. Rafe was hired by Lady Tottley to find me. Now that he has, he has written her to say that I will agree to give up writing my *Miss Darby* books on the condition that she sponsors me for the Season."

The colonel's brow furrowed as he considered this. "Well, that's a fine sight more respectable than the other notion."

"Yes, quite," Rebecca said. "And it also means we can go to London as we've hoped, so you'd best begin packing."

"We?" the colonel shook his head. "I'm not going there."

Rebecca's hands balled up and sat in jaunty angles on her hips. "You most certainly are going. I'm not leaving you here with only Mrs. Wortling to keep an eye on you." Rebecca lowered her voice. "And don't forget, the Harringtons are now suddenly off to town. The major must either know something about Lieutenant Purcell or he's discovered—"

She stopped short of revealing what Rafe had uncovered at Bettlesfield Park—that someone had been living there recently. She didn't want to frighten the colonel further, let alone admit she'd been there with Rafe. Alone.

Instead she continued by saying, "It isn't safe, and you know it. That note this morning said quite clearly you're next, and I won't stand for it. We have to leave. Now start packing or I'll have Mrs. Wortling do it for you."

"Bossy bit of baggage," the colonel muttered. "Don't remember putting you in charge."

I wouldn't be, she thought, *if you and Richard hadn't got involved in all this bad business years ago.*

She looked out at the empty road and thought of Rafe again.

The colonel was right. She probably should tell him the truth. But unlike the colonel she wasn't as convinced of the sincerity of Rafe's heart. She'd known Lt. Habersham for years and thought him sincere, but he'd fled her side the moment any hint of scandal had tainted her.

And with Rafe, she suspected she was merely a means to an end. Before she trusted him with her life, with her heart, she needed to know that once all this was over, he'd still return to steal a kiss.

The bell rang a half hour later, and Rebecca dashed for the door, half expecting to find Rafe standing on the steps, having realized that he forgot something . . . namely a kiss. But to her dismay it was the Gadbury sisters and Mr. Kitling.

"Oh, Miss Tate, you are home!" Miss Honora said, bustling inside without an invitation. Alminta and Kitling followed and were in the library settled on the sofa for a cozy visit before Rebecca could utter a word of protest.

Heaving a sigh, she followed them inside. "How nice of you to come by."

Miss Honora patted the empty seat beside her. "I thought you might not be receiving visitors today, especially after last night's humiliating dinner. I don't know what Lady Finch was thinking. If I were her I would declare Major Harrington unfit for company and see those upstarts ruined. Striking the poor colonel like he did." She paused for a breath, but before Rebecca could interject a comment Alminta was off and running.

"And the way that Miss Harrington giggled about you wanting a Season. Of course you are too old, but what business is that of hers?"

Rebecca forced a smile to her lips. Despite their wayward manners and less than circumspect speech, she knew the Gadbury sisters held her in good opinion and hadn't a malicious bone in their identical small frames. "Actually, now that you mention it, I may be going up to London for the Season."

"You don't say?" Sydney Kitling asked, leaning forward. "How unexpected! I mean to up and leave for town just like that."

"Oh, yes, quite!" Honora exclaimed. "Do tell!"

"I don't have the specifics yet," Rebecca said, "but I am quite sure I will be leaving very shortly for town and enjoying the remainder of the Season."

Alminta glanced at her sister and frowned. "Oh, that would never do!"

Honora nodded in agreement. "Certainly not! Not proper in the least."

"Why not?" Rebecca dared to ask.

"My dear, you can't travel to town unescorted. You need a proper chaperone," Honora whispered so as not to spread the disgraceful notion too far.

Shaking her head, Rebecca smiled at the concerned pair. "I wouldn't be going alone," she explained. "The colonel will come with me and we will be staying with a lady of some means and social influence. It is all quite proper."

"If you say so," Miss Honora said, though sounding completely unconvinced.

Rebecca decided it was the better part of discretion not to mention Rafe's involvement. For she wasn't so sure herself that she didn't need a very diligent chaperone to keep her safe from the man's all-too-tempting kiss.

Rafe woke bolt upright the next morning as frantic shouts echoed down the halls of Finch Manor. After having sent Cochrane on his errand to London, Rafe had spent the rest of the night outlining the facts of the Codlin case to Jemmy and Lord Finch in hopes that they might see a connection he'd overlooked.

Then he'd sought the peace of his solitary bed, only to find himself dreaming of India and a slight, red-headed minx in a crumpled bonnet and brilliantly woven shawl standing on the edge of a great precipice.

Don't move, Rebecca. I can't lose you, I love—

The rising shouts wrenched him from a confession that not even he was willing to admit. Even in a dream.

He glanced down to the nightstand and there lay *Miss Darby's Reckless Bargain*. Shaking his head, he snapped the book shut. Last time he was going to fall asleep reading one of her novels.

Certainly not when he found himself cast as Lt. Throckmorten in his own dreams. *Why the man is a self-important, preening twit and I'm . . .*

An idiot, he realized, digging in his valise for a white linen shirt that wasn't too wrinkled. A new volley of shouts caught his attention and he hastened to pull on his breeches and boots.

He didn't need to get downstairs to discover the news, for his door opened and Jemmy Reyburn came limping in.

Besides appearing exhausted from climbing the stairs—his face white and drawn and his mouth set in a line of grim determination—he looked as if he'd just walked off a battlefield.

"Rafe, my father wants you to come straight away," he said. "There's been a murder."

Chapter 11

You have but to ask for my aid, Miss Darby, for you already possess my heart.

Lieutenant Throckmorten to Miss Darby
in *Miss Darby's Reckless Bargain*

The next morning, Rebecca knew something was wrong the moment she opened her eyes.

Downstairs someone was moving about. Mrs. Wortling was up? Before she had to be nudged and prodded to do her job?

That was an ill-sign indeed.

Whatever could the woman be doing at this early hour?

Rebecca tossed on her wrapper and padded her way downstairs, only to discover the housekeeper struggling out the front door with her well-worn valise in one hand, and a Wedgwood vase in the other.

"Mrs. Wortling! What is the meaning of this?"

"I ain't staying here," she declared. "Not when there's murder about. I'm a decent, law-abiding woman and I won't be killed in my own bed."

Decent and law-abiding? While she was in the process of stealing Rebecca's sole remaining possession from her mother?

But then the rest of the woman's words stopped her. *Murder?*

"What are you talking about?"

"Murder! And it is coming here," she declared.

"Someone was murdered?" Rebecca asked. Dread filled the pit of her stomach.

Rafe! Hadn't he said he was going to confront Harrington? Given the major's temperament, anything could have happened.

"Yes, killed most foul. Got it from Mrs. Benton across the way. Her screeching woke me up."

Rebecca reached over and caught her arm. "Who? Who was killed?"

Mrs. Wortling shook her loose. "Major Harrington, that haughty, tightfisted fellow. He was found this morning on the south road." She blew out a long disgruntled breath, as if to say, *serves the pompous fool right*. "Not that it wasn't bound to happen eventually, him being so mean-spirited and all, but lawks, I don't think you need to gut a man to get your point across."

"Gut?" Rebecca gasped, feeling her stomach drop. Just like Codlin . . .

"Uncle!" she cried out. "Oh, dear heavens."

She raced past Mrs. Wortling, theft and employment issues aside. Up the stairs she flew, down the hall, and into her uncle's room.

She came to a breathless halt before his bed. To her relief, he lay fast asleep, his chest rising slowly and evenly. "Uncle," she whispered in a little sigh of relief.

He stirred, and she quietly and quickly backed out of his room.

Downstairs the hallway was empty and the front door wide open. And the candlesticks on the sideboard were now missing as well.

Drat and hellfire on the woman.

Wrapper or not, Rebecca sped out the door and

caught up with the miscreant housekeeper at the gate. "Where do you think you are going?"

"I don't rightly know," the woman said. "But I know one place I ain't stayin'."

"Mrs. Wortling, you can't just quit like this." *Especially not with nearly every valuable we possess in your valise.*

"I can."

"Then hand over the candlesticks and the vase."

"I am owed wages," the woman said with a righteous indignation she had no right to possess.

"The candlesticks alone are worth ten years of your salary, so hand them over."

The housekeeper shook her head. "Hardly all that. They're just plate, not full silver. Not even worth a year's pay at what I git here."

"I paid you your quarterly wages last week. And considering the amount of brandy that has gone missing over the past year, I would be more inclined to believe you owe me."

"Harrumph. Don't see that that's the point," Mrs. Wortling huffed. "More important is that I won't be killed in my bed. Murdered with the lot of you." She glanced at the colonel's window. "He's next, and I don't aim to be here to clean up the mess."

"Next?" Rebecca's gaze narrowed. "What are you talking about?"

The woman's jaw worked back and forth, her gaze fixed on the ground before her. "I know there was a note left here yesterday morning. Someone was in the house. He got in and left the note on the front table right under our very noses. Could just as well slit our throats, and I don't aim to stick around and find out if he's gonna."

She gathered up her belongings, and those that weren't, before she continued out the gate. "And yes, I heard you and the colonel talking about it. Not ashamed to say I was listening at the door, but a person can't be too careful. Too many strange doings around here. Packets from London. Letters always coming and going. I won't be part of this." Her eyes narrowed. "I should be the one going to the magistrate what with how deep you and the colonel are in on that Codlin fellow's death." She shoved the gate open and set off, her bony nose stuck in the air.

"Why you—" As stunned as Rebecca might have been, she wasn't about to let the thieving, snooping housekeeper leave. Not just yet. "The vase and the candlesticks, Mrs. Wortling. Return them immediately or I will have Constable Holmes called and see that you are dealt with most severely."

The woman froze. "I'll tell everything, miss. Everything I know."

"You do that, Mrs. Wortling and I'll tell them about the mark on your shoulder."

The housekeeper's mouth fell open.

" 'Tis a brand, isn't it? For stealing?"

"It is no such thing. 'Twas an accident when I was just a bairn."

Rebecca crossed her arms over her chest, unwilling to listen to the woman's bluff. "Do you prefer hanging or transportation?"

Mrs. Wortling made a low growling noise.

"I believe a second offense is worthy of either," Rebecca said, "and I'm sure the magistrate, who you must realize is the colonel's cousin, would be inclined toward leniency by sending you to Botany Bay."

Mrs. Wortling shook a bony finger at Rebecca. "Oh, you're an uppity one. You ain't so nice as everyone says. That handsome Mr. Danvers won't be none-so-pleased when he discovers yer shrew's tongue." Her eyes narrowed. "But then again, mayhap he already does and doesn't care. Just as happy to take his pleasure and leave like the other one did."

Rebecca's cheeks grew hot at the woman's vulgar suggestion. She held her ground, inclined to show the housekeeper just how shrewish she could be. "Give me the candlesticks and vase now, Mrs. Wortling, before the magistrate has another murder on his hands."

The housekeeper stood for a few moments longer, before she started grumbling and digging into her valise. She produced the candlesticks and the vase and tossed them onto the grass at Rebecca's feet.

"Not like you'll have need of them for long, not if that note is right," the woman said. "And then I'll be back to get what is owed me. What I'm due." With that the woman trudged down the road toward the village, lugging her valise along.

Rebecca suspected that the only reason Mrs. Wortling had given up the candlesticks and the vase was because she'd probably taken enough other valuables to finance her flight from Bramley Hollow.

She'd send a note to Lord Finch immediately and he'd see that she didn't get very far.

Seething with anger, she stormed back inside the cottage, returning the vase to the mantel and the candlesticks to their rightful place.

Yet her fury was soon overridden as she realized just why the housekeeper was fleeing.

Major Harrington was dead? Murdered?

She tried to breathe, to tell herself that they were safe, but her body began to tremble with well-deserved fear—the kind that reached all the way down to her toes. She caught hold of a chair and dropped into it, feeling faint and nauseous and terrified all at once, for it seemed their time of reckoning had finally come—and there was nowhere that was far enough to save them this time.

But, Rebecca thought, as she looked out the window and at the road to London, it didn't mean she couldn't try.

Rafe stood over Major Harrington's body and shook his head.

It was Codlin's murder once again.

On the far side of the road, Lord Finch was bent over the ditch retching.

Poor fellow, Rafe thought. Hardly a regular day in his orchid house.

The Harringtons' Indian servant, Mahesh, approached. The same fellow who'd shut the door in his face with stony resolve.

"*Sahib*," he said, addressing Rafe now with a more revered tone. "I understand you have knowledge of the other one . . . the one such as this."

Rafe nodded. "I've been looking into Sir Rodney's murder, yes." If ever there was a suspect for the case, it was this Mahesh. The murderer was obviously proficient with a sword, as well as a knife.

Both of which Mahesh wore tucked into the belt wound around his robes. It would be easy to point a finger at the foreign fellow and be done with the matter, but Rafe wasn't looking for an easy solution. He wanted to solve this crime. Put an end to these killings. Especially now that he knew Rebecca and Colonel Posthill were connected to both victims.

"I did not do this," the servant told him in carefully enunciated English. "I can see in your eyes that you have your suspicions about me."

Rafe didn't say anything and for a time the two just

stared at each other. He did have his suspicions, but in his gut he doubted Mahesh had anything to do with this.

The servant bowed slightly. "You leave me to fill the silence. Well done. Not all English are so canny. So I will say it again: I did not murder the major. I would never defile myself by touching such as this." He shuddered and looked away. "Does it not bother you as well?"

Rafe sighed and glanced away. "Yes. It does. But I was in Spain for most of the war, and have seen this and far worse, so perhaps I am not as shocked."

The servant nodded. "You must believe that I am not responsible. I was in the house all morning supervising the packing. I even advised the major not to go out." The man paused for a moment and studied him. "But you already know all this."

"Yes." Rafe motioned for the footmen who had arrived with a wagon, to carry out their duties. "Whoever did this would be covered in blood, and you are wearing the same robes you began the day in. So the other servants tell me."

Mahesh eyed him. "You are wise and thorough. Good. Then I can entrust you with this." He reached inside his robe and pulled out a piece of parchment. "It was posted over the young memsahib's gown yesterday." He paused. "You know about the dress?"

Rafe nodded. He'd just finished questioning the game warden.

"I found the note this morning in the *sahib's* jacket. After he'd left. For if I had seen it before, I would never have let him out of my sight."

Looking down at the foreign lettering, it struck Rafe as familiar. Exactly the same characters that had been on the shred of paper he'd stolen from Rebecca yesterday.

"Do you know what it says?" he asked, digging in his pocket and producing Rebecca's note. "A friend of mine found this recently."

Mahesh paled as he glanced first at the note in Rafe's hand and the identical one in his own. "Yes. It is a warning in Benjali. It says, 'You're next.'" He shook his head, tears glistening in his eyes. "A warning the *sahib* should have heeded. A warning your friend must not take lightly or they will share my master's fate."

Rafe's blood ran cold. *Rebecca*.

"*Dios!*" he cursed and ran for his horse.

In the library, sorting her notes and research and the colonel's various translations, Rebecca heard the front door crash open and reached for her father's pistol.

She'd dug it out not long after Mrs. Wortling had left and had kept it close at hand all morning.

Drawing it up before her, she pointed it at the library door, her thumb pulling the hammer back.

But she failed to even get a shot off as a looming figure strode into the room, filling the doorway, his dark greatcoat swirling about him like a cape. The treacherous light in his eyes, the determination in the set of his jaw was enough to frighten her—if it hadn't been for the way the dangerous man stole her very breath, sent her heart racing.

Rafe.

She felt like cursing his blasted hide for breaking into the house like a marauder, while at the same time thanking the heavens he'd come.

But if she thought he was about to profess his relief that she was safe, she was wrong.

"Demmit, Rebecca, you'll be the death of me," he said, yanking off his hat and throwing it down on a nearby chair. "If I weren't a gentleman, I'd—"

"A gentleman? How dare you!" she said, still pointing the gun at him. "How dare you come here and scare me out of my wits."

"You're scared?" He began ripping off his gloves. "Good! Because you should be."

"Well, what am I supposed to think? You come barreling in here as if you were shot from uncle's cannon," she said. "Most people in Bramley Hollow knock first."

"And do the good people of Bramley Hollow also keep a loaded gun at the ready?" He nodded at the pistol in her hand.

She glanced down and bit her lip. "Oh, dear. So sorry," she said, letting the hammer fall slowly back into place and setting it carefully down on the side table.

"Were you expecting someone else?" he asked, tossing his gloves atop his hat.

Rebecca eyed his discarded outerwear. Drat. He meant to stay. And from the look of him, he wasn't going to be easily put off. "I don't know what you mean," she said, turning her back to him. "As you can see I have packing to finish, and so many things to attend to before I can—"

"*You're next*," he said, with such cold, deadly calm, that for a minute she considered reaching for the pistol anew.

She glanced over her shoulder at him. In his hand he held a familiar piece of paper. Then she looked back at the fireplace. How had he . . .

"So, now you've taken to pilfering my private correspondence. That's hardly proper. Why I should—"

"It's too late to be worried about what's proper, Miss Tate. If you'd seen what I saw today, you wouldn't be agonizing about what to pack but rather would be locked in the cellar with the colonel's cannon at the ready."

She cringed. So he'd seen Harrington. The village had been abuzz all day over the major's murder. Not an hour earlier, the Misses Gadbury and Sydney had been over to relay the details of Harrington's grisly murder, so she knew Rafe wasn't being facetious.

"*Dios*, I feared I'd lost you when Mahesh translated this for me." Then he strode across the room and caught her in his arms.

Rebecca tried to breathe as the heat of his hands seared through the thin muslin of her gown and sent tremors of longing through her limbs. And as he stared down into her eyes she thought she was going to drown.

"Why didn't you tell me?" he asked, his voice choked with emotion she couldn't fathom why he possessed. At least not when it came to her. And yet . . . the way he looked at her made her hope. Made her believe . . .

He pushed back the loose strands of her unruly hair. She thought he was going to kiss her, but instead he asked, "What is in London that you think is going to save you?"

Rebecca's mouth fell open, and then just as quickly, snapped shut. Damn him. He was too smart by half. He must have realized she'd agreed only too readily to go to London, to give up her writing.

"Silence, Miss Tate? How uncharacteristic of you," he said, pulling her closer. "Demmit, Rebecca, you cannot stop this yourself. And whether you like it or not, you need me. If you'd only told me the truth, I might have—"

"Stopped Harrington's murder?"

The question came from the doorway, where her uncle stood, tall and ramrod straight.

Rebecca sprang from Rafe's grasp, embarrassed to be caught so.

Her uncle cocked a brow at the pair of them, and then marched into the room. "Mr. Danvers, you couldn't have helped Harrington even if you'd known the truth. Stubborn fool that he was, he was always convinced he could protect himself."

"Colonel Posthill, sir," Rafe said. "My apologies, sir, for—"

"Never mind," the colonel said. "I'm glad you're here, and glad to see why." He smiled at Rebecca. "Go fetch a tea tray, Bex. Mr. Danvers and I have much to discuss." He took his chair by the fire, and motioned for Rafe to take the one opposite. Once Rafe was seated, he continued, "You couldn't have prevented this morning's tragedy. Harrington placed himself on that path years ago." The colonel shook his head. "But you may be able to save Rebecca."

"Uncle, you aren't well," she said, rushing forward, and grabbing his arm to lead him from the room like the invalid he was supposed to be.

He shook her free. "No, Bex. No longer. It is time we told someone of our plight. Found someone to help us." He turned to Rafe. "My apologies, sir, for my earlier displays. I fear my behavior was part of a ruse Rebecca and I have been using for years, the purpose of which was to keep us out of the deadly game that took Codlin's life, and now Harrington's."

Rafe's gaze flew from the colonel to Rebecca and back to the colonel, his dark eyes narrowed to a dangerous pair of midnight slits. "You aren't—"

"Ramshackled? Addled? Around the bend?" Her uncle grinned. "Only when it suits me."

Rafe glanced at Rebecca and she nodded, albeit reluctantly.

"Do you know who murdered them?" he asked her uncle.

The colonel shook his head. "No. I wish I did. It would certainly make the job ahead easier."

Rebecca felt the sting of tears fill her eyes. For so long she and her uncle had hid behind a web of deceit and lies to protect themselves and now the colonel was handing this man their very lives.

"Uncle, don't say another word. Don't tell him anything. How can we trust him on such a short acquaintance?"

"Because we don't have a choice, my dear girl."

"We don't even know him, sir," Rebecca was saying.

Rafe watched the byplay between niece and uncle, still a little amazed to discover that the colonel possessed his wits and had been able to fool so many people. Himself included.

Colonel Posthill sat up straight. "I saw enough last night to tell me that we can trust him. That we need him. Now more than ever." Level and calm, his voice held none of the frantic timber from the night before. In fact the only evidence of the evening's escapade was the shining bruise ringing the colonel's eye.

Rebecca shook her head. "He means to take away everything from us. Our means, our livelihood—"

"I would never—" Rafe began, but he stopped as the colonel raised his hand.

"No need to explain, Mr. Danvers. Whatever reasons brought you here to Bramley Hollow, I believe they have changed, haven't they?" His chin tipped up.

The man was astute as well. Obviously his fall from grace hadn't been for incompetence, or mental failings as had been asserted the night before, but for something else.

Something that had killed Codlin and Harrington,

and was now, Rafe would bet, determined to see Posthill gain the same grisly fate.

And the colonel was right about another thing. Rafe's reasons had changed.

"If you need my help, sir, you have but only to ask," Rafe told him.

The man nodded. "You've already started helping us, by arranging our travels to London."

"What is in London?" Rafe asked.

The colonel looked up at Rebecca and nodded at her.

She crossed her arms over her chest, determined and stubborn to the last. But when he nodded a second time at her, she sighed and said, "A chance to find the same thing the murderer is looking for—the Kailash ruby."

"A gemstone? This is all about a jewel?" Rafe asked, incredulous.

"A very valuable ruby," she said.

"But never forget, it is protected by a curse," the colonel added. "He who disturbs the goddess of Kailash and her dowry shall never know a moment's peace."

Rebecca's gaze rolled upward and she shook her head.

Rafe had no doubts as to her opinion on the subject—a curse was the least of their worries.

"Pay no heed to my niece's skepticism," the colonel said. "Her father was the same way. Wouldn't listen to me when I warned him that not all treasures merit pursuing."

"Uncle, that ruby is worth a fortune," Rebecca said. "And it was just sitting there for the taking."

"But at what price, Bex?" he shot back. "How many lives have been lost to gain it?"

Rebecca crossed her arms over her chest and frowned.

"Perhaps you should tell me what happened, sir," Rafe suggested, gauging that this was an old argument and not one that was going to be settled now. "From the beginning."

The colonel nodded. "Yes, I suppose you want to hear the story. That is the best place to start." He sat back in his chair, his brow wrinkled. "I was never a very successful military man. My uncle bought my commission for me and sent me out to make my fortune. I would have been much better suited for the Church, but my family had always sent a son into the King's service and I was the designated representative."

Rafe nodded in understanding. He'd been tossed out of the Navy and the Army, trying to live up to the Danvers' heritage of serving England.

"But despite my failures in the field, that didn't stop me from learning wherever I went, studying myths and legends and languages. Fascinating stories. Did you know there is rumored to be an island in the West Indies where a Portuguese sea captain hid a bounty of gold and gems that is just waiting to be discovered?"

"Uncle," Rebecca interjected, "the Kailash ruby please, not your speculations on other lost treasures."

"Practical chit!" the colonel complained to Rafe. "Thinks all my work and research are just fool's errands. Now where was I?"

"The ruby," Rafe prompted.

"Ah, yes, the Kailash. The ruby of eternal life. It is said that if you can swallow it, you will be protected from your enemies for all time."

Rafe grimaced. "That's why Codlin and Harrington were split open."

The colonel nodded. "Looking for the ruby, the desperate fellow."

Rebecca shuddered. "Swallowing it! What sort of fool would swallow a priceless gem?"

Rafe resisted the urge to smile at her. He had to admire her mercantile heart even in the face of danger.

"Yes, well," the colonel began, "Rebecca's father, Philip, sailed to India with the intention of discovering it. At first I must confess I shared his enthusiasm for locating it, but now I realize the entire plan was folly."

"And no mere legend," Rafe said.

The colonel smiled. "No. It was real. And even after Philip died of fever, Richard and Rebecca and I continued his search."

"It took nearly three years to locate it," Rebecca said. "And then when we were just about to mount an expedition, all our notes and research were *lost*."

There was something about the way she said it that made the word sound more like an accusation. And apparently it was.

"Richard and I were deceived," her uncle said in his defense.

"Yes, with a cask of Madeira and poor judgment," Rebecca shot back.

"We needed money to finance the expedition," the colonel explained. "Richard had a talent for cards—"

"Harrumph." Rebecca crossed her arms over her chest.

"As I was saying," the colonel continued, "Richard had a talent for cards and thought he could win enough to hire the drivers and supplies we would need."

"Was this game with Harrington and Codlin?" Rafe asked.

Rebecca nodded. "And another man named Mayne."

"Where's he?" Rafe asked.

The colonel shook his head.

"Dead," Rebecca offered. "Killed a few weeks later trying to leave Calcutta with the ruby."

Rafe shook his head. "So if all three of them are dead, then who is still seeking the ruby?"

"We don't know," she confessed.

"So back to this card game, you suspect they cheated you?" Rafe asked.

"Most decidedly," the colonel complained. "Plied us both with liquor and then when I was incapacitated—which mind you, had never happened before—"

There was another loud "harrumph" from Rebecca.

"They stole our notes," the colonel said, "all our research, including the map I had just finished piecing together from various local legends."

"Then what happened?" Rafe asked.

"The worst thing imaginable," Rebecca said. "The lot of them went and stole the demmed thing."

The colonel huffed. "If they had bothered to read my research they would have known that they simply couldn't ride into the temple and take the ruby. But no one bothers to read the critical details."

"So did they or didn't they steal the ruby?" Rafe asked.

"Oh, they stole it," Rebecca said. "Murdered the temple scribes and pillaged more than their fare share of the place and then rode off."

"But," the colonel said, "they hadn't counted on the temple guards."

Rebecca picked up the thread and continued the story.

"We were awoken just after dawn by the shouts. Our outpost was under attack. The fools had led the temple guard right back to the outpost."

"I was still at the officer's mess, working on—"

Rebecca coughed.

"Well, perhaps I was sleeping there. It was better than returning home and having a peal rung over my head."

"To say the least," Rebecca muttered.

"Suddenly I was in charge, but luckily for us, Lieutenant Habersham was also there. He was able to rally the men and we drove the angry fellows back into the dust and hills."

Habersham? He glanced over at Rebecca to find her cheeks rising in color and her face turned away from him. "And the trio?" he asked, holding back his curiosity about this other fellow.

"Harrington claimed that Mayne was killed, but I later found out that he had gained the ruby and continued on downriver, making for Calcutta. He'd promised Harrington and Codlin their cut if they'd just declare him dead and lost."

"But that wasn't the end of it," Rafe said.

Posthill shook his head. "We were recalled to Calcutta for an inquiry. Two other outposts were attacked as a result of the ruby being stolen. Worse still, the East India Company was losing money right and left with trade being interrupted, though they weren't about to admit any wrongdoing by Codlin and Mayne."

"And the ruby?" Rafe prodded.

"Not to be found," the colonel told him. "Richard and I began searching high and low through Calcutta for Mayne, as were Harrington and Codlin."

"But to no avail," Rebecca said. "Then Richard disappeared one night."

"Disappeared?" Rafe asked.

"Aye," the colonel said. "He heard a rumor of an Englishman trying to book passage on the sly to England, and went down to the docks to catch him."

"What happened then, we aren't too sure," Rebecca said. "But Richard later wrote us that he had managed to gain the ruby from Mayne, and had taken his place on the ship. Once here, he sent word that the ruby was well hidden."

"But you never discovered where?"

"No," Rebecca said. "The next thing we knew, he'd joined a regiment and shipped out for Spain."

"And so you two returned to England as well," Rafe said.

"Yes," the colonel said. "After the debacle with the ruby, I was given the opportunity to retire and retain my half-pay. Not that I minded. It freed my time for my studies."

"But what about the others, Harrington and Codlin?" Rafe asked.

"They were furious," Rebecca said, continuing the tale. "They were convinced we knew where the ruby was and were returning to claim it from Richard. They vowed to gain their share if we ever discovered it."

"So what happened next?"

"On our trip home, uncle was struck by a fever," she said. "He was desperately ill, ranting and raving, and everyone was so afraid of it spreading, that they left us completely alone."

"So you decided to continue the charade," Rafe said, nodding with approval. "And keep society at arm's length."

The colonel snapped his fingers. "Exactly. I was no threat to anyone if I was completely out of my mind. And as long as everyone believed I was incapable of continuing the search for the ruby, there would be no need to seek us out."

"But Harrington did," Rafe noted.

"Yes. He moved his family here about a year ago, setting himself up like a country gentleman. I think he hoped he would catch me on a lucid day and learn where the Kailash was hidden."

"So you kept him at sixes and sevens," Rafe said.

"Yes. Deuced hard. Harrington was no fool. You don't know how often I've wanted to tell him what I thought of him."

Rafe laughed. "I think you did a demmed good job last night."

"Suppose I did. If that isn't proof that the thing is cursed, I don't know what is. Harrington was a sensible enough fellow until he got hold of it, and look how he ended." The colonel shook his head. "When we find it, it is going back where it belongs."

"Uncle—" Rebecca's voice rang with a warning.

"Not another word, Bex. That dashed thing has wreaked enough havoc. It is going back to the safety of the temple and that is the end of it."

"You mean to return it?" Rafe asked, looking from the colonel to Rebecca.

She nodded, albeit reluctantly, for her uncle's sake. However, the moment he glanced away, she shook her head and mouthed an emphatic, *No.*

"So if you have avoided society, why is it that you are so eager to go to London?" he asked. "It certainly isn't discreet to go to town and make a showy Season."

The colonel and Rebecca exchanged glances that spoke more than if they had shared their confidence out loud.

"The ruby is in London?" he asked. If it were in London, then the killer wouldn't be far behind, and then it would be easy to set a trap and . . .

But Rebecca and her uncle weren't all that forthcoming.

"Well, is it?" he asked.

The colonel opened his mouth to reply, but Rebecca furiously shook her head.

"There is a murderer loose," Rafe said, more to the colonel since obviously Rebecca was of another mind. Demmit, why wouldn't she trust him?

Perhaps because you kiss her senseless one moment, and suggest she go to town to find a husband the next . . .

"I mean to catch this villain," Rafe told them, ignoring the other conflicts he was battling. "Will you or won't you help me bring him to justice?"

"Of course we will help you," the colonel said. "In fact—"

"Oh, no you don't," Rebecca burst out. "Don't tell him another thing."

"Why ever not?" Rafe and the colonel asked at the same time.

"The reward," she said in an aside to her uncle.

"Ah, yes. The money." The colonel let out a long suffering sigh and then shrugged at Rafe.

Rebecca's gaze narrowed like a seasoned gamester. "Half."

"Half of what?" he asked.

"Half of the reward that the Company is offering for helping you find this fiend."

So this is what it was all about. The reward. Rebecca wasn't just a practical minx, but a bloody mercenary. Though he had to admire her brass and audacity—for he'd do the same thing—but half? Was she out of her mind?

"No," he told her.

"No?" she asked.

He crossed his arms over his chest. "No. That reward is mine." Besides, once he got done reconciling his outstanding debts, putting a sum away for Cochrane, there would barely be half left.

Not to mention that he'd started considering putting some of the Company's money to work on Bettlesfield Park. Fix it up a bit in case he decided to keep it.

Rebecca rose and crossed the room to the study door, opening it and pointing at the hall. "Then good day, sir. We've given you enough free advice."

The colonel looked ready to say something, but she shot him a hot glance and he snapped his mouth shut and gave Rafe another sympathetic shrug.

"Why of all the high-handed, blackmailing—" Rafe spat out.

"Do you really want to discuss high-handed methods?"

Demmit, it wasn't like he'd twisted her arm or anything remotely high-handed. Why he'd offered her a fair trade to quit writing and she'd agreed to it.

Despite his moral indignation, a twinge of guilt rifled down his spine. For he knew the truth—she'd had no choice.

She stood in the doorway, staring at him, unblinking.

Her brother and uncle should have let her play that fateful game of chance. They would have had no need to go chasing fortunes—Rebecca would have cleaned out the lot of them.

But now she was gambling with her life, though you couldn't tell that from her steady, unwavering gaze. Azure eyes capable of piercing his very soul.

Dios, the woman was going to be the end of him. And damn her, she knew he'd capitulate. Knew he was as determined to catch the killer and claim the reward with a steely determination so very like her own.

She knew him better than he did himself, for she was willing to bet that he wouldn't leave her unprotected.

And demmit if she wasn't right.

"Fine," he said. "Ten percent."

She laughed, and the twinkle in her eyes told him she knew only too well she had him on tenterhooks.

"Twenty five," he said, regretting the offer even as he made it.

She yawned and glanced down at her nails.

"Thirty five," he said through gritted teeth. That would still leave just enough for his debts and Cochrane's share.

"Done," she told him. "And we get to keep the ruby."

"Thieving wench," he muttered.

"Foolish man," she replied. "I would have settled for fifteen."

Chapter 12

It is said that by traveling one will gain a thorough understanding of the world. But no matter how many miles you traverse, I don't think it's possible to gain an inkling of the mysteries that lurk in a man's heart.

Miss Darby to Miss Cecilia Overton
in *Miss Darby's Perilous Journey*

With the deal struck, Rebecca and the colonel told Rafe everything they knew, including their carefully thought out plans to locate Lt. Purcell without drawing too much attention to themselves.

Of course, he objected to everything they wanted to do, stomping around the library and casting his orders out as if he were in charge. Did he truly think she and the colonel had survived this long by sheer luck?

And though she had seethed inside, Rebecca smiled and let him think that she was going to sit idly by while he risked his life to stop the killer.

And find *her* ruby.

Just before darkness fell, Cochrane had arrived with Lady Tottley's reply. The countess's letter had been full of bluster but eventually she'd acquiesced to the offer.

Cochrane, done with his duties, hurried on to Finch Manor for a promised dinner of beef pies.

Rebecca had been sent upstairs to finish her packing, and had gone, albeit reluctantly, for she knew it was futile to protest. Rafe was determined to keep her well out of harm's way, and she was willing to let him think that he was in charge. So she'd left the pair of them to their plotting, while she put the time to good use putting the finishing touches on her own plans.

With the door to her room open, she could hear the pair of them discussing strategies for finding the elusive Lt. Purcell. If they had bothered to ask her, she would have provided a fine list she'd already compiled on the man's previous residences and acquaintances.

She looked down at the gown she had just crumpled into a ball instead of carefully folding and shook it out. Well, it was patently unfair of them not to include her.

Downstairs, she heard her uncle bidding Rafe a good night. Oh, that was the other part of her vexation. He had announced he was spending the night, muttering something about seeing his interests safeguarded.

Spending the night under their roof? Sleeping just downstairs in the library . . . a handful of steps from . . .

Rebecca picked up a pair of slippers and dropped them atop the rest of her jumbled packing. Truthfully, she was ever so thankful to have him in the house. Not that she was going to tell him that.

No, having him here meant her uncle would live to see another day. She didn't imagine any killer, no matter how ruthless, no matter how strong, would stand a chance against Rafe Danvers.

The man's utter mien spoke of unforgiving strength and competence. She'd been in the company of enough officers and soldiers during her tenure in India to know the difference between a man who could stand to the challenge, and those who fled in the face of adversity.

Rafe Danvers stood his ground. She admired such courage, but did he always have to stand his ground against her? Stop, when she wanted him to kiss her until she was senseless, until she understood the whispering need that he left in his skillful wake.

Actually it was his contradictions that had her in such a muddle.

Instead of hearing Rafe make dull statements about "safeguarding his interests," why couldn't he make the declarations her heart longed to hear?

I will not let you risk your life, Miss Tate, for you are more precious to me than life itself.

She paused for a moment in her packing and considered writing that line down for her next *Miss Darby* novel. She was halfway to her desk when she recalled she wasn't supposed to be writing.

"Botheration!" she muttered, flopping down on the corner of her bed. Give up writing, indeed. Who did this Lady Tottley think she was demanding that Rebecca disavow her livelihood? And what about Rafe? What would he say if someone told him to give up his dangerous profession?

He'd fight to the end of his days for his independence, yet take away hers without a second thought, the infuriating rogue.

Her uncle came up the stairs just then, ambling down the hall to his chamber. "Good night to you, Bex," he called as he strolled past.

"Good night, uncle," she replied as she rose to close her door and make her own evening ablutions.

Glancing at her reflection in the mirror, she wondered why it was Rafe called her a "thieving wench" and a "bluestocking" one moment, then arrived today like a knight errant, making his stormy demands to her confused heart?

Could she believe, even dare hope, that he wanted to

protect her, safeguard her for reasons beyond his own financial gain? That the passionate light, the elation of relief that had burned in his eyes when he'd come crashing into the library earlier meant he cared for her?

Could Rafe Danvers actually have fallen in love with her?

She shook her head. It was a ridiculous notion. Men like him didn't fall in love with bookish spinsters who spent their days penning romantic nonsense.

But it wasn't nonsense, her heart clamored. And, as Prince Ranjit had once told Miss Darby, *The heart's desires will always remain a mystery when its secrets go unspoken.*

There was only one way to find out what Rafe's heart wanted, she realized, crossing the room, her trembling fingers tugging the latch open.

Then Rebecca crept down the stairs, hoping she possessed the nerve to reveal her desires.

Rafe spun around when he heard the tapping on the library door.

"Is there anything I can get you, Mr. Danvers?" Rebecca said, poking her pert little nose inside.

"Rafe," he told her, not surprised at all to see her. She'd probably been upstairs for the last hour plotting how best to undo his plans and substitute them with hers.

"Pardon?"

"I thought we'd already discussed that. Call me Rafe."

"Rafe," she said, coming into the room like some shy miss, her back to the bookshelf, her teeth having captured her lower lip.

He found himself thinking about doing the same.

Covering her mouth with his, tugging at her lower lip with his teeth, before he—

"Is something wrong?" she asked, glancing down at her plain, serviceable gown.

"No, nothing, I was just, uh, looking at that book—the one over your shoulder." He came across the room and stood before her. Reaching over her shoulder, he caught up the volume and plucked it from the shelf. "I thought perhaps I might read a bit before I turn in."

"*Antiquities of England: A Traveler's Guide*?" she asked, glancing up and into his eyes. "You're a fan of Mr. Billingsworth? He strikes me as rather dry for someone of your, shall I say, mettle?"

Mettle? She thought he had mettle? That was a fine sight better than arrogant and loutish.

"A new line of study," he told her. He needed to step away, move so he was out of reach of her, but he couldn't.

Fortunately, she did it for him, ducking around him and moving to stand in the middle of the room. "I came down to see if you would like some more tea? Or if you need another coverlet?"

The only coverlet he wanted was her naked body.

Demmit, he needed to stop thinking like that. At least about her. Really, how did one tell a lady like Rebecca that you wanted her in your bed?

Oh, he had no problems getting women in his bed, it was just this lady wasn't, as Jemmy had said, one of his London lightskirts.

No, Rebecca Tate was much more of a challenge, to his heart and to the mettle she seemed to think he possessed. She'd cast a spell on him the moment she'd turned around in the village post office and pinned her skeptical gaze on him.

She made him want to be more than just the man he'd been for far too long.

Arrogant and swaggering. Charming and roguish. Those were accomplishments in themselves and they served him well, but they weren't enough. Not to someone like Rebecca.

It wasn't enough to solve the case, to gain retribution for the wrongs done, now he wanted more. He wanted to see the light of approval in her eyes, he wanted to tell her his thoughts and fears and, yes, his desires.

"Perhaps I should just leave you be," she was saying, slipping past him and heading for the door.

Was it his mistake, or did she sound disappointed?

"More tea would be fine, though I hate to drink alone," he told her hastily. "That is, if you'll join me."

Now what had he done? Invited her to join him?

To his chagrin and delight, she smiled and said, "Yes, that would be lovely. I'll be right back."

Rafe slapped his forehead. *I hate to drink alone.* What was he thinking inviting a tempting spinster to join him in the middle of the night for an innocent cup of tea?

Oh, there was nothing innocent about Rebecca Tate. Just temptation after temptation. And notions of waking up to her restless stirrings and silken kisses.

There was no saving him now. He was going to have to endure an hour or so of polite conversation before he could even consider sending her packing upstairs.

And send her packing he would.

An hour suddenly sounded like a painful lifetime to his thrumming senses.

Or worse, she'd start berating him about her lack of involvement in their plans. Passionate and persuasive, Rebecca at her obstinate best was quite a sight.

No, that was not a good idea, he decided. A passionate Rebecca only made him want to gather her up in his arms and unleash her ardor, stoke it into a blaze he would quench with his own untimely needs.

Glancing over at the long sofa that had been about to become his lonely bed for the night, he envisioned her sprawled across it, naked and inviting, wagging a finger at him to come and join her, to undo the pins from her hair, to . . .

No. No. No, he told himself. *She is your partner in this endeavor, your client.*

From the kitchen the telltale sound of the kettle hissing told him he hadn't much time to shore up his defenses.

Rafe paced the room, searching for safe topics of conversation.

The weather. Yes, that was it.

Hasn't it been rather warm of late, Miss Tate?

Too hot, she might say, tugging at her bodice in hopes of catching a hint of the evening breeze fluttering through the window. The type of hot night that called for cool cotton sheets on which to lay one's sweaty, sated body after hours spent making love.

Rafe raked his fingers through his hair. That didn't seem such a proper subject of conversation. Why was it then that everyone always suggested discussing the weather as a safe topic?

He needed to find something that wouldn't excite any passions. Maybe he could tell her about some of his cases.

She'll think you're bragging. Or worse, you'll frighten her.

No lady needed to hear the details of his work—they certainly weren't a fit subject for delicate ears.

In the kitchen something hit the floor, breaking into a thousand pieces, and he swung around, wondering if she was hurt. The crash was followed by a very unladylike curse.

A curse no lady should ever have heard, let alone use.

He grinned. Perhaps he could give her the restrained version of his life. Knowing Rebecca she'd want to hear about his work, his life in Spain, his escapades as a guerilla, probably even his long history of expulsion from every school in England for imprudent use of cannons.

After a few minutes of sorting through his repertoire of stories and discarding most of them as generally unsuitable, she arrived with a laden tray in hand.

Looking at the mound of provisions, he wondered if she ever planned on going to bed.

Maybe not, he found himself wishing against his better judgment. He sat down warily on one end of the sofa.

Rebecca settled the tray on the low table before him and sat down on the other. Primly folding her hands in her lap, she looked up at him and said, "Tell me what you like in a woman."

Rafe blanched. "Pardon?"

"Well," she said. "What do you think I'd want to discuss in the middle of the night? The weather?"

So much for his theories on female delicacies.

She plunked three lumps of sugar into his tea, without asking. Not that he minded, but he couldn't help but wonder how she knew he liked his tea sweet?

"Can we talk about something else?" he asked, accepting the cup and shifting in his seat, wishing there was another foot or so on the couch to separate them.

She shook her head. "No. I want to hear about what type of ladies you like. Do you have a mistress? Have you had more than one?" She scoffed at that. "My apologies, you've probably had dozens of mistresses. What is it about a lady that makes you want to give her your *carte-blanche*?"

Rafe had chosen that moment to take a sip from the scalding liquid and spewed it all over the sofa. "My wha-a-a-t?"

"Your *carte-blanche*, your protection," she paused, a blush stealing up her cheeks. "Your bed."

She should be blushing, the shameless wench.

He set down his cup. "Miss Tate—"

"Rebecca," she admonished, easing closer to him on the sofa.

"Miss Tate," he said, unwilling to yield an inch to her. He would stand his ground or be lost forever. "I hardly think my private life is a proper subject for examination."

She tipped her cup up to her lips and said over the rim, "And what would be proper, Rafe?"

Rebecca Tate flirting? He was in trouble now. If not from her batting lashes, then gads, there were once again her bare toes wiggling enticingly from beneath her hem.

Bare toes? That was only the merest step from bare limbs . . . Didn't this woman own a pair of shoes?

Rafe set his cup down. He needed to take control of this conversation quickly, before it got out of toes . . . no, hand.

"Perhaps we could discuss your Season," he suggested. "I understand the plays being offered this year are quite good."

She glanced upward, as if asking the heavens how he had ever acquired a reputation as a rogue. "Fine. My Season, if you insist," she agreed.

Too readily, he thought, wary already.

"Tell me about the debutantes this year," she said. "How do they compare to years past? Do you think I'll fit in?"

"You?" he stammered. "Fit in?" He managed a short laugh.

"What is so funny about that?" She set down her teacup, her hands balling into fists at her sides.

"For one thing you aren't like any of the other misses and ladies in London." He'd meant it as a compliment, but from her outraged moue he realized she might not have taken it so.

"I may be a bit older than the other young ladies, but I don't see what about me is so different."

Everything, he wanted to tell her. From her outspoken manners to her infuriating self-reliance to her bluestocking sensibilities. She wore her scandalous notions and opinions out on her sleeve for all to see, while a proper London miss would have been doing her damnedest to hide such unwanted ideas.

How could she not see that? It was what he loved most about her.

Loved. Rafe tried to draw a breath, but his chest seemed locked in a panic. In love with Rebecca Tate? It couldn't be.

"—and I intend to in London," she was saying.

"Do what?" he asked.

"Fit in," she insisted. "I intend to take full advantage of Lady Tottley's offer and use this Season to find a husband."

A husband? Over his dead body. Not when he . . . "I thought you were going to London to find the ruby," he pointed out.

"Of course I want to find the ruby, for it should make a nice dowry, don't you think? Besides, I have you to thank for all this, because it was your idea."

"Well, yes. I mean no." She would have to bring that up.

"No what?" she asked, a wry smile on her lips.

"Well, you can't marry," he said, a little too adamantly.

"Why ever not?" Her eyes twinkled slightly, capturing his heart.

Oh, he was lost. "What I mean is that I thought your desire for a Season was just a ploy. To find the ruby. To gain your fortune . . ." His arguments trailed off as he saw the resolve in her eyes.

She truly intended to marry.

"I must," she whispered.

"Why?" It came out as a plea. *Don't marry someone, Rebecca. Please don't do this. Not when I . . .*

"Because, Rafe, unlike you, I must marry. Especially if we never find the ruby."

He had no one to blame for his dismay other than himself. Wasn't it his demands that had put her on this path?

To stop writing in exchange for a Season. And that is why young ladies had a Season, to find a husband. She would go to London and find another source of income, another form of indenturement. Only this one was marriage.

And when she did find a man, which he had no doubts the practical and efficient Rebecca would, Rafe would have to let her go, walk away from a job well done, satisfied that he had done what had been promised.

She smiled at him, then shifted back to her original subject. "So if I don't fit in with the ladies in town, what about the men? Do you know any who might make a good husband? I want to find a respectable man, a man who'll appreciate my bluestocking ways, a man who doesn't mind if I don't fit in." Rebecca sat up straight, her hands folded primly in her lap. "I've always thought I would make a good vicar's wife. Vicars are usually very patient and quite sensible."

A vicar? Here he had thought the colonel's suggestion the other night had been another of the man's ravings, not any indication of the lady's true desires. Now he laughed until tears streamed down his cheeks. "You? With a vicar?"

"And why not?" she said.

"Because, well, because—"

She sat there, a picture of passionate outrage and everything a vicar didn't need in his scholarly, respectable life.

But she was everything *he* needed, and as he made that realization, it felt as if the earth beneath him had shifted, his equilibrium lost. As if he was standing on a precipice, like the one in his dream, only he was the one at the edge and she was there to coax him to safety. A crossroads of sorts, like the old matchmaker had told him.

And if he didn't choose wisely, he may never have another chance.

"Oh, hell," he said. "Over my dead body you'll marry some nearsighted old vicar." Then he caught her in his arms and began to kiss her.

She protested with one short "mew" until she opened her only-too-opinionated mouth to him and responded with an eagerness that met his own.

If Miss Tate had a crossroads, Rafe guessed she'd just leapt over hers with heady enthusiasm and no regrets.

His fingers found her breast, rolling over the nipple back and forth until it was hard and full. He deepened his kiss until she was moaning, pressing her body against his.

And when she was panting with need, clinging to him like a tigress, and begging him in a breathless voice, "Love me, Rafe. Love me now," he set her aside.

"That's why," he told her.

"Why what?" she gasped, tossing aside her tangled hair. Her eyes blazed with desire. A fire he intended to slake, but not until he'd made his point.

"Your vicar would be in for a surprise when you arrived in his bed and made your demands. Your very passionate, unspinsterly demands. You don't want to marry a vicar."

She bit her lip and frowned at him. "How do you know what I want?"

"I know," he said. And proceeded to prove his point as no vicar ever would.

Love me, Rafe. Love me now.

What the devil was she saying?

Oh, I've fallen into it now, Rebecca thought, as Rafe caught her once again in his grasp and tugged her up against him.

Giving herself to this man she barely knew? Didn't trust.

Loved so very much. It was madness, delirium.

It was heaven.

When she considered Miss Darby's romantic dreams of a tender kiss and an appreciative glance from her Lt. Throckmorton, Rebecca realized she had cheated her poor heroine, her readers. Tender kisses and appreciative glances be damned, and that honorable and insufferable Lt. Throckmorton as well.

Rafe's fingers wound into her hair, pulling her few remaining pins free and teasing it loose with his fingers until it fell unruly and untamed down past her shoulders.

He held her in place, refusing to give quarter, demanding and taking from her as if it were his due.

And she was more than willing to give herself to him—for she suspected he was the only man who could cool the fire spreading down from her gut and into a place so intimate, so demanding.

He hauled her closer, her breasts pressing against that wall of strength that was his chest, and she felt her nipples respond in kind, hardening and rising in ruddy peaks, aching for his touch.

He answered her silent plea. Masterfully, he undid her bodice, freed her breasts from her corset.

It obviously wasn't the first time he'd undressed a lady, and instead of being piqued, she was thankful for his skill.

In her current state, she doubted she could have done such a good job.

Then his lips left her mouth, if but for a few moments, before he claimed one of her breasts, sucking and lapping at one then the other until their pebbled peaks ached.

"Oh, Rafe, what have you done to me?"

"I haven't even begun," he promised.

Rebecca sighed. *Take me,* her heart clamored with a trembling beat, as her fingers uncurled from the folds of his shirt to splay over his chest and tug at the white linen in hopes she could remove it with as much finesse.

Instead she ripped it.

"Oh, dear me," she sputtered, looking at the torn seam. "Did I do that?"

"Miss Tate, you surprise me." Then he grinned and ripped it the rest of the way, until it was tossed aside.

Her mouth fell open as she surveyed the muscled expanse spread out before her eager hands. She wanted to touch him. To claim him, as he was claiming her.

She glanced up and found his dark gaze devouring her, like a moonless night, pitch black and so very dangerous.

That abyss excited her, teased her, drew her into nameless temptations.

Take me. Please, take me.

As she arched toward him, urging him on, he slipped his hand beneath her breast, cupping it for a moment. Then he made a low noise, like a growl, and it brought her no small measure of satisfaction to know that she excited him.

His thumb found her nipple and he rolled his finger over it, teasing circles that left her weak in the knees. He bent her back over the sofa, his bare chest towering over her. She clung to him as he kissed her, his lips teasing hers, leaving a trail of passion from her mouth, down her neck, to the curve of her shoulder.

A log in the fireplace sputtered, sending crackling sparks upward. She now understood what it was like to be on fire, to feel as if one's body might combust—for she wanted him to take her and suckle her, to tease her breasts and send those tangled threads of passion spiraling through her limbs yet again.

The ones that left her begging.

"Rebecca," he whispered, his voice thick with need, "I want you. All of you." His confession emboldened her. The light in his eyes pleaded for her acquiescence while his fingers plied at her gown.

She knew only too well what he wanted. Her naked and beneath him. Oh, and she wanted him just the same. Naked, over her, in her.

In her?

The thought was followed by a ripple of panic. The

practical Rebecca wondered if a spinster had any business having such thoughts.

And as Rafe pulled her gown over her head, unlaced her corset and consigned it to the farthest corner of the room, and she was all-too-quickly naked before him, all her maidenly fears came to the forefront, overshadowing her unfamiliar wantonness.

"You are so beautiful," he whispered.

What had he said? She was so beautiful?

Perhaps her passion-enthralled senses had left her hearing muddled. *Beautiful?*

"I am?" she whispered in disbelief.

"Oh, yes," he said with a nod and a lascivious grin on his lips that suggested his hunger went well beyond kisses. His fingers reached up and pulled a strand of her hair down so it fell over her breast. "Your hair is like heaven, as soft as silk." His nose nudged the tendril out of the way and he sought out her breasts again.

She closed her eyes and sighed.

"*Dios, mi ángel*, where have you been hiding these? Never wear that corset again." He paused. "No, do wear it. I don't want any other man to know what he is missing."

She laughed, languid and glowing beneath his praise. Until he dipped his head lower, laying a trail of kisses down past her stomach to her thighs.

"Oooh," she managed to gasp, catching hold of his shoulders as his fingers tenderly parted her fevered flesh and his tongue darted forth to savor that place. "Oooh, Rafe," she gasped as he started to lap at her. Her breath caught in her throat, her world began to spin out of control.

"You taste like something forbidden," he murmured. "Sweet and forbidden."

"No, don't," she gasped.

"No?" he asked, glancing up at her.

"No, don't stop," she pleaded, her legs falling open, her hands pulling him closer.

He laughed, his breath hot and steamy. Then he continued, stroking her, teasing her. And when she thought she couldn't stand it any longer, he pressed a finger inside her, easing her open. He moved it gently, but she was past that. She needed more.

"Oh, please, Rafe, please save me from this madness."

His tongue flicked over that sensitive point, over and over, until her insides coiled so tight, she thought she'd burst from longing, her hips rising to meet each stroke.

Then all of a sudden . . . like the sparks in the fire, she combusted, a fire erupting inside her. Spasms of release coursed through her limbs and she writhed and shuddered with pleasure.

"Oh, Rafe," she panted, grasping for him as she fell from the dizzy heights to which he'd carried her.

He caught her and held her close, kissing her, teasing her still with his gentle touch.

Breathless, she looked up at him. "Oh, my!"

He laughed, a sound that spoke of his own pleasure in her pleasure. "Did you like that?"

"Oh, yes," she whispered.

"I wanted to see you well pleased."

"I am," she laughed. "But what of you? I think you deserve your pleasure as well."

And she reached up and caught his strong, rugged jaw in her hands and pulled him toward her for a daring kiss.

Rafe didn't think his body could get any harder, but when Rebecca caught hold of him and hauled him down atop her, her legs winding around his thighs, he thought he would burst with need.

Need for her, his tempting little spinster.

He wanted nothing more than to bury himself inside her and stroke this madness, release this fire from his veins. To feel her body arch and rock as she reached her climax.

He wanted to hear her call out for him again, to plead with him. For her cries, her needs, only echoed his own.

And despite being spent and sated moments before, she was alive with desire once again—her nipples taut and pressed to his chest, her hands combing over his shoulders, down over his body to his breeches. Impatient and greedy, she tugged at his waistband.

And she called him reckless!

"How do you get these off?" she complained.

Helping her, he loosened them, and to his surprise and delight, she finished the task, tugging them free and tossing them aside, a victorious and hungry light in her eyes.

If he'd had any second thoughts, any fears for her maidenly delicacies, they were forgotten as he watched her gaze at him with a mixture of awe, and then longing.

She glanced up at him and smiled, sly and feminine, like a cat ready to seize her prey.

And take him she did, with her hands at first, caressing him, as he had her, running her fingers up and down his length in tantalizing strokes.

"You'll unman me doing that," he gasped, his body taut, the familiar rising rush of his climax starting to rob him of his senses. "No," he told her, taking her hands away. "I want to be inside you. I want to feel you around me."

Rebecca grinned and stretched beneath him, her

thighs opening, her legs tangling with his, pulling him closer. "Come to me, Rafe. Fill me."

He kissed her first, letting his tongue lap at her, tease her. He stroked her breasts, loving the feel of their response, of the soft moans that escaped her at his touch.

Reaching down further, his fingers delved into her honeyed center, opening her up, delving inside her still trembling flesh, teasing her back to a feverish pitch.

Only too quickly she was ready for him again, as he was for her.

"Please, Rafe," she whispered. "Love me."

It was all the encouragement he needed. He poised himself over her, and looked down at her trusting gaze.

Then it struck him. Such doe-eyed innocence meant only one thing.

Rebecca was a virgin.

"I shouldn't be doing this," he stammered. Widows and mistresses were one thing, but virgins? He avoided them at all costs. The price was far too high.

"Rafe, please," she whispered. "I know what this means, and I want to be with you."

"But—"

"Ssh," she told him, putting a finger to his lips, her hand moving to stroke his brow. "I want you so very much."

And he wanted her. More than he'd ever wanted any woman. But what left him bowled over wasn't her trust in him, or her faith that he would do the right thing, but that he wanted her not just for this night, but for the rest of his.

"This may hurt," he told her, still more than a little taken aback by the revelation that left him stunned.

He wanted her, wanted her always.

"I know," she whispered, now with a hint of impatience to her voice. "But right now, I need you ever so much. Please."

Rafe gave in to her demands. He'd never known a moment so freeing as the one when he pressed himself inside her, felt her body enclose him, felt his desire run hotter than he'd ever thought possible. He filled her quickly, pressing past the slight hesitation of her barrier, and only stopping when he was all the way inside her.

She had winced as he'd breached her, but now with him buried inside her, she rocked against him restlessly, clawing at his shoulders. "Oh, again," she pleaded.

He drew himself out, slowly, enjoying the feeling of her as he slid free from her captivity, and then just before he slipped loose, he drove himself in again.

This time, she cried out, the pleasure of her cries like the hail of trumpets to his desires. She called his name, she pleaded with him to go deeper, go harder, her hips rising to meet him until her body tensed and then shuddered around him, devouring his control and wrenching his own release from him like a torrent of cannon fire.

He continued to stroke her through her crowning, trying to prolong every surging peak that raged between them.

"Rebecca," he gasped. "Oh, Rebecca."

They collapsed together on the sofa. The few candles in the room now burned down to shallow stubs, bathing their naked and entwined bodies in shadowy wavers of light.

The garden window was open and a soft breeze fluttered through the curtains, the gentle wind cooling their heated flesh.

After some time, Rafe leaned up and looked down

at her. "There will be no more talk of vicars, do you hear me?"

"Yes, Rafe," she promised, drawing him back down into her arms. "No more vicars."

And then to prove his point, he loved her again.

Chapter 13

Forgetting the past is as difficult as realizing you've mismatched your gloves. Why, no one forgets mismatched gloves.

Miss Cecilia Overton to Miss Darby
in *Miss Darby's Perilous Journey*

Rebecca wandered downstairs the next morning, nervous and anxious. What had she done? Gone and given herself to Rafe Danvers like a foolish nit. Hardly practical in the brimming sunshine of a May morning.

But it hadn't been just foolery. It had been glorious. And if she never gained his attentions again, at least she knew what it felt like to be loved.

Loved? How easy it was to believe such things in the intimate, lonely midnight hours.

She paused at the foot of the stairs, perched on the last step, her hand clutching at the post. Could a man like Rafe really fall in love with her?

Oh, who was she to compete with the best coquettes and flirts in town? What did she have that would spark any man's attention?

Your hair is like heaven . . . Where have you been hiding these . . . You taste like something forbidden . . .

Rebecca's cheeks warmed as she remembered Rafe's words.

Her practical side told her those were just the phrases a man told a woman to gain what he wanted.

But Rafe already had everything he could want from her. Her identity as the *Miss Darby* author. Her help in finding Sir Rodney's murderer.

So could she dare believe that he had been trying to gain her love? She bit her lip and wondered what one said to a man you'd just spent the night with? Making wild, passionate love, until he'd carried her spent and exhausted up to her own virginal, narrow bed and kissed her softly as she'd drifted into an exhausted sleep.

In the kitchen her uncle was speaking to someone. With Mrs. Wortling gone and his deception out in the open, at least before Rafe, he was obviously talking with someone other than the imaginary Trotter who had been his faithful ensign all these years.

Rebecca suspected the colonel would miss the poor beleaguered lad. She knew she would.

She strained to hear Rafe's deep voice, struggling at the same time to gather together enough nerve to face him.

And why shouldn't I be able to face him? she asked herself, rallying her failing courage like a regiment of untried recruits.

It wasn't as if *she* had anything to hide.

A wicked little voice inside her laughed. *It isn't like he hasn't seen every part of you.*

She cringed and wished she hadn't thought of that. She went pink from the top of her head to the tips of her toes and in all the places in between that Rafe had explored with explicit detail.

Finally, she discerned that the second voice in the kitchen belonged to Rafe's assistant, Cochrane. So where was Rafe? She turned around to go take a peek in the library, when something ran between her legs.

"Oh dear, oh my," she cried out, as her feet tangled with Ajax, who yowled in protest. His indignant meow seemed to say that he was only offering her a good morning caress and there was no need to trod all over him in return.

"Ah, Rebecca, there you are," the colonel called out. "Thought I was going to have to fire off the cannon to get you to arise. Can you manage a bit of tea and eggs for Mr. Cochrane here? He's a might peckish."

The boy nodded enthusiastically.

She smiled and gathered up the kettle and settled it over the fire. "Where is Mr. Danvers?" she asked as innocently as she could.

"Danvers?" the colonel said. "Gone to fetch Lady Finch's carriage."

"He'll be back presently, miss," Cochrane said.

"Noisy fellow," the colonel complained. "Rattled about the library last night until all hours."

She cringed and tried to maintain her composure. That is until a knock on the door brought her attention straight up.

Rafe.

She bit her lip again, and this time looked down at her gown. She'd never been one to worry overmuch about what she wore, but suddenly this morning, she wished she had a new muslin to wear, for she felt like a regular dowd in her old bombazine.

Botheration, she sounded as silly and impractical as Charlotte Harrington and Lady Victoria, fussing over ribbons and laces.

Still, she couldn't help wonder what Rafe would say when he saw her with her soon-to-be-had town polish and silks?

Take them off, she thought wickedly and hopefully as she flung the front door wide open.

"We're all packed and ready, dear Miss Tate!"

Standing on the steps before her were Miss Alminta and Miss Honora, dressed in identical traveling gowns. It if hadn't been for their bonnets, Miss Alminta trimmed in blue, Honora in red, it would be nearly impossible to tell them apart.

And out in the road, sat a grinning Sydney Kitling, decked out in a bottle green great coat and tall beaver hat, whip in hand, his phaeton and matched set ready for the journey. Filling the tiger's seat to overflowing was a collection of small trunks and valises.

"What is all this?" Rebecca asked, fearful of the answer.

Alminta's words from the other day returned like a warning. *My dear, you can't travel to town unescorted. You need a proper chaperone.*

"We've decided to join you," Honora was saying, confirming Rebecca's rising panic.

Oh, dear lord. Not both of them. And from the look of it, whither the Gadbury sisters went, there went Sydney. How was she ever going to explain this to Rafe?

"You mean to see me to London?" Rebecca asked weakly, hoping this was all the sisters intended. To see her safely ensconced at Lady Tottley's and then having discharged their neighborly and moral duty return promptly to Bramley Hollow.

To her disbelief, both ladies shook their heads, bonnets and ribbons aflutter.

"Oh, no. We've decided to join you. For the rest of the Season!" Honora declared.

Rebecca clutched the doorpost. Never mind Rafe's reaction. What was Lady Tottley going to say?

"Where's Danvers?" Kitling called from his phaeton. "We've a town to conquer!"

Just then, the Finch carriage ambled up the road, Rafe riding ahead on his mount. He glanced at Kitling and then up at the Gadbury sisters, then his gaze bore down on Rebecca.

Of all the things she had thought he would say to her this morning, she would never have imagined his first words would be, "Over my dead body!"

So much for a spinster's dream of romance.

Rafe leapt down from his horse and stormed up the walk.

Stormed was good, Rebecca thought. It made him look all that much more formidable, all that more dark and dangerous.

That's because he is, she reminded herself, suddenly realizing just how fearsome he could become, this stranger she'd given her heart to.

He swept past the twins, caught Rebecca by the arm and dragged her into the house. Now this she could get used to. Her imagination, now well fueled by a passionate night, sprung forth, offering lines that could as well have been from her next novel.

> *He slung her over his shoulder and carried her up the stairs, tossing her onto the bed and throwing himself atop her, his lips catching hers in a kiss that—*

Only much to her disappointment, Rafe came to an abrupt halt in the hall. Nowhere near the stairs and nary a bed in sight.

"What is all that?" he asked, jerking his thumb at the front door and the newly added collection of Bramley Hollow hangers-on.

Before she could answer, the colonel came down the stairs, Brown Bess in one hand, valise in the other.

"Danvers, ah, there you are. Starting to think you weren't coming after all and we'd have to—"

Rebecca stopped him with a carefully launched coughing fit, their agreed upon sign that now was a good time to act a bit deranged. She tipped her head slightly toward the open door.

The colonel glanced outside and his brows rose at the sight of the unwanted additions. Then a sly smile rose on his lips. "Leave this to me," he muttered, continuing past Rafe and Rebecca as if nothing was unusual about Mr. Danvers holding her by the arm.

Because he was. Still holding her by the arm.

Rebecca hadn't bothered to shake him loose. She was almost ashamed to admit, but she didn't want him to let her go.

Literally or figuratively.

"What are they doing here?" Rafe demanded.

"The sisters were horrified that I was going to town without a proper chaperone," she whispered.

"Your uncle is going with you, as am I," Rafe countered.

The colonel answered that one for her by firing a shot over Sydney's phaeton and sending the man's skittish set racing down the road, Kitling clinging to the reins and shouting orders at the frightened animals.

Rebecca's brow arched. "A proper escort doesn't carry a Brown Bess."

Rafe worked on that one for a few moments. "And what am I?"

"I think you are what they are going to protect me from."

"Well, they're a bit late on that note," he muttered.

"I can hardly tell them that," she shot back. "Unless you are of a mind to be standing before a parson before the day is out?"

Again, his jaw worked back and forth, his feet shuffling.

Rebecca's earlier fears came to the forefront. He regretted making love to her.

"About last night—" Rafe began.

"Yes?" she asked, just as Cochrane came staggering past with Rebecca's trunk in hand.

"This is the last of them, sir," he told Rafe. "And not a moment too soon. Saw that matchmaker prowling along the road last night when I was on my way to Finch Manor. I was afeared I'd wake up with some strange chit this morning." He glanced from Rafe to Rebecca, and then to Rafe's hand on her elbow. "Seems she wasn't after me at all." The boy grinned and then went about his duties, whistling happily.

Rafe turned back to Rebecca. "As I was saying . . . I meant to say, about last night—"

Outside, Kitling had returned, his horses dancing and prancing at being put back in the general vicinity of a madman.

"Come back for more, have you?" her uncle shouted. "Demmed Frogs never do know when they are beat."

"Miss Tate, would you do something about your uncle?" Kitling pleaded. Though a skilled hand with cattle, he was having some difficulty.

Rafe swept past her, first catching up the colonel's gun and tossing it to Cochrane, then marching out into the road without breaking a stride. He caught the front bay by the bridle and said something to the horse, running his hands over its muzzle and the animal settled right down, the other following suit.

"Lawks, Danvers," Kitling said, rising from his seat and staring openmouthed at his unusually docile animals. "What did you say to them?"

"Something my grandfather taught me. He had a talent with horses."

Kitling nodded. "Seems you've inherited it. If you ever decide to give up this runner nonsense, you should consider breeding horses. Probably make a fortune at if you can turn such a lively lot into a pair of overfed housecats."

Rafe glanced at the horses and said something else to the bay before he walked back toward the house. The bay nickered, and the other answered with the same horsey laughter.

"What did you say to the horse?" Rebecca asked.

"I expressed my sympathy to them for being owned by such an idiot."

Rebecca grinned, for no sooner than she could attempt to ask him what it was he'd been trying to say to her before, Miss Honora rushed forward.

"Mr. Danvers," she said, taking him by the arm and leading him along the path. "It is so good of you to include us in your party and under your protection."

"I fear, Miss Gadbury, I don't remember inviting you," he said, glancing helplessly back at Rebecca.

Miss Honora laughed, her gloved hand covering her giggles. "How droll you are, Mr. Danvers. But of course, our dear Miss Tate can't go alone to London with just you and the poor colonel."

"So I am told," he said, shooting one more glance at Rebecca.

She smiled smugly back down at him. He may be able to tame wild horses and kiss a woman senseless, but he was no match for the Misses Gadbury.

"Are we off then?" Miss Alminta asked.

"I need to get Ajax," Rebecca said, rushing back into the house.

"Ajax!" came the collected gasp.

Right after the colonel, Ajax was the most avoided creature in Bramley Hollow. He'd battled every cat within a five mile radius. And his fury had not escaped human notice either. Not even Esme, who was known to be a soft touch for any creature, would reach out a kindly hand to the ginger terror.

Rafe followed her into the house. "You can't be serious," he said, glancing over at the ottoman upon which Ajax lay curled up, sleeping like an apparent angel.

The ottoman gave evidence to the contrary, with its shredded legs and rag-tattered covering. "How can you even think of bringing along that devil?"

"I can't leave him behind," Rebecca said. "No one will take him in. He'll starve or worse if I were to abandon him."

Rafe looked about ready to settle the problem with the colonel's cannon.

Rebecca moved quickly, sweeping the cat into the basket and settling the lid securely down before Ajax knew what had happened.

The cat let out a yowl of protest that sent Kitling's horses to dancing again. Rebecca clung precariously to the now quaking basket, unwilling to leave her beloved, well perhaps not so beloved, pet behind.

Rafe grabbed the basket from her. "I would hardly say taking a deranged tom to London is a practical idea."

No, it wasn't practical. But Ajax had kept her company for several long years, and she wasn't about to abandon him now. He'd earned a place by that cozy fireplace she'd always envisioned. "I'm taking him."

"I doubt Lady Tottley is going to be that accommodating," he told her. "About all of this."

"Serves her right," Rebecca muttered under her breath. Before she could say more, the colonel took center stage.

"Not bring the artillery, sir?" her uncle was crying, his hands waving broadly. "Why, that's madness! Once we take the ridge, we'll need a good cannon to get those devils on the run. Why we'll—"

Rebecca suppressed a smile. There really was a majesty to his madness when he had a good audience. The Gadbury sisters and Kitling stared openmouthed first at the colonel, then at the much loathed cannon and then back at Rafe to see how this latest snag was going to be resolved.

Rafe took on his role as the keeper of the resident lunatic with less aplomb than he had before he knew the colonel's maladies were self-induced.

"Miss Tate!" he bellowed when her uncle went completely into Bedlam by throwing himself over the nine pounder and declaring it was him or England. "Miss Tate, I am not adding artillery to this menagerie."

So it was Miss Tate once again.

Harrumph.

"He is rather fond of that cannon," she said, if only to annoy Rafe. Mr. Danvers, she corrected herself.

Proper, restrained, and all business Mr. Danvers. When had he become so stuffy and practical?

Luckily, Cochrane stepped in and saved the day. "Colonel, sir," he said. "There's no need to bring that cannon. I've scouted the road to London, twice now, and there's no sign of the enemy. Besides, you'd hate to deprive Bramley Hollow of their only means of defense, should it come to that."

The colonel appeared to consider this advice, then nodded. "Good point, lad. You'll make an excellent officer when the time comes." He rose from the cannon,

his hand giving the long iron muzzle one last affectionate pat. "Do hate to be without such a fine piece."

"Oh, they've got some great ones at the Tower,"
Cochrane said, playing along with the finesse of Kean
in Covent Garden.

"Yes, the Tower," her uncle was saying, rubbing his
chin. "We'll gain our replacements there, if need be."

"Aye, sir," Cochrane said, winking at Rafe as he led
the colonel to the carriage.

Rebecca followed, snatching up Ajax's basket from
Rafe and heading toward the carriage Lady Finch had
loaned them.

"Miss Tate," Rafe said, having helped the Gadbury
sisters up into Kitling's phaeton and now returning to
her side. "I had something I wanted to discuss with
you."

She stopped in the middle of the path and looked
at him.

As did everyone else in their party.

When he glanced around and realized they had
about as much privacy as on the dance floor of Almack's he muttered a curse, that thankfully was in
Spanish, before he turned and marched back over to
his horse.

Rebecca considered echoing his sentiments.

Well, she wanted to demand before all of Bramley
Hollow, do you love me or not?

By late afternoon, their procession picked its way
through the crowded streets of Mayfair, Rafe leading
the parade to Lady Tottley's fashionable town house.

He should be thrilled to have found the *Miss Darby*
author and gained his prize, and even more happy to
be depositing the odd collection behind him at the
lady's doorstep.

Then he could wash his hands of the entire affair.

Affair.

The word made him cringe. If only it was an affair. Those he knew how to start and how to end, quite expertly really, without the hint of hurt feelings.

But not so with Rebecca. He loved her. How the devil had she done it, an opinionated spinster from Bramley Hollow, when the best of London's flirts had been unable to crack his stony reaches?

And from Bramley Hollow, no less. His brothers would have a fine time teasing him about being "matched." He'd never hear the end of it.

He stopped his horse to let a pair of elegantly clad young ladies, their beaming mothers, and trailing retinue of maids and package laden footmen cross the crowded street.

Now that he'd found her, he didn't quite know what to do with her. He'd never proposed marriage before. And it wasn't just the proposing that had him over a fence.

It was the what came next that had him trembling in his boots. Taking Rebecca into his dangerous and highly irregular life was one thing, but along with her came the colonel and Ajax. How could he give her the regular life she longed for when he could barely keep himself housed and Cochrane fed? Not to mention keep the colonel in cannon balls—for Rafe suspected the old fellow, even when he was able to discard his madness, would be inclined to periodically fire off a round or two.

And there was another rub. Rebecca would insist he keep Bettlesfield Park. Keep that tumbledown wreck? There wasn't enough gold in England to save it.

And demmit if the chit didn't have him already considering that foolish notion.

"Ah, the riches of town," Kitling was saying, as he pulled his phaeton to a stop beside Rafe, judiciously tipping his hat at the young ladies' mothers. The Gadbury sisters had retired to the comforts of the Finch carriage hours ago. "Yes, surrounded by rich treasures, plump and ready to be picked, wouldn't you say?"

Rafe shot the man a sidelong glance. There was something about the way the man had said "treasures" that caught his attention. He suddenly recalled that at Lady Finch's supper party, Kitling had given all the talk of lost fortunes a great deal of interest.

Mayhap too much so?

And hadn't he been in Calcutta at the same time as all the others? And returned mysteriously wealthy. Enough so to be able to bestow his generosity on the Gadbury sisters.

Perhaps Kitling wasn't merely the useless nit most regarded him as.

He cursed himself for not seeing all this before. "Where are you planning on staying?" he asked.

"Staying? Well, with the ladies, why of course," Sydney proclaimed.

Leave him under the same roof as Rebecca if he had anything to do with the Kailash murders? *Not as long as I have anything to say about it.*

Rafe shook his head. "Lady Tottley will never allow it. She's rather a high stickler."

"Hmm. Hadn't considered that. Where do you room, my good fellow? Perhaps they have a vacancy there?"

"Seven Dials. Near the Rose and Lion."

Kitling paled, then burst out laughing, assuming Rafe, the son of a gentleman was joking about living in London's most notorious neighborhood. "Ah, you had me going there, sir."

Rafe just stared at him blandly.

Kitling's features paled when he realized Rafe wasn't kidding. "I suppose there is my father's club," he said, glancing back at the Finch carriage with a look of frustrated regret.

"White's or Brooks?" Rafe asked offhandedly.

"I don't even dare say it aloud in Mayfair. I fear it is a mercantile association in Southwark," Kitling offered. "My father is far too tightfisted to ever consider wasting money on a membership at any reputable establishment." Again there was another look of longing.

If Kitling supposedly had all this money, why didn't he just join one of London's more infamous male bastions? Or take a suite of rooms at one of the finer hotels? And why didn't the man have a valet? Or any of the other ostentatious accoutrements of the typical nabob returned from his exile in India?

As happenstance would have it, Tottley House was on the same block as Bridwick House, his brother Colin's London residence.

Rafe rarely asked his brother for a favor, but Seven Dials was too far away to keep an eye on Rebecca. And Kitling as well. He'd station Cochrane at Bridwick House as his lookout and figure out how to repay Colin and Georgie later for their emptied larder.

Before he had time to direct any further queries at Kitling, they were in front of Tottley House. The footmen came pouring down the steps like a well-trained troop, with Crumpton leading the charge, as unsmiling and disapproving as ever.

As Rafe looked up at the imposing marble façade of Lady Tottley's town house he told himself once again he was doing the right thing, leaving Rebecca here. No killer, no matter how desperate, would risk seeking her out here amidst the busy household. A lonely Kent road or a solitary bachelor residence was one thing, but the Tottley town house wouldn't be so easy to penetrate.

And until he could make an offer worthy of her dreams, it was best to leave her here. He could only hope that she'd see the sense of it as well.

"Mr. Danvers," Lady Tottley's butler was saying, "her ladyship requires your attendance inside. Immediately."

"Is my assistant still alive?" Rafe asked the stuffy butler. Rafe had possessed the forethought to send Cochrane ahead with the news that she should be prepared for not two houseguests, but four. "Or did the old dragon kill the messenger?"

He thought he detected a slight smile on Crumpton's lips. Or perhaps the ancient fellow was just finally cracking like one of the stony megaliths outside Wiltshire. "Mr. Cochrane is in the kitchen. Being fed."

"Still?" Rafe asked. Cochrane had probably arrived a good two hours before them.

Crumpton snorted. "Your assistant has a remarkable capacity." That was the end of his lively humor, for from within the confines of the house came a strident cry.

"Is that Mr. Danvers, here at last? Bring that thieving, underhanded wretch in here. Now!"

"The dragon awaits," Crumpton said, this time deigning Rafe with a real smile.

Rafe suspected that it was because he was about to be sacrificed and Crumpton was finally going to gain some justice in his original reluctance to allow the likes of Rafe Danvers inside the hallowed walls of Tottley House.

"There you are, you scoundrel!" Lady Tottley said, as Rafe was shown in. "Our agreement did not include me housing the entire village of Bramley Hollow. Now

I see there is another gentleman in the party. Don't tell me I'm expected to house him as well?"

"As I'm sure Cochrane informed you, Miss Tate did not think it was proper to travel without her companions, and by bringing them it would reduce your responsibilities to see her suitably chaperoned."

Lady Tottley snorted, though she could hardly object to a young lady who took such grave care with her reputation and with her hostess's obligations.

"As for Mr. Kitling," Rafe continued, "he is a friend of the Misses Gadbury, and did not want them to travel unprotected. I assure you, he is not here to stay. He will be taking rooms at his father's club." He deliberately left out the club's location or name.

Her sharp eyes narrowed as she considered this news. "And who is Mr. Kitling's father?"

"Sir David Kitling. Lady Finch assures me they are a respectable family."

"Lady Finch says that?"

"Yes, ma'am."

"And Mr. Kitling is his father's heir?"

Rafe could see the wheels turning. A wealthy enough baronet wasn't the perfect son-in-law, but Lady Tottley had two more unmarried daughters behind Lady Lucinda and there weren't enough available heirs to dukedoms for all of them.

"No, Mr. Kitling is the younger brother. But he spent time in India and is rumored to have returned home well-favored, though he is too much of a gentleman to discuss such matters."

The lady nodded. Mr. Kitling may not discuss his income, but such information could be easily had for a mother determined to see her daughters well matched.

"I find all of this very high-handed," she complained. "I only agreed to all of this because of Evaline's recommendation that it was the best solution."

Rafe cocked a brow. So Lady Finch had stirred the pot a bit. It didn't surprise him that the baroness had added her blessing to the situation.

"Then is all this settled?" he asked. He could hear the servants coming up the stairs with the luggage, and it was only a matter of time before Rebecca would be here as well.

Panic struck him as he realized he needed to say something to her, but what? *I must leave you now because I love you so very much?* He'd sound as spineless as Lt. Throckmorten.

"I suppose it is. But mind you, Mr. Danvers, if I discover this gel divulging her radical notions to anyone, I will toss her and her party out into the streets without the least bit of hesitation."

"I think you are going to find Miss Tate is actually a very sensible young lady."

Lady Tottley made another snort, a sort of "we'll see about that," that spoke volumes of her general disbelief. "If you are going to take your leave, do so," she told him. "And take that assistant of yours with you. Cook says he's eaten all of the meat pies that she'd made for Lord Tottley this evening and just about all the custards and tarts." The lady shook her head. "You sent him on purpose, I assume. Why he's probably eaten more this afternoon than Bettlesfield Park is worth."

Rafe smiled. If that was what the lady believed to be the worst of her troubles, she had yet to meet the colonel and Ajax. And speaking of Bettlesfield Park . . .

"About the property—" Rafe began.

"Your payment, sir, is contingent on this author undoing her damage."

"That was not what we agreed to," Rafe shot back.

"And I didn't agree to finance some chit's Season either," she said. "The deed to Bettlesfield Park will be in your hands the day my daughter is the future duchess of Hemswell. Not a day before. Undo these troubles, Mr. Danvers, that is what I hired you to do."

Rafe let out a frustrated sigh. "Yes, my lady." After making a proper bow, he stormed from the room, running straight into the colonel.

The man blustered his way past, ignoring Crumpton who was poised to make the introductions. "What are your artillery positions, madam?"

"My wha-a-at?" Lady Tottley stammered.

"Your cannon. I have seen no cannon so far in my inspection. How can you make a proper defense of this hill without a cannon?"

"I—I—don't know."

"Bah! Greenlings, all of you. I'll have a full inspection at dawn."

"Dawn! Sir, I never arise before noon," she declared.

"Noon? Shameless. We'll have to rectify that immediately." The colonel saluted her, then took a chair in the corner, picking up the paper and ignoring everyone as he leafed through the day's news.

"What is the meaning of that man?" Lady Tottley managed to ask.

"Colonel Posthill, ma'am," Rafe told her. "He gets a bit confused at times."

"Confused? Why, he's nicked in the nob."

"Unfortunately so. But truly he is harmless as long as you don't let him near any firearms or cannons."

"Cannons?" she gasped.

Rafe smiled at her. "Oh, and here are the Misses Gadbury. Miss Honora and Miss Alminta."

Lady Tottley looked at the twins and then looked again.

The pair started chattering at once, offering their appreciation for her kindness, her generosity, asking her advice on modistes and complimenting her on the beauty of her home and gorgeous lace on her gown. When they paused for breath, Lady Tottley swayed as if she were about to fall over, dizzy and overwhelmed by the talkative pair.

She closed her eyes, her hand on her brow.

"And this is Miss Tate," Rafe told her, parting the way and escorting Rebecca forward.

The lady opened one eye, as if she were afraid to see the final guest in her home. Even as she caught sight of Rebecca, the lady's lips turned in a smile as her worst fears evaporated.

"Lady Tottley, it is my sincere honor to meet you," Rebecca said, curtsying deep. "I am so very sorry to hear of the despair I have caused you and your friends. You have but to ask and I will do everything in my power to see the situation brought in hand."

The countess heaved a sigh of relief, like a storm tossed boat finally finding a friendly port. She brightened immediately. "My dear Miss Tate," she said, taking her by the arm. "Come let us see about getting your things unpacked. We have much to do if you are to catch up with the Season—what there is left of it—but you are here to save the day, I see, and for that, I am most grateful."

"As am I," Rebecca told her, "for you are providing me with the means to attain my dearest wish, a good and sensible husband and a home of my own."

A husband? Rafe spun around and gaped at her. She needn't sound so enthused about the idea. And worse, she looked like she truly meant it. Hadn't last night meant anything to her?

And what had she said she wanted? *Good and sensible.* Bah! He could be those things.

On occasion.

"And a husband we shall find for you. Just as every wise girl should desire," the lady was saying, approval beaming from her sharp eyes.

Rafe found himself forgotten as they left the room en masse, talk of silks and brocades and hats and shoes fluttering through the air like autumn leaves.

Had she forgotten him so quickly? Demmit, he wasn't going to stand for this. He was going to—

"Rafe?"

Suddenly she was there and his chest tightened.

"Rebecca," he said, forgetting that he shouldn't address her so intimately. "I'll find Purcell. I'll get Richard's haversack. I'll stop this—" His words tumbled out, promises and vows of everything but the one thing he should be offering. Himself. A life together.

But would she want such a miserable offer once she'd seen the glories of Mayfair?

Rebecca was, after all, a sensible lady.

"I know," she was saying, her teeth nibbling at her bottom lip. "You must use undue caution. Do you have my list of residences that Mr. Purcell has used in the last two years? His previous employers? My instructions?"

"Yes," he said, stopping her and placing a chaste kiss on her cheek. "I have everything I need."

Everything but you.

"I could come with you," she offered.

He shook his head. "No. You'll be safer here." This is

where she belonged, in the safe confines of Mayfair. And if he was half the man he professed to be, he'd leave her here and never come back.

Let her find her reliable and prudent vicar.

Afraid of his own weakening resolve, he bid her a hasty good day and fled toward the front door.

"Rafe?" she called out.

"Yes?" He came to a stop and prayed his voice didn't sound as hopeful as he felt.

"Be careful," she finally said. "Don't jump into anything without judiciously considering the consequences."

It was too late for that, he wanted to tell her.

Some hours later, after everyone had gone to bed for the evening, Rebecca wandered down the stairs, in search of a book to read, for she couldn't fall asleep, her thoughts awash in grief over Rafe's desertion.

Oh, why had he left her without any word of last night?

As she crossed the hall in front of Lady Tottley's salon, she heard an odd noise inside the elegant room.

Crying.

Rebecca bit her lower lip and considered what she should do. Leave the person to the privacy of their tears or interfere. She knew what Lady Finch or the Gadbury sisters would recommend.

Tapping on the partially open door there was no reply, so she pushed it open a bit further and poked her head in.

To her shock, it was Lady Tottley, alone and prostrate on her settee, sobbing as if it had just been announced that the Regent was knighting every merchant from Brighton to York.

"Lady Tottley," Rebecca whispered, coming into the

room and closing the door behind her. She knew the countess would not appreciate the staff seeing her in such a state of distress. "Is there anything I can do for you?"

The lady sniffed and sobbed some more before she managed to say, "I fear it is too late! Lord Barwick was seen this afternoon out driving with Miss Thayer. A cit's daughter! Can you imagine such a thing? When my dear Lucinda was so close to being his bride." She drew her handkerchief to her trembling lips. "All is lost!"

"This is my fault," Rebecca said, coming to sit beside the lady. "I wish I'd never written that last book."

The lady wiped her tears away and gazed intently at Rebecca. "I do believe you mean that."

"I never thought Lieutenant Throckmorten's death would be so ill-received. I only meant to get rid of him because I truly tired of his unwillingness to propose marriage."

Lady Tottley stared at her, and then of all things, burst out laughing. "You mean you got rid of him because he was being a typical man?"

Rebecca nodded. "Wait until my next book."

Lady Tottley's iron brows arched.

"I mean," Rebecca corrected herself, "the one I have stopped writing. Miss Darby discovers that Lieutenant Throckmorten had a betrothed in London and one in the West Indies. He was a regular Lothario. She is well rid of him."

"This man, who has every miss in London mourning, was a cad?"

"A wretched one."

The two of them laughed until Lady Tottley finally caught her breath. And then she sighed and shook her head.

"Miss Tate, you would probably cause a riot if you published that book. Who knows how the younger set would react. It is better that Miss Darby's misadventures never again see the light of day."

Rebecca didn't agree, but she wasn't about to argue with Lady Tottley. Perhaps in a few weeks, once everything was set to rights, the lady would allow her to continue writing.

"My daughter is so terribly headstrong," the countess was saying. "She got that from her father, bless his heart."

Rebecca wisely chose not to comment on that either.

Lady Tottley glanced over at the fireplace, the last of the flames lingering in the grate. "I know she is fond of Lord Barwick, and he of her. All things together, I think they suit, and that is all I ever truly wanted for Lucinda. I want her to be happy, as I am with Lord Tottley."

"Then let me tell her the truth," Rebecca implored. "That I wrote the *Miss Darby* novels and that I never meant for Lieutenant Throckmorten's death to become this grand statement against marriage."

The countess shook her head. "She'll see my hand in your arrival and not believe you. No, she needs to come around on her own." Lady Tottley sighed. "You have a good heart, Miss Tate, though a misguided pen. It cheers my heart to know I'll have your willing assistance when the time is right."

"I am at your service, Lady Tottley," she said, bidding the lady good night and returning to the solace of her room. But as she closed the door on the elegant chamber, Rebecca felt a twinge of guilt. For there sat her dispatch box, and hidden inside it was *Miss Darby's Terrible Temptation*, awaiting its final chapter.

In truth, how could she finish it when she herself was starting to think the Darbyites had it right—

marriage was a fool's dream. She crossed the room to the window and stared out into the darkness. She couldn't see much, beyond the lights that twinkled in the other stately homes of Mayfair.

"*Rafe*," she whispered like a prayer to the single star she could discern. *Please come to me.*

But she knew the truth. If he truly loved her, he would have declared so this morning. She turned from the window and made her way to her bed. Drat the man!

Oh, she had only herself to blame. For throwing caution to the wind and diving into life with the same reckless abandon as her plucky heroine.

But fiction and real life, she realized, rarely found common ground. Hadn't she started writing the Darby novels in answer to her own broken heart? To find a place where happy endings truly did exist.

Then as her despondency reached new lows, she thought she heard the garden gate squeak and she rushed to the window.

He'd come for her!

But darkness obscured the garden and she couldn't see a thing. After standing at the window for an indecent amount of time peering into the shadows and willing Rafe to appear, she finally gave up. Without a book to read or anything to distract her wayward thoughts, she found herself staring at her desk.

What would one page hurt? she found herself wondering. And before she knew it, she had a quill in hand and was seeking solace in the one thing that never disappointed her.

Rafe had asked his brothers to meet him at the Rose and Lion, Pymm's old haunt, for he needed their help and was more than willing to swallow his pride to gain it.

"Now let me get this straight," Colin was saying. "You seduced this innocent girl and then left her without a word."

"It wasn't quite that bad," Rafe told him. "I tried to ask her to marry me, but I couldn't get the words out. Besides, I'm not sure she would have said yes." He took an unwitting swallow from the tankard before him and choked on the foul brew. "You didn't see her face when she saw Lady Tottley's house. And what can I give her? A one room flat in Seven Dials and a share in my disreputable life? Besides, she's always fancied herself married to some vicar—you know, a sensible sort."

"Put that way, you'd have to wonder about any lady who would say yes to you," his brother Robert commented.

Colin wasn't so convinced. "You should have got down on both knees and with every bit of sincerity and charm you possess asked the lady. Then before she had the chance to refuse you, carted her off to Gretna Green and married her."

This, Rafe noted, from the man who'd almost married the wrong woman.

Robert leaned forward. "What do you need us to do?"

"Yes, why exactly have you dragged us down here?" Colin asked.

Finally, Rafe decided, his interfering family was going to be an asset. Right down to Colin and Georgie's seventeen-year-old daughter. He glanced over at his eldest brother.

"With Chloe being out this Season, I suppose you're being dragged about to all these balls and other nonsense?" he asked.

Colin's brow knit together and nodded.

"Good. Keep an eye on Miss Tate for me. If she starts

to show any marked preference for anyone, get rid of the fellow, then send me word immediately."

Colin glanced at Robert, who just shook his head. Then both brothers launched into a fit of laughter that drew every bleary eyed gaze in their direction.

"Gads, Rafe, you are an idiot," Robert said, once he'd recovered enough of his composure to speak. "What do you expect Colin to do if some fellow does take an interest in this paragon, challenge him? I think Georgie might take exception to her husband following around a woman, shall we say, half his age?" Robert chortled, while Colin shot him a black look.

"Perhaps, I haven't thought this thing completely through," Rafe admitted.

"Not much, I'd say," Colin muttered.

Leaning back in his chair, Robert asked, "Since I'm obviously not here for spying on your lady love, what do you need of me, little brother?"

"Your connections, Hobbe," Rafe said, using his brother's old nickname. "I need to locate this man." He dug into his pocket and pulled out Rebecca's list.

Robert whistled as he looked over her tidy script. "Thorough chit."

"You don't know the half of it," Rafe said. He pointed down to item thirty-six on the page. "We need to find this Purcell. But with the utmost discretion. Don't let him know we are looking for him. According to Miss Tate, he's a bit of a gambler and moves around frequently. Debts and all. If he thinks someone is looking for him, he'll bolt. And foremost, I don't want anyone else to find him first."

Colin's gaze narrowed. "Now you sound like Pymm. What is this all about, Rafe?"

He shook his head. "I can't say anything more than that."

His brothers exchanged glances and then grinned.

"An adventure!" Colin declared. "Gads, how I envy you. Since the war ended, I haven't had a single excuse to fire a shot or go skulking about the wharves looking for information. Quite dull, really."

Rafe considered introducing Colin to the colonel if he thought his life was lacking in peril and excitement.

Robert nodded in agreement. "Count us in. We'll find this Purcell fellow *and* make sure there isn't a vicar in sight of your future Mrs. Danvers."

Rafe nodded, and then headed for the door.

As Colin and Robert watched their brother leave, Colin said "Do you think it is ethical for us to help him gain this bride?"

"God help her, saddled with him for the rest of her life," Robert said.

"I rather felt the same way for Olivia when she went to the trouble of saving your miserable hide," Colin teased.

"Still," Robert mused, "I can't figure one thing out."

"What's that?" Colin asked absently.

"Why does Rafe believe he has nothing to offer this Miss Tate?" Robert wondered aloud. "Lord, father left him enough money in trust to marry half this Season's debutantes."

Both brothers paused, staring at their drinks, then looked up at each other.

"You did tell Rafe about his fortune when he came of age?" Robert asked.

Colin's eyes widened as he realized the truth. "No, I thought you had—"

They stared at the now empty doorway and laughed. A few moments later, Robert wiped his eyes and rose from the table. "And here we thought for all these years he just favored living in utter poverty to keep himself well out of the parson's trap." He started to go after Rafe, but Colin stopped him.

"Let's not tell him just yet."

Chapter 14

There isn't a man in England who doesn't think he can't do anything he sets his mind to, Miss Darby. And every woman in England knows he'll succeed with her help.

Lady Lowthorpe to Miss Darby
in *Miss Darby's Perilous Journey*

A sennight later

"**A**bout time you arrived," Lady Tottley said to Rafe as he was shown into her drawing room. "You're late. I specifically told Mr. Cochrane that you be here at one. Now it is nearly half past two and my callers will be arriving within the hour and I don't want anyone seeing you—"

"My apologies, milady," he said, cutting her off. "I've been gone all morning. On business. I just got your message and came as quickly as I could."

"Yes, your business. Well, that isn't my concern, but what is my concern is Miss Tate. She's still writing!"

"She's what?" he ground out. Not that it surprised him. It had probably been too much to believe that Rebecca could stop just like that.

"Yes. I caught her yesterday afternoon in her room

scribbling page after page!" Her brows rose. "You know what this means don't you?"

Yes, he knew. If Rebecca continued writing there would be no Bettlesfield Park. "It might have been letters or some of the colonel's correspondence," he offered.

"It wasn't!" the lady said. "It was more of those novels." She went to a sideboard and opened a drawer, pulling out a handful of pages, shaking them before him.

He passed on reading them. If Lady Tottley said they were further adventures of Miss Darby, he believed her.

"I will speak to her," he said. Threaten her was more like it, though he was afraid if he offered bodily harm, Lady Tottley would demand a public flogging.

"If that was just all!" Lady Tottley declared. "Her uncle is a Bedlamite! Why he has the staff marching each morning and has demanded that Crumpton be armed to 'protect our perimeter.' "

"The colonel is relatively harmless," Rafe assured her. "And your staff will survive. They are well trained and well chosen." He made a note to chat with Posthill about maintaining his ruse without driving Lady Tottley's servants into full revolt.

"And then there is the matter of that," she said, pointing a long finger at what was probably once a very expensively covered chair. The fabric was in shreds and the legs looked liked they'd been run through a grist mill. Atop this domestic ruin, lay Ajax, curled into an innocent ball of yellow and white stripes.

"That evil creature is single-handedly trying to destroy my house. Not to mention terrorizing the maids."

"He's just a cat," he said, though he wasn't all that convinced of the fact himself.

"I caught him yesterday hanging by his claws in my new drapes. It took three footmen to get him down."

Just three? he resisted asking.

Ajax's ears twitched and he poked his head up, his one eye opening.

Rafe swore the damn thing smiled, as if proud to hear his accomplishments recounted with such detail and aggravation.

Lady Tottley sighed, a loud lament that rang through the room. "And finally, Mr. Danvers, I blame you for bringing that odious Mr. Kitling into my house."

Rafe crossed his arms over his chest, suddenly wary. "What has Kitling done?"

Cochrane had been watching the man's comings and goings, so Rafe knew that the man had been spending an inordinate amount of time at the countess's house.

Mostly around meal time, a sin that Cochrane saw no fault in, and truly neither did Rafe, considering Lady Tottley's chef was coveted by half of Mayfair.

"He is a fortune hunter, sir! And his father is no gentleman."

"He's a baronet," Rafe pointed out.

"Raised to that position after he helped negotiate a trade agreement with the Russians. Commerce! Why the man is a *cit*. And his son is nothing more than a sponger. An impoverished one, at that."

Not unlike half the *ton*, Rafe wanted to point out, but Lady Tottley didn't appear ready to listen. But one thing did catch his attention. "How do you know he hasn't any funds?"

Lady Tottley's gaze rolled upward. "Mr. Danvers, you aren't the only one capable of ferreting out the *ton*'s secrets."

Rafe had to imagine not even Barclay and Company would deny her access to their clients' accounts.

And if Sydney Kitling had no money—then where

were the funds that supported his fondness for all things fashionable coming from?

In the meantime, while he pondered these developments and how best to uncover Sydney's secrets, Lady Tottley had rung for Crumpton. The butler arrived so promptly, Rafe suspected the old fellow of eavesdropping at the door, *à la* Mrs. Wortling.

"Bring Miss Tate here," she intoned, much as Henry VIII must have called for Catherine Howard when he discovered her infidelity. But if Lady Tottley thought she could berate Rebecca into submission she was about to find herself sadly mistaken.

Meanwhile, Lady Tottley continued listing her complaints from the last week. The disgraceful mess Ajax had coughed up on Lady Funtley's slippers—while Lady Lucinda was pouring the tea, no less. The colonel's demand that the countess invest in a cannon. Nothing extravagant, just a nice six pounder that would send a good shot into Cheapside. Not that she minded Cheapside being laid siege to, but really, what would her neighbors say about the noise?

It was all Rafe could do not to laugh at her laments. How was it that Rebecca could be such a practical and sensible woman, yet wherever she went, chaos swirled from her serene hemline like a West Indies hurricane?

Upheaval and commotion he'd come to enjoy. Missed so very desperately.

His brothers had been right—he should just catch her up and marry her. Damn his worries, and his pride. He'd find a way to keep her in silks and the colonel in cannon balls.

And he would do it today, this very afternoon . . .

Rafe had his determination fully in place by the time the door opened behind him, and Rebecca's dulcet voice called out, "You asked for me, my lady?"

But when he swung around, he wondered where she stood, for before him stood a striking London miss, coifed and dressed to perfection like one of the figurines decorating Lady Tottley's mantel.

"Rafe!" the lady said, coming forward and nearly tripping over Ajax who had jumped down to greet his indulgent and understanding mistress.

Then it hit Rafe that this vision was Rebecca. What had Lady Tottley done to her? He'd only left her in the lady's care a week ago!

The generous red and topsy-turvy curls he loved, were now piled artfully atop her head, perfect coils spilling elegantly to her shoulders. And then there was her dress—what had happened to the sacklike monstrosities she usually wore? This gown, what there was of it, revealed the generous swell of her breasts and the nip of her waist, the curve of her hips. The curves he'd caressed, the body he'd found as close to heaven as a man could venture without sticking his fork in the wall.

"Rafe, you've come back!" she exclaimed.

Was it his mistake or did she sound glad to see him?

Lady Tottley's brows had risen at this familiar use of his name. "*Mr. Danvers* is here to discuss our agreement. The one you have so blithely ignored, despite taking full advantage of my patronage."

Rebecca opened her mouth to protest, but Rafe beat her to the punch. "What have you done to yourself?" he asked, circling her.

"What I was promised," she replied tartly, glancing over her shoulder at him. "Set myself up to find a husband."

"In that?" he sputtered. "Do you know what kind of men you'll attract? There isn't a vicar in England who would find you sensible now." *Dios*, it was hard to manage a sensible thought with her decked out so!

Lady Tottley laughed. "A vicar? That is who you thought Miss Tate should marry? Sir, I promised the girl a good marriage and that does not mean she'll spend her days toiling in some drafty manse. Miss Tate has already been called upon by Pease. Twice."

"Pease?" he said. "Who is this Mr. Pease?"

"Viscount Pease," the countess corrected.

Viscount Pease? Not Vicar Pease? Oh, his ever effi-cient Rebecca had outdone herself.

His decision to declare his intentions suddenly seemed laughable. What did he have to offer against a viscount? A poor flat in Seven Dials and a broken down estate?

He couldn't afford the gown she was wearing, let alone the fancy slippers peeking out beneath the lacey hem.

"He doesn't count, Lady Tottley," Rebecca said quickly. "He's just an old friend from India."

Old friend? The words stuck Rafe like a knife. There wasn't a man alive, old friend or not, who would look upon her and not have some other idea of friendship.

Besides, an old friend implied one certain man.

"You don't mean Habersham?" he asked.

Her chin tipped up. "Yes. Lieutenant Habersham. He's Viscount Pease now. Quite unexpected, but his cousin died and the title passed to him."

"What is *he* doing here?" he asked. She seriously couldn't be considering the man. Besides, he'd be damned if he'd stand by and let this Habersham-cum-Pease hurt her again.

"Hopefully planning to take her as his wife," Lady Tottley said, confirming his worst fears. "But only if you stop writing." Arms crossed over her ample bosom, she glanced at Rebecca and heaved an indignant sigh. "Tell her, Mr. Danvers," she said to him. "Tell her she is to stop writing. Immediately."

Rafe gazed at Rebecca again, wincing at the handsome, elegantly clad woman before him. The only thing familiar was the stubborn set of her jaw. The same look she'd held when she'd challenged him to prove she was the *Miss Darby* author.

Rebecca didn't wait for his admonishment. She launched into her own quite readily. "Lady Tottley, you need not have called Mr. Danvers away from his obligations elsewhere just because I am finishing my book. As I told you yesterday, I have no intention of sending it to my publisher if you succeed in helping me get married. Besides, how can you expect me to stop on the mere promise of a successful Season? I am five and twenty, a factor not in my favor."

"I wouldn't be touting that fact so loud, Miss Tate," Lady Tottley said. "I've been telling everyone you are only just this side of twenty. But it matters not if you are one and twenty or one and forty, if you do not stop writing these *Darby* novels!"

"And if I find myself unwed at the end of this Season, what then? I will still need to eat this coming winter and I will still need to care for my uncle."

Lady Tottley muttered something about putting her cat to good use.

Rebecca ignored the suggestion. "I will not stop writing, but I will not send it to my publisher either. That was what I agreed to—not to publish any more of these novels."

"My dear," the lady cajoled, "you all but have the viscount's declaration."

"His wh-a-a-at?" Rafe sputtered. Habersham wasn't wasting any time reacquainting himself with Rebecca.

His Rebecca. Where the hell were Colin and Robert? They were supposed to be keeping an eye on her, not watching her waltz off with this cad.

Rebecca sighed. "Lady Tottley, I sincerely doubt Lord Pease is going to offer for me."

"Pish, posh! I haven't spent the last thirty years in London society not to know when a man's smitten and when he's playing a lady false. The viscount is going to propose." The clock struck the hour and Lady Tottley glanced over at it and frowned. "Lawd sakes, is it three so soon? And you aren't even dressed yet." She pointed at the door. "Miss Tate, go change into your new muslin, the one with the green trim."

"But I have something I would like to discuss first with Mr. Danvers," Rebecca said. "In private."

"Unless he is here to propose, there will be no *tête-à-têtes* in my house," Lady Tottley said. "State your business so we can see him gone." She pointed one finger toward the door and planted her feet like a giant oak.

Rebecca heaved a sigh of resignation, then turned to Rafe. "I've been making some inquiries and I've found Mr. Purcell."

"Inquiries?" he asked. Her broken promises to Lady Tottley aside, what about her vow to him to stay out of harm's way?

"I found Mr. Purcell," she repeated, a proud smile turning her pert lips. "I've been able to make great headway here in London with just a few letters, some social calls, and after a visit to the Adjutant-General's office yesterday I was able to obtain the address were he collects the payments for his commission."

Rafe crossed his arms over his chest trying very hard not to admire her thoroughness and attention to detail.

Not even Robert with his vaunted contacts to Wellington had been so lucky. Yet how could he tell her so when she was putting her life in danger?

"Miss Tate," he ground out, "you aren't supposed to be involved."

Lady Tottley let out a triumphant "harrumph," one that suggested she was glad to find she wasn't the only one so ill-used by Miss Tate. It also didn't appear that she was going to tolerate much more of this scandalous sleuthing in her house.

Rebecca must have realized this as well, for she frowned and said to him hastily, "Do you want the address or shall I call on Mr. Purcell myself?"

Rafe's temper got the better of him. "You will do no such thing," he told her. "As it is, I also have Purcell's address, and intend to go there this very afternoon."

She nodded. "Good, then I shall accompany you to Spitalfields."

"Spitalfields?" he asked. What was she talking about?

"Yes, Mr. Purcell has taken a rented room above the Royal Thistle in Spitalfields. I have the directions upstairs," she said.

Rafe shook his head, feeling a bit smug. Perhaps her meticulous methods weren't so superior. "I beg to differ, but the man is living in Shadwell, near the docks."

Rebecca's jaw set. "Spitalfields, above the Royal Thistle."

This was the lady he loved, stubborn and passionate. He couldn't help but be pleased that no amount of Town bronze could hide that.

"You are most decidedly wrong," she told him.

"I am not."

"Enough!" Lady Tottley declared. "Enough of this nonsense. Obviously, Mr. Danvers has business to attend to, and you, Miss Tate, have callers to dress for. No

more of this talk of gallivanting off to Shadwell or Spitalfields. The viscount left his card yesterday, so he is
assured to be here this afternoon. And so will you, Miss
Tate, awaiting his proposal."

This afternoon? Rafe glanced at her again. As enticing
as she looked she'd be engaged before Crumpton was
through announcing the fellow, if this Pease had any
sense. Then again, this was the same fellow who'd
abandoned Rebecca before, so that spoke volumes of
the man's character.

So did you, his conscience prodded, leaving his gut
twisted with guilt. And regret.

"I leave you to your callers, Miss Tate," he said, making his bow. Even as he turned and left, she followed
him, a final admonishment ringing in his ears.

"Rafe, you are wrong. Mr. Purcell is in Spitalfields.
You must go there without delay."

Dios, he cursed as he marched down the front steps
and hailed a hackney. He was going to go to Shadwell,
get her brother's haversack and return to Mayfair before the afternoon was out and deposit the blasted
thing in her lap for all her callers to see.

After all, he'd spent the entire night drinking with a
dull lot of fellows from her brother's regiment to locate
Purcell. That's how things in his line of work were
done.

Meticulous research and calls to the office of the
Adjutant-General. Bah! The London offices barely
knew where their units in the field were encamped, let
alone where to find a solitary Scottish officer who'd
sold out his commission two years earlier.

Rafe wasn't about to let his ringing head and well-
spent money go to waste chasing off to Spitalfields.

Why a lady's place wasn't running after murderers
and lost treasures, it was . . .

He ground his teeth when he realized just exactly what a lady was supposed to be doing.

Sitting in Mayfair being courted by a viscount.

He tapped on the roof of the carriage and told the driver there would be extra coins if he could make it to Shadwell and back in good time.

If only to see this Pease and send the bounder packing.

Lady Lucinda had been outside in the hall long enough to hear her mother's upraised voice.

Stop writing these Darby *novels!*

Miss Darby? That had caught her attention, and drawn her to the door in a heartbeat. And what she heard nearly sent her into a dead faint.

Miss Tate, her mother's mysterious protégée was the author of the *Miss Darby* novels? She drew back from the panel, stunned at what she had just learned.

Wait until she told Mary Mavery and Lady Penelope, and all the rest of her friends that she had the actual author of *Miss Darby* as her houseguest.

Lady Lucinda paused and glanced back at the door as she realized the true extent of her mother's intentions.

Miss Tate had been offered a Season in town to stop writing. And obviously she'd agreed to those terms. Oh, if it got out that Lady Tottley had been the instrument of Miss Darby's demise, Lady Lucinda knew very well where the wrath would fall.

"I'll be ruined," she whispered.

Oh, this had to be undone! Miss Tate couldn't stop writing. Not with Miss Darby's life in such a tragic state. She eased back from the door and went to the first landing on the stairs.

And here she had thought that her mother had summoned Miss Tate and her odd collection of friends to town, showered them with clothing and attention, as a way to jolt Lucinda out of her lethargy.

Her mother really hadn't needed to go to such lengths, for her own resolve had been starting to weaken. She hadn't considered that when she'd made the pledge with her fellow classmates that it would have meant neither dancing . . . nor shopping for new gowns . . . nor going for a ride in the park with Lord Barwick.

And it hadn't truly been a burden until she'd seen him pass the house the other afternoon with Miss Thayer beside him. The feckless girl had obviously set aside her convictions and put her attentions elsewhere.

On Lucinda's Lord Barwick!

How dare that *cit*'s daughter set her cap for the Duke of Hemswell's heir when everyone knew he was Lucinda's intended.

She glanced back at the doorway and wished she'd never made that ridiculous vow. Lucinda looked down at her dark gown and black armband and shuddered. Tugging the jet ribbon off, she tossed it behind a potted palm and raced upstairs to start planning.

Tonight was the Setchfield Ball, which she had airily told her mother she would attend, but would not enjoy. Mostly because she would be stuck in the wings with all the other Darbyites clinging to their promise of mourning like a pack of dim-witted fools.

Well, she had started this mess, and rising to her position in society, it was her duty to put a stop to it.

Rebecca followed Lady Tottley's orders to change by going up to her room and tossing on her new bonnet and pelisse, as well as catching up her dispatch box with all her notes and maps. But as she went to open her door to sneak out, she found one of the Gadbury sisters standing at the threshold about to knock.

"Oh, dear, 'tis me, Honora. Am I disturbing you?"

"Um, well, I was about to go out," Rebecca told her.

"Then perhaps later—" Miss Honora pressed her handkerchief to her lips and then burst into tears.

Rebecca glanced out the window where Rafe's hackney was now turning the corner, then heaved a sigh. Gathering Honora into her arms, she drew her into the room and gave the lady a shoulder to cry on. And Honora did, turning into a watering pot of tears and sniffles.

"What is wrong?" Rebecca asked.

"Everything," she gulped, trying to catch her breath beneath spates of tears. "Oh, just everything."

Rebecca led her to the small sofa in the corner of the room. "How can I help?"

"Oh, why did I ever come to London?" This statement brought a new round of tears.

Rebecca thought for a moment she was only suffering from a bit of homesickness, for she never could have imagined the real reason for Honora's despondency. "You didn't want to come here?"

The lady shook her head, still sobbing too hard to talk.

"You can go back to Bramley Hollow today if you are so unhappy here. I'll see to it immediately." Rebecca rose from the sofa, but Miss Honora caught her arm and towed her back down.

"No, I can't leave," she wailed.

"Why I am surrounded here with perfectly acceptable—"

She shook her head furiously. "I can't go. And not because of you," she said, hiccupping a few times. She drew a deep breath, composing herself. "If I were to tell you something, would you promise not to share my confidence with anyone?"

Rebecca swallowed. Oh, she wasn't very good at these things. It wasn't that she couldn't keep a secret, it was just that she feared she wouldn't know how to help the lady with something so obviously troubling. "Perhaps Lady Tottley or Miss Alminta would be a better—"

"No! Especially not Alminta. Why if she ever found out, she'd be despondent. I fear I need help, the type of help Mr. Danvers is capable of providing."

"Rafe?"

Miss Honora cocked a brow at her forward use of his given name, and then smiled. "He is a capable gentleman, don't you think?"

Capable of driving a woman to madness, Rebecca wanted to tell her. "What is it that you think Mr. Danvers can do for you?"

"I fear I've lost something," Miss Honora fussed.

Thinking the lady might have misplaced a broach or an earring, Rebecca tried to hold back the impatience in her voice. She really did need to catch up with Rafe before he ruined everything. "What is it? What have you lost, Miss Honora?"

"Oh dear, this sounds quite silly, and Alminta is going to be quite cross at me, but I fear someone has stolen our fortune!"

"Oh my," was all Rebecca was able to manage.

Twenty minutes later, Rebecca slipped out the servant's entrance. She had listened to Honora's entire story and was still trying to make sense of it.

She'd promised the lady she'd gain Rafe's aid in tracking down the sisters' missing money. She had her own suspicions where the money had gone, starting with Sydney Kitling. Though Honora had said they had helped Sydney from time to time, and she wouldn't hear a word that he might have stolen from them—why he was like their very own son!

Rebecca held her tongue on that matter. Rafe would get to the bottom of it and with evidence in hand, Miss Honora may find that their "dear boy" was nothing but a fortune hunting bounder.

But first and foremost, Rebecca needed to get her own future well in hand.

Once she'd slipped out of the house and through the mews to the street, she made a beeline for Rafe's assistant who was lolling about the corner. She took him by the elbow, steering him down the block and out of sight of the Tottleys.

"Miss Tate!" Cochrane protested, trying to shake her loose.

"Cochrane," she replied, hanging on for dear life. "Nice day for a walk, don't you think?"

He muttered something she chose to ignore.

"Fancy meeting you out here," she said. "What a coincidence, don't you think?" It wasn't a fluke by any stretch of the imagination. She'd spotted him every day for the last week watching the Tottleys' town house and keeping notes on the comings and goings. She also knew from asking the maids a few subtle questions that the handsome young man was staying at Bridwick House, the towering pile of white stone on the corner which belonged to Colin, Baron Danvers, Rafe's oldest brother.

"Yes, miss," he said. "A fine coincidence. Now let me take you back to Lady Tottley's afore you get lost." He tried to turn her around, but she planted her feet with resolute determination. "Ah, miss. It isn't proper for you to be out like this."

"Proper indeed!" she shot back. "Where did Mr.

Danvers go in Shadwell? I want the address and I want it now."

Cochrane's eyes narrowed. "I don't know where."

Rebecca pulled him to a stop. "That's a bouncer and you know it. You always know exactly where Rafe is and I must know where he's heading." She stepped off the curb and waved for a passing hackney. "I mean to stop him before he completely ruins this investigation."

"Miss!" Cochrane stammered. "I don't think that's a good idea."

"Tell me or I will tell him that you've been doing more than going out walking with Lady Tottley's up-stairs maid. Neglecting your duties rather shamefully, I'd say."

"That's blackmail," he complained.

"Call it what you will," she said. "But you will tell me where he's gone or I will do worse." Rafe and Cochrane weren't the only ones with a talent for investigations.

"And that would be?" the lad challenged as the hackney stopped beside them.

"I'll tell the young lady you've also been stepping out with Lady Danvers' scullery maid."

Rafe stepped out of the hired carriage and looked at the tumbledown, abandoned warehouse before him.

"Are you sure this is the correct address?" he asked the driver.

The man heaved a sigh. "Aye, sir. 'Tis what the man said down the way and the fellow at the pub up the road. This is it."

"*Mierda*," he cursed.

"Pardon, sir?" the driver asked, spitting over the side of his box.

"Nothing," Rafe said, pacing in front of the aban-doned warehouse. All that money on liquor for those fools and they'd given him a false address. He didn't even want to consider the smug satisfaction it would give Rebecca that his superior sources had proved him false.

Still, he wasn't willing to give up. There were still several businesses and a questionable house across the street that may have some information on Purcell.

But his inquiries proved unsuccessful and about a half an hour later he was about to give up completely, when a second carriage rolled around the corner and Rafe eyed it with suspicion.

She wouldn't have dared.

Rebecca got out and strolled up to his side. *Oh, she had.*

Rafe's jaw worked back and forth. "What are you doing here?" he asked more to a sheepish Cochrane who was skulking behind her, than to the smug lady herself.

Cochrane glanced away, but Rebecca wasn't so shy. "I would think that is obvious," she replied. "Assisting you with your investigation."

"But I told you—"

"Mr. Danvers, while we haven't known each other for very long, even you must realize that I am not easily naysaid." She tipped her head sideways and gazed at the dilapidated building before them. "Hmm," she mused. "Do you suppose Mr. Purcell is taking callers this afternoon?"

Rafe cringed.

"It appears to me that he may be out," she said. "Shall we go to Spitalfields now?"

"Oh no, you are going back to Lady Tottley's," he said, shaking a finger at her. "You have no business out here—"

"If you insist," she said, pushing his wagging hand aside. "But I would imagine that Lord Pease would take me to Spitalfields if I asked him."

Rafe took a deep breath and counted to ten.

Cochrane came up to his elbow. "She caught me much the same way. Mr. Pymm always said education makes 'em treacherous."

Rebecca only smiled, twirling her reticule in her hands. "My carriage or yours?" she asked, before flouncing back to her hackney, her dainty hemline swishing back and forth over the dirty cobblestones.

Rafe tossed his driver the money he owed the man and followed her to her carriage. "What are the directions?" he demanded.

She shook her head. "You'll not gull me so easily, sir. I have taken the precaution of already giving them to the driver and tipping him handsomely to forget them if I am not included in the party. So, are you coming along or not?" She patted the seat next to her.

Damn the little minx! Why did she have to be so sharp-witted? He was starting to think Pymm had been right about mixing females with a liberal education.

He took the seat opposite her, while Cochrane, having obviously already suffered enough at her hands for one afternoon, climbed up next to the driver. That, or he sensed the brewing dispute about to break out between them.

As the carriage started toward Spitalfields, neither Rafe nor Rebecca spoke.

He stared out the window, pretending to ignore her. But it was demmed near impossible when she sat there grinning like Ajax atop the wreckage of Lady Tottley's best chair.

"We haven't found the man yet," he pointed out.

She shrugged. "We will. Patience and meticulous research always works, Mr. Danvers."

"Rafe," he told her. "I thought we were past such formalities."

"So did I," she said, the accusation all too evident in her voice.

Tell her, he could hear his brothers urging. *Tell her you were a fool.*

He shifted in his seat, crossing and uncrossing his legs and in the process, tangling his boot in her skirt. He reached down to free it, as did she, and they came face to face.

Within a hairsbreadth of her lips, he inhaled the scent of wild roses that filled his starved senses.

"I will not be naysaid, Rafe. Never again," she whispered, and leaned forward to kiss him.

Her lips touched his with a moment's hesitation, and then they opened up to him with a pleading urgency.

Love me, Rafe. Love me.

He caught hold of her and hauled her into his lap, his lips devouring her. "Oh, Rebecca," he uttered between kisses.

"Rafe," she whispered back. "I feared you were lost."

"Not when I am with you."

He kissed her again. *Dios*, it was so easy to believe that she was his, that they were meant to be together with her willing lips teasing him senseless.

And the bold minx wasted no time, for before he knew it she was laying back in the seat and he was atop her.

She clung to him stubbornly, wantonly, her fingers winding in his hair, clinging to his jacket.

The kiss that had brought them together once again, deepened, bringing him to the brink of admitting everything. How wrong he'd been to leave her so abruptly, how much he needed her in his life, how much he loved her.

But what could he give her?

Love.

Her lips pleaded for his love, her eager touch pulled at him. And it terrified him.

Abruptly he yanked himself free.

She gasped for air, then glared at him. And she knew. Saw his cowardice.

"Rafe, you shouldn't have left me."

Oh, how her accusation stung. "I had to," he confessed. "Don't you see that?"

"No, I do not," she replied, sitting up and making a futile attempt to pat her wayward hair back into its London semblance of order.

He would have liked to point out that she was attempting the impossible now. She'd become once again his tumbledown spinster and he loved it.

Loved her.

"Why did you leave me?" she demanded. Ah, his unconventional Rebecca was never one to mince words.

"I had to."

She heaved a sigh that said only too well she thought him the biggest fool in London.

And demmit, she was right. Again.

"Rebecca, can't you see why I left?"

She crossed her arms over her chest and shook her head.

"Just look at you," he said, waving his hands over her elegant new ensemble. "How could I ever afford any of this?"

She looked down at herself and frowned. "Do you think I want this?"

"Well, yes."

To his surprise, she started to laugh. Laughed until the tears ran down her cheeks. "You are such a fool, Rafe Danvers." She pointed at her hair. "Do you know how long it takes a maid to do all this?"

He shook his head. His expertise with lady's clothing and hair lay in another direction. He'd never bothered with the getting a lady dressed part.

"Two hours. Two wasted hours. Bah, all a Season means is spending a good portion of the day sleeping and the rest sitting around while you are made presentable. Then you are wedged into some crush to be viewed and judged like one of Lord Finch's hothouse flowers." She shuddered. "And then the only topics of acceptable conversation are the weather and what everyone else is wearing." Rebecca took a deep breath. "I have eyes. I can look outside and gain a full understanding of the weather, and fashion I find tedious." She caught him by the lapels and tugged him closer. "And you would abandon me to such a life? Shame on you."

"You don't want all this?"

"Gads no. I thought a silk gown would be wonderful, but it stains terribly and this torturous corset must be left over from Cromwell's reign. My old bombazine was just fine and far more comfortable."

She leaned forward and kissed him again. "Besides, you need me."

"I do not," he replied, hoping he sounded firm.

She laughed and patted his jacket in place. "Of course you don't." She leaned her head against his chest and sighed. "Of course you don't."

"Rebecca, I haven't a fortune or a title or anything to offer you."

She struggled up off his chest and faced him, her eyes alight with a passionate fire. "But you do, Rafe. You can offer me a life. I don't want to spend my days idle, I can't. But most importantly, I love you. I love who you are and everything about you, impossible man that you are."

As the words fell from her lips, he felt his heart constrict with fear.

I love you.

He'd never thought those words would mean so much to him. Rebecca loved him.

But he didn't want her love, didn't need it, he tried telling himself. He'd certainly never sought it. But all those arguments sounded hollow, even to his most strident convictions to keep his heart unencumbered.

He wasn't the man for her, for any woman for that matter. Couldn't she see that? Yet, here she was, her eyes alight for him and him alone, and she saw in him the home and hearth that she'd always desired.

And like a candle in the window, suddenly he saw how much he needed her.

Besides, if someone as sensible as his Miss Tate could make such a declaration, who was he to disavow her? Not when he felt the very same way.

"I love you too," he said in return, waiting for the feeling of irons being clapped over his precious freedom, his independence, but instead his confession had quite the opposite affect—it let in a tempest of light that chased away the demons, the many regrets that had clouded his life for as long as he could remember.

"Truly?" she asked, disbelief surrounding her query.

"Yes. I love you. With all my heart." He'd never thought any woman would want to share his reckless life, so he had to be sure. "Do you realize what you are asking?"

"Yes," she told him, and throwing herself into his arms, her eager lips sealed their fate. Their destiny. And by the time the carriage rolled to a stop in Spitalfields, Rafe knew he'd never be able to set her aside ever again.

The Royal Thistle, Mr. Purcell's new hideout, was a fine sight better than the warehouse in Shadwell, which for that, Rafe was thankful, but against his wishes, Rebecca insisted on going in alone to inquire about the man.

"Rafe, if you go in there all scowls and bluster, the man will be out the back door and down the alley before you can bribe the serving girl for information." Rebecca smoothed out her rumpled skirt. "Better I go in and make a fuss. Then you and Cochrane can watch the doors and when he comes out, you'll be able to nab him."

Cochrane jumped down from his seat. "That ought to work."

"Of course it will work," Rebecca said. "It is how Miss Darby distracted Lieutenant Throckmorten's captors in *Miss Darby's Daring Dilemma*."

"Just because it worked in your imagination, doesn't mean that you can just attempt such madcap ideas in real life," Rafe told her.

"Actually," Cochrane said, "it's not a bad plan, sir, if you don't mind me saying."

"I do," Rafe told him. But Cochrane was right, her plan did make sense. And short of tying Rebecca up, there wasn't going to be any way of making her stay put in the carriage.

"You have three minutes," he told her. "Three minutes to set your trap."

Just then a watchman walked by, and Rebecca was at the man's side in an instant. After an exchange of coins, the man joined her as she entered the Royal Thistle, and Rafe and Cochrane made their way to the alley.

It took a total of two minutes for their quarry to come climbing out a back window and down a pile of crates. Rafe nabbed him before he hit the ground.

"Let me go," the man complained, his voice tinged with a hint of brogue. "There's some bird-witted lass in there claiming I left her in Scotland with a passel of bairns and no money to feed 'em."

"Mr. Purcell, I presume?" Rafe asked.

The man's eyes narrowed to flinty slits. "That depends on who's asking."

"Perhaps I can be of some help," Rafe said, catching Purcell by the collar and hauling him down the alley. "You see, I'm looking for something and I think you have it."

"I ain't got nothing of yours," he claimed, squirming and twisting at Rafe's steely grasp. "I don't even know you."

"Yes, but you knew Richard Tate."

Purcell stilled. "Tate?" He paled visibly. "Oh, the saints help me. I don't want to die," he wailed. "I told the gentleman that was here before that I'd get it for him. I just have been a mite busy of late."

Rafe looked at him. "What gentleman?"

Purcell appeared puzzled by this and stopped his caterwauling. "You aren't here to kill me?"

"First, you tell me about this gentleman, and then I'll decide whether or not you're worth killing."

Rebecca sat in the corner of the Royal Thistle, Richard's haversack safely tucked in her lap.

Mr. Purcell, it turned out, was only too happy to be relieved of the burden. "Are you sure you are Tate's sister?" he said, his head cocked to one side as he looked at her.

"Of course," Rebecca replied. "Why wouldn't I be?"

"Well, it's just because, well, it's because you don't look like—" He reached over and dug into the haversack, pulling out a small framed portrait.

"Oh, dear, not that," she muttered. The miniature. The one her brother had had commissioned in Calcutta. She had hoped that, of all his possessions, it had been lost for good.

Rafe caught it up and glanced down at it. Then he flinched. "Someone paid for that?"

She nodded.

"Not very flattering, Miss Tate, you must admit," Mr. Purcell said. "Now that I see you, I realize you got his eyes, and it's not hard to believe you are his sister. Tate always said you were a fine sight prettier than this, but the rest of us thought he was just saying that because you looked capable of giving a man a lifetime of nagging."

"You weren't entirely misled," Rafe told him, then shot her a wicked grin and wink.

She chose to ignore him. It was hard to be overly vexed with the scoundrel when the memory of his kiss still lingered on her lips.

"Why didn't you bring this to me?" she asked. "I sent you numerous letters and requests."

"That you did, but I've had my share of problems of late," he told her. In an aside, he whispered to Rafe. "Dice, I fear. A terrible temptation. Worse than a fine skirt."

"I wouldn't know," Rafe said. "But tell me about this gentleman who came to get Mr. Tate's haversack."

"He was a regular like gentleman. You know, nice coat, lofty manners. Told me he'd deliver it to Miss Tate for me, no bother. Found me at an inn in Richmond."

"The Royal Prince," Rebecca said. "The one before the place on Wilton Road and after the one in Bethnal Green."

"Right you are, miss," Purcell said. "You are a persistent one." He glanced over at Rafe. "There's no escaping her."

"How right you are," he agreed.

"But you didn't give Richard's haversack to the man," Rebecca said, hugging her brother's remaining possessions tighter. "Why not?"

"For good reason," Purcell said. "When I refused, he got real mean about it. Threatened me. Scared me awful bad, so I promised to get it for him and while he waited for me to go upstairs and fetch it, I slipped out the back and I've been running ever since."

"Why didn't you just give it to him?" Rafe asked.

"Because he knew Tate was murdered in Portugal."

"Murdered!" gasped Rebecca.

Purcell nodded. "Sorry, miss, to be so blunt, but your brother was murdered outside a Lisbon cantina."

"How?" Rafe asked.

Purcell's jaw worked back and forth. "Don't like to say in front of a lady." So instead, he took his finger and drew a line from his waist up to his neck. "I still wake up at night thinking of it." He glanced over at Rebecca. "Our commanding officer thought it kinder to let you think he died a hero, instead of in an alley."

"Codlin and Harrington's murderer," Rebecca whispered. "He followed Richard to Lisbon."

Rafe's blood grew cold. If the killer was desperate enough to go to such lengths to gain the ruby, no one was safe until he was stopped.

Especially not Rebecca.

She swiped at the tears spilling from her eyes. "I thank you for your honesty, sir."

"So if the official report said he was killed in action," Rafe said, pressing for details. "How would this gentleman have known differently?"

"That's what I asked myself," Purcell said, tapping his skull with a thick finger. "How did this fellow know about Tate unless he was the one who killed him? And then I figured if I gave the haversack to him, there wouldn't be anything to keep him from doing the same to me."

"Was there anything about this man that was unusual, anything that would help us identify him?"

Purcell shook his head. "Not that I can think of."

"Anything at all?" Rebecca pleaded.

The man swiped at his nose and appeared to be thinking hard. "Well, come to think of it, there was something that comes to mind. He had a fancy walking stick that pulled out and had a sword in it. A wicked looking one!"

Rebecca nodded, and smiled. "Anything else? Engraving? A gemstone?"

He snapped his fingers and said, "Now that you mention it, it was engraved. With his initial, I suppose. There was a 'K' on it."

"Kitling, I'll wager. It's got to be him." Rafe ground out. "I'll kill him when I find him."

"Not if I find him first," Rebecca said, in an equally deadly voice.

Not for first time, Rafe was relieved that the colonel had left his cannon behind in Bramley Hollow.

Chapter 15

*When attending an elegant ball, a proper lady always
maintains a respectable distance from scurrilous types
that often are invited against the hostess's better judgment. Miss Darby, did you hear what I said? A proper
distance.*

Lady Lowthorpe to Miss Darby and
Miss Cecilia Overton
in *Miss Darby's Daring Dilemma*

The Setchfield Ball was regarded as the highlight of
any Season. An invitation was a coveted prize,
mostly because the ball wasn't an annual event, but
whenever the whim struck.

And this year the duke and duchess arrived in town
unexpectedly and announced to their startled staff that
they were going to host a ball in less than a week.

Invitations went out posthaste and the piles of ac-
ceptances started pouring back in almost immediately.

Standing at the doorway to the ballroom, the duke
stood beside his beloved duchess. He leaned over and
whispered into her ear, "You've outdone yourself,
goddess."

"Not yet," the former Lady Diana Lamden said, her
lips pursing into a thin line. "Miss Tate is here, but
there is no sign of Colin's brother. I will ring a peel over
Rafe's infuriating head if he doesn't show."

"First my cousins, now you. I pity Rafe, with the lot of you plotting against him. Bad enough you've joined the conspiracy to see him leg-shackled, but his own brothers?" The duke shook his head. "I've never seen Colin take such joy in another man's fall."

"Not since yours, Temple," Diana said, a sly grin turning her lips. When they had met, her husband had been the Marquis of Templeton. Temple he had been then, and Temple he would always be to her.

"What about all this Darby nonsense?" he asked. "Do you think anyone will dance? Seems a demmed shame to have hired musicians when none of the young ladies are willing."

"I have Lady Tottley's promise that tonight will be the turning point in this crisis."

Temple snorted. "It had better be. I bet an inordinate sum down at White's that the Darbyites' resolve would crumble this very evening." He leaned over and kissed her forehead. "I have every faith in your capabilities as a hostess."

Diana harrumphed and crossed her arms over her chest. "It will have nothing to do with me," she said, "but Rafe's Miss Tate."

Temple looked over in that direction, but his gaze stopped as he saw a furtive figure sneaking in the door from the garden. He was about to call a footman to dispatch the uninvited guest when he realized the interloper was none other than Rafe Danvers. "What the devil is he doing?"

Diana followed his gaze and smiled. "You know how much he hates receiving lines and being announced."

"But do you see what he is wearing? Who tied that cravat?" Temple had once been *the* Corinthian of the *ton*, and had never quite shaken his eye for detail and fashion. "I'd wager that disreputable little thief Cochrane is behind that mess. I declare it looks like a hangman's noose."

"Oh, do behave, Temple. Why I haven't seen Rafe that well dressed, well, ever. Leave him be. He's obviously a man in love."

"His efforts will be for naught when his Miss Tate catches sight of *that* cravat."

Diana's gaze rolled upward and she swatted him with her fan. "Temple, you are incorrigible."

"That is why you love me so," he told her, slanting a glance at Rafe and hoping he found everything his heart desired in this Miss Tate. Everything Temple had found with his dearest Diana.

"I have a nice vicarage in Porterton. Perhaps you've heard of it?" the most respected and honorable Reverend Brown asked.

Rebecca smiled at the man before her, trying devilishly hard to recall what he'd just asked.

Luckily for her, Miss Honora stepped in and helped her out. "Porterton? Such a lovely village. I read about it in Mr. Billingsworth's latest travelogue."

The man preened. "Mr. Billingsworth did our small hamlet a great honor by including it in his book." The man slanted a glance at Rebecca. "Have you read Billingsworth, Miss Tate?"

"Um, uh, yes," she offered, wondering what it was she'd just volunteered. "Quite edifying," she added.

The vicar smiled, his wide set eyes blinking from behind a pair of dirty spectacles. He was fifty if he was a day, bald and sweating profusely. Lady Tottley had sent him over, Rebecca suspected, to give her a chance to see what the Fates held for her if she was fool enough to refuse Lord Pease.

Happily for her, Miss Honora stood beside her, giving the vicar her full and rapt attention.

Meanwhile, Rebecca continued her vigilant watch for Sydney Kitling.

She and Rafe had returned to Tottley House after finding Purcell, only to endure Lady Tottley's wrath—for the viscount had come and gone—until they explained the circumstances to her, and the danger that Kitling presented.

With the Gadbury sisters' fortune missing and two bodies, Lady Tottley had called for the colonel and ordered the man to take charge of the perimeter.

The colonel had been only too happy to comply, lamenting at great length the lack of cannon.

They decided not to tell the Gadbury sisters about Sydney's duplicity for they feared the kindly sisters would not believe them and alert their beloved friend to the grim future that awaited him.

Yet when the man failed to show up to escort the sisters to the Setchfield Ball, Lady Tottley, Lady Lucinda, Rebecca and Miss Honora went on to the Setchfield Ball, while Rafe and his brothers set a trap outside the duke's house. Alminta begged off, pleading a case of megrims, while the colonel chose to stay behind to continue reading Richard's journals in hopes of discerning some hint as to where the ruby was hidden.

"Kitling," Rafe vowed, "will not escape." Then he'd promptly told Rebecca she was to remain inside Setchfield House and well away from harm's way.

Despite Rafe's dire warning, Rebecca had spent the first hour of the party crisscrossing the ballroom, a vigilant gaze sweeping over the crush of people in hopes of spotting Sydney. That is until she'd been trapped by Lady Tottley's vicar. The man had droned on for the last half an hour about the joys of Porterton and the fine state of his vicarage, and his parishioners, until she thought she would have to borrow a page from her uncle's repertoire and feign insanity to be rid of him.

Instead, a familiar voice asked, "Who do we have here?" and with his words brought on a different sort of madness.

His Spanish tinged tones rippled down her spine like the memory of his lips on her bare skin. Her gaze flew to meet his.

"*Rafe!*" Even as she said his name, her hand went to her mouth as she caught herself. "Er, I mean, Mr. Danvers, how nice of you to join us. I would like to introduce you to Reverend Brown. He is the vicar for a lovely little village called Porterville."

"Porterton," the man corrected, his nose twitching.

Rafe grinned at the vicar and then at Rebecca. "It is so nice to meet you, sir." He held out his hand and gave the vicar an enthusiastic handshake.

"And you, Mr. Danvers," Reverend Brown said, glancing up and down at Rafe as if he wasn't too sure whether he'd be called upon to protect the ladies from this obvious cad or if he'd have to ask the ladies to protect him.

"You know, I would love some punch," Miss Honora announced. "Reverend, would you be so kind as to show me where the refreshments are being served?"

"Uh, well, I suppose I could," he said, glancing at Rebecca and then at Rafe. "And perhaps we'll run into Mr. Billingsworth. I have it from Her Grace that he is in attendance."

"Here?" Miss Honora said. She glanced around the room as if she were about to be introduced to Prinny. "*The* Theonius T. Billingsworth? I wouldn't know what to say to him—why he is *the* authoritative source on so many subjects. I believe I would be too flustered to speak in his presence."

"Would you care to join us, Miss Tate?" the reverend asked, holding out his arm, obviously still unconvinced that Rafe was proper company for a young lady, even in a crowded ballroom.

Miss Honora wrapped her arm in the crook of the vicar's elbow. "They will be just fine. He's an old friend of Miss Tate's," and with that, steered the man away, asking him, "Have you read Mr. Billingsworth's treatise on the great monuments of England? Why I have been dying to see Nettlestone Castle ever since I read his description."

Reverend Brown adjusted his glasses. "And I as well. Perhaps when we find Mr. Billingsworth, he will offer us a personal account of the property."

Honora beamed at such a prospect and the pair went off in search of the illustrious Mr. Billingsworth, leaving Rebecca with Rafe.

Once they were well away, Rebecca leaned over and whispered, "Did you catch Kitling?"

Rafe shook his head. "There's been no sign of him." He adjusted his cravat. "Did you have a chance to find any clues in Richard's haversack?"

She shook her head. "I only got halfway through his journal before I had to get ready for the evening."

She waited for him to tell her something, her dress was divine, her hair spectacular, but all she got was a puzzled look.

Why was he looking at her head so oddly?

"Is something wrong with my hair?" she asked, patting at the elaborate arrangement.

"It's all . . . all . . ." His hands waved in the air. "All up and pinned." He shook his head. "I liked it better before. Or rather *after*."

She tapped his sleeve with her fan. "You wicked, wretched man." What she didn't tell him was that she'd be more than willing to unpin it right this very moment if it would tempt him to take her away from the crush of society forever more.

"Are you going to ask me to dance?" she asked. "I saved the first waltz for you."

He turned and looked at her, his eyes so dark and black that they looked fathomless. She could well imagine he would sweep her away, as he had her heart.

But to her dismay, he shook his head. "No."

She sucked in a deep breath. "No? Just like that, 'No'?"

He leaned even closer and whispered into her ear. "Have you forgotten our quarry? I must get back outside and keep watch."

"What about your brothers?" she asked. Suddenly having him hold her, even in the confines of a dance, was so very necessary.

"They are out there this very minute fighting over a watch schedule. Colin is citing naval regulations and Robert wants to post scouts at regular intervals." He shook his head. "I'm about to declare war with France again, just to get them out of the way."

Rebecca laughed. "I doubt the situation calls for anything that drastic."

"You haven't met my brothers. Yet."

"It sounds to me like they are as stubborn, and opinionated, and resourceful as their brother."

"They are—mostly the stubborn and opinionated parts. That's why I left them for a time, so I could come inside and see that you were safe."

Safe? With him beside her? She slanted a glance into his dark eyes. Most certainly not.

"And I see I came just in time," he was saying, tipping his head toward the entrance where Viscount Pease had just been announced and stood in the doorway. "Your beau has arrived. Looks the type who would keep you in silks and satins for the rest of your days. More so than your very impressive vicar."

It was just on the tip of her tongue to deny her affinity for the viscount or poor Mr. Brown, but there was something in Rafe's voice, in the tension lining his jaw that said something else.

"You're jealous," she gasped, before she could stop herself.

He glanced over in the direction of the vicar. "Of him?" he scoffed. "I think not."

She whacked him with her fan again. "Not the vicar." She nodded toward Pease. "Him."

Rafe shook his head. "Do I have reason to be?"

"He's quite handsome," Rebecca said, easing a little closer to Rafe so her gown brushed against the solid muscled strength of his hip.

He glanced down at her, his gaze hungry and teasing. *But not so handsome as you*, she wanted to tell him.

He reached over and plucked a strand of her hair free from her elaborate coiffure. "Lady Tottley says this viscount of yours is one of the *ton*'s biggest catches of the Season."

Biggest catch? Biggest pompous nitwit, Rebecca wanted to tell him, but she was enjoying this game too much. Reveling in the undercurrent of passion flowing between them. "True, a fine catch. Do you think I should accept?"

"Do wha-a-at?" Rafe sputtered. Then he realized she was teasing, but still he shot a measuring glance at her soon-to-be former swain. "He hasn't tried anything, has he?"

"Nary even a kiss," she replied, her nose tipped at a

lofty angle. "He's been a *perfect* gentleman. Quite exemplary."

She watched with some satisfaction as Rafe shifted from one foot to another under the vast umbrella of Pease's supposed nobility.

Just then the viscount spotted her and smiled widely.

"There you are, Miss Tate," Lord Pease said as he made his way through the last of the crowd separating them. "I was having a terrible time finding you in this crush." He took her hand and planted a kiss on her gloved fingertips.

Rebecca made a note to lose her gloves before the end of the evening. Most likely in the nearest fireplace. "How kind of you to seek me out, my lord," she managed to say from behind a forced smile.

"Now none of that," he said, not relinquishing her hand and instead, wrapping it into the crook of his arm and pulling her out from Rafe's shadow. "We are old friends, Rebecca. There was a time you didn't mind calling me by my given name."

Rebecca glanced not at Pease but at Rafe and could see the murderous intent in his eyes. She eased out of the viscount's grasp, on the pretense of making introductions but more so because his cloying cologne was making her nauseous.

How had she ever thought this popinjay the romantic hero of her heart?

"Viscount Pease, may I introduce Mr. Danvers," she offered.

Rafe nodded, but didn't smile, looking the fellow up and down as if seeking something to dislike about him. Apparently he decided just to limit it to everything about the haughty lord.

"Ah, yes, the ruffian fellow," Pease said, casting a sidelong wink at Rebecca as if they shared some private jest on the matter. "You break arms or some other nasty business. Isn't that what that Kitling fellow was saying the other day at Lady Tottley's, Rebecca?"

Rafe decided he wasn't just going to wring Sydney's neck, he was going to give him a demonstration of his supposed arm breaking skills.

Pease turned his back to Rafe, all but dismissing him, while his complete attention showered upon Rebecca. "I was bereft this afternoon when you weren't at Lady Tottley's."

"My apologies, Lord Pease, but an unexpected errand arose," she said, trying to glance around him at Rafe.

"And what was so very important?" he asked. "A new bonnet or another of these enchanting gowns?"

"Believe it or not, I was retrieving Richard's haversack."

His eyes widened. "Richard's haversack? But I thought your brother's belongings were all lost in Spain."

"Mr. Danvers was able to assist me in locating them."

Pease spared a glance in Rafe's direction, but only for the briefest of seconds. "Why that is remarkable. And how lucky for you, Rebecca, to have your brother's possessions back in your tender care." He took her hand again, and this time appeared not as willing to be parted from the lady.

Rafe made a low growling noise and Rebecca discreetly jerked her elbow into his side.

"When I think of your brother, Rebecca," Pease said, "I always remember him with one of his journals jotting down ideas or translations or whatever struck his fancy. Quite an erudite young man."

Rebecca smiled. "Oh, you do remember him!"

"Let me guess, you found inside one of his note-books, along with a collection of dull nubs. He never did have a sharp quill at hand. Never!"

She laughed. "Yes, it was exactly as you described. There was his journal with the page creased over to mark his last entry and a collection of broken quills. I've just begun reading his observations of Spain and they are fascinating."

"I am sure they will be quite enlightening," Pease murmured.

"Uh-huh," Rafe said, elbowing his way back between Pease and Rebecca.

The viscount shot him an annoyed glance, but then like a *perfect* gentleman, included him in the conversation, if only to humor Rebecca.

"I hear tell you were in the war," Pease said. "As was I. Injured at Maguilla," he said, tapping his leg with his walking stick. "What regiment were you in, sir?"

"The 88th," Rafe said. "Until I deserted."

"*Deserted?*" Pease coughed as if he hadn't quite heard it correctly.

"Yes, after I realized my commanding officer was an idiot and I could better serve my country by fighting with the guerillas."

Pease straightened himself up, his knuckles white as he clutched the top of his cane. "And what country is that, sir?"

Rafe smiled. "I still haven't quite figured that out."

Rebecca coughed, holding her handkerchief to her lips.

The tension between the trio was momentarily broken as the musicians started tuning their instruments and struck up a waltz.

"Our dance, my dear," Pease was saying to Rebecca, handing his cane to Rafe like he was a servant.

Rafe didn't take it, rather he took the lady.

"I believe this dance is mine," he told the viscount.

Rebecca didn't argue, but Pease did. "I don't care for your reputation, sir. I demand that you unhand Miss Tate or perhaps you will find that I am capable of breaking arms as well."

Rafe leaned forward and whispered something into Pease's ear that sent the man reeling back, as pale as a January sun.

"Whatever did you say to him, Rafe Danvers?" Rebecca said, casting only the merest glance back at her former beau as Rafe led her to the dance floor.

"I told him he'd have a hard time breaking my arm from his grave, for if he tried to stop me, I'd finish off what the French had obviously failed to do."

But Rebecca was soon to find out, Rafe had no intention of dancing. Just before they reached the floor, he tugged her back into the crowd and then through a doorway that was hidden behind a set of drapes. It led into a hallway and after catching up the candelabra on a side table, he continued past a few more doors, before he shoved one open and pulled her in with him.

The panel slammed shut behind them.

Rebecca had never heard a happier sound.

Before she could speak, before she could even glance around to discover just exactly where it was he'd taken her, he snuffed the candles and his mouth covered hers, kissing her senseless.

She rejoiced at his touch, at his kiss. For it was a claiming that spoke of his need for her, his passionate desire for her. As she avowed for him.

His fingers pulled at her perfectly wrought curls, teasing them back into some semblance of the tumbled disarray he loved so much. Tugging her closer, so her hips met his, she could feel his hard desire for her.

She couldn't resist the urge and stroked the front of his breeches, teasing him until he strained beneath the wool.

How she loved the feel of him, but even more so, she loved him inside her, filling her. She moaned softly. "Rafe, I need you so. Can't we . . . couldn't we . . . ?"

He didn't need any more urging. Catching her up, he carried her across the room until they bumped into something, a desk she thought, and with a sweep of his arm, he cleared it, tossing her atop it and throwing her skirts up.

Her feet dangled over the edge, her slippers falling like fat raindrops to the floor.

Rebecca moaned as his mouth found hers again, while his hand, using his exquisite, expert touch began to torment the already fevered flesh between her thighs. There he enflamed her, parting the delicate folds, one at a time, until he found the very center of her passion.

It felt so good, this fire he was kindling, but she wanted more, she wanted all of him—without any preludes, for Rebecca had no need for tender inter-ludes at the moment.

She wanted to be claimed, to be taken quickly and fiercely by this dark and passionate man.

Tearing at his breeches, she freed his manhood, and wrapped her legs around his hips, tugging him closer until the very tip of his staff rode restlessly against her cleft. She felt fevered and anxious, hot and hungry, ready to be filled.

Somewhere in the distance, the musicians were play-ing a tune, a perfect, delicate waltz, but inside this darkened room, it was a ragged, wild beat that claimed them. Rafe entered her swiftly, for he seemed to understand her raging desire—though it might have been her instant pleas.

"Take me, Rafe. Take me now!"

Her fingers clung to his shoulders, to his hips, tugging at him to drive into her, stroke her until this madness went away.

"Oh, yes, please," she moaned as he pushed her backward on top of the desk, then covered her with his body, thrusting into her with long, hard strokes, until she came with a shattering explosion. He covered her mouth with his as she cried out, and he too shuddered inside her, filling her with his spent passion.

She clung to him, and rode through the storm that possessed them both. He whispered ragged words in Spanish that she didn't understand but knew came from his heart.

Finally he pulled back from her, and the cool of the night rushed over her fevered flesh. He tugged her up and off the desk and her skirts fell back into place. Her legs wobbled, still trembling from his explosive lovemaking.

He held her for a moment, kissing her one more time. "Don't consider dancing with anyone else," he said, as he released her. "Until later, *mi ángel*." Then the rogue slipped out the balcony window. "Duty calls," he whispered, before he was gone from sight.

Rebecca stared at the vacant space where he had stood but a moment before, her body still thrumming. "Damn your wretched hide, Rafe Danvers," she called after him. "Come back here!"

What about his duty to her? Not that he hadn't just done an admirable job, but she would have liked an hour or more of his time. *His expertise.*

Then she let out a short laugh as she glanced down at her ruinous state of *dishabille*.

How was it that when all she'd ever wanted was a predictable, sensible life, that she'd found her heart's desire with this impetuous rake? Life would never be practical with Rafe, but she wouldn't want it any other way.

Straightening herself up as best she could, Rebecca made her way back to the ballroom. She had every intention of finding the blackguard, when suddenly she found her path blocked.

"There you are, Miss Tate." Lady Tottley stood before her like the great dome of St. Paul's, vast and imposing.

Rebecca bit back the very unladylike curse that rose to her lips. In Spanish, no less. Oh, Rafe's influence was infectious.

"*Now*, Miss Tate," Lady Tottley said. "Now."

"Now what?" she asked, her hands to her lips, her heart still beating in a wild tattoo. She glanced around the room to see if Rafe had returned as well.

"To right your wrongs." The countess pointed to the ballroom which was mostly divided into two camps—the Darbyites on one side and the young men of the *ton* on the other.

"Here comes Lucinda," the countess urged. "It is time to tell her the truth."

Rebecca sighed, still glancing for any sign of Rafe. His disreputable coat shouldn't be that hard to spot amongst the colorful plumage of the *beau monde*. "Are you sure this is the best—"

"Now or never," the countess declared with tones that rang with finality.

Taking a deep breath, Rebecca reminded herself she had promised to help Lady Tottley, but the timing was horrible. There was a murderer to catch, and once that was accomplished, she had a word or two for Rafe Danvers.

Like when was he going to get around to proposing?

"Lucinda, darling, there you are!" the countess enthused. "I have something I want to tell you. About Miss Tate."

"If you mean, Mother, that she's the author of the *Miss Darby* novels, I already know."

Both Rebecca and Lady Tottley stared at her, mouths agape.

"You know?" the countess managed to stammer.

"Yes, and I think it was lovely of you to invite my favorite author as a surprise for me. You are the kindest mother in the world." Lucinda rose up on her tiptoes and pecked an affectionate kiss on her mother's cheek. Then turning to Rebecca, she said, "Miss Tate, would you mind being introduced to my friends?"

"No, not at all," Rebecca said, as the girl led her away.

But Lucinda had another surprise for Rebecca when the girl whispered almost immediately, "Oh, Miss Tate, you must help me."

"Help you?" Rebecca managed to ask. Not another person seeking her aid! She still had to find the Gadbury sisters' lost fortune. And help Rafe find Kitling. And then there was the ruby . . .

Oh, this profession of Rafe's was exacting.

"Yes. I need to find a way to end this wretched Darbyite pledge without delay. Miss Thayer has danced with Lord Barwick twice this evening. If she manages another set, they'll be as good as engaged. I must get her away from him."

Rebecca smiled but didn't say anything. Her promise to Lady Tottley wouldn't be any trouble to fulfill now.

"I have my place in society to consider and I will not

give it up to the likes of some *cit*'s daughter. If you could perhaps suggest that it wasn't your intention for all of us to mourn the loss of Lieutenant Throckmorten to this extent, I would be forever in your debt." Lady Lucinda paused, then smiled sweetly. "I won't even tell mother that I saw you leave the ballroom with that handsome Mr. Danvers. Or that you're missing your slippers."

Rebecca glanced down at her stocking-clad feet and then at the grinning girl beside her.

Oh, Lady Lucinda was going to take her mother's place in society without any help from her, or anyone else for that matter.

They arrived before the assembled young ladies and Lady Lucinda smiled brightly. "Everyone, I would like you to meet Miss Tate."

Obviously her identity had already been revealed for the girls surrounded her, each of them telling her their favorite Darbyism.

"*I thought for sure she'd never escape when she was kidnapped by those South Seas pirates—*"

"*And when she was at the dance waiting for word of her beloved—*"

"*No, no, the time when Lieutenant Throckmorten was trapped by the tiger and Miss Darby lured it away by—*"

One of the girls pressed forward and heaved a loud sigh. "Oh, why, Miss Tate, did you allow him to die? Lieutenant Throckmorten was the most perfect gentleman," she declared.

All around, heads nodded in agreement.

Rebecca's chance to change the course of the Season had arrived as if delivered by Crumpton on a silver platter.

"I fear ladies, you have all been misled," she told them, "much as Miss Darby was."

"Misled?" one of them said. "How so?"

There was a buzz of questions, but Rebecca held up her hand to stave them off. "Lieutenant Throckmorten was not as noble as we all would like to believe."

"Never!"

"I can't believe it."

"Yes," Rebecca told them. "Lieutenant Throck-morten harbored a dark and terrible secret."

There were gasps, and one silly girl, Lady Penelope Bittleman, she later learned, fainted dead away. Rebecca wanted to groan. Each of these girls should be placed on a limited income and forced to live in a cottage in the remotest part of Scotland for a year, in hopes that they would gain an ounce of common sense before they were allowed in society.

Still, she had her audience and she was a storyteller. "I fear now the truth will never be told, for Lady Tottley has asked me not to publish the next volume of Miss Darby's adventures."

"No!" half a dozen of them said at once. Several shot Lady Lucinda very dark and dangerous glances that said only too clearly her time as the bellwether of their society was about to come to an end.

"But you must tell us, Miss Tate," one girl pleaded. "For not to know is worse than knowing he is dead."

"When I tell you the truth, you will see why Lieutenant Throckmorten is better off lost and forgotten. For I fear, my dear friends, he was a terrible bounder. Throckmorten, though all but pledged to Miss Darby, was already betrothed."

Lady Penelope had just recovered from her first case of vapors when she heard the awful truth. Lt. Throck-morten already betrothed? She promptly toppled over yet again. No one gave Lady Penelope the least bit of concern.

"The cad!"

"*How dare he!*"

"*Oh, poor Miss Darby!*" rose the chorus.

"She'll be fine," Rebecca assured them. "She has a resolute spirit. Remember she's survived tigers and South Seas pirates and the time when the Prince's palace caught fire."

All around, agreement rose on that point. Tears were being wiped aside, as were the black armbands most of them wore to commemorate their once beloved hero.

"I would wager that if Miss Darby were here," Rebecca advised them, "she certainly wouldn't be wasting her time lolling about in the wings of a ballroom when there were so many eligible men about to which to be introduced—"

The stampede was almost immediate as the girls fled first to their mothers, aunts, and relations seeking the necessary introductions that had gone too long unwanted.

"Discreetly, of course," Rebecca finished to no one in particular. Even Lady Penelope had recovered and was taking the arm of a young swain. Lady Lucinda and Lord Barwick took their place at the head of the forming lines and soon the floor was filled to overflowing with young couples.

Across the room, Lady Tottley stood beaming beside a smiling Marchioness of Funtley as if the future of England had just been saved from unimaginable catastrophe.

By the time the musicians started the next song, the Setchfield Ball was declared the miracle of the Season. And the duke was planning a full day ahead collecting his winnings.

Now that Rebecca's obligations in London were done, it was time for her to find Rafe and her own happy ending.

"Perhaps we can have our dance now," said a voice at Rebecca's shoulder.

She spun around thinking at first it was Rafe, only to find Lord Pease standing before her. Rebecca did her best not to reveal her disappointment, before she shook her head and said, "I would rather sit this one out, my lord. It looks quite crowded."

He laughed and pointed toward the refreshment table with his cane. "Perhaps we can take a stroll and get some punch."

"My lord—" she began.

"Tsk tsk," he said. "So formal, Rebecca."

"Yes, well, while I find your attentions very flattering, surely you must realize that I am not the same girl I was in Calcutta."

"No, you aren't," he said, moving closer. "You have grown into a beautiful woman." He paused and drew himself up to his full height, striking an elegant pose—one that reminded her unfortunately of the same one Lt. Throckmorten had favored before his demise. "Rebecca, I was a fool to ever leave you behind. When I was recalled home, I should have just married you then and there, but I was an idiot. I can understand you were hurt, but now can't you find it in your heart to forgive me?"

"There's nothing to forgive," she told him, glancing around for Rafe, and not really listening to the viscount's words, until he made a fateful request.

"Please, allow me to put the past behind us. Would you, my dearest Rebecca, make me the happiest man in all of England, I daresay, and marry me?"

Unfortunately for Rebecca, Lady Tottley had arrived to see for herself that Rebecca wasn't "ruining her chances" and overheard the question. So before Rebecca could refuse, the lady replied for her.

"Why of course she will, Lord Pease."

Rebecca's mouth flapped open in shock, her protest lodged in her throat like a cannon ball. Meanwhile, the countess was not so afflicted and opened her mouth loud and clear.

"I do declare, we have the first engagement of the Season! Huzzah for Miss Rebecca Tate, the future Viscountess Pease."

"Where is he?" Rafe demanded as he stormed into Lady Tottley's salon.

The colonel looked up from his reading and shook his head. He sat in a chair before the fireplace, Richard's journal in hand, the man's haversack at his feet. "Sorry to have called you back here, Danvers," Posthill said. "But Cochrane was sure he saw Kitling in the neighborhood and I thought it best to alert you, though now it appears the lad was mistaken. Easy to do—spot some fellow and blow his head off, only to discover he was your advance scout. Sorry business, that."

Rafe shrugged, not sure he wanted the colonel to elaborate on that point. Still it was unlike Cochrane to be mistaken. He'd take a look around in a minute, but first he had another matter to attend to.

"As it is, sir, I wanted to come back here to speak with you. Privately, that is."

The colonel looked up from his reading. "In private, you say? Sounds serious." He set aside the journal. "Can't find a single reference to the ruby as yet, so I might as well hear you out."

Taking a deep breath, Rafe found himself tongue-tied. "It is, sir. I mean to say, that is—"

"Out with it, Danvers! No need to shilly-shally around." The colonel stood up. "Are you going to marry Bex or not?"

Rafe was so taken aback, he sputtered a hasty, "Well, yes." Then he added, "If she'll have me."

The colonel snorted. "She'll take you. And I'll give you my blessing on one condition."

"What is that?" Rafe asked.

"You agree to take the ruby back to India when you find it. No matter how much Rebecca protests, no matter the fortune that it would bring. I will not give you my blessing unless you agree to my terms."

"She'll have my hide." If Rafe was lucky that would be all she'd take.

"No doubt she will," the colonel agreed, "but better that than keep it and doom yourselves to a cursed existence."

Rafe wasn't all that convinced of the calamity the colonel seemed to believe was so insurmountable, but his blessing was important.

And though they didn't need it—Rebecca being old enough to marry without her guardian's approval—Rafe didn't like the idea of putting an estrangement between his bride-to-be and her only relation.

Giving up the ruby was a lot to ask, but there was still Bettlesfield Park and the Company's reward money to be had. It would be enough for a start. And knowing Rebecca and her practical, managing ways, she'd have them uncovering a fortune before he knew it.

He held out his hand and took the colonel's outstretched one. "You have my word."

Heaving a sigh of relief, with his duties to Rebecca now duly dispatched, the colonel retook his seat by the fire. "Suppose you'll want to marry her straight away?"

"Actually, I've already procured a Special License."

The colonel nodded. "Smart man. I'd suggest not

telling her about our agreement as to the ruby until after the blessed event."

Rafe laughed. "Just in time for my funeral."

They both laughed, but their jest was interrupted as a commotion arose in the entryway.

Lady Tottley's voice rattled the walls with its fevered pitch. "Miss Tate, I will not hear another word of this mutiny! You shall give Lord Pease your pledge immediately."

"The hell she will—" Rafe muttered, starting for the doorway, but the colonel stopped him.

"Is there somewhere private we can discuss this matter, Lady Tottley?" Pease was saying. "I have a proposition that I believe will convince Miss Tate of the seriousness of my intentions."

"Yes, we can go in my salon and—"

Rebecca interrupted her. "I don't see that anything you have to say, Lord Pease, is going to—"

Rebecca's words ended as Lady Tottley screeched, "Lord Pease, put that sword down immediately."

Rafe looked at the colonel and then at the hallway. *Sword?*

Pease's walking stick. It wasn't Kitling they were looking for, but—

"*You!*" Rebecca cried out. "It was you all the time."

"Yes, and now I've come to collect what is mine," Pease said.

Crumpton, Lady Tottley and then Rebecca came backing into the salon. Rafe dodged behind the door and let Pease enter the room. He'd already drawn his pistol and was about to put an end to the villainous viscount but to his dismay he realized the man had the advantage, at least for now—for the viscount had the tip of his sword resting under Rebecca's chin.

"Handy little stick, this," Pease was saying. "Found

it in my cousin Kemball's belongings after I inherited.
Much less conspicuous than my saber, but just as
deadly."

From the glint of the blade, Rafe had no doubt that it
was razor sharp. One false move and Rebecca would
end up like the rest of Pease's victims, split from stem
to stern.

So for the moment, Rafe remained concealed, his
body tense and his finger coiled around the trigger of
his pistol, awaiting his chance.

"Colonel Posthill," Pease was saying. "How nice to
see you again, sir."

"Habersham!" the colonel blustered. "Let Bex go."

He shook his head. "Not until I have what I came
for—Richard's haversack."

"Don't give it to him," Rebecca said, her voice filled
with resolve and anger.

That's my foolish, headstrong girl, Rafe thought. She'd
fight to the end to save what was hers.

"Miss Tate, I don't see that your uncle has a choice.
For if he doesn't hand it over, I shall spill your insides
all over the carpet, much like I did your insolent
brother."

"And Harrington and Codlin?" she brazened.

"Yes, those fools as well. Stealing your research like
the worst amateurs, when I was so close to laying my
hands on it by merely enduring your dubious charms."
Pease sneered at Rebecca. "Bah, how I deplored you.
Still do! But to gain a fortune, a man is willing to lower
himself to do almost anything."

"You mean your proposal wasn't honestly intended?"
This indignant question came from Lady Tottley.

"Madame, I hardly think that matters at the present
moment," Crumpton pointed out, still the model of ex-
cruciatingly polite decorum.

"Of course it matters," Lady Tottley said, outraged.

Pease's sword wavered under Rebecca's chin, but she only tipped her head up higher and stared him in the eye. "You would add my death to your list of crimes?"

"Happily to regain the Kailash," he told her, his voice rising in pitch. "It is more beautiful than any mortal can imagine. To hold it, is to hold eternity."

"You had it?" the colonel asked.

Pease nodded. "The night I gained it from Mayne."

"You killed him as well?" Rebecca gasped.

"Yes. And I would have added your wretched brother to my list that night if he hadn't been so quick. Stole the ruby from me. My ruby. And I swore, then and there, I would gain it back from him. But by the time I returned home as well, he'd already joined a regiment in Portugal." He turned to the colonel. "Richard's haversack, if you please. For I've had a devil of a time locating it." He held out his free hand, all the while the sword remained dangerously perched at Rebecca's throat. "You don't know how many times you've come close to this end. How many times I watched you at Bettlesfield Park, waiting for this day, to take my revenge on the lot of you and regain what is mine."

"It was you there," she whispered.

"Yes," he said. "So you figured that out as well. You never stop surprising me, Miss Tate. Now let us finish this game of cat and mouse and give me what I want. The Kailash ruby."

The colonel glanced in Rafe's direction and he nodded at him. Scooping up the haversack, Posthill went to toss it at Pease, but the man shook his head. "Nothing too fast, sir," the viscount told him. "Empty it out here on the table." Then he glanced over his shoulder. "And tell Danvers to step out from behind the door."

Rafe cursed, but slowly walked out from his hiding place.

"Rafe!" Rebecca cried out, her words like a silent plea.

But whether it was to save her life or save the ruby from Pease, he wasn't too sure. Knowing her mercantile heart, the fortune was paramount. But he also suspected she wanted retribution.

For Richard and the others.

"I thought I smelled your cowardly stench," Pease said, his voice filled with contempt. "Don't even think of taking a shot or you shall have to find another bitch with which to rut."

Rafe started forward, but the colonel stopped him with a curt shake of his head.

"The haversack, Posthill. Now!" Pease said, his madness growing more and more apparent.

The colonel upended the contents of Richard's haversack on the table beside him. Then he backed away, until he stood by his chair, and Rafe realized what the colonel was doing.

Though he had given Pease the haversack quite willingly, his real objective was to save the journal sitting safely and unobtrusively on the table.

Pease, meanwhile, was picking through Richard's belongings, tossing aside the remnants of his life as if they were but flotsam. His eyes grew more wild and desperate with each object, his motions frantic. To see him turning from an elegant gentleman into this crazed madman was alarming.

Rafe was starting to believe that perhaps the colonel was right, the Kailash curse wasn't to be taken lightly.

The viscount had come to the last thing remaining, the small portrait of Rebecca.

He held it up and examined it, then laughed cruelly.

"A fine likeness, Rebecca. Exactly as I remember you. Gads it was a chore to listen to your prattle, to offer you my lips. But ah, the prize. It was worth having to lap at your ragged skirts."

Rafe made a low noise in the back of his throat.

Pease turned to him and shot him a withering stare. "From the looks of you I would assume you've had the lady's favors. Not that I suppose her common qualities would be all that noticeable to someone of your ill-breeding."

If the man hadn't had the advantage already, Rafe would have seen him consigned to hell that very moment.

Pease took one last distasteful glance at the portrait and threw it against the fireplace, shattering it.

Then he turned a wild eye on the room. "Where is it? Where is Richard's journal? I want it and I want it right now!"

"Is this what you are looking for?" the colonel asked.

Rafe didn't know who looked more angry—Pease or Rebecca as they both saw what the colonel intended.

The cagey old man held Richard's journal over the licking flames in the fireplace.

"Let her go, Habersham," the colonel said, in a cold, determined voice. "Or I will make sure no one ever finds the ruby."

"You wouldn't dare," Pease said, as he drew the sword back.

Rafe knew that the madness that encompassed the man was about to take Rebecca's life, so he aimed his pistol.

And fired.

The ball hit exactly where Rafe had intended, and Rebecca screamed in agony—for it tore into Richard's journal, pulling it from the colonel's fingers and dropping it into the greedy flames. Almost immediately the fire consumed it.

Pease, his victim temporarily forgotten, dropped his sword and dove for the grate, scrambling across the floor to the fireplace. "Mine! It is mine!" he screamed, shoving his hands into the flames. He screamed as his flesh burned, though it didn't stop him from trying to catch up his prize.

But his agony didn't last long.

In a blinding flash, Lady Tottley snatched up a large vase from the sideboard and dashed it over Pease's head, rendering the viscount unconscious. "That will teach you, sir, to tender a proposal to a lady that you have no intention of honoring," she said in lofty tones, as if a fraudulent marriage proposal was the worst of the viscount's sins.

Chapter 16

Distance from the object of one's affections? Propriety is well and good if one wants to remain a spinster for the rest of her days.

Miss Darby to Miss Cecilia Overton
in *Miss Darby's Daring Dilemma*

Rebecca woke the next morning to an unusual noise. She'd thought she had finally grown used to the never ending din of London—which seemed to rise and fall with the hours but never ceased—from the first crunch of the trash man's wheels in the morning, to the cry of the night watch calling the hours. But this sound was something altogether different.

"Oooh," came the moan from the next room. "Oh my!"

Miss Alminta's room?

Rebecca rolled over to grab her wrapper and ran smack into the solid strength of a man's back.

Rafe.

Rafe in her bed? Miss Alminta completely forgotten, Rebecca sat bolt upright, and stared down at the magnificent man beside her.

Her husband.

She grinned and tucked her knees up under her chin, her hands folded in front of her, where a ring on her finger declared her newfound status as Mrs. Raphael Danvers.

For after Lady Tottley had dashed the vase over Pease's head, Rafe had ordered Crumpton to fetch some rope, and then the murderer was tied up and the authorities called for. And though it was apparent the madness that the colonel attributed to the ruby had taken its toll on the man, his confession to killing four men did not bode well for him. Not even his noble status would save him.

With the viscount dispatched to Newgate and the case solved, Rafe had turned to Rebecca and gone down on one knee and proposed.

Despite Lady Tottley's assurances that her chances to make an advantageous match yet this Season (despite her rather unfortunate, albeit short, engagement to a confessed murderer) were quite good, Rebecca accepted Rafe's impractical request. It was hardly sensible considering this was the same reckless man who had just burned Richard's journal and lost a fortune in order to save her life. But Raphael Danvers left her breathless and starry-eyed, and she couldn't imagine her life without him—no matter how many viscounts or vicars Lady Tottley could promise.

And when her reckless betrothed informed her there would be no need to wait for banns since he had procured a Special License, Rebecca gained a new respect for his impetuous practices.

In truth, when she considered it, his rash and imprudent methods were really quite practical.

Lady Tottley was still listing her objections to their match when Miss Honora, Reverend Brown, Lady Lucinda and Lord Barwick arrived home from the ball. Taking her mother aside, Lady Lucinda gave her mother a few sketchy details about what may or may not have occurred at the Setchfield Ball, including Rebecca's missing slippers, and the countess immediately pressed the vicar into action. Within minutes, the marriage was duly performed, with a beaming Lady Lucinda and Lord Barwick standing up with the happy couple.

As the newly minted Mr. and Mrs. Danvers shared their first marital kiss, a misty-eyed Crumpton passed around glasses of champagne. Toasts were made by all until the happy couple retired upstairs for their wedding night.

Rebecca grinned at the rest of the memories from her wedding night.

After making love, he had held her in his arms and told her the story of her wedding ring, which she had thought at first was nothing but a simple gold band. The ring had been one of a pair, gifts to Rafe and Orlando from their brother Robert when he'd gone into the army, leaving his two younger siblings behind. It had been a pledge back then of his protection, and now Rafe had carried on that vow, with his name and heart, by placing it on her finger.

She sighed and looked over at the romantic, rakish devil sleeping next to her. Was it proper, she wondered, to nudge one's sleeping husband a bit and see if she could gain his interest yet again?

Then next door, Miss Alminta groaned once more, and Rebecca knew she really should go see to the lady, yet . . .

Then another moan, one much deeper, echoed from the room. One that decidedly did not belong to Miss Alminta.

Her marital intentions would have to wait.

"Wake up," Rebecca whispered, nudging her husband.

He grumbled and caught her in his arms, tugging her close and nuzzling her ears and nibbling at her neck. A warm, lazy passion spread through her limbs. *Oh, yes* . . . she thought until once again Miss Alminta's cries broke her concentration.

Rafe's eyes flew open. "What the devil was that?"

"It's coming from Miss Alminta's room," Rebecca whispered. "I think she's in trouble."

Rafe didn't look so sure, but he got up, splendidly naked, a sight that Rebecca knew she should be blushing at, while at the same time thinking it a terrible shame to see him yank one of the sheets from the bed and wrap it around his waist.

"Stay here," he said, as he went for the door.

"Oh, no you don't," Rebecca told him, shrugging on her wrapper. "You'll terrify Miss Alminta if you go storming in there, besides wake the entire house."

"I don't care."

"You will if you rouse Lady Tottley before noon."

He looked about to argue the point, but the moaning started again and he stalked out of their room.

"I'm coming with you," she said, following him to Miss Alminta's room.

Without knocking or any preamble, Rafe flung the door open. Miss Alminta let out a piercing shriek that did exactly what Rebecca feared—woke the entire house—and brought the servants and Lady Tottley alike to discover what had happened to the missing Sydney Kitling.

He'd obviously spent a very comfortable night abed with Miss Alminta, her megrims quite cured.

"Why you fortune stealing—" Rafe started to drag Kitling from the bed, but was stopped not only by Alminta's further shrieks but Lady Tottley's loud protest.

"Mr. Danvers, that man is *unclothed!*" she bellowed. "Put him back!"

Rafe gave Kitling a good shake, then tossed him back under the sheets.

Lady Tottley shook her head, then dispatched every one back to their rooms to get properly dressed, despite Rafe's protests that he wanted to toss Kitling out without the decency of his clothes. With a warning shake of his fist to Sydney, he agreed to the countess's demands that everyone be clothed before anyone was thrown into the streets.

Rafe followed Lady Tottley's orders with the precision of a gunner, yanking on his clothes and then stationing himself outside Miss Alminta's bedroom to await his quarry. Rebecca followed suit and arrived just as the weasel poked his nose out. Rafe caught him by the scruff of the neck and dragged him from the room. He was about to give the man a very good example of his skills at arm breaking, when a pair of hands caught his sleeve.

"Mr. Danvers, please unhand him. I beg of you, do not harm him."

He glanced down to find Alminta anchored to his jacket. "Miss Alminta," he began, "you don't know what he's done. He's stolen your fortune."

"I've done no such thing—" Kitling protested, until Rafe gave him another good shake and his mouth clapped shut to keep his teeth from rattling loose.

"Oh, please let him go, Mr. Danvers," Alminta begged. "Mr. Kitling hasn't stolen anything."

"But someone has," Honora said, coming up the hall and pointing an accusing finger at Sydney. "I was at the bank yesterday to have drafts drawn to pay our bills and the clerk said all our accounts had been emptied."

"I didn't touch your money, Honora," Sydney stammered. "I swear it."

Rafe gave him another good shake to shut him up.

"Mr. Danvers, you must release Sydney, he has nothing to do with the missing money," Alminta said, her face having turned a deep shade of red.

"Are you positive?" Rafe asked, unwilling to let the man go just yet.

"Oh, yes, because I know who stole our money."

Honora gasped. "Who, sister? Who could be so dastardly to have stolen our legacy?"

Alminta looked down at her slippers, then up at her sister. "I did."

Down in Lady Tottley's salon, the countess sat preparing a carefully worded lecture as well as her plans for the removal of her ungrateful houseguests, when yet another cacophony of shouts and accusations arose.

She promptly tossed aside any thoughts of a most needed reprimand and an extremely discreet eviction to avoid the notice of her neighbors.

"Mayfair be damned," she told Crumpton as she flew past the crusty butler. "I will toss them into the streets myself."

But the lady's hasty expulsion had to wait until everyone was properly attired and assembled in Lady Tottley's salon, so that Alminta could finish her startling confession.

Rebecca stood beside Rafe, wide-eyed at the truth that came spilling from the spinster's trembling lips.

"Honora, I'm so sorry. I didn't know what else to do," Alminta said. "I wanted to be Sydney's wife, but mother's will forbids either of us from marrying without the other's permission." She turned to her audience. "It was established that way to ensure that neither of us were taken in by a scoundrel or fortune hunter."

Most everyone in the room was still just recovering from the shock that the sisters held a large fortune.

"I wasn't thinking clearly when I went to the bank the other day. I just asked them to send over all of it to the house and I thought . . . well, I thought I could convince Sydney to run away with me."

"Which I refused to do," Sydney said.

Alminta confirmed this with a mournful nod and began to cry anew.

Honora took her sister's hand and patted it. "Oh, Alminta," she said. "Why didn't you just tell me you were in love with Sydney?"

"I didn't think you'd approve, what with him being so much . . . so much—"

"Younger?" Honora said.

Her sister nodded.

"Not that much," Sydney said, rising to stand beside his lady love.

The Misses Gadbury exchanged a look that spoke louder than words.

"More than ten years?" Kitling asked, glancing down at Alminta.

"You haven't told him?" Honora asked her sister.

Alminta shook her head.

Honora prodded her. "Tell him. Tell him how old you are."

"Oh, if I must," Alminta sputtered back. She went up on her tiptoes to whisper to Sydney the mysterious number for him and him only.

Though every ear was pricked to catch a hint of the sisters' age, Miss Alminta's soft voice did not betray their secret, though Sydney's wide eyes gave every indication that it was well and beyond the ten years that he had suspected. The lady stepped back from him, her eyes once again on her slippers as if she feared to look up and discover the truth.

But Sydney surprised her. He reached out and tipped her chin up. "It matters not to me, Alminta, my dearest darling girl. I'll always love you."

"But it is scandalous," she protested. "I am so much—"

He stopped her by pulling her into his arms and kissing her. "It matters not to me if you are a hundred years older," he told her again. Then he glanced over at Honora. "Miss Honora, I apologize for my deplorable indiscretion with your sister but believe me, I love her with all my heart. And if you can find it in your heart to forgive us, I would be deeply honored if you would give me the blessing of your good favor to see us wed."

It might have been Kitling's need for money that had brought him into Alminta's life, but anyone looking at him now could see that in the process of gaining her *carte blanche*, he had also fallen in love with the lady. Deeply and sincerely.

"With all my heart," Honora told them, tears filling her eyes.

Rebecca swiped at her own damp eyes, and there were hugs and hearty congratulations all around.

Finally, Honora stepped back from her sister, and shook a finger at her. "Alminta, you must promise me to put that money back in the bank forthwith. Fifty thousand pounds shouldn't be just laying about."

"Fifty thousand—" Lady Tottley gasped, glancing at the ceiling above her where Alminta's room sat.

Rafe and Rebecca gaped at each other. *Fifty thousand?*

"I still think I ought to break Kitling's arm," Rafe muttered.

"Save it for another day," Rebecca told him.

*   *   *

As the money was being dispatched back to the bank, a maid came into the salon with a handful of pieces from the miniature that had been in Richard's haversack.

"Oh, Miss Tate," the girl said. "Um, I mean, Mrs. Danvers, I was cleaning up the room this morning, and found these. I thought you might like to keep them, being your brother's and all."

"Thank you," Rebecca said, barely giving her fractured picture as well as the broken frame a second glance, until she spied something odd. Taking a closer look, she spotted the corner of what appeared to be a piece of paper tucked inside the frame behind the portrait. Carefully she extracted it.

"What is it?" Rafe asked, glancing over her shoulder. "A love note?"

"I don't know," she said, though her fingers were shaking in excitement. Something told her this was the key they'd been searching for.

As Rebecca unfolded the scrap, her breath caught in her throat. The paper held a small map. A topographical map, much like Richard had probably drawn while mapping the Spanish countryside for Wellington.

But it wasn't Spain, she'd wager. "This is it. This is where Richard hid the Kailash ruby." She wound her arms around Rafe's neck. "We've found it! Our fortune!"

In her excitement, she didn't see the significant look the colonel shot Rafe.

"About the ruby—" her husband began.

Four hours later, Lady Tottley's vow to see Miss Tate and company out of the house, had yet to come to fruition, and happily Rafe was still alive, despite Rebecca's outraged reaction to the fact that he had vowed to see the Kailash returned to India in exchange for her hand in marriage.

"In the future, when we come into a fortune," she told him, "I shall be responsible for it."

Rafe had grinned and agreed to give her control of any boon they obtained, since it was the most impractical thing she'd ever suggested. Unless they stumbled upon a trunk like Alminta's, such a future was highly unlikely.

Instead, the entire household was gathered around the large table in the library trying to discern where in England the little bit of map represented. The mystery had everyone entranced.

In addition, Rafe had sent notes to his brothers and the Duke of Setchfield, and they'd arrived, wives in tow, to help discover where Richard Tate had hidden the Kailash ruby.

Colin's wife Georgie had spent her life studying sea charts and navigation, while Robert's wife Olivia was an expert in languages, though neither lady had been able to offer any help.

The colonel had pulled out all his maps, and Lady Tottley had fetched her husband's books as well, but to no avail.

"If only we could discern what that means," Rafe said, pointing to the drawing beside the "X" that marked where the ruby was hidden.

There were more such drawings all around the edge of the paper, until it looked like a stream of raindrops, along with an ancient staff and trees—yet what it signified, no one could determine.

Rebecca paced back and forth before the table. "Richard always did love a good puzzle."

"I fear that was my fault," the colonel said. "The boy loved treasure hunting as much as I. He probably thought it a great lark to hide his own treasure."

"There must be someone who would recognize what this all means," Rafe said.

"I have a suggestion," Miss Honora said. "I met a lovely man last night who might be of assistance. He knows quite a bit about England and has traveled all over the countryside."

"Mr. Billingsworth!" The Duchess of Setchfield exclaimed. "Oh, I don't know why I didn't think of him."

Temple groaned. "Not that odious man. The last time you consulted him, it took us five weeks to get him to leave."

"Not another houseguest," Lady Tottley protested. "I will not have any more cadgers in my house!"

"Oh, that doesn't even begin to describe the man," Temple muttered.

His wife ignored him and gave Crumpton Mr. Billingsworth's address and directed the butler to send their carriage to fetch him at once.

An hour later, Theonius T. Billingsworth arrived at Tottley House, the very picture of the absentminded scholar. He had nibs of pens sticking out from the pocket of his waistcoat, an unidentifiable stain on his cravat and the toady manners of a man used to living off the benevolence of his betters.

In other words, he charmed Lady Tottley with a recitation of the famed landmarks on her father's legendary estate in Northumberland, complimented the Marchioness of Bradstone on her latest treatise on an ancient Celtic tongue, and thanked the Duchess of Setchfield for her continued good graces.

The man knew his audience and how to keep his next meal properly in place.

With the introductions over and the situation explained, Mr. Billingsworth got out a great magnifying glass and peered over the small map with agonizing detail. As he hemmed and hawed, everyone in the room held their breath.

No one more so than Rebecca. Of course, she still held out hope that Rafe would come to his senses and agree to keep the ruby. Only long enough to sell it.

"Have you noticed these," Billingsworth asked, pointing at the raindrops. "There are forty of them. How very interesting. And this staff here—why I've seen one like it somewhere."

"What does it mean?" Rebecca asked.

The man scratched his chin. "I can't say directly. Not without consulting one of my older works, *Saints, Shrines and Holy Places of Olde*." He scratched his chin and sighed. "If only I had a copy at hand."

"I have one!" Miss Honora declared. "I have my copy upstairs." When she realized everyone in the room was gaping at her, she explained, "I have all Mr. Billingsworth's books and *Saints, Shrines and Holy Places of Olde* happens to be one of my favorites."

Mr. Billingsworth preened, adjusting his spectacles. "Miss Honora, you warm my heart."

She blushed. "As you have mine, sir, on the numerous nights I've spent with you . . . I mean with your books." Flustered, she went an even deeper shade of red.

Rebecca caught Rafe's eye. He edged closer to her. "Are you thinking what I'm thinking?"

She laughed. "Yes."

They shared a smile, for they knew that Alminta Gadbury wasn't the only one destined for the altar. There was no doubt Honora would very soon find her way into Mr. Billingsworth's good graces.

When she returned with the book and the man thumbed through the well worn pages, he finally came to a section and let out an "ah-ha!" that had everyone crowding around him.

"There are forty of these drops on here. Forty! And

this drawing is dated July 15th. Oh, now it makes perfect sense."

Everyone else looked at each other not as convinced as the illustrious Mr. Billingsworth that the answer was so obvious.

Noting their disbelief, he explained. "Mr. Tate is leading you to an ancient shrine dedicated to St. Swithin." He pointed at the little drawing. "These forty raindrops are from the old rhyme:

> St. Swithin's day if thou dost rain
> For forty days it will remain
> St. Swithin's day if thou be fair
> For forty days 'twill rain nae mair.

He finished his recitation and then smiled. "This 'X' most likely represents a well dedicated to Swithin."

"A well?" Rebecca and Rafe said together.

"Yes, an ancient well. The sort you'd find in a formal garden or even in a kitchen garden of an old house."

"But where is this well?" Temple asked.

"Bettlesfield Park," Rebecca whispered. "I knew it! I always knew he'd hidden it somewhere on the property. And to think of all the hours I spent digging and prying open—"

Rafe glanced over at her. "You put all those holes in my house! Pests indeed."

"Might I remind you, Mr. Danvers," Lady Tottley said, "that Bettlesfield Park is still mine until my daughter is wed."

"Then that shouldn't be for long," Lord Barwick announced, having just arrived. "Lady Tottley, I have come to ask for your daughter's hand in marriage."

Lucinda rushed to Lord Barwick and threw herself into his arms. Not even Lady Tottley could protest this unseemly display.

After all, Barwick was the heir to the Hemswell dukedom and that did call for some leeway in propriety.

As everyone congratulated the happy couple, Rafe pulled Rebecca aside. "I am taking the repair costs out of your cut of the Company's reward."

"You'll have to prove I did it," she teased.

"I can be very persuasive," he said, gathering her up in his arms and kissing her.

They were interrupted by an "uh-hum" from Colin. When Rafe continued to kiss his wife, Robert added a nudge into his brother's side.

Rafe cast them both an annoyed glance. "Can't you see I'm busy?"

"We have something to tell you," Colin said.

"It can wait," Rafe replied, turning his attention back to his eager wife.

"It's about your inheritance," Robert said.

"The fortune we forgot to tell you about," Colin added sheepishly.

Rafe pulled away from Rebecca, staring first at Colin and then at Robert. "My wha-a-at?"

"I thought he'd told you," Robert said, pointing at Colin.

"And I was under the assumption he'd told you." Colin laughed. "Quite funny, if you think about it."

Funny? He'd lived the last few years in a rat infested slum, and they thought it funny?

"You mean to say I have money?"

"Haven't you heard a word they've said? You're quite rich," Rebecca told him, catching hold of him and tugging him back into her arms. "There's thirty thousand pounds in trust sitting at Barclay and Company."

Then she tipped up on her toes to kiss him again, but Rafe wasn't so inclined.

He tore himself away from her. "How did *you* know about this fortune, when I've just been informed of it?"

She grinned. "Lady Tottley told me of it this morning. Apparently she was doing some checking and discovered quite by accident that—"

Rafe had heard enough. Now that he was a wealthy man there was only one thing left to do.

Kiss his sensible wife senseless.

Then he intended to break his brothers' arms.

Epilogue

India, 1818

The sun blazed overhead while Rafe and Rebecca stood before the ancient temple of Kailash.

"Must I?" Rebecca said, a small locked chest in her hands. "In truth, I think this curse is mere fiction on uncle's part."

Rafe smiled at her and nodded toward the waiting temple guard. He'd made a promise, and when he made one, he kept it. As he had discovered the *Miss Darby* author and helped capture Sir Rodney's killer, now he was determined to keep his vow to the colonel and see the Kailash returned to its rightful place.

"Rafe, this is worth a fortune, possibly more so than your account at Barclay's. You really mean to give this up?"

He did indeed. For one reason and one reason alone: He would stop at nothing, give up anything to see his beloved wife kept safe.

"We might as well have left it in the bottom of the Bettlesfield Park well," she was grumbling, as she went forward to meet the temple scribe, dust swirling around her boots.

Rafe grinned. Rebecca had been trying for the last eight months to wheedle and cajole him into keeping the Kailash—ever since they'd traveled to Bramley Hollow to excavate the ruby. Everyone had come along to help, and it had been exactly where Mr. Billingsworth had predicted—in the bottom of the well, right where Rafe had fallen.

Based on the colonel's dire warnings, so far no one had been allowed to touch the ill-fated gemstone. It had been transferred to a small locked box from the end of Rafe's trowel and hadn't been seen since.

Then it had only been a matter of traveling from England on Colin's ship, the *Sybaris*, to Calcutta. It had been a long and lazy honeymoon of sorts, with their nights spent stargazing and making love, while their days were filled with plans for the renovations of Bettlesfield Park.

With the money from Rafe's father's estate, as well as the Company's reward, the house and lands would soon be not only worthy of recognition in one of Mr. Billingsworth's travelogues, but also turning a fine profit.

The green meadows and pastures, Rafe had decided, would be perfect for raising horses.

Not everyone was thrilled about Rafe and Rebecca's plans to renovate and live at Bettlesfield Park. Cochrane for one had refused outright to move from London to Bramley Hollow, citing Rafe's marital fate as evidence enough to give the village a wide berth.

And while at first Lady Finch was delighted to know that her new neighbors weren't going to be some deplorable lot of nabobs, the joy soon turned to dismay when she realized the colonel would be living there as well. Within cannon range of Finch Manor. She'd immediately directed Lord Finch to start building a large berm between the two properties to prevent any errant balls from reaching the house.

Meanwhile, Rebecca had only one thing left to do, return the Kailash. Rafe nudged her in the back so she took another step forward. "Consider this a great les-

son in fortitude to use in your next *Miss Darby* novel."
With Lady Lucinda's bethrothal to Lord Barwick
firmly in place, Lady Tottley had released Rebecca
from her vow not to publish any further novels. *Miss
Darby's Terrible Temptation* had been published just before they'd set sail.

Rebecca's brow furrowed. "Miss Darby would never
be so impractical."

Rafe laughed, then planted a kiss on her forehead.
"What did Prince Ranjit tell your heroine in *Miss
Darby's Terrible Temptation?*"

"Utter nonsense, I'm quite sure," she said, as she
forced a smile to her lips for the benefit of the gathered
people around them. Villages from up and down the
river valley had sent elders and scribes to mark and
record this momentous event. The homecoming of the
Kailash would mean the return of their protection and
prosperity.

"Mrs. Danvers," the head scribe for the temple intoned, "you have given us the greatest gift, the dowry
of the Kailash. For your great sacrifice you will be re-
warded with good fortune for the remainder of your
days."

Rebecca heaved a great sigh and thrust her arms
out. With only the merest of hesitation, which Rafe
was sure he was the only one who noticed, Rebecca
handed the box with the Kailash back to its rightful
owners.

"*By the strength of your will, the pureness of your heart,
and the grace of your love, you will always have my protection, my deepest devotion,*" Rafe quoted softly to her, as a
cheer rose from the bystanders.

He thought she was going to offer him another of
Mrs. Wortling's infamous "harrumphs" but instead
she turned and threw herself into his arms.

"Thank you for helping me to do that," she told him. "I know it sounds quite ridiculous, but I think I was starting to go mad from that thing."

"You?" he teased, and then kissed her quite thoroughly, sending her heart fluttering with quite a different sort of madness.

Author's Note

I hope you've enjoyed this installment of the Danvers adventures. Having watched Rafe through so many books, I was delighted to finally be able to bring you his story. While there is no Kailash ruby, I would like to thank my friend, Darcy Carson, for her help with gemstones and their properties. I would also like to thank the staff at my local Starbucks for their unending support of my writing and for offering me their hospitality when I need a quiet place to work.

As for my future stories, rest assured that I will not leave Jemmy Reyburn languishing. Besides, he lives in Bramley Hollow—he can't escape the matchmaker (or his mother's infamous machinations) forever! His madcap adventure will be featured in an upcoming novella. In the meantime, if you would like to learn more about the Danvers family, take a peek at their family tree or learn more about my other books, please visit my Web site at *www.elizabethboyle.com*. Until next time!

Best wishes always,

Elizabeth Boyle